Vit. D .

Wimdu
Berlin appt?

MAZZERI

PETER CRAWLEY

MAZZERI

LOVE AND DEATH

IN LIGHT AND SHADOW

Matador
9 Priory Business Park
Kibworth Beauchamp
Leicestershire LE8 0RX, UK
Tel: (+44) 116 279 2299
Fax: (+44) 116 279 2277
Email: books@troubador.co.uk
Web: www.troubador.co.uk/matador

ISBN 978 1780885 384

British Library Cataloguing in Publication Data.
A catalogue record for this book is available from the British Library.

Typeset by Troubador Publishing Ltd, Leicester, UK

Matador is an imprint of Troubador Publishing Ltd

Printed and bound in the UK by TJ International, Padstow, Cornwall

For Carol

Prologue

The commonly held view is that man fashions the land to meet his needs and in so doing leaves his mark upon it. Only in the harshest of environments, in the great heat of the deserts and the extreme cold of the polar regions, is the reverse true and man is fashioned by the land. And yet, here and there, isolated chunks of rock protrude from the ocean floor providing little more than a bare platform on which life finds purchase.

Corsica, cradled in the corner of the Mediterranean between France and Italy, is one such granite isle; an isle where it is said 'bread is of wood and wine is of stone'.

The people, like their environment, are hardy and uncompromising, but they can also be gentle and hospitable. Over the centuries, their Menhirs, their megalithic stone warriors, have stood witness to the great nations of Europe, Africa and Asia battle for the right to number the island amongst their jewels. More recently, under the banner of the Fronte di Liberazione Naziunale Corsu, the Corsicans have waged their own separatist wars against their imperial masters, the French.

These days, their stone warriors watch silently as tourists of all nationalities flock to the birthplace of Napoleon to swim in the emerald waters, sunbathe on the flaxen sands, or trek through the crystal air of the interior. From the olive groves of the Balagne in the north to the high citadel of Bunifaziu in the south, Corsica is an island as beguiling as it is beautiful.

Outside of my own knowledge of Corsica, I have leant on the various staffs provided me by Dorothy Carrington, Stephen Wilson, Rolli Lucarotti,

Prosper Mérimée, Pliny and Homer. I trust they will not resent the weight of my frame.

Mazzeri is written from my experience of the island and many of the incidents cited are based on actual events, some of which I have had both the fortune and misfortune to witness at first hand.

At the end of one summer near Porto Vecchio, the matriarch of our village entrusted me with a notebook in which she had recorded local proverbs and aphorisms; many of those truisms and the atmosphere they engender are employed in the tone and resonance of *Mazzeri*.

I

---⊗⊗⊗---

Calvi
La Balagne
Haute Corse
1999

The old man sat forward and leaned against his long, dark-wood staff. Children skipping by stopped when they saw him, giggled, and then raced away to find their parents down on the beach. Tourists too broke the rhythm of their promenade when they noticed him. They smiled and remarked, rather too openly to be polite, that they considered him quaint, topped off as he was by his black, broad-brimmed hat. They envied him his peace; his tranquility. After all, was it not right that when one reached a certain age one should be allowed to devote as much time as one liked to the simple pleasures; pleasures such as watching Les Amis du Vent fly their kites at the Festiventu, the May festival?

Beyond the marina the windows of the citadel stared down at the many kites as they danced in the strengthening breeze. Red and white box kites, silver diamonds and stars, purple sleds, yellow and green deltas, and other intricate and extraordinary designs and devices decorated the blue sky. Along the beach at regular intervals, gaily coloured windmills whirled and tall flags fluttered. It was a jolly affair; a scene that would gladden the hardest of hearts.

Well perhaps most of them, he thought.

Occasionally a fanfare announced the arrival of a team of daring acrobats or lithe dancers, and the lilting harmonies of acapella and polyphonic melodies floated on the breeze, like Cistus petals on a gentle stream. The atmosphere was so clear he felt he could reach out across the Golfe and touch the Punta di Spano.

I

Days like this, he reminded himself, were rare. At least they were rare for him. He had only visited Calvi once many years before and he had never given much time to the idea of returning. This side of the mountains, *di qua dai monti*, as he knew it, was very different to where he had lived all of his life; for he was from the other side, *dila dai monti*, and the two halves of the island shared little in common. Through the years, up here in the north of the island, they had courted the Genoese, the Pisans, the English and finally the French. Down there, on the other side of the mountains, where he was from, they had never bent their knees to any imperial master. *Dila dai*, beyond the mountains, the spirits held sway, and, like the people, the spirits endured. They did not come and go like the seasons.

The old man sucked on his teeth.

No, here, he thought, *it is different*. And though the broad flanks of the citadel suggested the people of the Balagne had withstood many a siege, he knew they lacked that cold, bone hard inflexibility of people like him from the south; the south, where bread was of wood and wine was of stone.

He tugged at his beard and made to stand. But before he could get properly upright he slumped back down. Getting old was not easy; that he had come to realise, and his arthritis was born of his hard life just as much as his great inner strength-and that was what kept him going. He leant more of his weight against the staff and stood up into the breeze.

The *Maestrale* was growing in confidence. Soon there would be too much wind for the kites; maybe even too much for the ferry.

The last time he had come to Calvi was... fifty-five, no fifty-six years ago. Ah, what did it matter; it had been a very long time ago.

For the first half of the war they had smuggled refugees from mainland France into Corsica: spies, Jews, émigrés, escapees; all manner of people on the run; some wealthy, some not. For the second half of the war they had smuggled arms back the other way.

He had come to Calvi just the once during those turbulent days. He did not like the town. As a matter of fact, he did not like any town. He went to town only when going to town could not be avoided, for towns he had long believed meant trouble.

Calvi, he decided, was still the same only different. Perhaps there would be an old face he would recognise around the garrison in the citadel. Though, as he had seen earlier in the morning, the parachutists of the 2nd Regiment looked far too young to remember the old days. And anyway, it had been Mosca who had joined the Legion after the war, not him.

The marina was busy with early season tourists, so it took him a while to find a chair at the back of the café. He preferred to sit at the back; that way the string that tied his black trousers tight at his waist, and the collarless white shirt beneath his waistcoat, drew less attention.

He ordered ice cream, a glass of Chataigne and a pichet of tap water. The waitress easily picked him for a southerner. Even if she had been blind, she would have caught the hint of Gallurese in his pronunciation. But she was a little surprised when instead of drinking the Chataigne she saw him pour the rich, dark chestnut liqueur over his ice cream.

There was another reason he liked to sit at the back; it afforded him the facility of watching for any faces that might be turned his way. Since those hotheads had murdered the Préfet Érignac in Ajacciu, nobody was safe. Why hadn't they recognised a soft touch for a Préfet when they saw one? *Mind you*, he thought, *Érignac's successor Bonnet, whilst full of muscular rhetoric, had turned out to be something of a clown; the Affaire de la Paillote had shown everybody that. I mean really,* he chuckled: *those ridiculous GPS men scuttling about in the night pretending to be paramilitaries and setting fire to beach huts and, as it turned out, themselves.* He laughed so loud that a couple at a neighbouring table turned to see what it was that amused him so.

But assassinating Érignac had been foolhardy. Whoever had thrown that particular rock into the water ought to be ashamed. The ripples from that ill-advised stunt would be tripping ashore for the next ten years. That was why he had to be more vigilant. That was another reason why it was better for him to sit at the back of the café.

When he had cleared his plate he sat and stared into the distance. He toyed with the gold signet ring on the little finger of his left hand. Only the spirits knew why it should be his daughter who would lead him back to this place and then further on to the mainland. He could have flown of course; Paris was less than two hours away by aeroplane. But then he doubted the perspicacity of pilots even more than he doubted the virtue of sailors.

Sadly, while he sat reviewing his lifelong disdain for travel, the weather deteriorated. Tall, forbidding columns of cloud marched like an army of giants down from the north and the sea trembled before them.

He left the café and hurried along to the port, and as if to validate his lack of faith in all modes of transport other than his feet, he found the ferry cancelled.

It was another reason why he did not trust towns or the people from them.

He frowned at the desk clerk, a frown infinitely more threatening than the clouds outside; a frown which sent the apologetic little man scurrying for cover to the back office in case the old man's look should turn him to stone.

It was unusual; a ferry being cancelled. The rarity of the event did not help his cause or quiet the chill voices that murmured within.

But then, standing amongst the other disgruntled and disappointed passengers, he understood. Just as there were reasons why he should feel apprehensive at being back in such a foreign town for the first time in fifty or so years, and just as there were other more pressing reasons why he should be on his guard, he also knew there was yet another more compelling reason why he should feel so unpleasantly ill at ease.

Before he had set off from his home in the south, and even before his daughter had returned to him and turned his life upside down with her news, he had heard the spirits calling his name from the maquis and he had heard their footfalls as they passed by his window in the night. The spirits had summoned him. There was no point in denying it. He knew it as sure as he knew that a man dies only once.

He walked away from the ferry port and struck out uphill. He remembered from all those years ago a quiet hotel at the back of the town. He wondered if there was any chance it might still be there, wondered if there was any chance the same comely woman might still be the concierge.

The bright sunlight suddenly gave way to shade and heavy grey clouds pressed down on his hat. The hairs on the back of his neck stood up as the temperature fell away.

From behind came a sudden gust of cold wind, on the heels of which the rain hurried hard and fast. The streets cleared. Awnings were furled. Blinds were drawn.

He turned a corner and lost his footing on the wet pavement. He let go of his staff and spread his arms out before him to keep from falling to the ground. His hat rolled like a wheel into the gutter.

As he got back to his feet he was aware of hands helping him and he mumbled his thanks. But then a soft, sweet-smelling rag was closed firmly over his mouth and a blinding light burst from the back of his head. He realised he should struggle and understood he was being bundled into the back of a vehicle. He began to resist. He began to fight. But he was surprised more by his own curious impotence than by the sudden and overwhelming force that was being exacted upon him. All the strength he could normally summon had, for some inexplicable reason, deserted him.

If only these people, whoever they were, knew how much he disliked the north. He had always told others this was precisely the sort of thing that happened to you when you went to the north.

He decided, as the light began to dim, that he would not come north again.

It was his one last thought before the living abandoned him and he embarked on his journey to join those spirits who had so recently been calling his name.

2

La Forêt de Barocaggio Marghese
Alta Rocca
Corse du Sud
Six weeks later

They walked in the shade of holm oak and chestnut, shotguns slung on their shoulders and game bags empty on their belts. The air beneath the broad canopy of leaves was cool and moist and refreshing after their long climb. There had already been more rain this summer than last; that much they knew for certain. The lake at Ospédale behind them was full again and the steepening valley up which they climbed between the two points of Corbu and Diamante, led to the birthplace of two streams, each one flowing down to the sea on either side of the island.

Before, the two men would have met in one of the many bergeries dotted about the countryside, but these days they considered it wiser to take leave of their accustomed meeting places in favour of more isolated locations. They carried with them no mobile phones and they changed their route often, for they had learned that not only were the authorities triangulating their positions from their phone signals, but that the police had also placed cameras about the forest to monitor their passage.

"Did anyone see him arrive in Calvi?" the shorter man asked, not lifting his eyes from the trail before him.

"No, Mosca. But a waitress in a café at the marina is sure she served him. Her description of him is quite clear."

"What does she remember of him? How much detail?"

"She said he ordered ice cream and Chataigne, and that he poured the Chataigne over his ice cream."

The one called Mosca smiled and lifted his cap. His tightly curled hair was the colour of the *nevé*; the patches of snow high up; the small patches that survive through the year in permanent shadow. He scratched at a bead of sweat that ran down his neck.

"Ah! That would be him. He was always doing that. I don't know anyone else who would desecrate ice cream like that." He deliberated for a few steps, and then said, "Too much time has passed. It is too long. I have been to the *oriu* at Carbini; there is no sign of him having been there. We must assume the worst. I cannot believe no one saw him taken. No one at all?"

"It would appear not. The clerk at the check-in desk at the ferry terminal thinks he remembers an old man on that day, but apart from that no one saw him taken."

"The GPS?"

"No. If it was the Security Service, we would have heard," the taller of the two replied. "It must be the work of some other authority." He stopped, turned and laid his hands on Mosca's shoulders. Looking him directly in the eyes he said, "I know he was your friend. You knew him better than almost anyone.... "

"No," Mosca interrupted, raising his voice just enough so his companion would appreciate the importance of what he was about to say. "Better than that! I knew him better than all the others. Even his daughter. Even his wife – God rest her soul."

They walked on again.

After the older of the two men had been permitted time to calm himself, the younger man began again, "It has been said that the two of you argued; that of late there was no talking between you... some disagreement?"

"It was so," Mosca replied. "But," he continued in a tone firm enough to discourage any further enquiry, "it was not an argument that concerns the council. It was about the girl. It was family business, not political. If anyone suggests any different, they must suggest this to me directly. Do you understand?" His deep voice was suddenly raw with emotion, and he balled his right hand into a fist. "To me. Do you understand? To me." He glanced at the younger man, his eyes hard like the granite escarpment that soared above them. "They must say this to my face."

"I will tell them, Mosca. Have no fear, they will understand. I am sure of that."

"Fear?" he growled. "You think this is about fear; my fear? I tell you, my young friend, it is not about fear; it is about honour. It is always about honour. And in honour there is no place for fear. You do not fear to do something if it is right, eh?"

"What about the girl?"

They walked in silence for a while, the younger man waiting politely for an answer from his more senior partner.

Mosca raised a finger as if to confirm his point. "That girl, I tell you, is soon to be a woman. For a while her head was turned the wrong way, but now I think it is turned back to us again; to our ways again. She has learned her lesson, and learned it the hard way. This lesson will leave its mark, of that I am certain." He paused and then shrugged his shoulders: "But maybe it is not such a bad thing that she is this way now that the old man is gone."

They strolled on in silence.

"So, no more questions," said the taller man. He searched for the right words to reassure the older man that all of his enquiries were now satisfied. "That is the end of it."

"If only it were so," Mosca replied, "if only."

They arrived at a small clearing in the midst of which sat a smooth, oblong rock about the size of a modest headstone.

Even though the sun was well beyond its highpoint it was still hot, so they perched in the shade, ate smoked cheese and drank their rough wine. They waited patiently for the other members of the council to arrive.

3

La Baie de la Tozza
Porto Vecchio
Corse du Sud
Ten years later

He ran along the beach at a comfortable pace, some way short of an outright run but with a little more energy than a casual jog. He allowed only limited, efficient movement to his arms, which were slightly raised and bent at the elbow as though he was trying to run whilst steadying a heavy weight on his back. His path followed the narrow margin of firmer, damp sand at the water's edge. Ahead of him lay the long strip of beach, whilst behind him his footprints melted gently away, leaving no trace of his presence. He was naked and barefoot, evenly suntanned, except for the lighter skin around his buttocks, and lean in build, though not so lean he considered himself slim.

The pale yellow disc of sun off-shore was clear above the broad horizon and the purple sea beneath it flat and glossy, like polished rosso antico. The first breeze of the day was only just beginning to stir from its slumber and there was something almost virtuous about the cool, clear air, as though the natural vapours of the morning warranted his exposure.

When he reached the northern end of the long, curving beach he halted, turned, stretched his arms and legs and set off back the way he had come. Beyond the occasional and very gentle lap at the breakwater and his steady, easy breathing, there was no sound. There were no seagulls this morning; for them there was the promise of better rations to the north, over the rocky point in Zizula where a few of the local fishermen would be coming in from their labours.

The first hour after dawn belonged to Ric in much the same way as the hour before it belonged to the fishermen. Out in the still silence, his body working, his head light and uncluttered, he felt detached from influence. There were no external pressures or demands lurking along his route; no structures, no restrictions. This was his time; just him and the beach and the water, and another fresh morning. And over the past week or so he had begun to notice that both his mind and his body were once more working in close, if not yet perfect union.

He remembered reading somewhere that when pilots land they require a period of adjustment during which their heads and feet get used to being once more in contact with the hard ground; the longer the flight, the longer the period of adjustment required. He guessed it was the same for a truck driver after a long haul in his cab, or an office worker after a day spent staring at a computer screen. They too, he thought, needed an interval or space between their two worlds, a kind of no-man's-land in which to effect as gentle a transition as possible between the surreal and the real. There was no reason why he should be any different.

It came to him that though he had not seen a soul on his side of the hill, he could not help but feel that he was being observed. He tried hard to ignore it, but when the feeling took him he was naturally very conscious of his vulnerable state. He was perfectly at ease with his own nudity; it certainly did not bother him, but he was aware of his isolation and knew that his only exit lay up the narrow track down which he had come, and that he would be relying on his old and rather temperamental car to get him up the long, steep slope out of the bay.

Yet he felt oddly secure on the deserted beach; he sensed in his quieter moments a belonging to it.

Once, after his swim and his run, he had put on a pair of shorts and walked up through the maquis and the grove of umbrella pines, and searched for the tell-tale signs of another presence. But he had found no evidence of either intruder or intrusion. The forest floor was mostly hard ground and near the crest of the hill the pines were scorched and blackened by a recent bush fire. But deeper in the grove, where the fire had not reached, the floor was strewn with pine needles and here and there clumps of rye grass, and together they allowed for little evidence in the way of footprints.

So, as on most other mornings, he shrugged off his apprehension and finished his run back down towards the southern end, sprinting the last hundred metres or so.

Fifteen minutes or so later, by his car in the shade, he worked through his customary routine of cool down stretches, towelled himself dry, and then stood and sipped a bottle St George's water.

He surveyed the horizon out to the east. The light, like the air, was changing, emerging from the monochrome of dawn into the brighter colours of morning. The sea was still flat and pearly calm, and unbroken except for the odd, limp ripple that tripped idly onto the beach.

The bay was curved like the left half of a compass, the shore sloping gradually down to the points at north and south, and out almost in the centre of the bay between the points stood, proud and defiant, the tall triangle of rock to which he had just swum. From where he stood it seemed not much more than a bald cone, like an ice cream with the topping knocked off, but he knew from experience that its circumference at water level was a good thirty metres or so, and its height maybe ten. The craggy crown of the rock was mostly flat and wider than at the base, so the rock threw a large shadow on the water even through the hotter part of the day.

Over the many thousands of years the water line had fought a losing battle against the relentless sea, and beneath the water the rock tapered down another ten metres to where the seabed splayed out to all points of the compass. Below the waterline, the wall of rock was pockmarked with holes and indents in which lived the fruits of the sea; the cavities and faults playing host to the many crustaceans and molluscs. Above it, the sea birds nested in the valleys and crevasses; the upper surfaces being constantly eroded by the natural elements of wind, rain, sun, and the bird's own nitrous guano.

la Tozza was named so locally because it was literally a big rock. The French called it the Grosse Pierre, or more accurately the large pebble; dull and barren except for the dark striation that ran through it like the line left by the cut of a cheese-wire. The sea birds nesting on it held dominion over the clear shallow waters below; they reared their young and defended their territory noisily. As far as he could tell, no one had yet tried, or had been bothered enough to try, to master the slanting overhang from the sea up to the top of the rock.

To passing holiday-makers the upside down mushroom of granite was merely a picturesque feature of yet another picturesque bay; a surfeit of which he now knew lined the south-eastern coast. But to Ric it had become his morning ritual; the swim out to the rock, a half hour of fishing for octopus and a swim back with his catch on a loop attached to his belt, followed by a run along the beach. Most of the time he used a wetsuit, for he found that diving so early in the day in such cool waters reduced his core temperature very quickly. He had bought a mask and snorkel in a local store, a pair of long, pro-light flippers, and a weight belt, net and spear-gun. After his second outing he'd fashioned a climber's cam out of an old bicycle pedal and wedged it in one of the fissures of the rock. He then attached the weight belt to it so that he did not have to wear it every time he swam out. Some days he didn't bother with the fishing and on other days he swam back with five or six octopus; much depended on how the mood took him or how easy the catch came. Some days it was as though the octopus were absent and on others there was an overabundance, but he hadn't yet learned to read the habits of the cautious, watchful creatures. Initially he'd had trouble dispatching them, but, after asking one of the old fishermen from over the hill in Zizula, he'd soon got used to turning them inside out and removing their viscera, which was not always an easy task when treading choppy water. He usually gave his catch to the chef at the hotel in the village, who repaid him with a free meal in the restaurant once a week. It seemed a pleasingly natural and very reasonable trade.

A bird flitted about the scented pines, disturbing his light meditation. It was small and compact, with light blue wings, a dark head and not much in the way of a tail. The nuthatch scrutinised him from the lower branch of an Aleppo pine at the edge of the forest, twitching and turning its head as it watched.

He stood and looked back at it for a minute before pulling open the boot of the Citroen. The bird was probably waiting to see what his intentions were for the octopus he had caught. He took his catch from the bush upon which he had hung them while he ran and laid them in the boot. He dressed, glanced back along the beach as if to preserve the sight for one last time, and then sat down on the driver's seat, legs out of the car, to slip on his trainers. He swung his legs into the battered dome-shaped vehicle, pulled on a little choke, turned the key, pressed the starter button and applied some throttle to catch the start as the engine coughed into life.

He backed the Citroen up, wheeled it round, and stuttered in an effective, if ungainly, progression up the track.

Ric flipped up the lower section of the window to allow the cooler air in to freshen up the musty cabin. By now he was looking forward to *pain-au-chocolat*, his morning vice, but he was otherwise unconcerned by the day that lay before him. He was in a relaxed and contented mood, and very much unaware of the young boy studying him from the camouflage of the pines.

4

The small beachfront village of Zizula, just up the coast from Porti Vechju, lay in a protected bay much broader than its sister just to the south. Five minutes off the main road that traversed the eastern side of the island, the village had grown up around a beach-front, villa-style hotel, far more Italian in appearance than French, and a small number of bars and café-restaurants that straddled the road at the back of the beach. The bleached sands squeezed between the road and the sea at the centre, and the trees and maquis out wide at the ends, but it was a long strip like a stretched crescent moon and sported a colourful array of lounge chairs and parasols.

The southern end of the crescent swept round towards the east, ending in a shallow causeway that linked the bay with a small, barren island. The causeway, though under water, was just shallow enough to wade across, but also just deep enough that it deterred all but the most determined sunbather in search of solitude from crossing; on the low summit of the island stood the crumbling pile of a Martello tower. It reminded Ric of an unwanted chess piece; a castle discarded and forgotten; a testament to a game the players had lost interest in a couple of centuries before.

Either side of the hotel in the centre of the bay, two pontoons stretched out a hundred metres or so, the southern of the two playing host to a smattering of small, blue and white sailing dinghies.

The burnished shield of the sun wheeled slowly into the azure sky, too bright to look at but not yet too formidable to loiter in, and the cool of dawn was but a distant memory. Few of the late season holidaymakers were in any doubt as to the course of the temperature.

Late September was a favoured time for the more leather-skinned sun-worshippers and, with a few exceptions, the children had returned to school. There was still enough heat in the sun to bake a decent tan, but the searing white heat of full summer had long since passed. Much of the western Mediterranean had endured a mixed summer, but on the eastern coast of Corsica the earth was tinder dry from the lack of rain.

Ric heaved on the steering wheel and swung the old car into a parking space facing the *patisserie*. He crossed the road and handed his catch in at the kitchen door of the hotel; the portly chef beamed, inspected the octopus hanging slack on the loop and nodded his approval.

The street was quiet. The shops were only just raising their shutters, but the bakery had been open for a while. He collected his crusty loaf and chocolate croissant, which the brunette behind the glass counter handed him with a smile, suggesting her husband was unwise to spend so many nights out fishing. After that he strolled down to the small store, bought some *capellini* pasta, a dozen slices of the smoked ham the locals called *prizuttu*, and a wedge of *ottavi*, the hard goats' cheese.

Ric dropped the shopping onto the back seat of the Citroen, climbed in and reversed out into the road.

As he was half out onto the road an angry horn blared at him and a dirty, dark blue saloon swerved in exaggerated fashion to avoid him.

Ric lurched to a sudden halt and peered out the passenger window to catch a glimpse of a raised hand and behind it a moustachioed, chubby man mouthing a torrent of invective. The car, bearing mainland licence plates, sped away at considerable pace to the south, fish tailing a little as it went.

The brunette from the bakery appeared by the door. She looked towards the fleeing car, looked back at Ric, glanced up at the heavens, smiled with a hint of a raised eyebrow and returned inside before he could respond.

Ric exhaled slowly and shook his head, then reversed slowly out of the parking space.

After all, not even the local *Sapeurs Pompiers* en route to a recent bush fire had swept down the main road at such a speed.

He drove west out of the village in the direction of the main road to Porti Vechju, the same route out of the village as that of the urgent saloon. As he passed the hotel the sea came into view on his left and he noticed the dark blue hull of a large motor-yacht lying up in the bay.

5

The drive up to the villa, or bungalow as it really was, led by way of a three minute crawl up a dust bowl of a track near the turn off to the cluster of residences known as Cirindino.

To begin with, when he drove back from the beach up to the bungalow, he missed the track, but after a while he noticed just by the turning an isolated stone hut set into the hillside twenty or so metres from the road. He had reckoned it to be some kind of municipal deposit, like a refuse station, but reasoned it was set too far back to be so.

A few days before his curiosity had eventually got the better of him, so he stopped and wandered over to investigate it. The small bleached-stone house was a little larger than a garden shed and more solidly built. The roof, pitched in the centre, was overlaid with ridged terracotta tiles and the whitewashed stucco walls were weathered and crumbling in places. In the centre, which faced east down the hill, stood a doorway with a wrought iron gate of the kind one might expect at the entrance to a walled garden. Above the door a name was chiselled into the lintel; a singular and short family name. But the elements had long since triumphed in their battle to weather the stone, and apart from the first letter *P*, the others were too indistinct to be legible.

Ric had peered through the bars of the gate to read the legends on the casket plaques set into the wall at the back, but he'd not been able to make out much more than the odd name and date, none of which provided him with any clues as to the identity of the family interred. The tomb was so barren of any decoration that it could in no way be termed a mausoleum. The only grandeur was to be found in the fact that it remained alone and aloof on the hillside, as though the family to whom the tomb belonged was one of significance and very definitely not to be confused with other, perhaps lesser families.

He had first noticed the proliferation of tombs during his drive from Ajacciu down to Bunifaziu. Most were gathered together by the main road in or out of town in great allotments, as though each of the resident families was entitled to a plot on which to build their tomb and lay to rest inside it their departed; albeit in uncomfortable proximity to the relatives of their neighbours. Some, like the one at the bottom of the track, stood alone on a hillside, but in general the communities seemed to exist as two villages side by side; one for the living, the other for the dead.

In Olmeto, perched in the hills high above Proprianu on the west coast, the village of the dead appeared to preside over that of the living, such was its immense size and concentrated occupation.

In Bunifaziu, where he had stayed for a week in a quiet hotel, tucked away in one of the cobbled alleyways of the old town above the harbour, he had spent long periods wandering the Cimetiere Marin in the Bosco; the high citadel which had once been home to the Foreign Legion. Amongst tombs packed tightly together, like troops queuing patiently for embarkation, Ric had stumbled upon an extraordinary calm, a brief peace and tranquility he had not sensed for as long as he could remember. The irony of finding such a beguiling serenity amongst so many long dead strangers, strangers with strange names like *Chiozzi, Guiaro, Lavigne, Terrazoni, Casanova Zuria* and *Schmidt*, had vaguely amused him.

And beneath most of the names were inscribed the letters *Priez Pour Eux*; the demand that the living should pray for the dead. Perhaps, he had wondered after reading the many tributes and commendations, it was the fact that the dead still craved the comfort of prayer from the living which calmed him, as though the vain request for salutation from the living suggested that even in death there would be no lasting refuge from the despair of life. In some cases the tombs told stories of entire families who had perished in terrible disasters, and on a few of the rough-hewn stone crosses loyal troops had posted respectful affection for their brave officer struck down in Madagascar or the Sudan; the sword of the infidel and the lance of the mosquito having taken a heavy toll.

Some of the houses of the dead were in better order than those of the living, as though the grand houses were kept clean and tidy in case their former residents should reappear from the afterlife.

Around the corner from the Bosco he found the long abandoned garrison of the Foreign Legion; the cobbles of the parade ground worn smooth by many boots and bleached white by the unforgiving sun, the high windowed walls of the barracks watching and waiting in vain hope for the return of their heroes.

And it was perhaps at the high arched gate into the deserted garrison that Ric found an end to one odyssey and the beginning of another, for it was shortly after he left Bunifaziu that he chanced upon the crumbling edifice at Cirindino.

The track up the shallow incline to his *villa*, as the immobilière in Porti Vechju had described it, was pockmarked with potholes that had over time filled up with loose stones. Only God knew how the local builders had managed to transport the plaster and tiles up the bumpy cul-de-sac, and it was no wonder the local postman never called, even though Ric was not expecting mail from anyone other than the letting agent.

The Citroen was ideal for the uneven driveway. Seeing as the customary gait of the old heap consisted of a series of lurches, bounds, bounces and rolls even on a smoothly metalled surface, it was therefore a natural progression for it to behave in exactly the same way on the uneven gulley of a trail. Any other more modern vehicle would have shaken its teeth out in a week, whereas the Citroen had started life without any in the first place. He identified it as bohemian, even a shade aboriginal and quite literally 'earthy', as he had learnt by the sandy clouds that billowed up from underneath the dashboard.

Pulling up amidst one of those clouds outside the main door of the house, Ric realised that although he had spent much of the last couple of weeks completely on his own and that there was no one to look forward to on his homecoming, he felt a gentle, almost reassuring wave of pleasure wash over him every time he got back to the old place; his temporary quarters-his 'home' of the moment.

He gathered up his shopping and went indoors.

The *Paviglione*, as it was called, was nothing more than an adequate and functional, south-facing dwelling, square to the point of symmetry, with views down to the sea in the east and up towards the mountains in the west. There were no locked doors; there was nothing, except perhaps for the basin and shower in the bathroom and the fridge and gas stove in the small kitchen, worth stealing. Ric's few items of value, his passport, credit cards and cash, he put in a plastic bag and buried in the garden between two cacti; one small, green, plump and spineless, the other larger, with long, thin, flat ears which rose to a point like an Agave.

Outside, on the south facing wall, sliding glass doors opened onto a paved patio. The doors had been set into the old stone walls, but looked very out of place and were un-pointed, as if the builders had intended to return and finish them but had as yet not found the time. A modest pool was set into the patio; not much more than a plunge pool, a few strokes in length and a tall man's height in width. It was, though, an adequate relief from the midday heat. On the wall of the north side of the house sat a large boxed gas canister to which Ric had chained his motorcycle; apart from the Citroen his only other extravagant purchase. The garden, such as it was, knew neither manicured lawn nor boundary, and there was no evidence of any recent attention having been paid to it; the ubiquitous maquis that faded away down the slopes from the house being a mixture of rock rose, stonecrop, wild herbs in dry grass, and dense juniper, arbutus, lentisk, myrtle and other shrubs. There were not yet many flowers; they would come later, he supposed, with the autumn rains.

The inside consisted of a very square living room, a thin white carpet rug on the floor, a bedroom, a little ungenerous in its dimensions, and a rudimentary bathroom with a shower; the water flowed irregularly and was in the habit of discontinuing at the most awkward moment. The furnishings were functional, nothing more; a small dining table, sofa, and a couple of occasional chairs fashioned from dark heavy wood broke the hollow of the living space. The *décor* was all white-washed and the floor tiled throughout in pale terracotta.

The walls were thicker than those of the other holiday rentals he had seen; the brickwork was neither modern nor conventional, the blocks hand-hewn, rough and uneven. One stone in particular, in the lower part of the north wall, was more yellow in colour than the rest. It lay horizontally and, whilst it was similar in height at about half a metre, it was at least three times as long as any of the other, squarer blocks. The edges of the stone were rounded and the surface smooth to touch.

Only an optimist, Ric reasoned, would call it a villa, for really it was nothing more than a hut on a hillside, perhaps originally a dwelling for the goatherd; cool in the summer and dry in the winter. But after so many seasons the communion of old stones and recent glass had assumed enough form to earn the designation *villa*, and from it a meagre income was provided.

Ric had not wanted the disturbance of a maid, and even though there was no call for one in such a basic and humble abode, the agency had insisted. An elderly and plump crone, who knew only black attire and who whistled unintentionally when she walked, was deposited at the house once a week to while away an hour sweeping, polishing and dusting. They engaged in no conversation; there seemed little need. Ric tried his best to be absent on the Thursday of the week, but more often than not he misjudged her arrival. On the occasions when he was present, he would sometimes catch her staring inquisitively at him from behind her broom, at which point she would look away sharply.

He put the shopping away, slipped out of his T-shirt and shorts, and opened the long glass doors to the patio. Ric walked out, again untroubled by his nudity, there being no other property within line of sight, and fell with a loud smack on his back in the pool. The slap of his shoulders against the flat water gave rise to a stinging and then tingling sensation on his skin. Somehow the brief discomfort reminded him he was very much alive and that in turn lifted his spirits.

But, no sooner had his spirits begun to rise than the very same idea induced a low melancholy within him, for it pricked his conscience that he often felt so lifeless when there was so very much of life to feel alive about.

Shaking his head to disperse unwelcome and unwanted thoughts, he submerged himself beneath the water for a couple of seconds, then climbed out of the pool and went inside to clean up.

After a shave and a lukewarm shower, Ric called Manou on his cellphone.

She did not pick up, which for her was unusual. He left a brief message on her voicemail to let her know his plans, or rather his lack of them.

6

Ric sat by the pool and read the notebook she had given him. He was beginning to make sense of the Corsu without having to resort to the French translation, and that pleased him. He was keen to show Manou how much of the local dialect he was picking up, with her help of course.

Then a vision of Manou materialised right out of the text. She was standing in front of him wearing her dark green camisole and shorts, and not much else other than her brightly coloured headscarf. She was questioning him with those light blue eyes of hers; those extraordinary, compelling, morning-sky blue eyes. He had exchanged only a brief look with her at the beach bar, and it was her smile and her eyes which had caught his attention. She had provoked a fluttering in the pit of his stomach; an unusual reaction that had made him suddenly very self-conscious.

He put the book down and closed his eyes.

The image he conjured was Manou the first time he saw her. But what was it that set her aside from others? Was it how she stood; that slight arch to her back? The way she seemed to hold her shoulders very straight and a little further back? Further back from what he hadn't been sure, but it accentuated her slender breasts and hinted at a slight physical arrogance, not brazen or pushy arrogance, more a slightly proud and assured way in which she held herself. At first he had mistaken her as overly self-confident, and had decided she was a shade self-possessed. But later he had come to realise that her stance owed more to a put-up defence rather than aggression, and that behind her composure there lay a very different form to the one on show.

Manou was at once unpredictable and yet consistent. She could be at the same time diverse and yet constant. He knew whenever he was with her

21

he could rely on her to surprise him, and that every time she reacted to him she would react to him in a way he had not seen before, whether it was in conversation, in attitude, or in behaviour. It wasn't that her views-political, religious, social, sexual, or emotional-changed from one often animated discussion to the next; it was that her approach always came from a new angle, making it impossible for him to argue with her in any conventional way. She confused him much, but not unpleasantly. She was quick to excite, but possessed the strangest ability to be perfectly calm in an instant; a raging tempest one minute, a tranquil pool the next, and without any apparent physical effort or evidence of transition. Manou was possessed of a skill he had never been able to achieve: the abrupt calm after a storm.

Ric stood up and rubbed his forehead. His torso ran with sweat from the cradles at the base of his neck, and his skin felt taut. His heavy, dark sunglasses dimmed the glare of a sun which now hung high above him and he realised it was far hotter than he had at first thought. The mountains to the west shimmered in the haze and to the east the purple Tyrrhenian dozed flat and placid. With the temperature nearing its peak, the cicadas were murmuring their noisy approval and the air was thick with the heady aroma of rosemary and arbutus.

The world was still. There would be no relief from the heat until well after noon.

A familiar gecko skittered rapidly across the patio in front of him. He went indoors and collected a bottle of St George's water from the fridge and drained it in long steady swallows. It was colder than was good for him. The chill streaked down his chest, invigorating him, reminding him of the way Manou teased him with her nails.

7

Two weeks before he had been sitting in a beach bar at the southern end of the bay in Zizula, eating an early dinner of *salade niçoise*. Camille's beach bar was popular with the younger crowd, the atmosphere permanently scented with coconut oil and grilled sardines, and the conversation overlaid with eighties vintage Eurofizz that bubbled from a small speaker perched on the roof of the bamboo shack.

Ric was studying a rapidly emptying bottle of *Patrimonio rosé* when a group of half a dozen or so young locals breezed up from the beach and took over a table. They took a while to level it on the soft sand, laughing and joking as they did so. One of them went to the bar to order drinks and, judging by the chat and backchat passing between the table and the bar, they were all known to the patron. There was, he noticed, much familiar physical contact between them, much embracing and friendly pawing.

Hearing the brusque but jolly bar owner, Camille, call out "Manou," Ric turned towards the group to see who would respond, and it was when she got up that he noticed her.

He decided she was pretty; just that. She was wearing a green camisole and shorts, her rich, dark, curly hair falling untidily about her face, and every now and again she would casually push it back out of the way. Manou's almond brown skin was no stranger to the sun, but neither did she owe her colour to it, and her poise and ease, and the confidence with which she held herself, turned a few heads at the tables as she walked up to the bar.

Sometime later, in that curious, instinctive way in which one knows one is being observed, she must have become aware of his gaze for she raised her head to look over at him. It was then that he saw the unusual and striking light-blue of her eyes; an intensity and clarity that was as much beguiling as it was unsettling. But her look was not one of rebuke, which he had expected, although neither was it an open encouragement. Her look was simply an acknowledgement of him, nothing more.

A little self-consciously Ric then dropped his gaze and returned to examining his bottle of rosé. As he did so he realised how ridiculously obvious his reaction to her must have seemed and he coloured with embarrassment.

The low sun was throwing long, cool shadows out across the beach, even though sunset was still some way off. As he finished his meal he listened in on the group's conversation. Though his French was passable, the rapidly spoken Corsu with its Italian influence was not so easy to pick up. It was easy on the ear, he thought, if occasionally argumentative in tone.

As the shadows lengthened further so the bar emptied and he soon found himself sitting alone but for the larger group in which the young woman, Manou, sat and held sway. Ric finished his bottle of wine and vowed to order only a 'pichet' next time.

He paid at the bar and left, unable to resist the temptation to glance at her as he walked by.

This time she raised her eyes, inclining her head very slightly so that he was in no doubt, and smiled briefly at him.

Ric wasn't sure whether hers was a casual acknowledgement, or whether it was the Patrimonio trying to convince him otherwise.

As he buzzed the trials bike along the winding road back to Cirindino, the wind whistling around his unprotected head, he tried to guess her age. She was very much a woman, but there was something of the girl about her too. He realised that though every local female, teenage or otherwise, seemed to possess a confident, almost knowing air, she was probably older than she looked; perhaps roughly the same age as him; perhaps just old enough to be looking back at thirty.

As he rode up the track towards the house he felt her presence begin to ride up alongside him, and sure enough by the time he reached the house she had overwhelmed him.

8

Ric put the water bottle down and grinned at the memory. How stupid he had been to even try and convince himself that her glance had been anything other than casual at that first meeting.

In the kitchen he put a few slices of the ham and cheese and a couple of beef tomatoes on one of the bright orange plates and took it with the bread board out onto the patio. He put up an umbrella; it was far too hot to eat in the sun.

Ric sliced the bread and tomatoes and carved a sliver of cheese on top. He sat back and gazed into the hazy distance.

Two days after that first encounter Ric had driven the back road down to Porti Vechju and swung by Renabianca, a large camp site which lay in the next bay south. He had gone not exclusively out of boredom, although a change from his everyday routine had been on the cards, but he'd also wanted to find another outlet for his daily catch of octopus.

He'd driven down to the busier town of Porti Vechju on a couple of occasions. But in the City of Salt as it was known by the salt pans at the southern end of the bay, he had found himself feeling out of place and uncomfortable. Treading the cobbled alleyways he felt like just any other tourist, which, undeniably, he was. However, that had not been his intention, for Ric had no desire to be a tourist even though he found it difficult to discard the tag that so obviously hung around his neck. He held no grudge against them, tourists, but he was not inclined to join them in their aimless meandering. Being just another watcher, looking in from the outside, and being the stranger in another man's world, Ric had had enough of.

Perhaps it was his need to belong to a more local parish that drew him to Renabianca. And perhaps it was what she later referred to as providence.

To whatever it was, whether coincidence or luck, or to whoever it was that was responsible for his course, Ric was suddenly very grateful, as the first person he met when he walked into the reception at the campsite was Manou.

She was on the phone.

She smiled briefly and put up a hand to ask for his patience as she concentrated on her call. Her teeth were very white and even; her cheek bones proud and firm, smooth and rounded, soft with flesh not tight. Her slender jaw curved evenly to her delicate chin and her eyebrows were dark and crowned her eyes; eyes that were, he noticed again, that light blue of the Corsican morning sky. She was wearing a cream blouse, which offset her slender brown arms, but the rest of her was hidden beneath the counter. Manou was speaking quickly, smiling as though she was familiar with the caller.

She replaced the phone in the cradle and turned to him, waiting for him to speak, but he hesitated.

"Hi," he said before the silence grew too long.

"Hello," she replied, highlighting the 'he' and softening and extending the 'lo'. "How can I help?" she asked.

There was another overlong silence before he replied. "Sure, do you, I mean would you mind if I looked around?"

"No, of course not. Do you mean to look at Renabianca or just here at the shop and the restaurant? I can give you a map of the camp site. It's a big area."

"Thank you," he replied. "I was thinking of eating in the restaurant one evening, but then a look round the site would be good too." Good? Good for what? He wasn't going anywhere. "I mean I'm renting the villa over the hill and...."

"You stay up at *Paviglione*," she interrupted, smiling.

"Oh! You know that?"

"Yes," she inclined her head a little, the way she did when she had looked up at him as he left the beach bar. "Everyone knows where everyone is around here," she said with an impish grin. "It's a big place and a small place too, you know. There are many places to hide, but you will always be found-well, sometimes later than sooner."

"That's reassuring. I'll remember it the next time I get lost."

Silence followed, and then she beat him to the next question.

"You want to look round? It's a bit early for lunch. Come on," she offered, lifting up the flap of the counter, "I have to take some papers down to the beach. You can walk with me. I will show you the way."

He stood back at the doorway to allow her to pass in front of him. Her perfume was light, soft coconut and vanilla, perhaps a hint of lavender. Ric followed her out into the dazzling sunlight.

To the right behind them lay a small supermarket-style shop with a display of lilos, towels, wind-breaks and other beach paraphernalia. To the left of that stood a large, stone-faced restaurant flanked by mature plane trees which opened out in arches onto a circular, paved dance floor. A communal area hosted table tennis and football tables, and in the shade provided by the broad leafed trees lay a gravelled square for *petanque*. There were other wooden sheds and outhouses behind that, all wedged between well-aged trees. Many of the timbers were old, sun-bleached and twisted, and in need of replacing. The main building had at one time been a substantial residence; the campsite had simply taken root and grown up around it.

She led him in the direction of the sea, down a narrow tarmac road.

To break the quiet he said, "Great place you have here."

"Yes," she replied. Manou wore a calf-length, dark blue skirt to contrast with her blouse, and leather strapped sandals, the soles of which slapped a little as she walked.

"It has been here a long time, like some of the people who come here every year. They come back again and again. They like it. It is simple. They don't need more than the sun and the beach and the sea. We are lucky with our natural resources; our white sand, our 'Renabianca'." She smiled again directly at him, catching his eye so that he would know she was quoting her sales spiel and that he should not take it too seriously.

"I can imagine," he replied, "it must take some looking after."

Manou raised her right eyebrow as though he couldn't possibly know the half of it.

"All year round, I guess."

"Yes, it does," she said. And then realising what he was getting at she added, "I live here. It is my home."

They walked on, making small-talk. Ric felt a little scruffy beside Manou's office uniform, but she didn't seem to be aware of his awkwardness.

The closer they got to the beach the more densely the pines grew. The scent of the pines was strong and heady, but what struck Ric most was the dry heat thrown up by the scorching sand which was far too hot to walk on without shoes. Back from the dunes, spread out in the shade of the pines, stood brightly coloured caravans and tents, and every now and then service blocks with showers and basins around the outside. It was rudimentary but functional. Some of the caravans were well-established, as though they would provide year round accommodation.

"In the winter months we take the caravans to a park at the back," she offered, ahead of him again. "The *Préfecture* doesn't allow them to be here all the year, so we have to move them. And they are safer further away from the beach when the weather is bad. Some of the people have a lease on their positions. That's off the record, as you would say. But it keeps them happy. And," she paused, "what's good for the goose...."

"is good for the gander. Your English is far better than it has a right to be if you live here," Ric said, and immediately regretted his presumption.

"Oh, I get a lot of practice. Corsica is very popular with the British. After all, you used to be our masters." Manou spoke without a trace of resentment. "We have a great deal to thank you for, and this," she spread her arms wide, "this is how we show our appreciation."

He laughed, but didn't want to expose his ignorance of the island's history so he didn't pursue it.

"You didn't know it, huh?"

She did it again; she was ahead of him all the way. "No, I did not," he replied holding up both hands. There was no point in lying.

"Don't beat yourself up," she soothed, "it's your first time in Corsica, eh? Not many British people know it. The Americans, they go to Iraq, they think it's full of Iraqis. You British, you come to France, you think we are all French. But this is Corsica. We are not French." She paused. "Well, maybe not all of us."

He was about to mention Napoleon, when a little voice in his head warned him that it might be the reply she was expecting. So, not wishing to give too much ground, he turned to gauge her intention.

She was already looking at him with that mischievous smile, head slightly inclined, eyebrow raised. She knew what he had been about to say.

They laughed together; he at the trap she had set and she at his anticipating it.

When they reached the beach he left her to hand out her papers among the campers: British, Dutch, and Belgian, most of them retired couples.

Ric hung around, feeling a shade spare while Manou chatted and joked. She was popular with the dune dwellers and very much at ease in their company. In hanging around though, he provided her with a reason to cut short her conversations and return to him. He was her excuse, and he warmed to the role.

The beach at the northern end petered out round to a rocky point. The hill behind sloped down, via a saddle, then up again before ending out at jagged rocks. He wondered whether the saddle in the hill led directly into the bay in which he took his morning exercise. At the southern end the beach opened out into a wider and deeper strip and then rose up to small, reddish cliffs. Out in the bay a dozen speedboats nodded at their buoys, bobbing spectators to a similar number of brightly coloured windsurfers and Hobie-cats that zipped about catching the breeze.

They walked round in a loop back to the camp centre, talking about something and nothing.

Back at the office she gently dismissed him, claiming she had work to attend to. He didn't doubt her, but he backed away from suggesting they had lunch in the restaurant. Besides, he realised by the lack of diners that the restaurant at Renabianca was more probably an evening venue.

Manou walked slowly with him towards the car park. Ric's dusty Citroen sat rather self-consciously alone, baking in the heat.

"This is your car?" she asked, chuckling.

"It is."

"It is very," she paused, half suppressing a giggle as she searched for the correct term, "um, very, you would say, very *beatnik*? It is the same word in English, I think."

"Yes. I guess you could say that. More indigenous, I thought."

"Ah, yes. Sure," she replied, evidently turning his description over in her mind. "You could say it is *indigène*, perhaps native."

They laughed again.

"Would you say," this time he paused searching for the right words, "that if I did not know where to eat in Porti Vechju, you would recommend somewhere for me? Even," he carried on before she could reply, "show me?"

There ensued a silence, and the more it prolonged the more confident he felt about its outcome. Ric had always found rejection to be fleet of foot.

Manou studied the ground at her feet, letting Ric know her decision required careful consideration.

She looked up and smiled at Ric.

"No," she said, but then very quickly, "Yes, I mean, yes. I'm sorry, I would. I would like that very much."

9

That first evening out together they dined at *La Scorpina*. The restaurant faced the harbour of Porti Vechju from the south-eastern side of the bay beyond the salt pans. It took them forty minutes to drive to as the last part of the journey followed the small road towards the point at La Chiappa.

Manou had insisted on picking him up, saying it was she, better than he, who knew where they were going. After all was it not *he* who had asked *her* to show *him*?

And perhaps it was better that she had.

Though he had not so far managed to get himself lost when driving, most of the signposts left standing had seen better days.

It was rare, he noticed, to find a signpost which had not been defaced. The French name of the town or village was more often than not overwritten with a rough, black aerosol scrawl rendering the letters illegible. And that was only if the signpost hadn't already been so heavily peppered with shot that it resembled nothing more than a rusty colander. Usually the name of the town had been scribbled very hastily in its original Corsu beneath the illegible French. On newer signposts, the town name was written in both French and Corsican, but in most cases the French had nevertheless been defaced. It was also rare, Ric had seen, to find a signpost, advertising hoarding, bus-shelter or brick wall that had not been decorated with the initials 'FLNC'-the Fronte di Liberazione Naziunale Corsu. The supporters of the FLNC evidently wanted all and sundry to know they were still a political force to be reckoned with in spite of much of the crude graffiti looking dated, as though the defacement was more suited to a fifties film set rather than as it was, attempting to promote a very real and contemporary separatism.

Manou drove her cream coloured Peugeot Coupé a little too fast for him, but then he figured she knew the roads. At times there were precious few road markings, making it difficult for him to anticipate the long sweeping curves as they dipped in and out of the lengthening shadows. Ric recalled the overwhelming rush he had felt riding the motorcycle home that evening he had first seen Manou in Zizula, but made a conscious effort to rein in his enthusiasm.

They talked more small talk. There had been a *Levante* blowing for the past few days; a strong wind that blew from the east across the Tyrrhenian and which capped the mountains of the interior with white saucers of cloud. The sea was dirty with the debris blown shoreward by the *Levante*, but the season, if the weather settled and the sea held its temperature, she told him, might last into October.

The restaurant lay, in keeping with so many others, at the end of a dusty and bumpy track. But La Scorpina was different. It was a year-round eating place as opposed to a seasonal venue. A covered walkway shepherded them down to an established patio on a promontory of rock overlooking the sea. The food was brought on salvers down the walkway from the kitchens at the top by the car park. There were perhaps twenty tables at which were seated, Ric judged by their dress and complexions, mainly local folk and certainly very few tourists. La Scorpina was, he realised, one of those restaurants tourists rarely got to hear about-one of those locally kept secrets-and he was flattered that she should want to share it with him.

"*La Scorpina*," he said, trying his level best to pronounce it with as much French and Italian inflection as he could muster.

"Yes," she agreed, "but it is a Genoese word, not really French. So you must say it with a little more accent on the i at the end, but softly. *Scor-pi-na*," she broke the name up into syllables for him, slowly. "You cannot make a good *bouillabaisse* without a scorpion fish; the *rascasse rouge*. People confuse them with poisonous fish and think you cannot eat them, but it is only the spikes on the back fin that are poisonous. Maybe you would call them red snapper. But I think that's another fish."

Every table hosted the well-preserved head of a scorpion fish presented as a centre piece with a scented candle protruding from its jaws.

"Scorpion for the Genoese, the word also means 'a little ugly'," Manou added.

"Well," Ric surveyed the gaping mouth and vicious, needle-like teeth, "the Genoese got that right." Then not wanting to appear ignorant he added: "But they come in black too?"

"They do, but they are very small. Not worth the trouble." Then she leaned forward, frowning slightly and slowly arching her left eyebrow. "But then you know fish, huh Ric? Of course you do!" She grinned mischievously, her eyes bright with fun. "A man must know more than one fish if he is to make harvest from the sea, eh?"

He wasn't sure if she was being subtle, or if he was listening too hard. "A famous Corsican proverb?" he asked.

"No," she giggled. "I just made that one up. But we have many for sure." She wagged her finger at him, toying with him. "In fact we have too many sayings, but they all have a little truth in them. This one I like; *A macha, ochi un ha ma ochi teni*-The maquis has no eyes, but it sees all. You want it in French too?"

"No. Thank you. It sounds better in Corsu."

Manou nodded in appreciation. "Well it is an interesting language, Corsu, though it is not used by everyone these days. The government try to," she paused searching through her English vocabulary, "promote it, encourage everyone to speak it. They tell us that more and more of us speak it, they even teach it in schools now, and they tell you that you need it for the university at Corte. But only some of the old people speak it all the time. I know a few of the old proverbs that my grandmother, my father's mother, taught me. You know how grandparents like to talk in riddles, but...," Manou hesitated.

Ric assumed it was because she was searching for the right words in translation. But then it became apparent to Ric that Manou was studying him intently, looking directly and deeply into his eyes, as if she was trying to read his thoughts. The pause unnerved him enough to cause him to shift in his seat. He had been concentrating on what she was saying; he was intoxicated by her mid-Mediterranean, Latin accented English.

"Carry on," he offered, but not wanting her to have to lead their talking he said, "I've been listening to Voce Nustrale, the radio station from Cervioni, they air Corsu and French translations on a Sunday morning, about the same time we would normally have church service at home. Believe me, I know what I would rather listen to. Their play-list can be a shade dated, but it's a language that's easy on the ear. I heard some of the fishermen in Zizula talking to each other; didn't want me to understand what they were saying, I suppose."

"Yes, they will do that," she replied, grinning as though she remembered employing the tactic on more than one occasion. "But sometimes it's difficult for me to understand them too. There is a little Genoese, and Ligurian from the mainland. In Bunifaziu to the south you will hear a little more Gallurese and Sassarese from Sardinia. In Calvi they can't make up their minds and in the north, Bastia, it's very different again to how it is spoken here in Porti Vechju. Many people want to preserve the language. My grandmother used to say, *Una lingua si cheta, un populu si more*-a language silenced is a people who die."

They both let the proverb hang in the air for a minute. Ric was uncertain as to how to reply. He felt as though Manou was asking him to share in some kind of sympathy with the proverb.

She watched him and then, whilst still holding his eye contact, she turned her head left to address the waiter who had appeared at their table.

Manou spoke to the waiter in Corsu, smiling affectionately at him and asking after his family. She had the habit of pronouncing some words faster and some slower, dropping the ends off some of the consonants and rounding down some of the vowels; Greek *i-ou*, Italian *ese*, an almost Balkan harsh guttural *hrghh*, and all overlaid with soft, almost poetic lilting French.

She turned to Ric. "*Pietra?*"

"No, not beer, thanks. You choose."

Manou ordered Cap Corse.

The waiter reappeared with two rose-shaped glasses of the local red Vermouth. Ric found it had a slightly bitter taste, but not so bitter that it was unpleasant. The waiter also produced a bottle of white wine which he set in a cold bucket beside their table. There was no offer of a menu; they would eat Bouillabaisse along with all the other guests.

Ric asked whether there was any truth in the stories he had heard about the *bandits d'honneur* who, supposedly, still hid out in the maquis.

In return she fascinated him with lurid tales of the blood feuds of Santa Lucia di Talla; of how *Giovan-Battiste Quilichini* was murdered by *Luca-Luigi Giacomoni* in retaliation for the *Poli* breaking off the engagement of their eldest son to a *Giacomoni* girl; of how the mayor banned the festivals and the subprefect was forced to send in a detachment of *voltigeurs* to keep the peace. Manou spoke about a character called *Bucchino*, named so because he smoked too many cigarettes; a man known as *Buccino*, as in little pig because he was a gossip; and the deadly *Buciardone*, given such a title because he was the thrower of balls, or perhaps bullets. Nobody was certain.

"And all this," she added, "just last week." Manou hesitated and then frowned. "No. Perhaps I am wrong. Perhaps it was in the early part of the nineteenth century? These days it happens so often it is easy to forget where and when it takes place." She laughed to show him she meant no harm by pulling his leg.

"But our society is like most societies; it has a complex history. For instance, each village has a brotherhood. And each village makes a visit to the villages close by to exchange food, help in building a house, or maybe to share local information. The village with the largest brotherhood is more important than the village with the smaller brotherhood. The problem is that the smaller village becomes envious of the village with the larger brotherhood. Envy," she said, "*invidia*, it makes people want what they do not have. Envy is the worst of the cardinal sins because you cannot appreciate what you have if all the time you want what someone else has, eh?"

Manou studied Ric for a moment; her eyes roamed his face until, he noticed, she was very obviously looking at the small, round birthmark above his right eye.

He didn't shy away from her gaze. He had grown used to people sneaking surreptitious glances at the penny shaped strawberry mark, and he was way past being bothered by them. However, what he was not used to was another person studying his face in such an open manner.

The waiter brought the *bouillabaisse* in a large round tureen and served them in rustic clay bowls. Ric decided as he listened to her explain the many flavours in the fish stew that she was comfortable in his presence, which pleased and relaxed him. Then, just as the thought came to him, he reasoned that she would naturally be so in company, as she was used to dealing with the many holidaymakers of different nationalities at the campsite. She must have had to speak to them in all the various ways their particular native traits demanded. But she did seem to be very at ease in his company.

He realised he had stopped listening for a moment too long and that she had noticed him thinking his quiet thoughts.

"The *bouillabaisse* is not to your liking?" she asked. "For some they put in too much chilli and garlic. And there is for others too much shell fish and not enough sea fish. Some people, they make it with shark which I don't like. It's better with capone and bream. Bream is what I think you call it."

"No, I mean yes," he said, trying desperately to disguise the hash he was making of peeling a prawn. "It is delicious; all the different flavours. I'm not sure when I should stop?"

"Oh," she shrugged, "when you are finished. It's not a place to mind your appetite. These people are all here for the same reason: food, wine, company and conversation, the view across the water to the harbour, this atmosphere. It's like the *bouillabaisse*; so many individual ingredients that make the dish. When you have had enough of them, then you go home. It is simple."

And it was, so simple. But it was her company that was holding it all firmly in place and he wondered if it would be the same if he were not with Manou.

An inquisitive voice rose up inside and pushed him to ask her about her life, her family, her 'situation'. Was she single? Had she been married? Did she…? But he held back, managing to curb his impatience. Now was not the time for crossing borders; not yet.

Ric poured Manou more white wine. "So many flavours, so many influences and so many ingredients; they all blend together so well. Where do they all come from?"

"Well," she finished her food and dabbed at her mouth with her serviette, "from the Mediterranean. It is called this for good reason. It comes from the Latin 'Medi' – for the middle and 'Terra' – for the land, meaning literally 'in the middle of the land'. But I am sure you know this. So the list of the people who have come here is long; everyone from the Pope to the prophet Mohammed. And as they passed through they left us with a small part of their character. Some of the flavours here are Italian, many from Genoa, but then it is joined together with French cooking. For that we have to thank Napoleon," she sighed.

"Not fond of Napoleon?"

"No. Not much. He was always too busy looking after his own appetite in other places, not at home." Manou paused, expecting Ric to ask more about Napoleon.

But Ric understood that most other foreigners would ask and he didn't want to be like most others, so he kept quiet.

"You British helped us and gave us Pasquale Paoli, the Father of our

Nation. Then we had the French again, then Germans and Italians, and then after the war De Gaulle. With De Gaulle we inherited a lot of *pied noirs* from Algeria. They didn't all want to go back to the mainland, so some settled here. They were not all bad. They make some of our best wine. So, you see, there are many different flavours here. This does not include the flavours of all the travellers and merchants who have traded through Bunifaziu or one of our other ports. We are a very convenient... stop-over, is it the right word? We are a convenient stop-over for travellers going east to west and north to south? But then I think you have many different cultures in Britain too. Like us, you are an island race, but the similarities are not great. You have exported your culture all over the world. You are on the outside of the land, the 'Terra'. We have been given all of ours. We are in the middle of the land, Medi-Terra, Mediterranean. There I'm finished!"

Manou was silent for a moment.

"How much do I owe you?" he asked, reaching into his pocket.

Manou laughed a bright, long and lightly mocking laugh. "Yes," she said, "it's quite a speech isn't it? I used to recite it in my sleep. I should probably save it for the campers. I'm sorry."

"No, please, don't be. I'd really rather you weren't sorry," he replied rather too quickly.

"Yes. You are right," Manou said with a reluctant smile, "Sorry is for children."

"One of your grandmother's sayings?" Ric asked dead-pan.

"No," she replied, "another one of mine." Manou laughed loudly and her blue eyes shone bright with her enthusiasm. She was pleased with the small trap she had set and even more pleased he had walked right into it. One or two of the other younger guests turned to identify the source of the laughter.

They rounded off their meal with a glass of sweet *Muscat* to complement the soft *briocciu* cheese and afterwards Manou took his arm very naturally as they walked up the tree-lined path.

At the top, by her car, they accidentally turned in toward each other. Her eyes seemed to reflect the light of the stars, but beyond them Ric could not read her expression.

Manou did not allow the moment to last.

Throughout the drive home, Manou fascinated him with stories of how one village would be jealous of another because, when it came to the drawing of lots for conscription, one village might have to lose more of its young men to the army than the other, and so would lose the power afforded it by what had been its greater male population. How large families with strong blood ties maintained their position of strength and authority, extending their influence through marriage and the consequent loyalty the union procured; and of how it was that if the trunk of the family tree grew thick, then many healthy branches would grow from it.

When they arrived back at his house they parted rather formally. He thanked her, and she him. Ric rather self-consciously invited her in for coffee, and then wished he hadn't because he decided his invitation sounded contrived and obvious. By now he was beginning to understand that Manou didn't conform to any conventional social course. She shied away from expectation; something she clearly had neither time for nor interest in. Besides, Manou had left the motor running as a clear signal that she was not about to prolong the evening. He got out, but then as he was walking away from the car she lowered her window, smiled playfully and said, "See you, Ric."

Ric stood and watched her melt into the night. He could read that sign. There were no bullet holes in that one.

10

In his sleep, Ric became aware of the steady, soothing wing-beat of a humming bird somewhere in the distance. The humming grew steadily into a thumping, whopping, knocking until he understood that what he could hear was the rhythmic drum of an approaching helicopter, the mean whip of its blades reverberating against the mountainside.

Ric opened his eyes. All he could see was white. He blinked and lifted his head. He was in the living room, lying on the sofa. The sun shone in a great hot beam through the glass doors.

It was definitely a helicopter he could hear. And it wasn't part of the soundtrack to any dream he might have been wrapped in.

He rolled off the sofa, stood up and walked over to patio door. Ric slid it open and looked up only to be blinded by the blazing sun.

A shadow passed over him and the angry noise continued away over the house.

Ric walked out into the stark, searing light, mindful not to fall into the pool, and looked up in the direction of the disappearing helicopter.

Very soon the buzzing receded. It faded into the distance, and Ric stood working out the direction from which the chopper had come-the south-west around the southern end of the mountains of the interior, and in which direction it was going-the north-east, toward the coast and Zizula. And it was travelling at some pace, really at some pace; 150 miles an hour, maybe more.

The indecent haste with which Ric had leapt up off the sofa caught up with him. As though suffering under a vague concussion, he felt the ground heave beneath his feet and bright fireflies danced before his eyes. He staggered over to the table by the pool.

In the shade lent by the umbrella, Ric ran his hands through his hair, rubbing his scull as if to clear the message board of his mind.

He went back inside and checked his mobile phone in case Manou had rung and he'd slept through the ringing. She hadn't.

In itself her lack of response was not out of the ordinary. Aside from her administrative duties she was always busy with the campers; taking one of them to the local doctors or dashing into Porti Vechju for provisions for a birthday celebration or wedding anniversary. He had noticed on his few excursions to Renabianca that if anything needed doing, Manou normally saw to it herself. The camp revolved around her and her alone. She appeared to occupy every post, delegating only the more physical or menial tasks to the few staff Ric had noticed moping about the place. The consequence of her being so indispensable was that Ric had not seen her as often as he would have liked; that and the fact that she preferred to see him away from the gossips at the campsite.

He ambled round the side of the house, picked a towel off the line and rubbed himself down, unsure as to whether it was his dreaming that caused him to sweat so profusely, or merely the searing temperature encouraged by the sun and the granite radiator that rose high in the west.

Ric sat down at the table and watched a couple of large black ants transporting breadcrumbs twice their size towards the scrub. It seemed everyone was working but him. He wondered what Manou was up to, wondered what she was wearing, and remembered the first time they had sat at the same table and talked.

11

They were sitting out on his patio two days after their first dinner together. The sun was slipping behind the mountains of the west, casting a golden glow over the maquis as it went. The cicadas were enjoying a moment of rest and the world was calm and peaceful.

Manou drank *Pernod* with water and ice; he, a whisky with water. She had brought dark olives, calamari and salted almonds.

Her father, Gianfranco, had been the owner of Renabianca. She told Ric that he had been a reclusive figure; an authoritarian, very strict, very old-Corsica. And the more she told Ric the more he could not think of two more diverse yet blood-tied characters. However broad a pen he might use to compare both father and daughter, surely it was only their apparent stubbornness that marked them out as related to each other. In every other respect it seemed to Ric they were poles apart.

"He was just an old bandit who always wanted to be a young bandit," Manou said when Ric asked about him. "In the papers I think they call them 'brigands', the old Corsican independence rebels." She hesitated and then asked, "He was a bandit, or a brigand?"

"It's a little more romantic; brigand," Ric said. "I think a brigand is something of a pirate; a freebooter. A bandit is just a highwayman, a plain robber. Although I suppose there are highwaymen and highwaymen."

"Brigand, pirate, bandit, they are all alike; thieves and murderers," she concluded and fell silent for a moment.

"You weren't that fond of him?" Ric asked.

Manou stared out into the distance.

"Fond," she repeated, leaning forward, her hands on her knees. She wore a white T-shirt which accentuated the deep brown of her face and arms, and a knee length patterned green skirt and sandals, the leather laces of which were criss-crossed up her calves. "Fond is a word in English, but not in French; in French you 'like very much' someone or 'you have affection for' someone." Manou furrowed her brow. "I think maybe I had, or perhaps have some affection for him, but I am not saying I liked him. It's complicated."

"Do you...?" Ric began, but she cut him off with a shake of her head.

"No, I don't mind talking about him. It is different. I can talk to you about him. I can't talk to people here. Many of them knew him. They all have their own opinions of him. Some liked him. Some hated him. Some were even," she paused, "afraid of him. Some admired him. Others thought him a fool. But he was an old father to me and I think you would say 'he was very set in his ways'. It is how I have heard some of the campers describe him; 'very set in his ways'. It is the type of thing you English say when you want to make an excuse for someone without saying what it is that you don't like about them, n'est ce pas?"

"I suppose so," Ric replied. "I'll never know him, so...."

"He was very Corsican; we say *machjaghjólu. Ma-chya-yo-lu*," she repeated. "It means *homme de maquis*-man of the maquis."

"Like the resistance?"

"Yes," she replied, tilting her head as she considered, "almost. It means a man of the land; a true Corsican, one born, raised and lived on the island all his life. You must understand my father nearly went to the mainland once."

"Nearly?"

"Yes, nearly. There was a big *Maestrale* blowing in from the sea to the north on this day and the ferry was cancelled. He must have changed his mind, because he did not go in the morning when the boat left. My father did not believe France needed him and he certainly did not need France. I think he only went to Calvi twice." Manou threw back her head and laughed a carefree unrestrained chuckle. "He was like a Sameri, an ass; he would make up his mind and not even God could change it. But, *Sameri chi grogna, Un ti fà vargogna*-an ass who brays is nothing to be ashamed of. And believe me, my father could bray."

This time they both laughed.

"That's a bit harsh on your own father," Ric offered.

"Oh, don't get me wrong. I said I have affection for him, or maybe for his memory. Girls, for that is how all fathers see them; it does not matter how old we are, we will always be just girls. Girls will always have affection for their fathers. But when a father brays, his sons can ignore it or leave; daughters have no alternative but to listen. And even though I listened to my father only for twenty years, it was enough."

"Your mother–" he started, but she cut him off again, shaking her head.

"No. My mother died when I was very young. I did not really know her, only what other people tell me." Manou stopped briefly while he refilled their glasses.

When he sat down again he realised Manou was keen to go on, and he was happy, perhaps even slightly flattered, that she should want him to know these details about her life. He translated her openness as encouragement.

"My mother was Jewish. She came to Calvi during the war to escape the taking of Jews from France. She knew no one. She just arrived on a boat with some others; you would say she was brought here by the tide of the war. Many of them tried to hide in the *arrière pays*, the back country, but, like in many places, the good Catholics," she scoffed, "gave many of the Jews away to the Germans when they arrived. My father was young. He was an idealist and in those days he was still a little religious. It's ironic too that he hid my mother and some others in the Franciscan monastery at Santa Lucia-di-Talla; the monastery? Madness! Heh?

"After the war my father and mother were married. They tried to have a family, but these things are not always natural. Then, 'just like that' as you would say, I was born to my mother, but very, very late for her. She was too old to bear a child. But this Catholic island; it has a strict moral code, not like the code they used for the Jews, eh," she scoffed again. "My father insisted she have me. How would he look to his people if my mother did something else?" She hunched her shoulders in appeal. "It made her very sick and sadly she was never well again.

"Sometimes I think my father blamed me for this. He did so much to save her from death during the war and give her new life; maybe he believed I took her life away from him. I don't know. I think he saw it was my fault, which is not fair when you think about it. I mean he had as much, if not more, to do with it than I did." Manou fell silent again for a moment.

"There, I told you it was complicated." She smiled a slightly sad, apologetic smile. "But I am older now. I understand that there are many things you cannot change. For my father I think it was, for a long time, like yesterday was always today." Manou picked up her glass and sipped thoughtfully.

"*Bene! Adavanzu!*" she stated. "I have confessed everything to you. Now you know all about me, it is your turn. What about you?"

He waited for her words to fade, but without the help of the absent crickets there followed an awkward silence and he realised there would come a time when he would not be able to avoid his turn at the family confessional.

"I have the strangest feeling there's a lot more that you haven't told me. And," he added, playing for time, "it's time for us to eat." He looked down at her, wanting to pull her up and draw her to him, as much out of a desire to comfort her as out of his appreciation of her shared intimacy. By the way she contemplated the cloudy liquid in the bottom of her glass, Ric got the impression that Manou had not spoken of such things for a long time.

"Where would you like to go?" he asked, rising rather too quickly.

Manou stayed sitting, staring up at him with her wondrous light blue eyes. "Well," she drew out her reply, "I think it is your turn to talk. And I think it would be right for a gentleman to return the compliment that I have just paid him. Is it not the English way?"

Ric grimaced. "Not for now," he said and scratched lightly at his right temple in nervous reaction. "Too dull! Really rather boring for you as much as for me. Now where would you like to have dinner?"

Manou tilted her head and pursed her lips, considering. She drew the moment out. "Here," she eventually replied. "Here will do fine."

Ric shrugged. "I don't have what I need to entertain properly."

"Oh yes you do, Ric. I looked in your kitchen." Manou smiled at him that way she did when she wanted him to know she had anticipated his objections and therefore she'd already prepared her response. "You have enough pasta and wine in there to feed the *Grande Armée*. And what you don't have, I have brought."

Ric stood in front of her, not moving, not wanting to capitulate too readily. But then he rolled his eyes and raised his hands in surrender.

They went inside.

Not only did Ric surrender the initiative, but he also ceded all the authority he might have held over his kitchen.

Manou had bought *vermicelli* and a cold box of clams, *vongole*, the small clams, and a few *cannolicchi*, the razor shell clams.

They talked. She did not press him again about his family. Their conversation flowed naturally and fluently like her cooking, which she appeared to pay scant attention to. Ric stood back, leaning against the wall, leaving her full access to an area that had for the last few weeks been his domain. He found he didn't mind in the least.

She sautéed the garlic and chillies in oil and added the clams. The combined assault on his senses made him feel light headed. *Or*, he corrected himself, *was that the whisky?* As if to refute his own allegation he drained his glass and took a bottle of *Patrimonio* from the fridge.

Manou nodded her approval. She added a little of the wine to the pan and then reduced the liquid to make a spicy sauce, tossing the vermicelli and the vongole together, and topping it off with the razor clams.

They ate outside on the patio. The cicadas had taken up their instruments and their evening was lit by the vast canopy of stars.

The conversation roamed to less sensitive topics for a while, but as the evening slipped into night a vague foreboding crept up on Ric, as though he expected the custodian of his memory to appear at any moment and declare he had enjoyed himself quite enough and that it was therefore time for Manou to leave.

"What is wrong, Ric?" she asked, hauling him from his distraction. "What is it?"

Ric was embarrassed that she had noticed his lack of attention.

"Oh, I was just seduced by the moment," he replied, buying time. "Some places," Ric nodded towards the dark, "all this," he motioned up at the sparkling and twinkling stars, "it's one of those places that I could never have imagined myself ever being. I mean, not in a million years, sitting here looking at all those stars." He hoped he had diverted her from noticing his lapse in concentration. And with the confidence of initiative regained, he went on, "And being here with...."

"Enough, Ric!" Manou cut him off. "Don't ruin it. You," she hesitated, "I mean we; we were doing so well," she said it in a way that had any other person said it to him, he would have considered them deeply patronising. But she said it with such gentleness and held such a deep eye contact with him that he could not mistake it for any form of condescension.

Manou smiled; her white even teeth, her warm, almond-brown face and clear blue eyes alive in his soul.

"More wine, please," she asked, holding up her glass. She laughed that carefree chuckle again, averting her gaze from him and looking up at the stars in order to defuse the surge of electricity passing between them.

The bottle of wine on the table was empty so Ric fetched another from the fridge; the second. He wasn't counting; something he always told himself he didn't do, but he didn't feel as though he was at the mercy of the alcohol. Although that state of mind, he knew, only persisted as far as the alcohol permitted. He made a mental note to take it slower.

"You don't want to talk about your family, Ric?"

"Not much. No," he replied. "There is not much to talk about."

Manou leant forwards in a faux conspiratorial manner: "Life can be complicated, heh? Tell me Ric, did you go to one of those English boarding schools? One of those prisons where they keep you locked up until they think you are an adult? Until they think you are ready to be returned to your parents?"

"You know the kind?" Ric replied.

She grinned knowingly, as if by knowing she was a party to some degenerate secret. But Manou wasn't going to let him off so lightly. "And after school, after the prison of your childhood?"

"After school I went into the services. My father was in the army; in for the long haul like my grandfather and his father. I wanted the same only different, so I joined the Royal Marines."

He waited for Manou to ask if he had been to Afghanistan, but she did not. It was what he expected her to do; after all, everyone else did. Instead she nodded and said, "The same prison only different, yes?"

"In some ways."

Manou waited.

"I could have stayed in for longer, like my father and his father and so on, but I decided I'd had enough."

"And your mother?"

Ric studied the floor between his feet for a moment. "Well my father always put the army first and my mother second. She wanted me to be different. She hoped he would persuade me down some more benign path, I suppose. Absurd really! My mother never forgave my father for my going into the Marines, even though it was nothing to do with him." He paused for a second and then heard himself say, "What I mean is; although it was

46

my decision, my mother couldn't get it into her head that my father hadn't persuaded me against making it." Ric realised he had never spoken of his parents quarrel before. He had committed a good deal of thought to the subject, especially since his father's death the year before, but he had never spoken of it to anyone. Somehow, and he was not sure how, Manou made it all seem so easy, so natural for him to talk about it.

They sat in silence for a while as though what he had told her demanded some token silence of respect.

"*Làcrima di donna hè funtana di malizia!*" She pronounced the words slowly so that he could hear them clearly. "The tears of a woman are like fountains of malice. She would not forgive him for what he did not do?"

"That's about the bones of it, yes."

Ric was weighing up whether or not to show Manou the photograph of his great grandfather and explain to her why he had come to Corsica, when she got up and went indoors.

She returned a minute later having been out to her car. "I have something for you," she said, offering him a small, leather bound notebook. "It was my mother's. I give it to you while you are here, but when you leave I must have it back."

Ric wasn't sure why, but it piqued him that she had said 'when' not 'if'.

The notebook, just larger than palm sized, was tied with a red elastic band. The sleeve was dark-brown and worn, with a frayed red strip at the binding edge. Inside there was no title just unlined pages of off-white parchment with a paragraph of writing on each page. The scrawl, though a touch spidery, was French on the left hand page and corresponded with a translation in Corsu on the right. In the middle near the binding, but on the right hand page, was written a single word designating something of relevance to either column. There were maybe sixty or so pages, he guessed, the last ten of which were blank.

Manou leaned close to him. "This book belonged to my mother. When she came here from Paris in the war she wanted to learn Corsu. She wanted to, I think you would say, assimilate. I think it's the correct word. So as she learnt the language she kept this book of proverbs. Some of the writing is Haute Corse from the north, but you have the proverb in the local dialect on the right, the French translation on the left and in the centre the place the saying comes from; Porti Vechju, Bunifaziu, and so on. Some of them are very appropriate. Some of them are quite mad. There are also little *vignettes* about how she had to change, to adjust to her new way of life; customs, terms of endearment, you would say; character names even."

Ric was unsure of how to react. Clearly this was something of value; a family treasure. "I'm not sure what to say. But thank you. This looks very... precious, priceless?"

"It is to me," she replied, "but you may keep it for a while. If your French is not good enough to translate it, you can ask me."

They sat oblivious of the time and began to read the book together; Manou reading the Corsu, Ric reading the French, and then the two of them refining the translation into English.

As they shared the time going through the notebook, Ric began to understand the significance of her lending it to him. She had lent it to him not only to bring them closer together, to acknowledge some common ground she wanted to share with him, but also Ric thought it suggested the promise of a future, although it was not clear to him what shape either the promise or the future might take.

A long time later Ric noticed the soft down on her neck and arms begin to stir, and small goose bumps rose on her shoulders.

"It's cool now. Shall we go inside?" he asked.

Manou glanced at her watch, and frowned, surprised at the time. "No," she replied. "I have to go. It is late and I have a busy day tomorrow. I have to pay everyone and some of the campers will be leaving this weekend. I must go."

They rose from the table, their bodies touching accidentally as they did so. Ric felt the charge between them. As they stood facing each other he fought and triumphed over the temptation to take her in his arms and kiss her. For now, after her gift, he was more than a little confident that the right time would come. He was feeling unusually optimistic, not doubting that if he spurned the opportunity, he might regret it later.

Manou said, "Thank you, Ric. We have had a good time." And she kissed him modestly but slowly, and certainly with more contact than formal manners would normally permit, on either cheek. "I hope you find your octopus tomorrow morning and learn a few proverbs. I will test you," she teased. And then she left; her Peugeot ghosting away down the track into the darkness.

Once back inside, Ric tidied up the few dishes they had used. And it was when he was at the sink that he saw her card wedged in the tiles by the windowsill; '*Manou Pietri, Dirittore Camping* Renabianca', with her contact address and telephone numbers.

He smiled. Manou, he realised, made him smile.

12

Ric showered a second time and changed into Levis and a light blue shirt. He slipped on a pair of trainers, ignored his crash hat, and unlocked his motorcycle.

If Manou was busy, he'd find some other amusement down on the front.

The beach combers had yet to reappear from lunch even though the sharp edge to the heat was pleasantly blunted by a strengthening breeze from offshore. Out in the bay, white caps skipped and jumped.

He parked at the front and wandered round the southern curve. He thought of Manou when he saw the beach bar. It was where he had first seen her and somehow it threw a calming veil over him. Ric felt the thumping rush of excitement from his motorcycle ride tail off and his heart beat to a more gentle rhythm.

A table at the back of the bar was free so he ordered a beer, stretched out in the chair and clasped his hands behind his head, legs out straight.

Ric studied the panorama before him; the deeper purple of the sea sat dark below the light cornflower blue of the cloudless sky, and here and there around the flaxen sands gaily coloured parasols stood out like regimental pennants on parade. The contrast with Afghanistan, or Afghan as he knew it, puzzled him in as much as there the sky was purple in the mornings, whereas in Corsica it was clearly the divine right of the Tyrrhenian to wear the imperial colour throughout the day.

Then he noticed the large blue-hulled motor-yacht; the one that had arrived as he had been leaving from the bakery earlier that morning.

She was anchored a hundred metres or so off the northern pontoon bow out to sea, presenting Ric with a clean view of her starboard quarter. There was something of the Japanese cartoon character about her; all pointed features, dark glasses and attitude. She was thirty metres or so at the waterline and her bow extended forward in a raffish arc. A tender was tethered off the stern and a jetski sat on the transom. There was no evidence of any crew and it was impossible to see through to the interior as the windows were all heavily reflective.

She had the look of speed rather than comfort, but she was definitely no hair shirt. She was for Monaco one evening and St Tropez the next, for rubbing shoulders with glitterati, for mooring in Portofino or Porto Cervo and very definitely not for tying up on the public jetty. She was an upmarket residence for the alpha male who would tire of staying in one place too long.

Ric had seen her kind before, but only in well-thumbed, glossy magazines, the kind more usually found in doctor's waiting rooms. A touch of envy rose within him, and yet, he decided, she had brazen immorality scrawled all over her.

The helicopter that had dragged him from his sleep had set down in a field beside the town boundary sign. He had passed it on the way in. It was dark blue with windows tinted like those of the extravagant motor yacht before him. The two were connected. They were too much show in Zizula, too much technology not to be.

Zizula was a shade low profile for that kind of statement; a matching yacht and chopper wouldn't look out of place in other resorts and there was no doubting that Zizula boasted a fabulous beach, but that kind of flash could access beaches off limits to most ordinary tourists; a sleepy little coastal village like Zizula did not exactly twin with Cartier.

As he watched, two deckhands appeared and drew in the tender.

Three men and a woman appeared from the main lounge, walked down the steps to the transom and alighted. Even from a hundred metres Ric could make out the woman's long blond hair.

The tender set off at a steady pace to the further northern pontoon; the men sat, but the woman, wearing a dark blue beach robe, stood, rather ostentatiously attending to her very striking hair. At the pontoon the four passengers disembarked, walked along to the beach and disappeared into the hotel. A couple of the old fishermen stared after them, then turned and passed some remark to each other, which caused them both to lean back and laugh. The tender returned to its mother at the same regulation pace.

Ric wondered, without any great concern, where Manou would have got to by now. He sipped his beer and wished he'd brought along her book. There were a few middle aged sun-worshippers out and about; substantial stomachs extending over minute briefs; over-oiled, equally corpulent, women soaking up the rays behind supermarket sunglasses.

It certainly was a day for indulgence. Ric ordered another beer.

He was halfway through it when he saw the three men who had come in on the tender appear out of the hotel and stroll over in his direction.

They walked pretty much abreast of each other.

The one on the right took a line just above the water's edge. He was shoeless and kicked the sand as he strode in a casual, confident manner. He wore cream chinos and a white shirt unbuttoned to his midriff with the cuffs folded back. He sported reflective sunglasses, a moustache and his hair was thick and black. A gold chain hung about his neck, catching the sun every now and then. He was slim and moved gracefully. Of the three, he was very much the kingpin; the other two reacting to his talking, waiting on his words.

The centre of the three was shorter than those either side of him. He wore a light tan jacket over a blue shirt and jeans, and as they got closer Ric could see that the man's hair was greying and he was neither as tanned nor as well built as the other two. He was on the thin side and wore white deck shoes, and the delicate way in which he lifted up his feet suggested he wasn't comfortable collecting sand in them. He was subordinate, but not completely subservient to the first.

The third of the trio walked on the landward side. He wore the uniform of a deckhand: white short sleeved shirt and trousers, blond hair cut short with a flat top, and his skin slightly orange, as if tanned by spray rather than the sun. He was a different commodity to the other two. It was obvious by his positioning, walking as he did just half a step behind the others, that he deferred to both of them. He possessed the rolling, almost sauntering gait of an athlete; he was heavy set but light on his feet and he swaggered a little. As he walked he watched the beach a yard or two in front of his immediate path, only lifting his head now and again to sweep the beach like a human radar.

The fellow on the right made a quip and his companions laughed.

They strode up and sat down at a table right in the middle of the beach bar. They were a little over dressed and evidently unconcerned by the attention they were attracting or the view of the bay which they denied the people sitting behind them.

The boss of the trio surveyed the scene before him, then turned and glanced toward the bar.

The owner, Camille, a gravel voiced, curly-white-haired patrician, one who adopted the repose of having seen most if not all of it before, was smoking behind the bar. He caught the man's glance, looked over at Ric, raised his eyebrows, and reluctantly forced himself out from behind his barricade to serve the prospective client; a client who clearly misunderstood the house rule of collecting your own at the bar.

Camille, a man more used to shouting out the menu, donned a claret coloured apron, laid a dish cloth rather theatrically over his folded arm and presented at their table.

The man ordered *Pernod* in a loud voice.

Camille scratched his white head and marched back to the bar, much to the amusement of his audience.

When he returned with three glasses, a *pichet* of water and a bucket of ice on a lofted tray, the man smiled approvingly and nodded, playing along with the steward's little cameo. However, as the patron turned back to the bar his new customer asked him to return again, but this time with the whole bottle of *Pernod*.

Camille paused and turned back to face the man. He raised his right hand and rubbed his salt and pepper chin in an exaggerated mime of dismay. Then he looked slowly from one to the next at the table before him.

The chatter from the other guests around the bar quickly faded. They had all suddenly become an audience to the pantomime, uncertain as to which direction the scene might play.

But, whatever it was that Camille saw in the three individuals seated at his table, it unsettled him. He thought twice about extending his act and hastily pulled the curtain down on it before it generated any unwelcome applause. He walked to the bar without affectation and returned with the full bottle of *Pernod*, which he placed carefully in the centre of the table.

On his way back, Camille took an extended route and swept by Ric. As he leant down to pick up Ric's now empty beer bottle, he muttered out of the side of his mouth so that no one else would hear, "*Russes*–Russians."

Camille winked and made a strategic withdrawal behind the safety of his broad wooden counter.

The three newly designated Russians proceeded to knock back the bottle of *Pernod* to the accompaniment of a barrage of what were, judging by the volume and pitch of their laughter, coarse jokes and lewd tales.

Faced with the deprivation of their view and the constant eruptions of what they understood to be bawdy mirth, the diners behind them capitulated, rose like a herd of elephants disturbed at their watering hole and lumbered off down the beach.

Ric fetched another beer from the bar. He spoke no Russian, although he knew it when he heard it. So he wasn't bothered to listen in, as was often his habit when he sat alone. He returned to his study of the bay; the sun was well below its zenith and so softened the contrasts of colour between the yellow of the rocks, the green of the scrub and the turquoise margin at the water's edge. The white caps had gone home for a rest, the afternoon breeze slowly giving way to the cool of early evening.

The Russians went quiet, which made Ric look up. He saw the kingpin of the three looking away in the direction of the hotel, and Ric followed his gaze to see the blond from the tender striding, as though on a catwalk, up the beach towards them. She was medium height with blond-to-platinum, long, straight hair parted off centre. She wore large, oval sunglasses and she made sure that when she stepped forward on her right leg it extended outside the blue beach robe, exposing the cream flesh of her slender calf and thigh. The slight upward and to-the-side tilt of her face suggested an arrogant awareness of the attention she was attracting. She was very good-looking, perhaps even stunning, Ric mused. But then, possibly because she had nearly arrived at the bar and he felt hurried to come to a conclusion about her, he decided rather unkindly, that there was something of the moll about her.

The blond haired, flat-top in uniform stood to offer her his chair, but she walked right round him in a wide arc.

The world, and the rest of the customers at the bar, fell silent.

The blond bore down on Ric.

And sure enough she stopped by his table and pulled out the white plastic chair opposite him. "Is this seat taken?" Her English was heavily accented; very Slavic.

"It is now," Ric replied. He had hoped to look a shade less British after so long in the sun, but clearly he hadn't shaken off the trappings. As he began courteously to stand she sat down and crossed her long slender legs, exposing her right leg below the knee and arranging her beach robe discreetly in such a way as to suggest she was now composed, comfortable and ready for conversation.

"Drink?" she said. Her impatience suggested she was surprised at his lack of clairvoyance.

"Of course," Ric said, calming the startled ranks within. "What can I...?"

"Brandy with lemonade." She then added "please," with a scowl that almost cracked into a grin.

As an act, it wasn't bad. But it was every which way an act for her audience at the other table. Ric turned in his seat to convey her request to Camille at the bar, who, having heard her request as all those seated about her must have, nodded, his grey, bushy eyebrows chasing his hairline up over his forehead in amusement. Then, as Ric began to get up from his seat, the old boy raised his hand to suggest the brandy would be forthcoming in the new Camille waiter-style vein.

When he turned back Ric decided it would be best for the moment not to look in the direction of the other Russians.

Whilst they waited for Camille to bring her drink and time slowed painfully to a trickle, Ric stood and offered her his hand. "Ross," he said, "Ric."

"Pleased to meet you, Ric," the blond reached up and shook his hand. Her fingers were long and cool; her handshake was light and on the tepid side, not cultured. "I am Pepela," she said, removing her sunglasses. "People call me Pela."

"Pleased to meet you too, Pela." Ric sat back down. "You have a beautiful name."

She smiled a small, warm and grateful smile that did not necessarily twin with her recent, rather brash action. Pela's eyes had something of the doe about them. They were large and amber in colour, and a little narrowed at the centre below her wide forehead. There was a brittle element to her delicate facial features, but a defiant strength in her eyes; a defiance, judging by her action, she was keen to display.

Camille laid the brandy, lemonade bottle, and tub of ice on the round table and politely transferred cubes of ice into the glass until she nodded. He left without notice.

Pela sipped her brandy and shook her hair out as if to advertise how at ease she felt. "Not much of a hotel," she observed, "this one." She pointed a long, manicured finger up the beach in the direction of the one and only hotel lest Ric be in any doubt.

"Seems to me you have a far better one already," Ric suggested.

She shook her head in disagreement. "Boats, ugh!" she sneered beneath her breath. "Even when they don't move they are moving. How can you sleep when you are moving all the time?"

"It beats some of the hotels I've stayed in," Ric said.

"Last night," she went on, ignoring his response, "we have this storm. We come from Naples. All night, like sleeping in washing machine! And then, when it is time to get up everything calm down.

"I tell him I need to feel my feet on earth and sleep in bed that does not move," Pela continued, running her thumb and the middle finger of her right hand through her hair, scowling again as if reliving her night in the laundromat.

Ric studied her for a moment and decided that her hair was from a bottle, a very expensive one. Her eyebrows were a couple of shades darker than her long flowing locks. "So you put in here for a good night's sleep?" he asked. "In Zizula? It's not exactly the Ritz."

Pela ignored his observation. "So, Mr Ross, you are a tourist. You don't look like a tourist, but you are English, so you must be tourist."

"I guess you would say that, albeit an extended one."

The three Russians sat beyond Ric's new companion. By looking just to the side Ric could see the muscular flat-top rising from his chair only to sit down again rapidly after a short, sharp word from his boss, who maintained a casual indifference. Ric had expected the situation to spiral into a proper domestic and was intrigued when it didn't.

"So, a temporary tourist." She took a cigarette from a gold case and toyed with it.

"Your English is excellent, Pela. Where did you learn it?"

"Thank you, Mr Ross. I like compliments." Pela beamed. "But these days if you don't speak English how would you understand the compliments. You could wait a hundred years for a compliment from a Russian," at this she nodded in the direction of her newly-deserted companions, "and all you can be certain of is that it will be your last."

"You're Polish?"

"No." She grinned. "It's not only Poles who hate Russians. Everybody hates them! I am from Georgia; you call it the Cradle of the Caucasus, do you not?"

"I believe we do."

There was movement behind Pela. The two lesser Russians were leaving, and the flat-top was unable to resist the temptation to throw Ric a testosterone filled glower before he walked away.

After a couple of seconds the kingpin rose and walked casually over towards their table.

Ric felt an obscure need to look around for a defensive position even though he didn't know the guy from Adam.

Pela looked away, restless, perhaps even a shade jumpy. Without looking she had realised the Russian was on his way over.

He arrived at their table and introduced himself smartly before there was any awkward silence.

"Forgive my intrusion," he said in perfectly bland English; no trace of any foreign accent. "My name is Petrossian, Kote Petrossian." He held out his hand to Ric and lent forward politely. He hid his eyes behind his graded dark glasses, but his smile was wide and confident, his hair was a little unkempt and shaggy, and his jaw around his moustache was unshaven in the two-day-stubble style of a movie star. A gold chain and modest medallion hung down on the dark hairs of his thickly matted chest. "Kote Petrossian," he repeated again, reaching nearer, awaiting recognition.

"Ross, Ric." He reached forward and they shook hands; a firm, testing shake. Petrossian was strong; innate, bone strong like a guitar player.

"May I join you?" he asked very much in Ric's direction.

Ric looked politely at Pela, who looked away, much as a child would when expecting to be told off.

"Of course. Please sit down, Mr Petrossian. Can I get you something to drink? *Pernod*, is it?"

"Sure, that would be good of you." Petrossian pulled up a spare chair and sat down at the table, upright, but not quite at attention.

This time, Ric got up and went to the bar to fetch the drink. Camille had it ready and frowned enquiringly; a look Ric was not sure how to read. When he turned back to the table he could see Petrossian speaking very quietly and seriously to Pela, but as he approached their conversation ceased.

"So," Petrossian began, "you have met Pela. You must excuse us both.

You see we are very sociable people. We don't know anyone here. And there is only one way to meet people."

"You're welcome." Ric said picking up his beer. "Good health!"

"And yours," replied Petrossian, as if to display his grasp of English, and threw back a good slug of the cloudy drink. Pela sipped her brandy.

"You've come up from the south?" Ric offered by way of conversation.

Petrossian shot the woman a cool glance. "Yes, from Naples. It's not so much south, but it always feels like one is forever moving up the map. The journey was a little uncomfortable and Pela wanted to sleep on a bed that was not disturbed. And as her wish is our command, here we are. This hotel is not much." He looked across at the woman again, waiting for her thanks. When they did not come he went on, "Hard to please some ladies, eh?" Petrossian's gold medallion and chain swung as he rested his forearms on the table and leant forward at an angle that suggested Pela's part in their conversation was over-as if it had ever been otherwise.

"Nice boat," Ric remarked inclining his head.

"Yes," Petrossian said, dragging out his answer as though the question deserved lengthy consideration. He turned to survey the grandeur of their attention, "it certainly is, Mr Ross. It certainly is."

"Ric. Please call me Ric. Everyone else does."

"Thank you, Ric! Please call me Kamo. It's easier. After all, Kote Petrossian is a bit of a mouthful as you English would say." He went on, "It is a really nice boat. Not really mine, you understand. It belongs to a friend, but he is a very generous friend, very generous indeed. You like boats, Ric?"

"Can't say I have much time for them. Nice to have friends though."

"Oh, yes, I agree. Friends are important, very important." Petrossian nodded as though he was turning the concept over in his head. "Do you have many friends here, Mr Ross, sorry, Ric?"

"Not me. I'm just a tourist I'm afraid. I'm only here for the view."

Petrossian turned to look at Pela. "And what a very charming view it is too." He reached over and squeezed her cheek the way an uncle might patronise a niece.

Pela scowled and pushed his hand away. This provoked the briefest flash of menace from Petrossian, like an electric light switched on and then instantly off. Whatever it was in that look-violence, extreme displeasure, or both-the woman apparently knew it well. She straightened up and began to pay attention, discarding her sulky countenance. Pela ran her hand through her hair again.

At that moment Ric's mobile chirped like a cicada. "Excuse me," he said, pulling the phone from his pocket.

"Naturally," Petrossian offered.

The text was from Manou. She was at the house. Where was he?

"Ahaah! No friends!" Petrossian exclaimed, faintly amused. He studied Ric briefly. "But, of course, it's difficult not to make friends here, as Pela has. You see Pela is from Racha. It is one of the most exciting regions of Georgia. The girls from Racha are well known not only for their cool and calm temperament, but also their beauty, is it not so?" He sat back, raising his hand to indicate Pela in much the same way as a pimp might present his merchandise. "So they find it easy to make friends. Now she has introduced me to you and so we are all friends," he added. "But come my lovely Rachvelian Rose, it is time we were going." He pushed his chair back in the sand and stood. "Permit me to return the compliment of an aperitif another time, Ric?"

"Naturally, I'm sure our paths will cross again if you're here for long," he replied.

Pela rose obediently.

Petrossian nodded thoughtfully, something Ric noticed he did often. He was not one to speak without prolonged and careful consideration. "Yes, I feel sure we will meet again. We will be here for as long as it takes Pela to get her...," he paused, "what do you call them? Sea legs? Is that right; sea legs?" He offered Ric his hand. This time there was a little more pressure in the grip, but not so much as to be intimidating; real, but not so real as to be unfriendly.

Ric was not offered Pela's hand. However, she smiled at him as the other fellow turned away so that he could not gauge the unspoken and slightly apologetic appreciation her eyes suggested.

"Yes, I must be going too." Ric stood up, draining his beer.

"Ahaah! A woman," Petrossian mused. "Only a woman would separate a man from his liquor."

"Perhaps," replied Ric, "but if I indulge in Camille's hospitality any longer I'll be in danger of developing sea legs all of my own. *Au revoir*," he said to both of them, but mostly to the woman.

"See you. Until next time," Petrossian replied with that broad, confident smile. He put a large denomination note on the table and turned away.

Ric went to the bar to exchange his smaller note for coins.

Camille's eyes narrowed at him. "*Les Russes!*" he exclaimed beneath his breath, and then in pigeon English scoffed: "*Georgians, Armenians, Russes. Pah!* Like Chess! Always for reason! Everything they do, always for reason." And then he waggled a precautionary finger at Ric and added with considerable affectation in Corsu, "*Attinzioni!*"

Ric thanked him, and they shook hands warmly, something they had not done in the weeks since Ric's arrival. It was as though Camille wanted to confirm to Ric that he was now formally admitted into the local society of beach-barflies. He doubted his membership would make the wine or the sardines any cheaper, but it would perhaps gain him a familiar greeting whenever he pitched up; something, Ric had noticed, Camille reserved only for the most regular of his customers.

Ric chuckled inwardly, not wanting Camille to see his amusement at the old guard closing ranks.

He walked back to the road, noticing along the way that Petrossian and the woman, Pela, were nearly at the hotel. They did not walk as a couple. There was no familiar contact between them and neither was there any conversation. She trailed just to the side and behind him, but not so far behind him that she might drift out of his wake.

There were cars parked along the front now; early evening trippers come out to dine at the few terraced restaurants along the front. And the glow from the sinking sun bathed the curved beach in a warm, golden light that rested easy on the eye. Ric felt light bubbles of dizziness spring up in his head, as though for the second time in the day he had risen too hastily from his chair.

Parked next to his bike was a dark Renault saloon. It was dirty; dirty and sand-dusted as if it had been parked too long in the path of a storm. He also noticed it sported barely legible mainland number plates and a chubby man with a black moustache sat in it, his elbow leant casually out of the open window.

As Ric swung his leg over his motorbike the man spoke, "*Monsieur? Excusez-moi, Monsieur?* You know this man?"

Ric was trying to remember whether or not he had brought his helmet. "Sorry?" he replied. He was sure he'd seen this man before, but couldn't place him for a moment. "What was the question?"

"*Monsieur*, do you know this man?" He gestured towards the hotel where Petrossian and Pela were by now at the door.

Ric paused, looked first towards the hotel, then down at the driver of the Renault, still trying to place him, only half hearing him.

"Please, you know this man?" the fellow asked. He was irritatingly persistent.

Ric looked the man over again, searching, trying to locate his face from the many in his memory. No ready identification presented itself so he answered, "No, I don't know this man." He nodded towards the hotel as he said it, and then asked, "And you are?" He cranked the bike, stamping heavily on the starter pedal. It exploded into deafening readiness.

The stranger leant out to speak again, but without waiting Ric turned his growling steed out into the road and roared off. He was still trying to place the chubby face, convinced he had seen it before, as he sped at flat chat past a sign wishing him a safe drive out of town.

13

A couple of days after their dinner at the house, Ric had suggested to Manou that if she had some free time they might spend a day at the beach.

He wanted to take her to *la Tozza* and he was surprised when she very readily agreed. But she insisted they go to Zizula and not conceal themselves in the seclusion of *la Tozza*. Ric assumed her choice was motivated by a desire to conform to some local social more, so he was perfectly happy to acquiesce. He also assumed and hoped her consent to their being seen together during daylight suggested she was ready to move their relationship to a more open, and at the same time, a more intimate level.

That day Manou formally introduced Ric to Camille at the beach bar in Zizula.

Although Ric had been patronising the bar for some time and had even left it on occasion several sheets to the wind, Camille was warm, if not suitably cordial, welcoming him as if it were their first meeting and yet not being able to resist the temptation of a trademark raised eyebrow.

He and Manou swam far out beyond the yellow marker buoys, and the sea was clearly a joy to her. Manou's strokes were long, even and assured. He noticed she was relaxed in the water, very much at ease, as though born to it.

Later they picnic'd and rested on the sand. Their conversation was light and easy, and he dozed for an hour only to waken slowly to find her leaning up on her elbow, studying him.

Ric wore dark blue shorts in place of the briefs most of the other men wore. He was glad he was wearing them as it turned out, for Manou wore a black one piece swimsuit that complemented her brown arms and legs. Her toenails were not painted, which he liked, and her feet were natural and unmarked, not the kind used to being crammed into designer shoes. Her dark hair curled in tight ringlets when it dried.

He expected her to speak, but she did not. Whatever she was looking for in him, she was possibly also searching for within herself, so he returned her gaze, losing himself in the depths of her blue eyes. As he did so he wondered whether he was being impolite, holding her gaze for so long, but then he realised that she wasn't looking right at him, for her eyes had lost their focus, rather it was as though she was picturing him somehow.

"Camille has known you for many years," Ric offered, more by way of observation than question.

Manou smiled, bringing the world back into focus. "Yes, a long time. He has been a part of this place from the beginning. He used to run the hotel; he and my father before I was born. In those days people used to own land and there was no record of it at the *Conseil General* – the council. Well, there was no *Conseil General* before; it was just accepted that when you were in one place, you were the owner. Then afterwards comes the government from the mainland; they made people take the same laws they have, and everybody wants to know, 'When did you buy this land? Who said it belongs to you? What right do you have to it?' It was a big mess." She went quiet for a moment, probably wondering whether he would really want to hear about it.

"Go on," he encouraged, "please."

"It was a very big problem; a big mess. Is that right; 'mess'?"

Ric nodded.

"Well my father, he was very angry that these people come here from Nice and tell him that everything has to change. He knew that some of these officials were correct and he knew that some of them were, I think you would say, corrupt officials; people out to make fast money from Corsica but wearing the uniform of the government. So my father and Camille, and some other people made a big fight. They burned some houses belonging to some foreigners. They kidnapped one official who had come from Paris. They said they would kill him if the government did not recognise their right to the land. It was very stupid, but it was not simple." She paused. "Or maybe it was simple for them. I don't know."

"How long ago was this?" Ric frowned, thinking it sounded rather medieval.

"In the seventies," she replied. "At the end they all made deals. All over Corsica they made deals. My father gave them Zizula. They gave him

Renabianca, where we have the campsite. Camille, he took the beach bar. It was what he wanted. He said if he could not keep the hotel, he would keep the bay. To Camille the bay was always the most important part. When he goes," Manou shrugged her shoulders, "who knows?"

Her question hung in the air for a few seconds.

"And the kidnapped official?" Ric asked.

Manou lowered her brow, her mouth a little sad and down at the corners. "Oh, they killed him," she said as though it was nothing to her.

Ric considered this for a while, turning the information over in his mind, a shade embarrassed to have received such an awkward answer to his question. "I see," he said. "Well, let's hope he was corrupt and not correct."

Then she laughed generously and laid her hand on his shoulder. She had opened the door and he had walked right in, without thinking. They dissolved into a fit of childish giggles; he exposed and infected by her laughter and she responding to his amusement, her eyes wide and lively. She did not immediately remove her hand from his shoulder, as if it were a signal of some reassurance or a vote of confidence.

When their laughter subsided he was taken with an urge to move closer to her, but he was aware that they were in plain view of the beach bar and wondered whether or not it would be considered too public an advance. Instead, he broke her gaze and inclined his head towards where Camille was watching them.

"So, you and Camille have known each other a long time, long enough to eat a 'full cargo of salt together'?

At his question, Manou's eyes opened even wider and her smile grew even broader. "I see you have been reading my mother's book, Ric. That's wonderful!" She was clearly touched that he should have committed his time to her precious memento.

"Yes it is like the book says; 'to get to know people, you have to eat the cart of salt together'. It's not so poetic in English. It sounds much better in Corsu; *Par cunnoscia la ghjenti, ci voli a mangna una somma di sali insemu*," she said, pronouncing each word with a sensual reverence. "The important word is *cunnoscia*–to get to know," she added.

The way she said it sent a shiver down his back; right down, he noted, to the very base of his spine.

Manou removed her hand, turned onto her front and leant up on her forearms. "So, you don't have a problem with my mother's writing or the French translation, huh? You learn fast, Ric!"

"Thank you," he replied with heavy dose of false modesty. "But your mother is a good teacher, and I have the time. Mind you, 'too much salt isn't good for you'. That was one of my mother's sayings."

They lay and watched Camille, who, realising their conversation concerned him, beamed his jolly smile and saluted, raising and then draining his glass of red wine in one elegant sweep.

"Does Camille have a nickname; a character name like those in the book?"

"Ah, yes, of course." Manou smiled. The subtle rise at the corners of her mouth suggested she saw the humour in his question. She had, after all, given Ric the notebook.

"Come on then, let's have it."

Manou bridled at his request, dragging the moment out. "Okay, but you must not tell him I told you. He can be very sensitive sometimes."

He nodded. "Can't we all?"

"Camille is known as Moscaneva, or Mosca for short; it means like a piece of snow. How do you say that?"

"Snowball?"

"Not so big; a small piece that falls from the clouds?" Manou frowned as though she should have known the correct word.

Ric began to laugh. "Snowflake?"

"Exactly," she replied: "Snowflake. That is it: Snowflake, because of his white hair, it has always been this colour even though his eyebrows are grey. And Snowflake because he is always sweating when it is hot, like his white hair is melting, like the snow melts in the sun."

When Ric had finished with his laughing, he said, "I think Camille has seen too many seasons to be a snowflake. And besides, there's something pure and virginal about snow; I'm not sure you could describe Camille in such a manner. You might give someone the wrong idea."

Sometime later, after the sun had surrendered its harsh tenure of the beach over to the gentle pastel shades of early evening, they left and went back to his house. Ric had expected Manou to have to leave him then and return to work at Renabianca, but throughout the afternoon she had not once mentioned having to go at any particular time. His anticipation of her leaving fostered a hollow sensation deep within him. Irrational though it certainly was, the dull, deep vacuum of yearning for her to stay was not a wholly unpleasant sensation to Ric. Somehow, and rather perversely, it made him feel, perhaps even reminded him, that he was no longer averse to company, a state of mind he had, until her appearance, found out of reach.

Once back at his house, Manou tuned the radio into Voce Nustrale as Ric made aperitifs: 'vin de myrte' and a side glass of water for her, whisky with ice for him. He opened a tin of peanuts and assorted dried fruits and put them on a small alabaster bowl he'd found in the kitchen cupboard.

At the beach Manou had thrown a brown T-shirt and green taffeta skirt over her swimsuit. They showed off her figure as she stood, back arched, hips pushed just slightly forward, studying his few music cds. After a brief appraisal she went out to her car and came back with one of her own and put it on in place of the radio.

They sat outside in the warm evening air; the hiss-whispering of the cicadas giving way to the deeper tonal rake of the tree frogs.

Gently from inside grew the subtle harmonies of polyphony; a rich fluctuating acapella of male voices; folk music, almost Gregorian in rhythmic chanting, yet lamenting like the muezzin's call at dusk or the solemn echoes of a priest at Mass.

The sun had slipped below the high horizon of the mountains, but here and there shafts of light beamed through the saddles and valleys, like transcendental escalators leading up to an alternative world.

Neither felt a particular urge to break the silence for some minutes. Ric got the impression, from where he wasn't sure, that Manou was weighing him up, as though she was about to ask or tell him something of weight, something of importance.

Whatever it was that she had been contemplating, she put it to one side suddenly and came back to him, as if waking from the lethargy of her indecision. "Have you heard this music before?"

"On the radio a couple of times," he replied. "It's quite haunting. I can't say I understand the lyrics, it's all in Corsu?" He saw that she was watching him closely now, and because she remained quiet he carried on, assuming that she wanted him to.

"But it's a different sound and not unpleasant on the ear, as we say. It reminds me of something I once heard from Morocco; the Master Musicians of Joujouka. It has a similar trance-like quality, like waves the way the notes rise and fall, but without the great wall of sound that you get from those massed reeds and pipes. It is impassioned and at the same time constrained."

"It is so," she said. "It is like an emotion pleading to break out of a chained heart." Manou chuckled at the gravity of her analogy. "But it is our traditional style; very sacred. It is the singing of our festivals, of our history, and of our soul. Many people say it comes from the earth, but that is the same as our soul, yes? It has Latin roots and yet there is a very Moorish influence. It is similar to our National Anthem, *Dio vi salvi Regina*, and the song of our brotherhoods. Easter in Sartene is the best place to understand what our sound means to the Corsican people."

"*Dio vi salvi Regina*," Ric repeated and then realised. "God save the Queen?"

"Exactly! I told you. You British helped our patron Pasquale Paoli during the War of Independence, when Nelson lost his eye at the siege of Bastia. But I don't think we sing about the same queen, eh." She laughed more, her blue eyes somehow deep and yet vivid through the mild hue of last light.

"That Moorish influence, it is in the flag too?" Ric offered in an attempt to keep Manou talking as he floated, suspended in the weightlessness of her voice.

"Yes, Pascal Paoli made it the symbol of our country, but it comes from a legend which has another Paoli at the centre. A beautiful maiden called Diana from Aléria was kidnapped by the Moors and taken to Grenada. But this Paoli, he was her fiancé, he went to Grenada and freed Diana and brought her back to Corsica. The Moors came and, you would say, raped and pillaged and burned the island. When they came to Aléria, the Moors were destroyed by an army of the Corsican people in a great battle. Paoli made a journey around Corsica to show everyone the head of the Moorish commander, which he had on a stick. So the legend of the Moor's head with the bandanna was born into our history. Some say the bandanna should cover the eyes of the Moor, and that this is the symbol of our conversion to Christianity. But," Manou went on more seriously, "as long as we don't have to fly the Tricolour of France, it makes no difference if we have to sing 'God save the Queen' or have the head of a Moor on our flag." She finished and looked hard at Ric with a deep, questioning intensity, as though she was proud of her patriotic fervour rather than embarrassed by it.

"You hate the French so much," he said, measuring his surprise so his reply would not be taken as a rebuke.

Manou softened and smiled, a reluctant and begrudging, vaguely appeasing look that suggested a quiet regret for her show of contempt; a look that was not designed to extend as far as an apology. No sooner had her fire emerged into the light than it was very quickly extinguished again without any apparent trace or effort.

"Yes, it's true. We don't like the French. They make plans for us. They contain us. I remember when I was growing up I would look up into the sky and every day a French Air Force jet would fly past out to sea. Most days, they would fly once around the whole island; 'training flights', they said. Sometimes one, but sometimes two jets, just out to sea, not so far that we could not see them, but close so we could hear the big noise." She shook her head dismissively. "They did it to remind us who is the boss. There was no other reason; just that. They want us to remember who is boss; that is all." Manou fell silent. She smiled self-consciously and fidgeted a little nervously on her chair, aware that she may have revealed too deep a discontent.

"Well," he said, "I'm glad you don't live under the Union Jack, or is that a case of 'my enemy's enemy is my friend' I wonder?"

"Maybe," she pondered. "Pasquale Paoli died in England, you know. Even with the British he was a political pawn. So, maybe it is true. And maybe if we didn't have the French to despise, perhaps we would despise ourselves. It's how people are, n'est ce pas? Perhaps we all need someone to despise a little."

From inside the house Manou's mobile phone chirped into life. "Excuse me. Duty calls," she said, rounding and extending her vowels in perfect English.

She was extraordinary; the many facets of her character left him both amused and captivated. He was aware that Manou was making a call and talking for longer than a simple message ought to deserve.

When she came back out, Manou apologised, explaining that she had to return to Renabianca; something she had to deal with. She looked distracted for a moment, her thoughts perhaps consumed by the conversation on the phone. Then she shook whatever it was that bothered her out of her head and bent down towards him, leaning her hands on his arms and lowering her face to his. She kissed him twice, either side of his lips, but not so far from them. Manou looked deep into his eyes and held his gaze. She squeezed her lower lip between her white teeth as if in mock reproach.

"*A dopu,*" she said quietly in Corsu, and followed it with "*a bientôt,*" in French, and finally "later," she said in English, so that she knew her implied promise could not be misinterpreted.

Ric decided it sounded best in French. And the contradiction of her deep rooted dislike for colonial masters, and yet her convenient resort to their language when it suited, intrigued him. But surely, he noticed by the awakening of his more carnal senses, her lingering presence left him somewhat more excited than just intrigued.

14

Manou was sitting under the umbrella out on the patio when he got back to the villa.

He walked over to her, bent forward, placed his hands gently either side of her face and kissed her briefly once, but with pressure, on her lips.

When he let go she looked up and smiled up at him. "Shall we go to dinner?" she asked. "I will wait while you change."

Whatever she had been thinking whilst she sat waiting for him, she was not willing to discuss it with him.

They did not talk as Manou drove them out of town on the main road to Porti Vechju past the pink granite chambers at Casteddu d'Araggio. A battered signpost pointed the way up towards the village of Ospédale in the hills. They seemed to be chasing the last rays of the sun along the winding roads as it slipped down beyond the Massif.

In far too many places Ric noticed the blackened earth where a few years before fires had ravaged the forests. On the upland the Corsican pine and chestnut had escaped the devastation, but beside the road the many varieties of oak and the maritime pines had perished in the flames.

She was aware of him studying the expanse of scorched earth and read his thoughts.

"The Forest of Ospédale! They burnt some parts of the forest so that the grass would grow. They wanted to make pastures for the cattle. The European Commission paid them money, subsidies, for the cattle they keep; more cattle more money, more money more cattle, more cattle more pasture, more pasture less forest. They have stopped the subsidies now, but it is too late for the forest, eh." Manou spoke without taking her eyes from the twisting road.

"These are bad, greedy people, like Mafia. The money comes from

Brussels and goes straight into their pockets, and the people who need it don't see it. Between Paris and Brussels we get half a billion Euros a year in subsidies. They give us special privileges not to pay social security and we have special tax status. This money comes to build airports, marinas and roads like this one. But all that happens is the fat get fatter. The young have to leave the island to find work that pays enough for them to live. The immigrants from Africa take any job they can get because they need any money they can get, and so the wages do not improve enough to keep the young here. Like burning the forest; it goes round and round and round." Manou made small dizzying circles with her head.

"That sounds pretty hopeless," Ric said.

"For some it is. There is a saying in the book that I gave you; *Chi campa spirendu, Mori caghendu.*" She waited for him to repeat the proverb then translated it for him. "He who lives on hope dies on shit. Not so nice, but true, heh?"

"So why do you stay?"

This silenced Manou, as if it was a question she did not have a ready answer for. She slowed down to negotiate a couple of very tight hairpins, and when she accelerated out of the last one she said with reluctant resignation, "I left once. I did not like it. I did not like leaving, so," she paused, drawing out her words almost painfully, "I came back. Besides we also say *Tantu ch'eddu ci hè vita, ci hè speranza*-As long as there is life, there is hope."

A sobering and sombre silence ensued for which Ric felt somehow responsible, as if he had directed their conversation off the road into a ditch.

They drove on up to the village, the road becoming even more tortuous as it wound its way up the mountainside. By the time they arrived the sun was down, but by the light of the stars from the cloudless sky, Ric could make out the surrounding forest and the great outcrops of granite behind them. She took his arm as they walked from the car to the restaurant and the weighing mood lifted in the same manner that a dull moment between two friends can sometimes be put aside because it is not sufficiently dull to separate them further.

From the terrace of the restaurant they looked south over the Golfo di Porti Vechju towards Sardinia, just making out the glowing pearls of the port. And even though they were high above the coast the lights far away

71

glimmered and flickered, like lazy fireflies in the warm evening haze.

When they were seated Manou recommended, "Usually the aubergines are stuffed with ham and cheese, basil and parsley, and bread, but at this time of year to honour the pilgrimage to the Ermitage de la Trinité in Bunifaziu they use eggs instead of the ham. You will like it," she suggested.

Ric ordered a bottle of white wine from Toraccia close by Zizula and again, he noticed, as on the occasion of their previous evening out together, the staff seemed to treat Manou as one of the family. Ric, whilst self-conscious at being cast in the role of escort, felt the attitude of the staff to be a touch cool; he observed that he was lent no lasting eye-contact by the patron.

"I feel I could be here for years and not understand all the significance of the festivals," he said.

Manou smiled an eager if mildly apologetic smile, the mood from before being lifted. "It is true. There are many. Like I said; everyone, religious or cultural, has left their mark. The Ermitage de la Trinité was one of the first places for the Christians to worship in Corsica. It is a small convent across the water from Bunifaziu; a place where the religious hermits could hide from persecution. Some people make a pilgrimage there at this time of year. The dish is made with eggs in place of ham to demonstrate the privations, is it the right word-privations, of the people from many years ago. There were even some people, the *Giovannali* from Carbini, not far away from here; they were Franciscans of a sort. They lived by their *austérité*. I think it is the same in English. They believed in social reforms, in justice, in proclaiming the gospel."

"Sounds rather Presbyterian, rather Calvinist," Ric suggested.

"Yes, maybe," she allowed. "But when you consider what little they had, you begin to understand that what they believed in grew out of the hard lives they were living. They had to share to survive. They were hard people; it was a hard land. Without their sense of community they could not survive, mostly because of the fact that when they had something of value, food, shelter, identity or religion, someone would always come and take it away. Whatever they had; someone would always take it away," she repeated, and in doing so Manou became suddenly impassioned, her blue eyes bright and vivid again.

"They learned to live without the comfort you get from the cities of the mainland. They learned to adapt, learned to live by their own means."

But no sooner was she roused than her stirring subsided and she gazed at the reflection of the candle in her wine glass. "I suppose what little one has someone will always want it. It is the way of things, and it makes us Corsicans very independent; like our island, very insular."

Manou raised her head from her glass and studied Ric, a look that he considered was both calculating and questioning, maybe even provocative. She held his stare for a few long heartbeats and just when he felt she would unbalance him completely, her face softened and her eyes and mouth widened into a generous smile exposing her fine, white, even teeth. An amused and wicked smile danced across her lips.

"We have always had our own ways of doing things. *N'est ce pas?*"

Ric felt himself drifting with her, a little at her mercy and a little too uncertain as to how to resist her, whilst not really wanting to resist her too much. And, like shadowed ground cast into light by the arc of the sun, Ric realised his whole body had come alive. Nerves tingled along the back of his thighs and his calves seemed to flex involuntarily. He felt an acute physical awareness and a warm power in his torso he had not experienced for how long he could not remember. He also found himself momentarily embarrassed and tongue-tied, and was thinking how to broach comically the subject of her effect upon him when Manou, very obviously basking in his apparent discomfort, spoke.

"How do you do that, Ric?" she asked in a playful tone.

He leant forwards, drawn by her regard, her tide now close to overwhelming him. Ric shifted his weight onto the front of his seat and leant his arms on the table in an attempt to relieve the pressure building inside him.

"Do what?"

Manou toyed with him, giving him time to listen to the coursing of his own blood. "Do that," she replied. "Make me think of things I have not thought of for a long time," she replied, still holding his gaze. "Things I have forgotten. Things from the past."

The waiter appeared and served them the aubergines.

Ric barely noticed the lack of any standard portion of meat or fish on his plate, and whilst the serving would up until recently have been regarded by him as insufficient bordering on meagre, he understood that a deep vein of thrift coursed through the community.

They ate slowly and addressed each other casually, not over-politely.

They discussed their musical tastes, the various artists both modern and classical that they preferred, and books they had read, though they shared little in common when it came to books for his knowledge of the French Classics was slight. What was clear though was that Manou was relaxed in his company and happy to be seen with him by those who knew her well. When she spoke to him, Ric was 'in' her world, whereas before he had been 'around' it. Manou was accepting him into some part of her life that she had previously denied him access to.

She would not let him pay for their meal, and he saw no sign of her paying either. The reverential waiter merely bade them good evening after their coffee. She did not take his arm on the way back to her car and she didn't allow them to linger before driving away. He wanted to take her in his arms there and then, let his impatience run away with him, but Manou kept her distance, enjoying and not wishing to risk disturbing the strong currents that flowed between them.

Sooner than he expected they turned by the tomb onto the dusty track that led up to his small, dark house. When she braked to a halt with her door nearest the house, Manou, without reference to him, turned off the ignition and before Ric could speak, got out and went inside.

Having expected to be the one to extend a more conventional invitation to her, Ric was caught off guard.

Instead of hurrying inside after her, some anxious vein within him slowed him down and forced him to take his time, to hesitate and to stumble mentally.

Ric stood by the car and stared up at the stars. The many needle-sharp points, glinting bright and unmolested by the ambient light of cities far away, seemed to prick the bubble of his thoughts.

The vast and heady ceiling crowned around his head; a dome that he had seen somewhere before, yet for the moment he could not recall where. Some place somewhere, as he stared up, the sky had been just like it was now.

There was no sound but for the soft, restless hiss of the cicadas. It was as though the maquis was turning over slowly in its slumber; sighing in its bed.

Ric breathed deeply and recognised anxious hands upon his shoulders. They propelled him on towards the door; telling him to hurry on and not waste time, telling him she was waiting, expecting, demanding, and urging him on before the opportunity to be with her slipped away.

And then, following on from behind those cool hands of anxiety, the mean, chill voice of doubt began to whisper in his ear.

There were no lights on inside. There was no need. Manou was not in the living room or the kitchen and the patio doors were still closed. She was, he realised with a creeping claustrophobia, in his bedroom, in his bed.

Manou lay on her side facing him. He could make out the profile of the sheet on her body; the curve about her hips and down her legs, her hair loose about her exposed shoulders and her eyes shining through the shadow.

She was watching him as he stood in the doorway, waiting for him to come to her.

Ric exhaled slowly and quietly, and moved forward to sit on the edge of the bed; an act that must have taken him but a couple of seconds and yet in that very short time a hundred bastard thoughts were born.

Instead of Manou Ric was reminded of another. And in thinking of her he remembered only frustration and disappointment and hurt and torment and misery; a pain of countless sharp edges; a pain he had vowed he would never hold and cut his hands on again.

And the harder he tried to banish thoughts of her from his mind, the faster she came back to haunt him. Lithe tendrils of insecurity sprang up through his torso, and whereas a few minutes before he had possessed all the conspicuous physical evidence of his desire for Manou, now, so awfully quickly and suddenly, there was no substance to his want. There existed only a horror; a slack void within his loins, an area that was now unresponsive and far beyond his reach.

Moments slowed and dragged, and the realisation came to him that there existed nowhere for him to hide. There was no avenue of escape and no haven in which he might conceal his state.

Ric rubbed at his temple, desperate to erase the other image from his mind. His body trembled as he remembered her tender touch, her warm taste and the perfume in her hair. He told himself again and again he had not known this would happen, but for far too long the possibility of it happening had haunted him. Deep down within him, the treacherous voice of doubt had never quieted.

Some time passed; how long Ric wasn't sure. He felt a hostage to his incapacity and interned by his impotence. He was condemned to his own very private solitary confinement and in that confinement he lost all track of the time. Thoughts, puerile, futile, savage and merciless, flew like random flaming arrows inside his head; arcing, criss-crossing and colliding with each other only to fall spent and useless, smouldering and smoking on the pyre of his wretched inability.

Then he felt Manou's soft, guiding hand holding his own, ever so gently pulling his hand away from his forehead. He felt the smooth, tender silk of her breasts against his back as she knelt up to hold him, resting her chin on his shoulder.

Firmly, but tenderly she coaxed Ric to lie down on the bed and covered him with the sheet. At first he curled into an almost foetal, defensive ball, as though he expected some fearful kicking; a beating he felt perversely he deserved in return for his pathetic frustrations. But by turning his back to her he allowed Manou to curl around him, and even though she was some way smaller than Ric, she enveloped him with her arms, laying her form against his, comforting him. The press of her breasts and her stomach against his back and the warmth of her thighs beneath his buttocks soothed him, but in no way aroused him. He had moved beyond that place. Though there was much he wanted to tell her, he understood that there was little he could do to rescue himself from the pit of his desolation.

Manou did not speak. In the moment she demanded nothing from him, as if she too understood that there was nothing to be said.

15

Pale bands of diffracted light, like those cast down from high cathedral windows into dusty vaults, roamed across the sea bed. The colours below alternated through many shades of subtle gold to arctic white; their hues from sand soft to stone stark, and their touch from lukewarm to raw cold. It was as though some celestial organist was leaning his leaden foot on the swell pedal, unaware that beneath him his congregation already sat in mute attendance.

Today there was a complete lack of octopus, the ten or so lures-the small strips of foil-he had strung about the rock face below the waterline of *la Tozza* had attracted none of the curious, dead-eyed creatures. Even a closer examination of their customary small holes and crevasses proved a complete absence of any of the sentinel squatters. There were plenty of the small, timid hermit crabs, the tiny, reddish-brown chameleon prawns, and the little, aggressively resolute porcelain crabs; all the normal provisions required to satisfy the enveloping, compressing and consumptive appetites of the octopus. But today there were none of the shadowy predators present.

Maybe he had fished the rock too often. Maybe he did not have the eyes for them this morning. Or perhaps it was just one of those days when they were off doing something somewhere else. He had become well acquainted with their habits over the last couple weeks, but still he understood little or nothing about the conditions that governed either their abundance or their absence.

Ric dived down as far as the pain of the pressure in his ears would allow, almost reaching the corner where the vertical wall of the outcrop met the sea floor. He levelled out and tracked around the circumference of the rock. Here and there the many small fish drifted lazily, some even smaller than a newborn's hand: blennys; the speckled, the striped and the black-necked and black-faced with their small red bodies and black patterned heads, darting in and out of the green-fingered stackhouse fronds like trains accelerating in and out of stations. There were bright, multi-coloured wrasse, rainbow and peacock fish dozing amongst the red and green beadlet and pink gem anemones. He noticed the conspicuous dark eyes of an orange cardinal fish watching him from the shadows of the overhang. Sea urchins had colonised the striped granite face; the black clumps of delicate spines that infested the striated wall reminding him of anti-personnel mines dotted on a border fence. And all manner of sea life passed the time watching and waiting to feed on the morsels of whatever the ocean should deign to wash past their plot.

He surfaced round the far seaward side of the rock, exhaled and cleared his snorkel tube in a sharp spurt of water. He felt a slight cramp in his left calf so he pulled his mask back on his head and searched for a hold in the rock to rest. Reaching out with his right hand, he took hold of the rock and then stood his right foot against the face. With his left hand he reached down and removed the long flipper from his left foot, which he then jammed, along with his spear gun and his weight belt, securely into a crevice in the rock face.

Ric pulled back firmly on the toes of his left foot and gradually the cramp in his calf dissolved away.

He rested there for a half a minute or so, filling his lungs with the cool morning air.

When he felt sufficiently recovered he reached into the crevasse in which he had jammed his flipper and pulled it out; as he did so he accidentally dislodged a length of thick rope that he had not noticed before.

The rope swung down from the slight overhang above. It swayed slowly back and forth until it came to rest.

Ric replaced the flipper in the crevice and then removed the flipper from his other foot and added that to the first. He trod water evenly and took hold of the rope. He studied the strands of the cord. It was no thicker than his wrist and knotted in steady intervals of about an arm's length; it was rough and unsophisticated in its construction, and had been, judging by the harsh, salt-dried texture, in situ for a long time. He pulled and then hung his full weight from the rope. It held him.

Some strange apprehension caused Ric to look around, as if he had discovered something that someone else had sought to conceal. But there was no one about. As far as he could tell, there was no one watching him.

Unable to resist the temptation of finding out what might lie at the other end of the rope, Ric pulled himself up, hand over hand, walking his feet upwards against the face as he climbed up to the overhang.

Towards the edge of the overhang he felt tired, but not so tired that he contemplated giving up. His feet slipped off the surface.

He hung until his body ceased swinging and, with his torso limp, pulled himself up using only his arms. Once over the lip he used his feet again and scaled fairly comfortably up the last couple of metres through a maze of seagull's nests. They squawked and screamed and beat their wings threateningly at him. He skinned a knuckle and an elbow climbing awkwardly over the last ridge onto the top where he lay for a while staring up at the sky, catching his breath. He wasn't certain he had climbed the face in the proper textbook fashion, but he had made it.

Ric rolled onto his side, sat up and took off his mask and snorkel. He looked round. The surface at the top was squarer than at the waterline and when Ric got to his feet he noticed that in the centre there was a small hollow just large enough to accommodate two or three people and just deep enough to provide shelter from the off-shore winds. The grey granite sides in the depression were blackened with the signs of a fire in one corner; a fire that had been lit and extinguished many times right upon a rich seam of the black stratum that ran through the rock. Also strewn about the hollow was the litter of a fisherman: some shreds of line, a lead weight, an old pen knife and a hard dark-wood stick about half a metre long and thick enough to hold in one's fist. The ends of the stick were bulbous, which gave it the appearance of some sort of animal bone, which it was not as it was clearly made of wood.

He banged the stick against the rock; it was so hard and cured that the blow left no mark on it.

Ric put the curiously shaped club back with the other items.

It was strange. He had not noticed the basin in the rock surface when looking down from the road above the small bay. The colour of the rock and the angle of the sun helped conceal the hide from view.

About the surface there were signs of old birds' nests and the ready stains of their inhabitants. There was nothing of value. Perhaps some hungry soul had collected the seagull's eggs for food over the years.

Ric stood and surveyed the bay before him; the thin strip of beach, the dusty track that led up through the trees and out of sight over the saddle of the hill towards Zizula. His position was not high enough to see over the ridges into the adjacent bays, but, shading his eyes from the glare of the morning sun, he could make out the pale scar of a footpath that wound its way out of the trees and over to the south, into what he supposed was Renabianca.

"Oh," he sighed, "Manou." He'd not thought of her for at least an hour, he lied to himself. And, even though the surface of the rock was now beginning to reflect the heat of the day, a cool hand ran down his spine as he remembered the touch of her breasts against his back.

He was in the act of looking away, just turning his face, when a movement at the tree line by the path caught his eye.

Ric turned back and watched where the movement had occurred, by the entrance of the pathway into the trees, perhaps some 350 metres distant. The tree line was not straight like a plantation; the pines just petered out further up towards the ridge.

He waited, staying completely still, not taking his eyes off the spot.

Some minutes passed; a time in which he was aware only of his own breathing and the gradual rise in temperature of the air around him.

Then, just as Ric was beginning to think he was mistaken, a figure ran out from beneath the trees and started to climb the short path to the top of the ridge.

It was a child, or a young adult, dressed in a light coloured shirt and shorts; a brown skinned kid with dark hair.

That was all he could make out from the distance between them. The path was maybe fifty or so metres long and the figure took only half a minute to make it up over the top and out of sight.

He wondered what the kid might have been running away from; him? There would be little sense in that. Ric was a good 200 metres of a swim away to start with.

Ric surveyed the rest of the bay, studying slowly the hill and its ridged sides. But he saw no one else. The trees and the maquis could hide a small crowd, but nothing looked out of place, and, more importantly, Ric felt no other presence.

Maybe it was the kid he had felt watching him some mornings while he exercised?

Whoever it was, he or she had disappeared over the ridge in the direction of Renabianca. He would mention it the next time he saw Manou.

And for the second time in ten minutes he sighed, expelling all the rank air from his lungs, hoping in vain that the departing breath might take with it all the dismal history of the previous night.

So to avoid any more reflection he threw his mask and snorkel down into the water, and whereas on another more confident day he might have dived the ten or so metres off the top, with his mood as it was, he jumped.

Judging by the slap to the soles of his feet, the distance down was someway more than ten metres.

Ric quickly retrieved his gear, set the rope back into the rock, reattached his weight belt to its fixing and set off on the swim back to the beach.

Now the sun was high in the sky and the shafts of light less angled through the water. He swam through thick shoals of small anchovy, and way below him flashes of white and silver bounced off the flanks of bream and bass as they grazed on the sea bed.

Ric pushed himself hard through the water; willing the power back into his limbs, banishing the feeble sensations of the night before. He reached out in front, reaching for great handfuls of the sea, and he thrashed his legs and feet, propelling himself on and on in the hope of leaving it all behind.

For a while it worked. For a while there was just Ric and the water and his action. But, as he neared the beach, Ric realised once again that his respite lasted, as it always lasted, only for a while.

16

Usually, Ric knew exactly where to go and what to do after his dawn ritual. His appetite saw to that.

This morning however, in spite of the restoration and regeneration provided by the salty water, he felt himself peculiarly stalled and at a loss. He did not run as he would normally have done after the swim. Though his legs ached, which, he decided, was their acid retribution for his having failed to deliver the desired sensations of the night before, he did not possess the latent will for further exercise. So he stretched out on the sand and banished his thoughts into the various shades of green at the back of the beach.

The constant observer of his drill, the inquisitive nuthatch, flitted down from the pines. The dark head of the tiny bird twitched and turned, scrutinising him, hanging on his every movement.

Ric wondered what it made of his presence. He hadn't as yet brought it any food, so it must have been the vague expectation of what he might bring that attracted the bird's attention.

He studied it for a while and it studied him back.

He must have fallen asleep, for now the sun beat hard on his shoulders and the back of his legs. His skin felt tight and his head thumped with dehydration. Ric scolded himself.

When he'd drifted off to sleep he had been thinking of Manou; of how she had left him in the cool hour before true light; of how she had thought him to be asleep, he judged, by the way she had kissed him tenderly at the base of his neck and slipped out of bed.

In truth Ric had been more awake than asleep, but had thought better of stirring.

He opened his eyes to see the nuthatch no more than a couple of feet away, still patiently watching and waiting. He raised his head, but the small bird, evidently perceiving no threat, just looked straight back at him.

Ric got up and checked the time on his mobile phone, which he had left in the dusty Citroen. The air inside was hot and dry like that of a Turkish bath, so he eased back the folding roof and left the door open. He was surprised to see that he must have slept for a couple of hours. The *patisserie* might still be open, if he hurried.

The nuthatch flitted back up into the trees, where it sat recording his habits.

Ric took a long look around the bay and then gathered his kit. Whatever misgivings he held for himself, he felt a very natural empathy for the colourful landscape. There was an unhurried peace to the island; an island where he felt himself to be alone and yet not totally so, as though there was a comforting presence around him at all times. Not one that sat in judgement of him, but one that he identified with. Perhaps he was merely becoming more familiar with the place and more familiar perhaps because of Manou.

He packed up and drove off up the bumpy track to the top of the rise. He could have sworn that the little nuthatch was following him. It seemed to be perched on a branch of pine every time he glanced out the window.

The *patisserie*, as it turned out, was shut. And the *figatellu* on offer in the modest store was too heavy and rich for his reduced appetite. So he sauntered over to Camille's beach bar, where the genial host, with all the wan and foggy demeanour of the all night reveller, was muttering sweet nothings to his plastic chairs and tables as he set them out beneath the wooden shades. Ric lent him a hand, which Camille appreciated, but with no more than a cursory nod of his head.

The old boy wore faded white shorts and a vest that he must, judging by their crumpled look, have slept in, and the top of his back where the vest did not cover it was dotted with irregular clumps of long white hairs. In one of the bare patches on his right shoulder was tattooed a small blue ring, banded at the top, and from which issued seven pointed flames, the outside of the two curling round and down, crowning the band beneath.

Camille removed the panels that secured the front of the counter, carried them around to the back, and then disappeared inside the little hut for a few minutes.

Ric stood with his arms folded against his chest and watched the small bay. It was now late in the morning. There was spare sand still to be claimed, but not much of it. The tanned young beach boys were going about their duties arranging sun-beds, opening out umbrellas and waiting on their more prosperous clients. The sun was high enough in the sky to prohibit the pilgrims from loitering on the baking sand for too long, so there was not much movement. The large blue motor-yacht of the fellow Petrossian dwarfed the little blue and white sailing dinghies as they swung ponderously on their moorings. Except for a jetski buzzing up and down a couple of hundred metres out in the bay and the odd radio issuing it's banal accompaniment of euro-fizz, there was not much to intrude upon the peace of the beach.

Camille appeared from behind his counter and handed Ric a cold bottle of beer. His hands were thick and marked; hands used to hard weather and the constant abuse of wind-born salt, on one finger he wore a black-stoned, gold signet ring.

It was a touch early, but Ric was not about to upset the welcome advances of his new found friend. And besides, the top was already off the bottle.

After the second bottle of beer they sat down at one of the tables in the shade and shared a third along with a saucer of small sweet olives, the stones of which Camille spat with practiced ease and accuracy into a small porcelain bowl that doubled as an ashtray. They talked about the season, the tourists and the weather; small talk, much as two comparative strangers would when sharing a bench in the park. Ric's rather fifth form French skills were improving and he had Manou to drive his renewed interest in talking to the locals. But now and again Camille would address Ric in English; usually, Ric noticed, when Camille wanted to make sure his point was understood. It piqued him somewhat to think that Camille's English was some way in front of his French and that Camille only made the effort to speak it when it suited him and not when it suited Ric.

But then, Ric reasoned, he was sitting on Camille's stretch of the beach, his island and his corner of the Mediterranean, so he was as entitled as anyone to speak how he wanted when he wanted.

They watched the jetski plough relentlessly up and down, throwing great arcs of spray in the turns, leaping clear of the water, and speeding furiously out to the points of bay and back again. On one occasion when it came into the shallows, they could see the pilot was Petrossian, the cocksure and self-possessed Georgian, who had come with the blond woman Pela to the bar the day before.

"*Russes!*" scoffed Camille, who then, with his right hand pressed against his groin, made a vulgar, suggestive gesture with his thumb. "*Battellu grandu; Minghitello, eh?*"

"Sure." Ric chuckled and nodded in agreement. "Big boat-little dick. I figured the same yesterday."

"But money, eh?" said the sly old fox, rubbing the middle finger and thumb of his right hand together in the internationally recognised sign of the filthy lucre.

Camille got to his feet and went to busy himself behind his counter.

A young woman arrived. She wore a tie-dye headscarf over frizzy dark hair, beneath which large round earrings dangled. She was very slim and hard boned, with pointed facial features and the proud bearing of a gypsy. Upon seeing the empty beer bottles she glared menacingly at Ric and rinsed Camille in a hot staccato of Corsu.

Camille gestured towards Ric, rubbed at his white curls in dismay, and then shrugged his shoulders in mock apology – as if there had been any way on God's earth a mortal host such as he would have possessed the ill manners to allow his guest to drink alone. He winked playfully at Ric.

There was not much else to do; the day was very much upon Ric and still he had no plan. He guessed he would pick up with Manou at some stage but, still feeling a little tender about the night before, he was in no great hurry. He found himself to be pretty comfortable where he was, sitting with a beer, watching the world at rest and play. That seemed to be a pretty steady way to be. After all, how often had he longed to be somewhere with a view, with nothing to do and even less to care about? How often in the past had he promised himself that he would come to a place just like this and do exactly as he was doing? What was there to care about? Except, of course, the future. But then the future would take care of itself.

Ric knew his eyes had glazed over. His daydream, probably triggered by the beer and compounded by the lack of any more solid nourishment since the evening before, both calmed and enabled him, settling him in an indifferent yet confident mood.

He needed to eat, he reminded himself; a *pan-bagnat* would crack it. Camille made a great Nicoise sandwich. A vision of the small, round, flat loaf with the tuna and anchovies, tomatoes and pickles, onions and egg, basil and capers, all soaked in olive oil, leapt into view. That was exactly what he needed, and as he thought it his taste buds started to tingle and his mouth started to water. His eyes came back into focus as he began to see the *pan-bagnat* in all its attendant glory.

But as was so often the way of things when, in the very second his body knew absolutely what it wanted, some outside influence wrenched that knowledge and desire from his grasp, like something glimpsed for a split second in the beam of a moving flashlight.

Ric awoke from his trance to see Petrossian speeding on his jetski towards where he sat.

As the Georgian hurtled towards the beach, he seemed as though he might plough straight up the sand into the enclave of the bar. But Petrossian's morning had not been wasted out in the bay. With well-judged timing he swung the front of the jetski round, the wash and swell from behind caught it up and lifted the noisy machine over the breakwater, to settle it tamely on the beach.

Petrossian dismounted, without getting his feet wet, and walked purposefully up to the bar.

It was a masterful display, Ric considered, but not one for which the man appeared to expect any applause. He wore dark glasses, a Grateful Dead T-shirt and black swimming briefs.

"Two beers," he called out to the gypsy woman behind the bar who glared back at him. "And olives," he added and sat down opposite Ric in the chair recently vacated by Camille.

"What a fantastic day," he remarked with theatrical embellishment. "You think so too, Mr Ross?"

"Could be worse."

"Bah! You English! Life has to be so perfect for you," he dismissed, ladling his pronunciation with a thick Georgian drawl. "You need the sun at this angle, the wind from here, the chair facing that way, the waiter from there, the temperature of the tea no more than this. It must be difficult to be satisfied. Impossible. How do you get it right?"

"Well, I guess that's why we come here," Ric replied, "because it's so close to perfect."

"Ah, that is true," Petrossian said, "it is close. But I think on the Costa Smeralda in Sardinia the girls are prettier." And as he said it a young girl, naked but for a wafer-thin wrap knotted at her waist, strolled past them. She had olive skin, long, straight, light-brown hair and breasts and hips that swayed in happy union. She was, Ric reckoned, in her late teens; young enough to discount the two men watching her, but not so young as to be unaware of the attention she was attracting.

"Ah! Maybe just more expensive on the Costa Smeralda," the Georgian corrected, nodding in appreciation.

The waitress came to the table and set down two chilled bottles of *Pietra* and a bowl of the larger, more acidic olives.

"So, Mr Ross...."

"Ric," he interrupted, "please call me Ric."

"Thank you, Ric. Of course, I forget Pela has already introduced us. My friends call me 'Kamo'. It is because they say Petrossian can sound a little, mmm... aristocratic, eh?"

Petrossian held out his hand. It was the same very firm shake Ric remembered from the day before, like that of a guitar player or barber, and he wondered if the man was the sort to have many friends.

"So, Ric," he began again. "Now that we are friends, how was your date last night?"

"Well, I suppose it could have been worse," replied Ric. "How was your evening? Were you in the hotel or on the boat?"

"Ah, yes," Petrossian considered. "Pela. Well, we had a small party on the boat; some wine, a little music, some dancing. But Pela, she stayed in the hotel. She can be a little... a little unsympathetic when she wants to be, especially when she is tired. But she is no different from other women. They want what they want when they want it, and if that is not what you or I want, then.... " He shrugged his shoulders, appealing to a higher authority. "It is true huh?"

"Maybe," replied Ric without any great commitment. "Depends what they want, I suppose."

"Mmm," Petrossian was searching for an adequate come-back. "Who knows what women want, eh? Who knows?" He paused. "If you find the answer, please tell me. I would like to know and I will make us both a fortune."

"Looks to me like you've got one already," Ric said, inclining his head towards the vast pile of ostentatious hardware wallowing in the bay.

"The *Kohar*? I told you. She's not mine, Ric, not mine." Petrossian allowed no note of regret in his voice. Then he sighed long and hard. "You would say it is a tool of the trade; the plaything of a friend. Even for me, this is a little pretentious, too much profile you would say. My friend uses it to entertain people when he wants something from them. And fortunately for me he sometimes wants something from me, so he lets me use it when I want."

Ric hesitated to ask who his friend was, or what it was Petrossian did for his friend that warranted such fantastic reward. But there was something about Petrossian that suggested questions were for Petrossian to ask, not for him to answer. Anyway, Ric concluded, there was probably precious little chance of getting a straight answer out of him.

"Would you like to see it, Ric?" Petrossian offered, leaping to his feet, draining his beer and wiping his moustache with a napkin. "Come on, I will give you a guided tour."

That caught Ric by surprise, and without really thinking about or intending to reply he said simply, "Sure! Why not?" And as he rose he found himself agreeing with his own reply; it wasn't as though he had an alternative plan for the day.

The glowering waitress appeared, no doubt doubting their intention to pay.

The Georgian hesitated.

Ric paid. Of course, 'Kamo' had no room for cash in his rather diminutive designer briefs. He finished his beer and turned to walk towards the quay from which he assumed he would be collected by the tender.

"Hey, Ric," called Kamo, "where are you going? There's room on the jetski."

So he turned back, took his shoes off and tossed them behind the hut. As he did so Camille, who happened to be around the back attending to a gas bottle, whispered, "*Attinzioni!*" and repeated the same suggestive sign with his thumb in his groin.

Ric chuckled, shook his head in mock reproach, then said "Thanks, Uncle Mosca," and went back round to the breakwater where Petrossian was waiting for Ric to help him persuade the jetski out into the water.

They pushed the vivid green-liveried jetski off the beach and were about to get on when Kamo stopped, turned to Ric and said, "Hey, why don't you drive, Ric. It's easy. Go on." And with that the smaller Georgian moved to the back and left Ric no alternative but to mount in the front seat.

"I'm not sure I know how to start one of these things," said Ric. He had ridden many machines, but somehow never a jetski.

"It's easy," replied Kamo. "There is a code pad, but we don't bother with that because no one can ever remember the sequence. So all you have to do is put the cord around your wrist, I think you call it the dead man's handle, press the green button and pull the lever on the right handle bar and off we will go. But treat the throttle like you would treat a woman, eh, otherwise we will take off. Or, who knows, even fall off." He was grinning, a wide confident grin that showed pearl-white even teeth. "This thing is a supercharged, fuel injected, water-cooled rocket. It weighs 400 kilos and makes 250 horse powers. So, treat her with respect."

Ric got onto the front seat, slipped the cord over his right wrist and pressed the green start button; the motor growled. Tentatively Ric pulled back on the throttle lever and the small craft eased out towards deeper water. The handle bars steered like a bicycle rather than his motorbike; he had to pull in the direction he wanted to turn, rather than just lean.

There was a line of buoys about fifty metres out marking the swimming area into which boats, and jetskis, were not allowed. The Georgian had ignored them when coming into the beach, but no one had tackled him about it. So Ric just squeezed the lever and allowed the jetski to idle its way out of the restricted zone.

Once clear of the buoys though, he squeezed the lever tight in his fist and the machine responded by leaping skyward straight out of the water.

The force of the acceleration threw them both backwards off their seats into the sea.

Ric swore as he landed on top of the Georgian behind him, pushing him further down into the water. For a moment their arms and legs fought each other as each one tried to get back to the surface.

When they did, the Georgian was coughing, spitting and laughing all at once. "You won't hang on to a woman for long if that is your understanding of respect, my friend."

"My apologies," said Ric. "I had no idea she was that frisky."

The green jetski sat bobbing patiently, like a mischievous horse waiting for them to remount.

"Hey Ric," began Kamo, "better get on from the back. If you try it from the side it will fall over on top of you – and I think we have provided enough amusement for the people on the beach for one day, no?" Kamo laughed easily and generously as he trod water, waiting for his pilot.

And though Ric felt the warmth of embarrassment rise up in his face, the feeling was not followed, as was normally the case, by the frisson of humiliation.

He mounted the jetski, clambering awkwardly up onto it from the rear. When he was seated, he felt the small vessel lurch as Kamo remounted behind him.

"Okay, Ric, take two!"

The motor of the jetski was dead, so Ric plugged in the safety cut-off, depressed the starter, took hold of the handle bars and squeezed the lever again. This time he opened the throttle progressively and they accelerated smoothly away.

"You want to take her out of the bay, on your own?" Kamo shouted above the roar of the motor.

"It's a great offer, thanks, but would you come to Italy to pick me up?"

They laughed and Ric steered them over to the mother ship where a deckhand appeared and held the jetski steady as they both dismounted onto the transom. Steps led on the left side up to the aft deck.

The Georgian clapped Ric on the back in an open and familiar gesture: "Anytime you want to have fun with this toy, you can, Ric; even if we have to come to Italy to rescue you."

Once up the steps he turned and said: "Welcome on board the *Kobar*, Ric. Come, it is customary to make a toast the first time you are on board."

Ric followed Kamo up the steps and forward into the stateroom. He felt a shade underdressed and grubby considering his shirt and shorts were soaking, but his host appeared oblivious to the water they both dripped onto the plush carpet. A young, Asian looking, uniformed steward appeared with thick bath towels and matching robes inscribed with a Georgian monogram.

The stateroom was panelled in teak and mahogany, the elegant furniture fashioned from the same wood. The joinery was ornate and expensive, and Ric wondered how much hard-wood had been rendered to create such an elaborate effect. The long windows allowed in more light than their dark, reflective exterior promised. There were no familial photographs about the tables and shelves; no evidence of any long term resident or owner. And Ric felt the place had all the ambience of a hotel suite. Where there ought to have been character there was chic, but it was generic and sterile like a hospital ward; there was no inherent personality in the surroundings. The singular saving grace was that even in the heat approaching midday, the atmosphere inside was cool almost to the point of being cold.

At the back of the stateroom, away from the stern, stood a semi-circular bar behind which Kamo was fixing drinks.

Ric didn't fancy the bathrobe; it was all a little effete for him. So he rubbed himself down with the towel and ran his hands through his hair.

Kamo suffered from no such concern; he reappeared wearing the robe and a different pair of graded sunglasses.

The Georgian handed Ric a drink, a cloudy cocktail with ice and mint in a highball glass.

"Cheers!" exclaimed his host, who then smiled broadly and tapped his glass against Ric's.

"Good health!" Ric took a long pull at the cocktail. It was sweet and whilst the lime fought a decent battle with the sugar, it couldn't mask the rum: a Mojito.

"I know what you are thinking, Ric; is it okay to mix Cuba with Corsica?"

"Well, we're not exactly in Hemingway country, are we?"

"It's true. There is a cocktail called a 'Corsican', but it is made with orange liqueur and lime. It's strictly for the girls. This is a man's drink. And rum is so much more refreshing, heh, especially when the sun is out?"

"I assumed it would be vodka," said Ric, really just to see what the reply would be.

"You should not assume, Ric. We are not all so very stereotypical, and besides, vodka is so, so yesterday." He leaned conspiratorially towards Ric; "You have a saying in English: assumption is the mother of all fuck-ups. It's true, no? I tell you it is true. I have made this mistake before, so I know it. Don't assume! And never underestimate! These are my two rules."

"Only two?"

Kamo looked very directly and very seriously at Ric through his darkened glasses. "Well, two is enough for one day, eh? Maybe I will have some more by tomorrow." Then he stood back and laughed a loud but ironic, self-congratulatory laugh that Ric found difficult not to yield to.

"Now," Kamo said, "now we must find something to amuse us." He set down his Mojito and rubbed his hands as if he expected a genie to materialize from between them. "My guess is, Ric, that you are a backgammon man and not cards. Am I right?"

Ric was surprised at the Georgian's uncanny instinct. "I've played a little, but I might be a bit rusty."

Kamo went to a side cupboard and pulled out a black leather-bound backgammon case. He set it very carefully on a low table and opened it up.

The case contained exquisitely carved ebony and ivory counters and the base was constructed with delicate and detailed marquetry. The intricacy and varied colours of the wood inlaid caught Ric's attention. Unlike the surroundings, the board was clearly an intimate treasure.

"Ah, I see you understand a thing of beauty when you see it, Ric."

"Well that is something for sore eyes, Kamo. But a man who keeps a board like this must also know how to use it."

"It's possible, Ric, possible," he said, stroking his moustache in contemplation. "Let us see, shall we? Let us see." He paused, watching Ric, evidently trying to sum him up in some way. "But, what shall we play for, Ric? For what shall we play? There must be something that either of us wants from the other."

Ric looked up from the board. "Well I can't imagine what in the world I might have that you could want. Seems to me, Kamo, you have most things a man might need."

There followed a silence during which the Georgian appeared to be deep in thought. Then he said, "It is true this board is very precious to me. I can see that you understand this. But I cannot play for the board, losing that is a risk I am not prepared to take. Some things should not be left to chance. And to play for money would, I think, in some way insult our new friendship. So, let us say that whoever has the most points at the end will be able to call on the other for…, for a favour." Kamo's eyes lit up. "Yes! I tell you, I have thought of something. You English are always so keen on doing favours for people, is it not so? For sure, let us play for a favour. After all, for an Englishman it is a national pastime. Is it not so?"

Kamo was still turning thoughts over in his head as he studied Ric, a feeling that Ric was not altogether sure he liked. The nuthatch doing it didn't bother him half so much. But Ric knew he was being played, perhaps even goaded, and knew enough, even given that he had only met Kamo the day before, and that he ought perhaps to be a little chary of the Georgian.

But there was an appetite in Ric that needed satisfying, an appetite fuelled as much by the beer and the Mojito and the lack of food, as by the smouldering disappointment of the night before. And it was his appetite which now spurred him on. Though Ric could think of many reasons why not to, he smiled and said, "Sure. Okay, for a favour. Why not?"

17

At first the scores followed a regular pattern, and as their enthusiasm swelled with each game the time drifted by unnoticed.

Both men were, in the initial games, prudent with the doubling dice, resisting the temptation when falling behind to be flamboyant in their play. However, as they became accustomed to each other's relative strengths and weaknesses, particularly their preference for forward or back strategies, so the tempo of their games began to rise. This rise in tempo was soon matched by the frequency of the rum cocktails, and before long their play grew more animated and less cautious in equal proportion.

As if to put a brake on the gathering momentum, the steward appeared and summoned Kamo very reverentially to the phone.

"Excuse me, Ric. This call I must take. Perhaps it is for the best-to take a break. I will ask the chef for something to eat." He stood up, taking a mental picture of the checkers in each of the quadrants with him.

A cluster of blinis appeared on a silver salver; the caviar and crème fraiche were cool on Ric's tongue and satisfied his appetite.

He got up and stretched his arms and legs, and just as he did so the steward materialised at the door. Ric smiled politely at the white coated young Asian and walked out of the stateroom to breathe the natural warm air outside.

The sun was still very hot and the lively wind that usually blew up around midday, the wind Camille had called the *Mezzogiorno*, had not so far prospered. Perhaps the wind had met with the same amenable lethargy that seemed to be visiting him for the time being. He walked round to the starboard rail; with the ship's head to sea, he had a broad and clear view of the southern side of the bay and the island with its ancient watchtower.

There were no customers at Camille's and he could see the old man sitting out front at one of his tables, turning his head every now and then to converse with the waitress as she busied herself behind the counter. Behind the beach, on which a good number of the hardier sun-worshippers were littered, the hill swept up in an abundant curtain of dark maquis, shrouding the little seaside town like the reassuring arms of a protective parent. The colours were rich and heavy; emerald and azurite separated by lean strips of light ochre parched by the relentless assault of the Mediterranean sun.

"It's beautiful, huh?" Kamo interrupted.

"It is," said Ric.

There was a pause as though each man equally appreciated the simplicity of the scene set out before him.

"What brings you to this part of the world, Kamo?"

The Russian smiled, acknowledging Ric's sharp timing, but thought for a moment before answering. "Like you, Ric. Probably like you; a little vacation, a little time to relax, take time out, isn't that what you say, take time out?"

"Well I think that might be an American saying; basketball or football, I think."

"Bah! American, English," he scoffed. "There is no difference these days. It is all the same. We all speak the same. There are no differences between people anymore; no languages to separate them, no borders to keep people apart. We come and go as we please; from the Black Sea to the Atlantic, from North Africa to Scandinavia. No one can stop anybody anymore. There is just a land in the middle some people choose to call Europe. It makes them feel comfortable to think they have some identity- the Europeans, some kind of nationality to unite them; some unity to protect them." Kamo paused, but, when Ric didn't offer any counter argument, he ploughed on, his inflection rising towards the end of each sentence, as though only a fool could not see that which he understood to be plainly obvious.

"People think there is some security in belonging to one nationality or another. The Americans think God supplies them with an automatic ticket to security. Let me tell you; there is nothing divine about being American. They forget where they came from; all over Europe, from Russia, from China, from Africa, from everywhere. But they think because they call themselves American and they live in the land of the 'free', they have some special right to be secure above all the other people of the world. They think they are the 'world police', isn't that what Chomsky called them? While the rest of the world fights everyday just to exist, the Americans fight for the right to preserve their consumer society: a new house, a new washing machine, or a new automobile." Kamo almost sneered when he used the word 'American'. He softened the damnation in his tone with an air of fatality, but it fell some way short of disguising his base opinion.

"But the world is too small a place now. And Europe is nothing more than a little piece of land for everyone else to fight in." He paused and leant against the rail, hanging his head.

"Europeans," he muttered to himself as much as to Ric. "They will all quickly remember which country they live in when their European subsidies run out and the rioting starts. They won't give a damn what happens to their so called member states. They will conveniently be German again, or Italian, or French, or even you English. Except maybe you will have the intelligence to be part of America," he mocked gently, his spleen for the moment vented.

"America! For you it may be further away than France or Germany, but in another sense perhaps it is closer than the others, if you get me?" Kamo smiled a contemptuous, toothy smile; gratified that he should have the opportunity to show off his proclivity for American slang.

Ric, though keen to lift the conversation away from the muddy drowning pool of nationalism, saw his chance.

"Tell me Kamo; where do you call home? Is there anyone out there you like enough to want to belong to, or do you hate them all?"

Kamo chuckled, a slow broken exhalation that bordered on a sigh. "No," he said standing upright and turning to study Ric from behind his dark glasses. "No! I am lucky. I hate everyone. I do not discriminate. I hate all of them, everyone except my family."

Before Ric could point out that he had answered only the third of his questions, Kamo went on swiftly, "That is all that is important now; that is all that is left, family. Come, Ric," he put his arm around Ric's shoulder, a curiously intimate gesture for a man who hated everyone but his family, "let me show you around our little technological ship of dreams. Then we will play some more."

They strolled forward. Kamo talked about the elegant lines of the motor yacht; of how she had been designed in Italy and built in Antalya,

Turkey, just the year before. Kamo reveled in his ability to quote the boat's statistics. He spoke with all the wondrous zeal of a college boy recounting to his best friend the details of his first date. "She has three MTU engines each developing over 2000 horse powers, a displacement of less than 100 tons, a top speed of over forty knots, and at a cruising speed of thirty-two knots, she has a range of over 600 miles. She is less than 100 feet at the waterline, draws six feet, and clears thirty foot, and she is slim at the waist," Kamo raised his eyebrows and grinned salaciously, "only twenty feet. That's pretty slim, huh? And only five crew, excluding of course my steward, my chef and one engineer. Come I will show you the bridge."

He ushered Ric aft and took him through the main salon and up into a world of electronic navigation and communication; a world of autopilot and gyrocompass, of radar and plotters, a cool nerve centre of LEDs and touch-screen controls bereft of the more conventional levers and dials that Ric had expected.

Kamo spouted figures and statistics, times and distances as if they were nothing more than hoops for the boat to jump through.

"Here," he said, pointing to a bank of screens beside what looked to Ric like a steering wheel from a racing car, "you turn it on." He pressed a green button. "Here you type in the destination. Let us say," he thought for a moment, "Rome." The screen immediately lit up with a host of figures, amongst which Ric could see the longitude and latitude of the city. "Touch 'yes', if that is where you want to go. And here we have a course out of the bay. And here we learn how long it will take at whatever speed we want, what the sea conditions and weather will be like, and what we can expect when we arrive; how much fuel we will use, how much we will have left, and so on." Kamo stood back to allow Ric a closer view of the screen. "All we have to do is put in the cruising speed, which we do here. And here we press 'yes' again and she will take us all the way to Rome without me having to give any more instructions. The radar and sonar will prevent us from crashing with any other boats or hitting any rocks. It's like this Distronic system you can buy for your car or the synthetic avionics you find in the cockpit of a modern jet fighter, except this works for a boat too."

Ric decided it possessed all the minimalist character of a flight simulator. He tried not to glaze over under the barrage of information.

"Seems to me you might as well take the plane. Besides, whatever happened to the key, the throttle and the helm?"

"Well my friend," Kamo replied, nodding thoughtfully, "for a start you need a passport to get on a plane — well, most planes, unless you are unlucky enough to be a guest of the American Intelligence Services, in which case who can tell if you arrive at the destination of your choice, heh? Besides, I'm not that fond of flying, it's a long way down when you get a bad pilot flying the airplane. And all we need here for security is a simple four digit pin code which you enter here," he pointed to an LED and keyboard on the left of the main, "just like you have for a bank account."

"And a very large bank account at that," replied Ric.

"Yes! It is true," Kamo said in almost solemn agreement. "With money one can buy many things."

After a short tour below decks, the two sat down to resume the backgammon. They also resumed their pursuit of the cocktails, feeling slightly more capable after breathing fresh air and stretching heavy legs.

The score was pretty much even, albeit with Ric lagging a little behind, but there was no good reason to come out aggressively in the second session and so he played a series of holding games. He was happy to hit loose checkers when the opportunity arose, but was more intent on making his bar and mid-points. His opponent, he noticed, would every now and again split his checkers early on, get in and mix his board, and then secure high anchor points before committing himself.

Through the afternoon Ric tried to assess his opponent's signature, intrigued to see behind the curtain of Kamo's play. But he was adept at concealing his intentions and seemed very confident in his manner and very flexible in his strategies. He split and consolidated irregularly. He was neither predictable nor apparently prone to any particular preference.

Sometimes on a big roll instead of racing, Kamo would hold back his counters and not lay himself open to being hit. He would build his position and wait patiently for the right combinations to appear before he ran for home. Then, every now and again, and usually when Ric least expected it, Kamo would abruptly throw caution to the wind, taking Ric's double when clearly disadvantaged and make his own counter-play; switching from defence to all-out offence when there seemed little hope of recovering his position.

On the odd occasion this tactic worked for him, Kamo seemed to draw more pleasure from his win than when he won by any of his more orthodox strategies.

Perhaps that was key to the player opposite him; the run against the play. Perhaps that was what drove him; gave him his buzz.

The games came and went; the Mojitos the same. And the great bronze orb beyond the tinted windows that guaranteed the sanctity of their ambience sank further towards the cover of the hills; hills that for so many years had themselves shielded and embraced the tranquillity of the small seaside village.

For a while Ric and Kamo just sat and played, wrapped up in the cloaks of their own individual thought, but sharing in the intimacy enjoyed between two people fastened together in common trail. They were oblivious of and unconcerned with the world beyond the dice.

Then, as with many of the more visceral physical perceptions that arrive without any warning, it dawned on Ric that he'd had too much to drink. He found he had to look twice to read his board correctly and he was someway down on points. The game had gotten a little way away from him; the alcohol was playing, not him.

He swore to himself, shook his head, and immediately wished he hadn't for Kamo looked up at him questioningly.

"What would you say, Ric, if we agreed how many more games we should play?" Kamo asked without any great concern. "Otherwise the evening will come and then it will be gone."

Ric fought to pick a card from the shuffling deck in his head. "Sure!" was all he could come up with, "but I'm a little behind."

"No problem, Ric Ross. You tell me how long you wish to play for. After all, you are my guest. So it should be your choice."

"Fine; thank you. Let's say," he hesitated, trying to appear, "let's say one more hour. Then we'll call it a day."

"Okay, okay." Kamo began to remove his sunglasses, but then changed his mind and left them in place. He consulted a large chunk of watch on his wrist. "Sure, one more hour. Nine o'clock. It's good?"

The next game went to Ric, just, and not by enough to make a huge dent in the score. Both of them ended up racing for home without trying to hit each other's counters on the way through; a straight dice race. The win served to settle Ric for the next few games, so much so that he was almost back on terms towards the end of the hour.

There was perhaps enough time for a couple more games when the steward arrived and called Kamo to the phone. He bridled at having to be called away.

"This is not fair for you, my friend. We have fifteen minutes. Maybe we should agree two more games after this. That would be fair, yes?"

"Agreed," replied Ric with renewed enthusiasm.

This time, Ric noticed, that when the Georgian left he didn't bother to take stock of the counters on the board. He just got up and departed in the direction of the control room.

Ric stood too, encouraging the blood, however diluted with alcohol, towards his extremities. He stretched his arms and legs, and felt better, but still he was irritated at having allowed himself to relax so completely. It wasn't just the drink, he rationalised; it was the comfort zone provided by the hospitality of his host and the empathy of their shared passion for the backgammon. He thought of Manou briefly.

Kamo reappeared. "I apologise," he begged, bowing, hands together, Buddhist style.

Ric nodded, not for a second considering that his adversary's action might be some kind of gamesmanship or some form of distraction.

Kamo sniffed, rubbing his nose as if warding off a sneeze.

Ric studied him closely, or as closely as his addled senses would permit. He could not see the Georgian's eyes, concealed as they were behind his sunglasses.

The game turned round on Kamo. He lost without having born any of his counters off; a gammon and a good score of six for Ric who had offered the doubling cube early enough not to lose his market.

They were almost back to parity; Ric nine points behind.

The second to last game started carefully for both men; they hit their anchor points, giving themselves good position from which to proceed. They sat forwards, leaning over the board, their heads close together as though conspiring or sharing some great secret.

Kamo raised his hands up and pressed his fingers to his temples in deep concentration. He sniffed loudly as if to clear his head and reign in his thoughts.

Ric watched and waited. He had a slight positional advantage, but he hesitated, unsure whether to grab the game by the scruff of the neck or exercise just a little more patience. And as he thought it his opponent with a big throw of eleven ran fast, splitting his high anchor and ignoring his other safety points and loose blots. There was no circumspection involved in the run. The move had all the hall marks of a rash, almost panicked dash for home. Such a change of heart surprised Ric.

Kamo surprised him even further by offering Ric the double, which he took and re-doubled to four at the next opportunity, not expecting his adversary to accept.

But, Kamo did accept, and then even more surprisingly he offered it back, which Ric accepted.

His opponent appeared to be frantic, even impetuous in his desire to finish the game. But, as fast as he ran, Ric hit Kamo's exposed counters and the bar became cluttered with the wreckage of his reckless dash.

Kamo held his head in his hands, sniffed loudly, then stood up and shook his head. He was staring down the barrel of a gammon, which would lose him the lead. He was uncomfortable with this new situation and it made him restless.

Then the dice deserted Ric. Though he had a good prime about his bar point and, as such, exercised good control of the outfield, he threw a run of low, odd combinations.

The dice now smiled at Kamo, and provided him with the briefest glimpse of shooting his opponent from the bar.

Ric, owning the cube, knew the prudent course was now to offer Kamo the double and keep alive the possibility of taking sixteen points from the game.

Kamo clenched his fists to his eyes, deep in thought. It was obvious to him that if he cashed in his game he would lose not only the eight points, putting Ric just one point behind, but also the upper hand and the initiative. If he took the cube, he risked losing a further sixteen, which would put Ric in front for the final game with enough points to play a simple holding game, a game in which he could easily limit his loss to maybe two or three points at most. There would be no point in Kamo offering Ric the cube. Ric would simply pass and forfeit the game. Even if Kamo won a backgammon, three points, the match would go to Ric; and that was a finale Kamo was not about to entertain; clearly not with one game still to play. He clapped his hands together and capitulated with a broad cheery smile. "Well done," he said.

One point behind; as good as parity. How fitting that after such a diverting and enjoyable afternoon the result should depend on the last game. And a draw would rest easier afterwards?

"Well, Ric. As you see, even I make the most stupid mistakes. I let my impatience get the better of me. Perhaps I lost my concentration when I left the board."

"Or maybe one can't always rely on the dice when you need to?"

They set the board for the last game and the steward arrived with fresh Mojitos. They rolled to determine who would start, and both dice came up threes. Kamo set the doubling dice at two on the bar. They laughed loudly and openly together; their humour without slant or expense.

"Of course," said Kamo between great peals of laughter. "Now it is both in and out of our hands. You would agree?"

Ric nodded. The draw was gone.

They opened slowly, both men rolling few doubles, making anchor points in their home boards and exercising caution in the outfield.

Then Ric threw a double four, which, with his two checkers still on Kamo's ace point, gave him his golden point. Now he could start to build a prime in his home board and close his opponent out.

But Kamo took his time constructing his outfield when the dice came to him, working slowly from his mid-point, going on to make his own bar point, and carefully crossing over when the opportunity arose.

The last game was very different to the previous games. It was no longer about the points, not about constructing a big win; a gammon or backgammon was irrelevant. Neither player felt inclined to warrant either the deep anchors required for a blitz, or the resilience necessary for a back game. It was all about being home first. It was the only result that mattered.

Yet Ric maintained his high anchor on the golden point, his two black checkers becoming increasingly isolated amongst a sea of red. Soon would come a time to decide: stand or run. To be caught between two stalls would be tantamount to defeat.

The Georgian sat unmoving except for his occasional rubbing at his nose.

Ric took his time, and took plenty of it. He realised the impatience within his opponent was escalating. He deliberated each move as though it were his last, now and then withdrawing his hand from picking up his checker, pondering another move, but without touching the checker; not committing himself to moving it.

Soon enough both had good primes either side of the bar; the only difference between the two fields being that Ric's high anchor on the golden point in his opponent's home board and Kamo's two checkers low on Ric's ace point.

Kamo could not run, he was corralled in Ric's home quadrant, and Ric had to follow his dice-had to play the blitz. If the dice were with him, he would win. It was as simple as that.

Kamo threw sixes, but could not use them to extract his two checkers on Ric's ace point. All Kamo could do was build in his home board, allowing Ric to move his two checkers from the golden point.

Ric threw four and five, and that made life difficult. He could run or risk breaking up his own precious prime. But if he ran he would have to split his two checkers on the golden point into the outfield and so leave them exposed.

He ran.

Kamo shrugged off his inertia. His whole form tensed like an animal preparing to strike. He grabbed the shaker and violently shook the life out of it. When he was convinced it would offer him no further resistance, he dropped the dice onto the board.

All he had needed was one of the dice to show only one point and he would be able to hit Ric's exposed checker.

He squealed with delight; double ones. Rapidly he plucked Ric's checker from the board and placed it on the bar. Then he stopped abruptly, realising that with three more pips to move, he would leave himself exposed not only to a shot from Ric's checker on the bar, but also from a further hit should the right numbers come up for his opponent. Even with three pips to move, he couldn't make all his open checkers secure.

There followed a number of frantic rounds as each player shot from the bar, hit loose checkers, and ran for home as fast as the dice would allow. The play descended into a kind of checker carnage; the kind of carnage Ric understood from bar room brawls; if it was open to being hit, he hit it whilst he could, uncaring of whether or not he might be hit by it later. And, in common with the many brawls, the episode seemed to last far longer than was necessary when in effect it lasted only a few minutes.

At the end, and Ric was not sure how the end came so suddenly, both players were faced with a straight run for home, with Ric to throw.

He counted up his points on the board. He had two in the outfield; one on sixteen and one on ten, making twenty-six; three on four, two on three, three on two and the final five on one. Ric ran the maths quickly through his head: fifty-five. Kamo had the better board, but the same fifty-five in total. Evens! Ric had a good home board, but had a couple further out in the outfield. It would be tight.

Evidently Kamo reached the same conclusion at the same time. They surveyed each other across the board.

"Your roll, Ric."

Ric threw six and five. He crossed over into his home board with his farthest checker, leaving only one in the outfield.

Kamo threw three and two, moving the last of his outlying checkers into his home board.

Ric threw five and four this time, and began to bear off.

Kamo's dice then deserted him. He was slowly bearing off his low numbers, but with four checkers on his six point he was up against it.

Steadily and, it appeared, relentlessly Ric rolled and removed his checkers from the board. His adversary twitched, fidgeted and rubbed his nose vigorously as if it might bring him luck.

Then, and against the run of dice, his luck did change and Kamo threw a pair of fives. It left him four out on his six point and three on his ace point.

Ric had two on each of his shortest three points; at worst three throws from home. He rolled two and one. Not enough, he thought.

Kamo snatched up the dice and shook the shaker furiously as he grinned at Ric. He splashed the dice out onto the board. Threes! He hollered out loud, cheered for luck and removed his three checkers on his ace point and moved one up from the six to the three.

Each player had four checkers left. A double three or over would win it for Ric. For Kamo it would have to be double sixes.

Ric threw twos, took the checkers off his ace and deuce point, and moved his remaining two checkers up to his ace point.

However, just as he pushed his checkers across from the three to the ace point, Kamo snatched up the shaker and rolled.

Ric's hand was still on his checkers.

The dice rolled out, bounced against the ridge of the bar, trickled back and stopped: sixes.

But Ric's hand had still not moved.

Both men looked up at each other, leaning across the board their faces ending up no more than a few inches apart.

Kamo knew he should not have thrown until Ric's hand had completed the move with the checker. Both men knew it. Both men also knew that Ric's only move could have been to transfer his checkers up to the ace point. There were no other checkers left to play. But Kamo had thrown early.

Would Kamo offer to roll again?

Ric wasn't sure he could allow the throw to stand?

The silence endured. The look between them lingered without promise of breaking.

Kamo stared at Ric, a strong calculating stare during which his shrouded eyes never wavered from Ric's; not even distracted by the birth mark above Ric's right eye.

Ric knew he was in the right. He knew there was no question of it.

Kamo knew he was in the wrong, but would his opponent force him to concede?

They waited, watching each other without malice or question; just waiting.

And then Kamo's mouth began to widen at the edges. His lips drew back and he showed his teeth. "So, Ric," Kamo said without any apparent hostility, "my favourite numbers come to me when I need them and yet I guess I have to roll again."

He picked up the dice and put them in his shaker. This time he shook gently and rhythmically, allowing the dice to bounce and clatter together in the shaker, the noise of their mixing loud and obvious. It was an act designed to deny the possibility of any kind of latent program to the movements of his hand.

Kamo grinned and rolled the dice out of the shaker.

They bounced across the hard wooden surface of the board.

They banged against the bar just as they had moments before.

They jostled and clipped each other, and slowly each came to its own standstill, their energies spent.

"Sixes," Ric said, stunned. "You've thrown sixes, again."

Even Kamo fell silent. Even he could not believe it. Then he swore beneath his breath in a language that Ric did not know, but the meaning of which he understood all too well.

"I'm sorry, my friend," Kamo offered with undisguised feeling. "I did not think.…" He let the words hang.

Finally Ric's faculties returned to him. "Neither did I, Kamo," he replied. "Neither did I. Congratulations."

They drank. Kamo commiserated. Neither of them mentioned the favour that they had played for. It seemed in the moment irrelevant that they had not discussed what the favour should be. The game was done. Talk of it would be for another time.

Kamo played music at a drowning volume; folk music from Georgia, strong, melodious, celebratory and cheerful music, with fiddles and horns and heartfelt verse. He danced around the room, arms outstretched above his head, legs kicking, head back, laughing. His was the triumph.

Ric found his new-found friend's enthusiasm both infectious and impossible to disregard. Sooner than he expected, his bruised ego healed from the constant, soothing balm of alcohol, and shortly after he felt his spirits restored. What little self-control he had left soon deserted him, gone in pretty much the same direction as his affection for the dice.

The woman, Pela, appeared wearing a yellow dress, tied at the waist but open beneath her arms, exposing her ribs and much of her breasts. She was followed by the surly looking crew member Ric had seen at Camille's beach bar.

Pela seemed amused by the state in which she found the two of them and joined in their cavorting and larking.

The crewman did not. He stared menacingly at Ric, as though Ric had led his charge into the arms of temptation, which Ric found even more amusing when considering that it was Kamo who had led him astray. It had been Kamo who had steered him into his current happy state. The more Ric laughed at the man's ridiculous stare, the harder the other man stared back.

Ric danced with Pela, as did Kamo. The three of them lurched about the room to the great, blaring wall of music.

Pela flirted with Ric. Kamo encouraged her. The crewman wandered in and out, his heavy presence anathema to the levity, a dullard in gay company.

Much of what happened thereafter escaped Ric. Pela was getting very fresh with him and he was aware his attempts to ward off her advances were some way short of effective. But, as surreal and blurred as his surroundings grew, Ric knew one thing for certain; he was beyond drunk in an unknown environment, with people he had only just met and in whose company he would rather not find himself given his condition.

Ric released himself from Pela's clutches and wandered out on deck. He tried to focus on the lights of the beachfront and the blinking Christmas tree lights draped about the *Kobar*, as though she was some Victorian pleasure steamer.

Focussing wasn't easy; even breathing was hard work. He forced himself to haul in as much of the cool evening air as he could manage. It tasted thin with a slight salty layer, but he needed it, and lots of it.

Then something hard prodded him in the back.

He turned round as quickly as his sodden reflexes would permit. But just in case Ric had missed the first message, the anthropoid flat-top, still smartly attired in his whites and sporting an ill-natured smirk as wide as his raw-boned jaw would permit, shoved Ric again full in the chest.

"English," he growled in a middle-European drawl. "Bobo says it is time for you to go."

The blow pushed Ric back, but he managed to keep his balance by stepping against the rail and putting his hand out to steady himself. "Hang on," he said.

But the man's muscles seemed to bulge beneath the constraints of his shirt. He raised his right hand; his hard fingers splayed, and shoved Ric back again.

Ric had no place to go. He swung his right arm with all the strength he could summon.

Although it was a spontaneous response, there must have been acres of premeditation about Ric's action. Even he was aware of far too much time passing between intention and action. His fist swung from below his hip, carrying all his weight from behind his body up to the target, on and up and through his aim-point, accelerating to achieve the maximum damage upon landing.

The other man merely swayed back out of the arc of Ric's reach. And, like a carousel horse passing by the grab of a latecomer at the fair, the man bared his teeth at Ric as his fist sailed by.

Ric missed-by a mile. He knew it and knew it even before his blow played out.

All at once Ric became aware of the results of his mistimed strike. He swore lazily and rather inevitably to himself. Stupidly, he had not moved his feet; they were rooted to the deck, and Ric, even in his remote state, remembered only too well the consequences of a drunk punch. The effort involved in the planting and then the pulling of the trigger left him no alternative but to follow the gravity of his actions. His fist blew out and he surrendered his balance.

For a brief moment, much was in that balance, but then the man opposite reached out and gave Ric a hefty shove.

Ric followed his punch beyond the rail and out into the space beyond; a space which only served to separate him from the dark sea water below.

He fell over the rail, cart-wheeling; aware, in a self-observant fashion, not only of the fool he was making of himself, but also of the fact that his feet were now above his head; an uncommon and unnatural state.

Before he hit the black, oily water Ric committed to his addled mind the smirk of the soul he had last seen; an image that would remain acidly etched on his psyche until he came by the chance to remove it.

Ric hit the water with a resounding splash. The loud noise not matching his hazy appreciation of the event.

He struggled to the surface in an effort to procure his lungs the air they so desperately needed. His legs stretched out, pushing backwards, searching for purchase to propel him away, not only from the danger of his surroundings, but also the confines of his inability. They hit some compact surface and he pushed off. Ric breathed hard and pulled in as much of the available air around him as his lungs would allow.

He struck out, not knowing whether he was going towards or away from the beach, but as long as he was going somewhere he didn't care. His arms reached before him; his legs kicked, driving him on, leaving the world behind.

Before too long, a creeping common sense moved him to lift his head from his laboured stroke and look up to see where he was. As he did so the movement of raising his head caused his back to straighten and his legs to push down.

His feet hit the pliant sand of the shallows and then, having stood up, he fell awkwardly forward onto his arms, taking in as he did so an unexpected mouthful of the lukewarm, salty water. Ric retched and coughed, and stumbled forward.

He rolled over and lay on his back in the breakwater. Ric felt clumsy and detached; his limbs waterlogged with a debilitating cocktail of brine, lactic acid and alcohol.

The sweet evening air eventually calmed him, but his need of it made Ric aware of his exhaustion. Like all those stirred to action when suffering under the influence, messages between his command and action centres took time to travel, as if when sober they were transmitted by wire and when inebriated they were passed by hand.

Ric rose, his movements crudely articulated, lumbering like an out of condition wrestler. He staggered up the beach, getting his bearings from the street lights in front of him as he went. At the back of the sandy strip he stopped for a moment, trying to remember where he had left his car some twelve or so hours before.

He saw his Citroen standing alone where earlier in the day it had been in the company of others. He felt in the back pocket of his sodden shorts for his keys and then remembered he'd had the sense to leave them on top of the driver's side rear wheel.

Reaching the dusty old car Ric rested against it, drawing in yet more welcome air.

Well, it had been a mixed bag of a day; he had lost, but he had.... Well, he had.... Okay, he had lost, but he had enjoyed it. And besides, he reckoned with a little convenience leant him by the alcohol, that strange Georgian would probably be gone in the morning.

Ric groped beneath the rear wheel arch in search of his car keys and found them. But just as his hands felt the cool steel of the keys, a figure materialised from behind the car and stood beside him.

Ric jerked upright, forgetting that his hands were still beneath the flimsy wheel-arch of the Citroen.

"Mister Ross?"

"Ow! Yes. I mean: What? Oui," Ric replied perhaps a little too slowly to conceal his intoxication. His eyes drew into focus and in the dim circle of the street light he recognised the man before him. This time he wasn't wearing the pork-pie hat, it may have been a little late in the day for hats, but Ric would not have forgotten easily the moustache or the round face from the driver of the dirty blue Renault that had nearly crashed into him the morning of two days before, or the same man who had the day before asked him whether he knew Kamo when he had first met him. "What do you want?" Ric snapped.

"I was thinking," the stranger said, "perhaps it would be better if you were not to drive home this evening."

"And what the... I mean; what has it got to do with you?"

"Well, Mister Ross, it has much to do with me," the chubby man said. There was no humour in his tone.

"Why? What are you?" Ric asked, lacing his question with an overdose of contempt as he hung unsteadily on the door of the car, "a policeman?"

"Why yes," he replied, "you are correct, Mister Ross. That is exactly what I am: a policeman."

18

Faced with the alternatives of searching out a taxi, walking the long and winding route home, or even worse, arrest and detention, Ric gave ground. The village taxi, if he could find it, might be reluctant to take his fare considering his waterlogged state, and besides he hardly possessed the energy to speak, let alone argue.

So, when the 'policeman' offered to drive him home, Ric accepted; in fact he accepted rather more readily than his gauche demeanour suggested. But he drew the line at the fellow dropping him right at the house and asked him to halt at the bottom of the bumpy track. Wet and weary as he was, and as grateful to the officer of the law seated behind the wheel as he felt he should be, Ric could not help but harbour a dislike for the man and decided it would be best if he kept him at arm's length. His testy diffidence towards his driver was born more out of the drunk being disturbed from his moribund progress than anything else.

When the heavy faced man pulled up at the turning, without, Ric noticed, having to ask for any directions, there followed a silence as though each man was waiting for the other to speak.

Ric was curious, confused and uncomfortably concerned by the man's appearance out of the evening shadows, but in his jaded state he couldn't come up with any sensible foreword to conversation apart from, "Thank you Monsieur, I mean Inspector, I mean whatever or whoever you are."

"Bosquet," replied the heavily jowled man. "René Bosquet. And I'm not Inspecteur. But for the moment it is not important what my rank is, Mister Ross. Let us just say that I have a rank, and we will leave it at that."

He looked at the policeman and rubbed his eyes, attempting to focus in case the man was a figment of his imagination or even a by-product of the minted rum and salted sea water commingling in his stomach.

However dulled his senses, he could see that Bosquet was middle-aged, or maybe older. Gravity had not been a friend to him; he carried a slack heaviness in his face and the fleshy, under part of his jaw hung down like the less attractive folds of a turkey neck. But then it was difficult to tell where his jaw ended and his throat began, for the policeman was criminally overweight. His neck swamped the collar of his white shirt and the knot of his dark, thin tie threatened to throttle him; his body strained to burst out of the confinement of his jacket, which looked a couple of sizes too small for his lax and corpulent torso. There was, in spite of his weight, an owlish aspect to his face, and though his mouth was small, his top lip wore a neatly trimmed, dark moustache. His full eyebrows met in the middle above his hawkish nose, like arrows pointing the way to his eyes.

Given the disconnected lines of communication between his mind and his senses, even Ric knew the look of a watcher when he saw one.

"So, what is it about Petrossian that makes him so interesting to you, Mr Bosquet? And don't start asking too many questions about him," he said. "I met him a couple of days ago in the bar, and today we spent the day, as you are no doubt aware, drinking on his boat. He's no slouch at backgammon and has a shed load of money, or knows someone with a shed load of money. He has a pretty handy bird to sing him to sleep too, and a gorilla for a boat-boy." Ric recalled his feeble attempt to thump the gloating expression which had led to his falling overboard; colour burned in his cheeks.

"Apart from that, I don't know him from Adam. I'll say this though; he makes a mean Mojito." Ric's stomach knotted.

The older man sighed the way someone does when exasperation has finally triumphed over toleration. "I realise you don't know him, Mister Ross. If perhaps you knew him, you would probably not pass your time with him. And as I understand it you are not a fool, well perhaps this evening is for you an exception, Mister Ross, or should I say Ric. Your full name is Richard Ross is it not?"

"Correct. It is," he answered far too quickly as though responding in an interrogation. This Bosquet really was a policeman; he had a way of asking questions that demanded answers. "Why do I get the feeling you know it is?"

"It is my work to know. But it is also my work to know that this man who says his name is Petrossian, is not who he says he is. And I also know that he is not," Bosquet hesitated, "you would say, not for the naive. So I offer you caution, Mister Ross; be careful. Do not be defined by the company you keep. Don't think you are the same as these people. You are not. This man and his animal, Bobo, they don't use the rule book the same way you and I use it."

Ric's immediate thought was that the man must have meant the backgammon rule book, but then realised he was talking about something else entirely.

He hauled himself up off the door. He had heard enough. He had listened politely and in doing so had paid for his lift home. It was time to go.

"Thank you, Monsieur Bosquet, both for the lift and for the advice. Don't think I don't appreciate it. All of it," he finished with a little too much sarcasm. He was in the process of shutting the door when the Frenchman came back for a final bite.

Bosquet leant over from the driver's seat. "Don't thank me, Mister Ross. But in the morning remember what I have said. Be careful of the company you keep. Sweet dreams! Au revoir."

As Ric pushed the door shut the dark Renault saloon pulled off the dusty verge, wheeled round in one noisy sweep and took off down the road.

He narrowed his eyes in concentration as he watched the tail lights of the car disappear round the bend, fine particles of the dust cloud thrown up by the tyres settling about him, like icing sugar on a sponge cake. He patted himself down, which only served to coat his fingers with the sticky emulsion of dust and sea water.

Ric swore as loud and as long as his lungs would permit and shook his clenched fists at the bright lights of the dance-hall dome above his head. Frustration erupted from deep inside him; frustration directed at everyone and at the same time no one.

Of course, he understood as he yawned, he should have been shouting at himself.

He laughed a little hysterically; a stuttering, exhalation of breath through his nose that gradually increased in tempo until he was laughing out loud; laughing and then coughing out all the stale air from his lungs. His convulsions grew steadily in strength until they threatened to overwhelm him, and then very suddenly they subsided.

19

Ric came to lying on his back at the side of the road.

He sat up, drew his knees up towards his chest and rested his elbows against them, holding his head in his hands. He tried to raise some saliva in his mouth, but all he could taste was acid and salt, and an overriding alcoholic remorse.

Standing up a little gingerly, his limbs scraped, cut and bruised in the manner of unidentified drinking injuries, Ric began to assemble in his addled mind the catalogue of errors that had combined to place him swaying unsteadily a fair hike from his bed. Flashes of information appeared before him like spotted rushes from his father's old sixteen millimetre film. But no sooner had one image jumped onto the screen then it was replaced by another random image out of sequence with his dim memory of the evening's events. The odds of assembling any of his recollections into a coherent order were not much in his favour, so he gave up.

Ric found his feet and ordered them across the road and onward up the dusty track in the general direction of the tranquil villa.

With the movement of his feet and the pumping of blood to encourage them, Ric's faculties gradually returned. He stumbled and lurched up the track; there was evidently a gaping chasm between what he perceived to be his intended path and the one his legs were wont to follow.

Ric was relieved to see the form of his destination taking shape before him, but discovered it was the old tomb, not thirty metres up the track from the road.

He stopped to breathe, hands on his hips, and looked around; his progress stalled.

The night air was cool. The stars in their firmament were bright and in the crowded sky seemed to compete for their own rightful plot. The brighter the star the greater the space it occupied and the maquis at the side of the road glowed as though painted with aluminium. The hissing of the cicadas and the resonant murmuring of the frogs in the background died away around him, as though some invisible conductor had abruptly tapped his baton to silence his orchestra. All at once Ric perceived a presence nearby and a shiver feathered up his back. Someone somewhere was marching over his grave. It made him start, made him straighten and then tense, and as he did so he recognised the familiar creep of fresh adrenalin through exhausted muscle.

Ric turned round, expecting to find himself in company, but even though the track, the verge about him and the surrounding maquis were well lit by the phosphorescence of the night canopy, there was no sign of any other person.

He tried to order his mind into thinking what Corsican wildlife might live in the maquis; whether there might be anything dangerous lurking in the maquis; perhaps a wild boar or a wild sheep, the kind with the huge curled horns. He tried to remember the word Manou had used to describe his old Citroen, but gave up.

Then the pleasant evening cool tumbled alarmingly down the temperature scale and Ric shivered, this time from the base of his spine right up to the top of his head, and his footfall, although on a dusty trail, sounded loud, unreasonably so, as though his senses were coming alive. Ric became very aware of the world around him and its enormous silence.

He shrugged, blamed the alcohol and turned back to the track, not realising that he had been standing for some time facing the tomb. But as he turned away he realised what had caught his attention, a pale light flickered from within the mausoleum and at the same time he heard a noise from the area around the old building; not an animal scuttle, but more like the rustling of clothing through undergrowth, perhaps the dragging of feet across stony ground.

"Who's there?" he called out, immediately feeling ridiculous that he should react in such a childlike fashion.

No reply came.

Of course, who the hell would be wandering around in the maquis at such a late hour? Well, who the hell else apart from an idiot inebriate like him, he thought.

Then the noise came again, this time louder still, from beneath the eve of the building, or perhaps from behind one of the pillars.

"Come on, who's there?" he asked again. In his heightened state he was sure he could hear a laboured breathing from the direction of the pale grey, flickering light. Half of him said he should investigate it and yet the other half of him was reluctant to; not really nervous enough to stay where he was, but not necessarily confident enough about his parlous state to walk over and make sense of what was going on.

Ric was in the middle of conjuring up a curse about not being easily spooked by things that went bump in the night when the sound occurred again, louder; a sound like that of a man squeezing through a confined space, maybe a man passing through a narrow gap between two walls; a watcher sliding into position. And then he heard the unmistakable scrape of dry iron hinges swinging open and shut.

"Oh for Christ's sake, come out and show yourself will you?" Ric shouted. "Look, it's my day for making friends. Come out," he ordered, mustering as much authority as he could manage. "Really, I mean come on. One more new acquaintance won't hurt, surely." It wasn't as though Ric offered any sort of threat, was it? Well, not in his current state, he decided.

The dragging sound came once more, but more softly, receding as though whoever it was that had been hiding had decided to leave without showing himself.

Ric was again in two minds; sorry that the person had not revealed himself, but at the same time relieved that whoever it was had chosen not to.

The sound and the curious pale light faded away in the darkness beyond the tomb.

Ric shook his head and shrugged. What could he do? He wasn't about to go stumbling around in the dark after someone who would rather hide.

He stood, rocking on his feet as he tried to stay upright and stationary.

Ric looked up at the stars once more; the stars who saw everything, but who said nothing. They offered no opinion. They didn't judge him the way people did; the way he did.

A shooting star streaked across the sky; a fine burn of piercing white light that flew between the other stationary points, dying almost as soon as it was born. The beauty and the brevity of its life humbled Ric and provoked a slow change of mood. A tiny seed of hope germinated within him and lifted his spirits, a sudden escalation that peaked with his feeling that life was perhaps not so bad after all.

And the still silence that suspended him in that moment was replaced by the re-emergence of the orchestra conductor, who flourished his baton and summoned the equally invisible multitudes in the maquis to take up their instruments once more. The steady murmur of the crickets and frogs returned, the night regained its balm and Ric's own self-awareness stepped back down to an acceptable level. He felt neither as sodden with alcohol as he had a few minutes before, nor as tense. He felt calm again; soothed by the accompaniment of the noises about him and consoled by the reward his bed promised him.

He turned his feet to the track and applied himself to the job at hand; his mission was to get back to the house, and soon. He realised he was ready for sleep, perhaps in spite of all he'd consumed even thirsty for it. He felt as though he would sleep for a week.

20

What woke Ric from his sleep was the oppressive heat that lay upon him in much the same way as his weight pressed down on the bed beneath him. A sheen of sweat wet his brow and a puddle of it had collected in the small of his back.

He could hear an erratic tapping noise that came from the living room. *Probably some insect frantically beating its wings in vain against the glass of the patio doors*, he thought.

Messages proclaiming distress arrived from all points muscular and orthopaedic, and at the same time muddled images from the night before arrived on the flickering screen of his consciousness. They competed for attention with his physical requests, each one more critically important than the last, and every one needing to be dealt with more urgently than the next. The only notable absence amongst the confusion of claims was the rather more conventional dose of alcoholic remorse that usually followed the morning after a night before. That, strangely, Ric did not feel.

Neither did Ric feel the need to analyse the night before. What he needed was to deal with his physical self before he could administer any emotional or intellectual consolation.

In spite of all the noise though, Ric was aware that he had slept as well, if not better, than he had for many weeks-perhaps even months.

Ric got up, stood for a moment, rubbed his hands through his hair and staggered out into the kitchen in search of some sustenance for his beleaguered and acidly sensitive stomach.

Instead of the more standard relief he expected to find in the kitchen, what he got was the little old cleaning lady, grey hair tied back in a bun and grey apron tied about her black dress, straining over the sink, attending to the dishes he had left out on the sideboard; evidence of his pathetic attempt to eat before he had wandered to bed and passed out.

Ric was naked except for his stubble.

The woman looked round, aware of his presence but in no hurry to acknowledge it.

Perhaps it was his anticipation of her reaction to his exposure that focussed his attention so directly and caused him to take note of every craggy feature of her face, for he suddenly noticed that the crow's feet at the corners of her eyes ran deep enough to collect shadow.

She looked at Ric, but at his chest not at his face. Then her gaze wandered down to take in his natural state.

Almost as though she suffered from dimmed sight she scrutinised him for a moment, not believing what she was seeing.

When she looked back up, she grinned and hooted all at once; a whooping, whistling sound that seemed to rise up inside her all the way from her miniature black shoes. Her lips contorted between the hoots and hollers, displaying a gap-toothed, small-tongued mouth, from above which suspended a few long grey hairs, like vines trailing over the entrance to a cave.

A witch with a sense of humour! He turned about face and strode back into the bedroom, fast awake.

As he threw on a pair of jeans and a T-shirt, he could hear the old crone chuckling to herself, and Ric supposed if nothing else, he had at least supplied her with a story to tell at the *veillée*, the gathering of friends and neighbours in the cool of the evening, what Manou had described to him as the 'evening whispers'. He retrieved the shorts and shirt he had worn the previous evening. They were lying where he had struggled out of them, on the living room floor, still soggy from his swim back to the beach. There were a handful of congealed notes in one pocket and a counter from the backgammon in the other. And at the sight of the counter, more of the previous evening's events came flooding back to him: Kamo, the jetski, the motor-yacht, the game, the bet for the favour that he had lost, the woman Pela getting far too lively with him, the ape he had tried to punch, the swim.... The news reel played on.

Busy night for such a sleepy place, he thought, and he realised once more that he hadn't really come to Corsica in search of the kind of partying he had chanced upon the evening before, and he was pretty sure there was some of it he did not recall.

When he came out of the bathroom his senses told him that the old crone was attending to more than just the dishes. She was cooking on the gas stove.

Ric wandered into the kitchen to find her frying a couple of eggs, a large beef tomato and some sausages. She had made a pot of coffee from freshly ground beans, and there was a flat loaf on the side so fresh that it threw out a steamy basil-scented vapour.

He was surprised, if not a little confused; he hadn't been to any of the shops in town yesterday, and he hadn't asked the agency to supply a maid. He presumed the old crone must have brought the provisions with her. He didn't feel like arguing or even asking the how or the why of it, so he took some cutlery from the drawer and sat down at the table in the main room.

After a few more minutes, during which time expectation played havoc with his taste buds, and the dull, sand-blasting throb in his head and neck calmed to a bearable level, the gnomed paragon of domestic virtue set before him a glass of cold grapefruit juice and a full southern Corsican breakfast.

Ric surveyed her composition. He was lost for words on two accounts: one that he could never, even in his wildest dreams, have expected her to cook for him, and the other that he was unsure of how to thank her.

She stood, rubbing her hands on her apron, and watched Ric in much the same way as the nuthatch watched him on the beach; she was anxious to see whether or not he would appreciate her efforts.

So he set to and got on with it. The sausages were armour-plated, thick and compact; they were a task to dissect, let alone chew. The woman had cooked them whole, frying them in their own fat. They were wild boar sausages packed with local herbs and wine, and they took to his tender stomach like an assault brigade hitting a beach. The tomato she had sliced thick and decorated with the two perfectly cooked eggs.

The more he ate, the more she nodded in approval. The more she nodded the harder she rubbed her hands in her apron and displayed her gap-toothed grin. By the time he had cleared the plate she appeared to have grown a couple of inches and broadened perceptibly. She had produced a hangover cure to savour. As Ric mopped his plate with a hunk of the basil flavoured bread and drained the pot of coffee, the old lady returned to the kitchen and finished the washing up.

Ric sat back and wondered what he had done to deserve such attention.

For sure he had not bought or asked her to buy the food, so rather than be thought presumptuous, when she returned to the room he picked up the handful of soggy notes and began to separate a few of them to pay her.

"*Nò!*" she said when she saw what he was about to do. "*Nò, sgiò. Micca eiu! Micca eiu!*" she repeated, showing him her clean palms as though she was not to be held responsible.

Then, as he stood beside her, Ric took her hand in his, lifted it up and kissed her rather bony knuckle.

She beamed up at him, her mouth split wide in a shallow, w-shaped smile he had the feeling she reserved for very special occasions. Maybe it was such a contrast from the restrained look she had worn since he had first met her, but he couldn't understand why he felt this look was so exceptional; it was so striking and affecting, like that of a rare orchid which would come into bloom only once in a very long while, or like the sudden glare from a match struck in a darkened room. As she looked up she withdrew her hand from his and reached up and gently traced the outline of the red birthmark above his right eye, studying it as she did so.

The old lady mumbled "*lotchu*", and then repeated the word more slowly, spinning out and rounding the first syllable and then thinning her lips, whispering out the second. She seemed to show some kind of understanding of it, or perhaps of him.

Ric had no idea what she was saying, but he was reluctant to interrupt her.

Then the old dear's look shifted from wondrous scrutiny to that of an inquisitive frown, as though by touching his mark she might have caused Ric pain or that she had glimpsed a light now dimming in the distance. It was as though she had gained some kind of access to his thoughts and hadn't liked what she'd read.

The moment, whatever it meant to her, passed.

Ric was aware that he ought to have felt unnerved by her familiarity, but to his surprise he felt nothing of the kind. Rather he felt a soft calm settle about him; a calm similar to that which had come upon him at the very end of the evening before as he had strolled, or perhaps more accurately stumbled, up the dusty track in search of his bed.

Then she turned and was gone; a brief unlacing of the apron, a sweeping collection of her black handbag and frying pan from the sideboard, a swift departure out through the front door into the car he had not heard arrive, and off down the dusty track; almost all in one fluid movement.

And suddenly Ric was alone.

He was not sure what to make of it; the breakfast or the old lady. He was not sure of much except that his car was still in town, and in the old Citroen were his mobile phone and sunglasses – that was if they hadn't been requisitioned by some light fingered Algerian.

It could wait. It could all wait, he thought.

Ric looked around the room for something to do other than be faced with the bother of retrieving his car and phone. He saw on the long sofa the small leather book that Manou had given him, and then logic took over.

Of course: Manou! Somewhere in the appearance of the old lady and the sumptuous breakfast lay Manou's hand. He was certain of it. Certain and yet he could not fathom why on earth she should lay it all on for him. After all, he had not phoned her the previous day as she had been entitled to think he would.

He picked up the brown palm-sized notebook, collected a bottle of St George's water from the fridge and headed outside to sit beneath the umbrella beside the pool. Perhaps the recuperative perfumes of the rosemary, thyme, lentisk and the other heady perfumes of the maquis would repair his dulled senses. Physical exercise was very definitely off the agenda.

The small leather bound book was not the easiest of reads, but it was fascinating. The unlined paper was only yellowed at the edges, suggesting it had not been exposed to the fading influences of sunlight over the years. Perhaps Manou had not lent it to others the way she had to Ric. The handwriting, in an ink which had purpled with age, showed a fine, elegant and very feminine hand. The calligraphy was educated, with distinctive curls around the tops of the taller letters and the tails of the fallers, like delicate and ornate filigree. The accents were precise in length and angle; the script suggested an educated and ordered mind as the drafting was both neatly horizontal and carefully measured within unmarked margins. It struck him that Manou's mother had retained both her literacy and her schooling from the years prior to her refuge on the island.

It took Rick some time to translate from the French, but the Corsu was almost impossible to break down as it leant further towards the Italian, his knowledge of which did not extend to the more obtuse vocabulary. But there appeared to Ric to be many extraordinary similarities between the slogans of his youth and the sentiments expressed in the book. Many of the proverbs and aphorisms were commonplace to those of his native language. Simple mottos like *La maison rend toujours ce qu'elle prend* – The house takes, the house returns, a version of What goes around comes around. *Si on te donne un cheval, ne regardes pas des dents,* translated literally as Don't look a gift horse in the mouth and *Aide-toi, le ciel t'aidera,* which amused Ric as it had been one of his father's preferred aphorisms: God, or heaven, helps them who help themselves. There were other more obscure quotes that he would need Manou to explain, such as *C'est dans le sac les problèmes* or The problems are in the bag, which sounded to Ric like a clue from a cryptic crossword.

But even in the small personal history of parochial phrases there appeared the footprint of the many foreigners who had trodden the island; foreigners bearing not only their own colonial aspirations, but also moralists and philosophers convinced of their duty to peddle their intellectual ideology. A biblical quote about not letting the left hand see what the right hand was doing, was followed by Kant informing the world of the futility of doing good, and Nietsche; *Ce qui ne vous tue vous fait grossir.*

"*What doesn't kill you makes you stronger,*" he said quietly to himself.

He sighed long and loud and looked about the view, searching the horizon for some explanation as to why Manou's mother should have gone to so much trouble to preserve so many common, if slightly obscure, proverbs.

Spread out before him lay a rich, green baize criss-crossed here and there by the odd footpath or vehicle track. Beneath the protective shade of the umbrella, Ric watched and bathed in the relative peace and quiet of the Corsican landscape; a landscape, he concluded, that to the casual observer appeared picturesque and forgiving. The sky was a deep azure blue at its crown and with the heat graded to almost chalk white where the maquis struggled up to meet it in the south; the beach was a flaxen strip of sand that lined the purple water to the east; and inland, the mountains stretched green and grey, high away to the bare peaks of the west. Out on the patio, soothed by the embracing and overwhelming perfume of the maquis, calmed by the constant whirr of insect life and heartened by the great warmth of the midday sun, it was difficult for Ric to imagine a life less elementary.

And yet now that he had met Manou, he was coming to appreciate that to the people of the island there existed a landscape entirely alternative to the one perceived by the many passing Sybarites; a habitat as rugged as any he had trekked, trudged or stalked through; one that could be harsh and unforgiving, the great heat of summer giving over to the intense cold of winter; a habitat that mirrored the people who existed within it – a people with an inner strength, possessed of both great kindness and enduring patience, but perhaps more fundamentally, possessed, like those bare peaks away to the west, of a granite resolve.

Ric's thoughts turned to the kindly old cleaning lady; his new housemaid. Her dark-olive face was lined from years of squinting in the sunlight and her eyes were beady, just like those of the nuthatch. Her nose, squashed into the centre of her face by her bold, purple-tinged cheekbones and round chin, was not much more than a button. He had seen her once or twice when he'd first arrived, but after he'd committed to his morning routine he hadn't been in at the time she had come to clean. There was something chiselled or hewn about her appearance, as though her features had been fashioned from the same granite upon which she perched.

Ric thought of Manou's mother; smuggled into the hinterland of the island from a cosmopolitan mainland over fifty years before, desperate to escape those who would have murdered her, only to find herself confined to a life far harder than she could ever have imagined when growing up in the city. Much like the people of the island during the occupation, who had no alternative other than to adjust to the harsh conditions pressed upon them by their new masters, the land and its climate, Manou's mother could not simply have left because she found the island life hard. Her choice was either death or life; a life governed by conditions and customs as unsophisticated, and at times as brutal, as those that had existed anywhere in Europe for centuries; a death, purely a disappearance into anonymity. Just as it was with the local people in Helmand, southern Afghanistan, in southern Corsica, in the place Manou had described to him as *dila dai Monti*, it was the land that fashioned the character, and not the reverse.

But Manou's mother had retained some of her very individual character from her time before Corsica, from her time before she had become governed and disciplined by influences far beyond her want or control. The small brown notebook was perhaps evidence of the distance she had maintained over the years between herself and the island. Perhaps it was through the book that she had kept herself apart and different from the rest; by observing and recording. It was proof that she had held on to that other person she had been before she came to Corsica; her previous, other identity that had risked being washed away by the very same tide of war that bore her to the island.

Ric wondered why she had stayed and had not left after the war.

21

Sometime later, and for the second time in one day, Ric awoke more than a little uncertain as to his whereabouts.

This time he was lying on his back, on a towel on the patio, beneath the umbrella. Away beyond the shade a few small puffs of white cloud lazed about, precursors of more to come; the sun was going to lose the day.

He had to get his car from the village, or at least he had to retrieve his phone and whatever else he had left behind the night before. A picture of the drooping and pasty face of the policeman jumped into his mind.

Ric needed a word with the man Bosquet. He had possessed neither the requisite energy, nor the mental faculty when the man had driven him home to ask him too many practical questions. Although in the dim light something in Bosquet's face had suggested to Ric that he wouldn't receive an honest reply to any question he might have asked. Bosquet looked too shrewd to hand over any more information than he wanted Ric to know. Besides, in his tired state Ric may not have proved the most receptive of audiences.

But there was nevertheless something about the fellow Kamo that interested the policeman, and that intrigued Ric. Perhaps it was the fact that he had little to keep him occupied that meant the intrigue appealed. Perhaps it was the Georgian's money, so evident and undeniable in the glitz on display, which pricked Ric's curiosity; that slightly uneasy, almost unclean feeling, like the itching from a borrowed shirt, which almost always touched Ric whenever he found himself in the company of such affluence.

He went inside, showered, shaved and changed, and grabbed a beer from the fridge. He still felt a little stale from the after effects of the night before, but the hair of the dog – the cold refreshing *Pietra* – soon chased his second hand blues away and buoyed his somewhat contemplative mood. He should go and retrieve his mobile from the car, phone Manou and make a date for dinner.

Ric felt better for a plan; direction and decision, he decided, was and always had been good for his soul.

He slipped on a pair of cross-trainers, closed the patio doors and back door, and wheeled the trials bike out from the side of the house. He didn't bother kicking it into life; he simply rolled it down the drive and, when it had gained enough speed, he dropped it into gear, slipped the clutch and the beast growled.

As he passed the white-washed tomb at the bottom of the drive he recalled the strange sounds he'd heard from around it the night before. Naturally, and given his absolute inebriation, he assumed that his imagination had been playing tricks on him. But his memory of the episode caused him to laugh out loud at his own childish response, and very soon he was sweeping through the smooth turns down to Zizula, a vague and airy euphoria blowing about him.

When he got there, the big blue boat was still at anchor, Camille's bar was busy and his old Citroen sat patiently and apparently unmolested exactly where he had abandoned it the evening before. There was something quaintly loyal about the battered, snail-like form, and he felt a nascent sympathy with it; not with the shape, he countered, but with the way it sat apart from the other cleaner, more modern vehicles, like a favoured old brogue set amongst newer shoes.

His keys were still on top of the rear wheel and, more importantly, his cellphone was on the floor underneath the plastic mat. He pocketed it and locked the car up again; the keys were so flimsy, and the design of the lock so basic that even an amateur car thief would have broken into it in seconds. He might as well not have bothered to lock it.

Then he saw the note on the windshield. *Demain matin* and *M* was all it said, but Ric knew her hand. Her mother may not have taught Manou to write, but there was no mistaking some of the style; he wondered how much form they shared.

As sure as he could be, he had not seen the note the evening before. Even in his parlous state he hoped he would have seen it. Anyway, he reasoned, examining the paper, the morning was long gone and he had not seen her, so she obviously meant tomorrow.

With that the sun surrendered to the gathering clouds and the beach began to clear.

22

The dawn broke bright and uncommonly sharp. The late afternoon breeze, the *Terrana* of the previous day, had swelled into a sizeable gale from the north-east, which had driven the sun-worshippers early from the beach, whipping up the sand to flay their broad flanks, like gravel tossed at a cumbrous herd. In consequence this morning there was clarity to the atmosphere promoting the illusion that, to the west, the mountains stood close enough to touch and, to the east, the horizon was but a neat pencil-line drawn upon a blue wall.

Ric had dreamt, but not unpleasantly. His images had not been those to which he had grown used, images that more often than not turned his night into nightmare; rather they had consisted of his being born along through light and dark, as though he was being swept through a universe of shadows, each one a different depth of darkness from the last, the gloom broken only by occasional glimpses of the stars. His smooth and fluid voyage seemed to last hours and terminated in a small, enclosed vault into which streamed a single shaft of moonlight from a high casement. The dream was possessed of a lightness which left him rested and calm, and somewhere along the way Ric had sensed Manou's presence, as though she had been watching over him throughout.

He had risen early, having left his windows open so that the light and sounds of the new day might call him from his sleep. He had ridden his motorbike down to the beach and, as his diving kit was still in the boot of the Citroen, he did not fish for octopus as he would normally have done. Instead he had swum out around *la Tozza* and had not found it necessary to break his journey for a rest at the island; the second good night's sleep in a row had fuelled the energy reserves upon which his long swim depended.

When finished, he'd not even paused to stretch before embarking on his run; he'd simply swum in, stood up, waded out of the water and turned up the beach at a vigorous pace, working the morning stiffness out of his legs and wind-milling his arms as he went.

To any casual observer, and Ric had seen no evidence of the youngster's presence, it would appear that the naked man running at the water's edge possessed not a care in the world. Even Ric thought it to be true, for he had woken not only thinking of Manou but also glad that he had been doing so. And though this was not a significant departure from the morning after the first time he had met Manou, he found himself infused with a heartening conviction about the day ahead; a rare and very welcome feeling.

Manou arrived at the house at eleven. He knew she would have laughed had she known he had been ready for her since not long after nine. And when he opened the door of the Peugeot for her, he perceived an almost coy and boyish abashment about his actions and hoped she would not notice his self-consciousness. Ric also thought he looked the part in blue checked shirt, white chinos and espadrilles.

"Good morning, Ric. You look very, mmm, smart," Manou said, reaching up for his hand as she got out. She put her left hand on his shoulder and leant forward to kiss him, once on both cheeks and then a third time on his lips. "Somewhere nice to go today?"

Ric was still reeling from her kiss, or kisses. They empowered him and filled him with a breezy confidence. Half of him wanted to gather her up and carry her indoors, but his other more cautious half held him back.

"I don't know where I got it from, but I am somehow under the impression that we were going out today," he countered.

Manou was wearing a buttoned beige shirt, khaki shorts, and ankle-length boots that had long ago been cobbled for hiking. Her hair was tied back behind a green head-scarf. She looked up at him, her light-blue eyes questioning; searching for something in him.

He felt there was something she was waiting for him to tell her, but he had not the faintest idea what it was. His mind raced down a progression of avenues until it arrived at the moment of their last uncomfortable parting, when she had left him lying cowed by his inadequacy in the early hours before dawn. The memory was still raw in him like an undressed wound.

But he was wrong, for as soon as he thought it she seemed to sense it and understand that this was not the conclusion she had intended him to draw. Manou had been looking for something else.

"You are a little overdressed for what I had in mind," she said teasing. "You want to go into Porti Vechju and play sight-seer? Mmm? Or shall I take you away for the day? I think it would be more fun for you to get away from the beach tourists for the day. I hear that they are not so good for you, eh?" She giggled, taunting him some more.

"I hear they make you swim in the dark, Ric. It's true, no?" Manou moved closer to him, her mouth raised at the corners, an eyebrow arched as she made fun of him; all acts designed to ensure he did not mistake her poking fun at him for anything other than exactly what it was: fun, even if it was at his expense.

"Don't tell me," he replied, "the maquis sees everything."

"Yes Ric. You know it now; everything! There is no escape, no hiding place." And she kissed him again full on his lips, pulling slightly at him with her mouth before standing back.

Her touch both reassured and inspired Ric.

And Manou knew it, for she turned away towards the house in a swift, elusive movement, withdrawing out of range. "Come on, I will make us coffee while you change into something more suitable for walking."

She drove them up to the main road and turned north to Solenzara. They left the windows down to allow the warm morning air to blow through the car as they traced the curls and loops of the coast road for half an hour.

On his side lay the Tyrrhenian, aquamarine and emerald at the shoreline and purple in the deep, laying a sparkling trail towards the brightening sun. He saw the old Genoese watch tower at Fautea and the beautiful Catholic church gracing the bay at Favone.

On her side the maquis and the woodland rose higher and higher up to the peak at Telica.

Manou pointed out the skyline which rose up to the higher *Pietra Bianca*, in turn dwarfed by Monte Piano, and then the long slope down from Monte Santo to Togna. All of a sudden the granite mountain knelt down to meet the sea at the small estuary of Solenzara.

Manou turned inland onto a road less broad and smooth than the one they had just left, but a road more used than the one out of Zizula. There was more traffic now; coaches on day trips and trucks hauling trailers over to the western side of the island.

"Today I am going to take you to the *arrière pays*," she said, turning to look at him. "The land behind," she added for his benefit. "The road is tricky; many turns, many hairpins, I think you call them. If you feel...?"

He shook his head and smiled.

The signpost in the small sleepy town of Solenzara pointed the way to Zonza and the Col de Bavella. It had not escaped the customary defacement from the separatists. It seemed as though the initials of the FLNC were scrawled wherever you could not avoid seeing them and Ric wondered whether they were the rages of a passing generation, or the voice of a continuous struggle. The styles of the graffiti appeared quaint, yet the messages seemed recently applied, for many of the signs did not carry the weathered and abused facades of others.

The road followed the tight, winding, white and turquoise stream up into the hills. High cliffs leaned in on them from either side. Rocks, smooth, white and grey threatened to crush them and push them into the narrow gorge below.

They climbed on upwards, up over the Col de Larone, up into the more open country, twisting and turning. Bald mountain tops sat proud on either side and they passed orange escarpments and gnarled pines, and lines of rough and jagged granite teeth keened up at the sky as if from a petrified jaw.

"Monte Incudine," she said, pointing at an enormous collection of crenelated peaks away to the north. "Up here we have *névé*, as we call them: the place of eternal snow, but there are not so many of them as there used to be. This route we are taking, it is the long way to where we are going, but I thought you would like to see the mountains." She took her eyes off the road to check and see if he was either bored or interested.

"It is so different from the coastal plain," he replied to her questioning look. But, impressive as they were, they didn't compare to the towering ranges he had seen in Afghanistan, yet they shared a stark desolation in common; as though they offered promise, or perhaps only the promise of hardship. And although he felt like a tourist, regarding the stunning views from the comfort and security of Manou's car, he didn't object to playing at it for a while. The wind blew the cobwebs away and the scenery stole his thoughts from less negative paths, and, probably more importantly, being in Manou's company, Ric simply didn't care either way.

They stopped at the Col de Bavella. She showed him the white statue of the *Notre-Dame-des-Neiges*; the lady of snow praying for the souls of travellers, perched high upon the pile of dark granite stones and votive plaques, like a hapless ghost reading and discarding books about her feet. He bought Manou an ice-cream. But, they didn't linger amongst the gaudy sightseers and the corpulent, smoking coach-drivers.

Zonza was busy with its fair share of day-trippers, casual walkers, hikers and climbers, and even a troop of horse-riders. Ric was hoping that Manou might pull up for lunch in the centre of the pretty village, but, instead, she took a right by the war memorial and dropped down out of the village, winding through the forests of holm oak, sweet chestnuts and maritime pines.

After much twisting and turning they came to Levie, a small village assembled around the road that traversed the broad hillside. Old farmhands sat at a café that spilled out into the road and Manou had to slow to a crawl to pick her way through the weary hikers and absent-minded dogs that wandered along the narrow road.

Leaving the smattering of small restaurants behind, Manou turned left and again dropped down towards the valley floor, the road zig-zagging like an eager snake through the forest. Their path undulated and curved through sprawling deciduous woods; here and there mountain spring water seeped from gullies and wet the grey tarmac, and plaques on railings preserved for posterity the actions of the resistance during the war. Then, as they wound their way up again towards the village of Carbini, Manou turned right off the road up a lane that led deep into the forest. The lane tailed off into a track, and when the going became too rough she pulled over into the shade of the trees.

It was cool beneath the apron of the forest, and the barks around them, though dry, were dressed with moss and lichen.

"Ospédale, where we had dinner, is over beyond this mountain," she said unbuckling her seatbelt. "Punta di u Diamante is to the east," she pointed upwards. "The village of Levie, which we have just come from, is there," she pointed, "to the north across the valley. The monastery at Santa Lucia di Talla is down the valley and beyond the ridge to the west; and to the south above us is di a Vacca Morta. It is the highest of the three mountains."

"Dead cow?" Ric asked.

Manou shrugged. "Mmm, I suppose so. Well, I have a *pique-nique*, but we will walk a little first. Okay?"

"Okay by me."

Manou took a back pack from the boot of the car and began to shoulder it.

"Why don't you let me do that, Manou? Seems to me I've had enough practice at it."

At this she hesitated, looking at him with her brow furrowed, evidently wondering whether she should deny him his gallant offer, or just plain give way to his presumptuous gender.

Ric liked it that she did not brush his offer aside; that she thought about him, about them.

"Sure," she said, smiling, slipping the strap off her shoulder and handing him the backpack.

He swung it onto his back. It was not that heavy; maybe ten pounds.

Manou reached back into the boot, pulled a second backpack from within the confines and swung it up over her own shoulder before he had a chance to intervene.

Ric cringed.

She laughed out loud.

And then they both laughed; she at his discomfort and he at her pleasure. They laughed, challenging each other, now daring each one to catch the other out the next time an opportunity presented itself.

Manou led the way up the mountainside at a comfortable strolling pace. She walked with little apparent effort; an athletic and rolling gait that suggested she walked often. "The earth here is very dry, huh? Usually by this time of year it would be moist."

Ric saw that the ground was rutted and parched. The path was dry and had crumbled in places to expose the grey of the granite beneath.

"It has not rained for too long," she carried on. "Okay we have had the storm sometimes from the *Maestrale*, but that rain is not enough for the *ruisseau* – the little streams, to water the harvest. We need more consistent rain to fill the lakes. The météo, the weather forecast, says the rains will be a long time coming. Even last night, we have the *Grecale*; it comes from the north-east. It was cool this morning and the air was very clear. Did you see it?" she asked, glancing at him as if to gauge her pace to his effort.

"Sure," Ric replied, "like you could touch the mountains!" He smiled at her to let her know he had no problem keeping up.

"Sometimes the *Grecale* brings rain, but not this time," she concluded.

"Today it is dry. We will have to wait now for the rains, perhaps wait until we are in the autumn."

They walked on down and then up through the forest. Here and there the path narrowed so much that Ric had to walk behind Manou. His gaze alternated between the stony ground beneath his footing, the tall gnarled holm oaks and chestnut trees, and the soft curves of her figure as she led him up the slope. Her legs were toned and held their shape. She was, he decided, very fit. No, he decided, she was not just fit, she was strong too. As with her swimming, her progress did not tax her breath, and she accommodated interruptions to her stride without any noticeable effort.

Ric wondered as he watched whether it was as much her mind as it was her physicality that drew him to her. Or maybe even it was that the one matched with the other? Her slender buttocks were firm and taught, and they rose and fell in even rhythm.

She must have recognised his silence, for she broke it with a chuckle. "There will be more to see when you get to the top, Ric?"

Ric was lost somewhere around her hips. "I can't wait," he replied.

In front of him, Manou chuckled again.

The air in the forest was cool and clean-scented, not sultry as Ric expected it to be, and he noticed a complete lack of sound apart from the muffled padding of their footfalls; the forest floor was an uneven carpet of grass and earth, dusty and parched, devoid of any sign of wildlife.

Ric tried to keep his bearings as they walked, but the sun streamed almost straight down through the trees. Only tell-tale lichen on the tree barks suggested north from south.

They skirted round and below a tall bluff and, he calculated, they were above the level of the village they had been approaching when they turned off the road. Now and again their path was cut across with partially concealed, ankle-breaking ruts; ruts not much wider than a child's step or deeper than an adult's hand. They were formed, she told him, by the seasonal melt-waters running down from the rocks above.

And it was as they came to one of these narrow, dry channels that Manou hesitated for a moment and then stopped so abruptly that Ric ploughed straight into her back, grabbing her not only to steady him, but also to stop from pushing her over.

"Whoa," he said. "Hand signals, please?"

Manou had frozen still. She was routed to the spot.

He could feel beneath his hands that she was rigid, as though her body had contracted in readiness for some enormous physical demand. And strangely, she had begun to whistle; a gentle, continuous and bell-like carillon.

Ric moved to her side, not sure what to expect.

Immediately to Manou's front a dry furrow crossed the path. It was perhaps a shade larger than several they had crossed, but still simple enough to step over without changing stride. Over the years the run-off had cut its own tortuous channel through the forest, finding the path of least resistance through the granite screed, trailing down and round to the valley floor.

But it was not the barren bed of what should have been the life giving stream that had halted her so suddenly; it was the human skull that lay in it.

Without realising it, he had pulled Manou back behind him. She stopped whistling, but mostly because Ric was holding her so tight she could not breathe.

"Ric?" she whispered at his chest. "Ric?"

"Wait," he replied, "just a, oh…," he relaxed his grip on her shoulders, "sorry. I, er, I mean I wasn't sure what to…."

"No, of course you were not," Manou replied some way between irritation and frustration. "I don't think he is going to hurt us now, *n'est ce pas?* And the people who put him there, they are probably dead by now too, eh."

They both stood up; Ric a little more guardedly than Manou, who brushed herself down as though Ric had thrown dust over her to camouflage her.

"Why were you whistling?" he asked.

She took off the backpack, took out from it a handkerchief and wiped a light sheen of perspiration from her face.

"Oh, something that my father used to do. For a man who was not superstitious, my father had some very irrational habits."

Ric knelt down to pick up the scull. It looked clean, as though it had recently been placed in the narrow culvert, and it was small, not large enough to be that of an adult, but it was without doubt old as she had suggested. The skull was grey and held no teeth. Just as he lifted it, an enormous blue fly emerged from the left eye socket and buzzed angrily at him, startling him, causing him to drop the scull back onto the hard ground. It bounced with a dull, hollow knock and began to roll away down the slope. He wasn't sure if she wanted him to retrieve it or not, but when he turned he saw the quizzical look in Manou's eyes.

"You want to take it with you?" she asked, amused. "A souvenir?" Manou shouldered the backpack again. "Come on! There is a place for us to stop just around the mountain." With that she turned, stepped over the furrow and started off up the trail.

Ric stood for a couple of seconds and stared at the skull as it lay upturned, exposing the inside of its hollow cranium, baring thoughts too late to be concerned with its own disconnected predicament. A tingle of guilt invaded Ric as though he felt wrong at dropping and deserting the shabby vestige of the poor unfortunate, as though perhaps he should have taken it and buried it. But when he turned back, Manou was some thirty metres away, so he set off after her.

They emerged from the forest at the foot of a high granite cliff that swept up out of sight. The slope down to the west spread out below them, like a vast deciduous apron covering the valley. Not far above them the forest discontinued its march up the mountain and gave way to a barren, granite-grey scarp with a bald summit.

The sun to their left hung high and blinding in the shimmering blue, but there was the gentlest hint of a breeze from the south-west which, as they had lost the cooling umbrella of the forest, served to take the edge off the baking heat.

A little further along the path they came to a curiously misshapen outcrop of rock, like a gnarled hand whose closed fingers pointed west towards the horizon. The upward angle of their pointing produced an overhang, around which blocks of stone had been piled to create a wall that stretched up from the ground to meet the hand three metres above. The overhang and the angle of it provided for a small cabin into the side of which was set a low doorway, and a window of sorts had been fashioned high up in the front face; a window just large enough to allow in light but not so large that it would let in much rain. There was a fantastic contrivance to it that reminded Ric of a Disney cartoon, or of one of those quaint but ultimately useless model cottages he had seen at airport gift shops. And yet the roof of the cabin had been fashioned entirely by the upheaval of cooling magma spewed from the depths and then forged smooth by the natural elements.

"We call it an *oriu*," Manou said.

Ric walked around it to the back where he was able to climb up onto the smooth curved surface of the roof; the back of the hand. The walls had been filled and pointed with some pale, chalk-like cement, and the blocks, rocks and stones had been cut very accurately square, giving the cabin the look of a carefully constructed residence.

"People live here?"

"Some of the time," she called out from below, "the shepherds take shelter in the *oriu*. Well, they used to. It is more of a refuge from bad weather. They live here in the summer sometimes; but they are also used for storing grain and food. Some people say that they were the hideouts for *bandits d'honneur*; others that they are tombs for the lost souls who walk the mountains."

Ric jumped back down and stood by the wooden door: "Like the kid who left his head back there?"

"Mmm, no," Manou replied between sips from her water bottle. "The skull in the bed of a stream without water has a different meaning. It is put there by the rainmakers to encourage the rains."

"Rainmakers?"

"Yes. Naturally we have rainmakers. In fact most people have them. You have harvest festivals in Britain. Everyone has festivals for hoping that the harvest will be *abondant* – you say bountiful – and everyone has festivals to give thanks. So, here it is no different." Manou paused. "Except sometimes we have a long time without rain, so we have people who make the rains come. Or maybe they make the people think they make the rains come. That is a little more mysterious," she went on. "Perhaps how it is, is that we like to think we have people who can make the rains come. It helps us forget we are always," she struggled to find the right words, "*à la merci du temps?*" Manou looked to Ric for help.

"At the mercy of the weather," he offered. "Bound by the elements."

"Sure! Bound by the elements," she repeated, committing the phrase to memory. "We know we are bound of course, but it is no bad thing to think we have some influence."

Ric carried on when Manou paused, "And so the rainmaker puts the scull in the dry riverbed to summon the rains?"

"Sure," she replied. "Sometimes they put the ears of the corn, but, sometimes a skull. It does not have to be the skull of a particular person; it is not like a sacrifice. The *Mazzeri*, as they are called, they ask for the rains to come. The water is a great part of our lives."

She paused and looked at Ric, waiting for him to respond. When he did not, Manou continued, "The spirits of the dead live near the water. We have many stories of people meeting the spirits near water. Some of the old people still throw stones into water before crossing the ruisseau to scare away the spirits. Maybe that is why my father used to whistle; to frighten them away. They say that the skull of Sampiero Corso, one of our heroes, ahah!" Manou laughed, a light and self-mocking chuckle that sounded like water flowing down the mountain streams of which she spoke. "We have had so many heroes in our past. They say his skull was placed into a riverbed to bring the rains, and afterwards the heavens gave us the rain." She shook her head in amused apology.

"Well, there's nothing wrong with having heroes, but skulls in the riverbed, rain dancers... that all sounds a little prehistoric." Ric had not intended his response to sound so dismissive, but his tone gave him away and immediately he regretted it.

Manou frowned at Ric as though his scepticism was misplaced. "*Mégalithique*, not *Préhistorique:* between 3-4,000 years before Christ."

Ric sought to atone for his disrespect. "The *Mazz... Mazzeri?* Rain dancers?"

"More or less," she replied. "The *Mazzeri* are our shaman, our clairvoyants... our mediums if you like. And yet they are not only our psychics; they have many roles in our society. The tradition is that they foretell death. They see things in people others cannot see. There are not many *Mazzeri* left now. Like the stone carvings, they are from the *Mégalithique* times. But they are flesh and blood the same as you and me, so unlike the stones they live for only so long."

He hesitated before entering the tight doorway of the *oriu*. He glanced at Manou. "Should I knock?"

Manou laughed again, a bright, long and cheerful laugh that echoed against the rock face. She shook her head in disbelief. "You can go in."

"Well," Ric said, "first the skull, now the tomb. I can't imagine what you're going to pull out of the hat next."

He ducked in through the makeshift doorway. It was dark after the blinding brightness outside and it took his eyes a while to adjust before he could make out the confines of the *oriu*. There was enough space inside for a disagreement between two residents, but not enough for a full blown argument. There was a low wooden bed at the back with some kind of uneven and unappealing straw-filled mattress on it. In the front corner nearest the door on a rough, hewn wooden surface sat a tin bowl; a bowl that had once possessed the white of enamel. And in the other corner below the high window a hearth was set into the stone with a hook fashioned over it. The walls and ceiling were smooth, like that of the exterior of the roof, and a shaft of light, like that from a searchlight, issued from the high window. Ric was reminded of his dream. It was cool in the tiny room, almost to the point of feeling cold, and Ric tried to imagine the kind of hardy individual who would dare dwell for more than one night in such a place.

Outside, on a flat rock she was using as a table, Manou had set out their picnic: a couple of small round loaves, a hunk of cheese, some cold sausages and a bottle of red wine that wore no label and was stoppered with a very second hand looking cork.

Manou unfolded her scarf and set it on her head to shade her brow.

They ate in silence for a while, the walk having charged their appetite, and took in the view down the valley to the village and the hills beyond. The cheese was sweet and smoky in flavour.

"*Ricotta,*" Manou said as she chewed. "It is from Porti Vechju. It is the same name as the Italian, but it is quite different. It's good, eh?" She handed him the wine bottle.

He eased out the rough cork and took a swig from it; a modest swig in case the flavour was as unusual as that of the cheese. It was sharp, full and rough, but it went well with the sweeter cheese. She broke one of the round bread loaves in two and handed him one half. The top of it was browned, as though over-baked like a hard pastry, and inside mixed into the dough were hazelnuts and raisins.

Ric bit off a chunk. The bread too was delicious, slightly lemon flavoured. "That's good," he mumbled between mouthfuls. "What's it called?"

Manou watched him, a knowing and mischievous smile spreading over her face.

"What?" he asked, returning her look, knowing she was about to pull his leg in some way. "Come on, Manou? What's it called?" he asked again with some resignation.

140

She laughed as she replied, small lines of pleasure forming at the corners of her lively blue eyes. "We call it *pan di morti*," and she exploded into a fit of giggles like a young girl. "Bread of the dead!"

Ric shook his head in disbelief, "Bread of the dead? I should have known."

Her laughter eventually subsided and she casually wiped a small fleck of cheese from her lower lip with the back of her hand.

He decided she was even more beautiful when she laughed, like the first rays of sun that chase away the chill of dawn. He raised the bottle to his lips.

"We leave this bread out with wine on All Saints Day," she said more seriously. "It is for the dead when they come back to visit. It is so they don't return to the underworld and say we have not been hospitable to them."

Ric put the wine bottle down on the rock. He found himself in no man's land again; literally uncertain as to whether or not Manou was still teasing him, as if her reference to the dead was very removed from her joking about the bread they ate. It wasn't so much the seriousness of her tone that alerted him; it was more the way she looked at him, as though she was watching for his reaction to what she had just said; testing him to see whether or not he could accommodate the concept of the dead revisiting their homes.

Curiously though, it wasn't the concept that bothered him. It was the dead themselves who suddenly occupied his mind, their grim countenances etched in the further corners of his sanity, their actions playing like looped film, over and over: laughter and tears, darkness and light, laughter and tears.

Manou watched him until the silence between them grew awkward. She pointed over towards the north-east where the bell tower of a campanile peered over a rocky outcrop. "Over there is the village of Carbini," Manou began, "you can see it and the cemetery below it. Carbini is a small village; a *paisolu* or *hameau*. But it has perhaps 400 inhabitants; 100 people are alive, living in the houses and farms, the other 300 are dead, they live in the cemetery. This side of the island to the south-west is called the Sartenais. From here the springs flow down to join the Fiumicicoli below Carbini, and the Fiumicicoli joins the Rizzanèse below Sartène, and the Rizzanèse flows into the Golfo di Valinco at Proprianu." Manou paused, looking ahead at the view, not at him.

"It begins up here, in these mountains," she went on. "Everything has a beginning somewhere. For now the *ruisseau* are dry, but the rains will come and they will feed the mountains again. Maybe not soon, but it will happen. Then we will have *vino di petra*, or wine of stone, again. For that is what we say; *pane di legna, vigno di petra*-bread of wood, wine of stone. We make bread with the flour of the chestnuts from the chestnut trees, and we have our water from the mountains. *Pane di legna, vigno di petra*," she repeated for him.

Ric bent to pick up the small bottle of wine. He raised and drank from the bottle; a long, slow pull and he held the dry sharpness in his mouth for a second before swallowing.

Manou talked on, filling the silence. "There was a Franciscan called Ristoro, he came to our island in the fourteenth century. He was one of the Poor Brothers of Penitence from Provence. Ristoro preached the virtues of shared poverty; a kind of spiritual poverty that should be endured by everyone. The people of the church of San Giovanni in Carbini, you can see the tower over there," she pointed again at the tall tower away to their right, "they took his teaching and rebelled against the wealthy families who were supported by their masters in Pisa. The authorities said they were extremists who took part in shameful orgies and who defiled the name of the Virgin. Others think that they shared the ideology of the Cathars. But their beliefs were like the beliefs of Saint Francis, who visited our island in the thirteenth century: kindness to all, animals and man, rich and poor, all the same."

Ric sat down beside Manou, leaning forward, his legs drawn up and his arms resting on his knees. He recalled she had mentioned the people from Carbini before.

She glanced briefly at him and went on: "They were excommunicated by the Pope. Of course, they were a threat to his authority and to his wealth. To survive they armed themselves and moved north to *di qua dai Monti* and became a part of the rebellion of Sambocuccio d'Alando from the Bozio. D'Alando introduced the *Regime Populaire*; a kind of egalitarian ideology." Manou paused again, glancing at Ric, trying to catch his eye, but he stared at the light grey of the rock between his feet. "But," she continued, "it is a problem with ideology, heh," she tapped her forehead. "It works in the head and not in the hand. In the end the rebellion only changed one master for another; in those days it changed the Pisans for the Genoese. The Poor Brothers of Penitence were not for our island. They were exploited by the ambitious." She paused again, raising her arm and pointing away to a line of rugged peaks across the valley. "Over there," she added, waiting until Ric looked up to follow her direction, "there, you can just see the cross on the top of the small, round hill behind Carbini. That is where the last of the *Giovannali* were murdered by the soldiers sent by the Pope.

"But," Manou carried on, "what they stood for has stayed with us: the sharing of life with each other, sharing among the people. Hah," she scoffed, "the poor sharing among the poor perhaps, not the rich sharing with anybody. They do not need to share, heh?"

She lost herself in the mist of her own thoughts for a few minutes, then Manou turned and knelt in front of him, separating him from the view and making it impossible for him to avoid her clear blue eyes. They calmed and comforted Ric the way the shaded pools of an oasis provide hope and rest for a weary traveller.

She leant forward, took his head gently between her hands and studied his face, searching, wondering.

In turn Ric looked back. There was a light sheen of perspiration above her dark eyebrows and the suggestion of the same on the fullness of her upper lip. There was a slight freckling to her cheeks, which he had not noticed before, and Manou wore no make-up around her eyes; no mascara, nothing. The blue of her eyes glowed against the deep almond of her skin and he detected the faintest perfume of lavender.

Afterwards, he realised that it was Manou who had kissed him, rather than the other way round.

As they walked back down the path through the forest to the car, Ric could still feel the hot, moist warmth of her lips on his, as though Manou was trying to move some part of herself into him through her kiss. She had not opened her mouth to him completely; she had not given herself up to him. But as they kissed, so Manou lapped four times at his lips with her tongue, savouring him, but not intruding far into him. Four times, he would not forget. Ric felt she was telling him and at the same time testing him; leaving him in no doubt that she wanted him, but also sampling him; saying to him that although she wanted him, she wanted to know his taste first.

Manou had rested her hand on the bare skin of his thigh as she kissed him, and through the connection between her mouth and her hand passed a warm and unmistakable current.

23

Manou drove them back through Levie and Zonza, and rather than head straight over to the coast the way they had come, she headed south and they wound their way up through the forest to the lake above the village of L'Ospédale where they had taken dinner three evenings before.

The narrow road weaved its course in tight turns and short straights, and she spoke a little as she drove, pointing out where the stumps of the trees that had been felled in order to extend the lake up to the barrage were now visible because the water level had fallen so low. She mentioned places of interest and told anecdotal stories about the small hamlets through which they passed.

"My father used to take me walking up here in the hills," she said. "He told me it was important for me to know the *pays*, the flowers and the herbs that grow and the ones we use for natural medicines."

"Natural as in homeopathic?"

"For sure," Manou said, "but they are more than *homépathique*. You know," she went on, "in the *arrière pays* there is not a pharmacie around the next corner and it has always been the way in Corsica for the old ones to pass the knowledge of the medicines on to the young. It has given many generations the power to survive the hard life in the mountains. We use wild garlic," she glanced briefly in her rear view mirror and then across at him to check that he was still interested, and went on, "for healing wounds and infections, sometimes for rheumatism, and for breathing problems; fennel for digestion and even for bronchitis. It is right; bronchitis?" Manou asked, taking her eyes off the road for a second, longer look in her mirror.

Ric sensed she had stiffened a little as she spoke, as though the conversation was not to her liking. But he was beginning to understand that she glanced at him often to reassure herself that she was not boring him. So he nodded, which Manou took as an encouragement to carry on.

"*L'arbousier* we use for treating kidney stones; *l'aconit* napel for shivers and sweats; *le rossolis* for respiratory problems. The verbena is for *vervaine*, for worms and gout; the lime blossom for *tilleul*, a sedative, and the camomile for *tisane*, for, well, our female tensions. I am sure you understand." She smiled a turned down crescent of a vaguely apologetic smile. "These last ones are all infusions: teas."

Then Ric noticed Manou looking in her rear-view mirror again, but this time for too long.

The next bend was upon them too quickly and Manou had to brake harder than was comfortable, getting the Peugeot a little out of shape in the corner. She seemed unusually tense.

Tea, of course, for tensions. He could hear his mother saying, as though tea was her own personal panacea, "Have a cup of tea and you'll feel better." Who needs a field dressing or a clotting agent when you can have a brew? Certainly his mother could. Bleed to death? No. Have a cup of tea. Ric chuckled to himself and as he did so realised he had made more noise than he had intended.

"Tea," he repeated. "There's nothing quite like a cup of tea," he quoted, hoping the mention of it might relax her from whatever it was that troubled her.

Manou braked very suddenly and slowed the car to a crawl, apparently to allow a vehicle to pass. But when it did not pass, she accelerated again.

As they rounded the left hand bend, Ric was presented with the vast panorama of the coastal plain below. He realised her driving had become a touch ragged and strained. The verge at the apex of the corner gave way to a sheer drop of several hundred metres and all that separated him from the plain below was the car door and a low stone wall.

Ric risked a look over the edge and felt giddy. He was relieved she appeared to know each and every contour of the winding mountain road by heart.

But, Manou was preoccupied with something or someone behind her. She stared into her mirror and anticipated, rather than saw, the next bend.

"You don't believe these herbs are good for medicine, Ric?" she asked with a sharp, disapproving edge.

"No," he replied, "it wasn't that. Really it wasn't. It's just that whenever tea is mentioned it reminds me of my mother. She'd have you believe tea would cure venereal disease."

This time Ric realised she had allowed her eyes to linger in the rear-view mirror for too long.

"Manou," he said in as loud and as firm a voice as he could manage without shouting. But his warning didn't wrest her concentration from the mirror.

As they entered the bend Ric realised they wouldn't make it round unless she looked where they were going.

"Manou," he repeated louder.

She blared the horn repeatedly, looked to her front and then pulled on the steering wheel. The car swerved round the broader, flatter curve on the outside of the hairpin, but on the exit they were impossibly close to the low wall. Manou was now looking round out of her window at the vehicle behind them. She shouted over her shoulder and waved frantically, ushering and encouraging the car past.

Ric involuntarily lifted his left leg like a spectator at a high jump competition. "Manou!" he shouted in desperation as he struggled against his seatbelt to get away from the precipice beside him.

The car hit the wall and for a moment ran down the side of it, the rough cut blocks scraping and tearing the sill of the door beside him.

As her Peugeot bounced back into the road, a shiny grey saloon raced alongside them and swerved towards them, squeezing them back up against the low wall.

Manou inched as close as she could to the wall, her natural instinct commanding her to turn away from the other car.

But then she hit the low wall again and this time rode up it, the nearside wheels of the car running for a moment along the top of it. The car bounced and shook and thumped and screeched as it careened along the wall.

The mountain below him swept away in one yawning and terrifying drop. Ric didn't have any alternative; it was either straight down to the plains several hundred feet below or smash left into the other car.

Ric reached over and grabbed the wheel forcing it and them over to the left, into the side of the grey saloon.

The driver sensed their intention and instantly raced ahead.

The Peugeot bumped down off the wall and swerved into the now vacant space.

Manou hit the brakes and wrestled control of the wheel from Ric before they went too far left and hit her side of the mountain.

The car slewed and then swapped ends as they spun down towards the next corner.

Ric was thrown first towards Manou, then away from her.

The tires squealed on the tarmac as they were forced unnaturally sideways, and in the blink of an eye Ric saw the valley, the road behind, the mountainside and the coming corner, and he knew they had no chance of making the next curve.

And then the car stopped.

The silence, an infinite, shocking and thunderous silence, made the cold, bloodless paralysis to his limbs all the more absolute. Before him spread the wide vista of the olive plains playing out to the yellow strip of coast, and beyond the yellow strip of coast the Tyrrhenian lay motionless, like purple baize unbroken all the way out to the broad horizon.

And Ric and Manou were parked, albeit a little casually on the apex of the bend, *deux amants* enjoying the warmth of a late afternoon sun and making good use of the rare opportunity to steal a moment's peace and quiet in their automobile.

Ric could just make out the grey saloon on the black strip of road that writhed like a languorous snake through the forest below.

Without turning to look at him Manou said: "So, you think you can remember this, Ric? For venereal disease we use the flowers of the clematis."

24

Manou dropped Ric in Zizula to pick up his car.

They did not speak as they completed their journey. She was, very naturally, shaken by the moment and seemed more than a little put-out that he'd felt the need to grab the wheel from her, as though she hadn't had the situation under control, as though his intervention had been completely unnecessary and wholly unwelcome.

Ric, in turn, resented her reaction to his help. Either way, he concluded, a little atmosphere between them was preferable to what would have been their swift and effortless progress to the plains several hundred feet below.

He had hoped, and almost expected after their day together, that she might want to spend the evening with him. But, as he had been about to mention it she had cried 'work', deposited him by his old Citroen and waited rather impatiently for him to get out.

"Later?" he asked.

"Oh yes. Maybe," she replied, more than a shade offhand. "Maybe see you later."

Ric watched her drive away.

The sun had not quite called time on the afternoon, and although common sense suggested to Ric that the last thing he needed was alcohol, he abandoned common sense at the side of the road with his Citroen and wandered over to the beach bar.

A few of the more leather skinned denizens of the beach were feeding and watering under the protection of Camille's umbrellas. The stern, disapproving stare of the waitress followed Ric's path to a table at the side.

Kamo's monument to Mammon still lay dwarfing the bay. There was no discernible movement on deck. It had the look of a pleasure boat dozing in between bouts of excess.

Ric felt a firm hand squeeze his shoulder.

Camille stood behind Ric, following his gaze. But as he turned and looked up, Ric noticed that Camille's left eye was sporting the blued swelling of a sizeable bruise. Ric raised his eyebrows in quiet question, but Camille's gaze remained fixed on the boat.

"Uh-huh," said Ric, at which the old man pulled up a chair and sat down beside Ric, depositing two bottles of cold beer on the table. "Rough night," Ric said.

Camille shrugged his shoulders.

"*Si*," he said. "Sometimes it happens." His accent, though still nuanced, was becoming less obvious; as though in the affinity Camille was developing for Ric, the old bar host was losing his need to play-act, opening a less affected and more straightforward communication to a young man he now considered more of a friend and less of a fish from the revenue stream.

"Bastards, Russians," Camille muttered, letting his words hang for a moment before going on. "We have them here for many years; white Russians, émigrés, deserters who join the *Légion Étrangère*, Russian Jews, spies, communists; mostly in Calvi and Ajacciu. They all come here to look for something; sometimes maybe just looking for a place to go. Maybe they bring something interesting to our island, I don't know. But this kind?" He nodded towards the boat, shrugged again and drank from his bottle of beer, considering, qualifying.

"This kind, they are like the cold wind; the *Levante*. It comes from the east. Very strong, eh! It comes from the east, and it goes direct across the mountains." He made a chopping motion with his hand, like a blade through flesh. "And then, after the mountains, it goes on to the west, right out to sea. It is like the island means nothing, like it cuts right through without problem. It kills everything, and it can drive the people mad. It leaves nothing good. Greek, Persian, Roman; like leprosy. I tell you Ric, nothing good comes from the east, except perhaps the Jujube." He drank again, a long slow pull, savouring the pale yellow beer on his palate as though it might be his last. Then he rubbed at his curly white hair.

"But this is *dila dai Monti*, this side of the mountains, so, they will learn. They will understand. Everyone understands in the end; enfin – in the end, eh?" The subject was done; closed with Camille's own version of a question that supplied its own answer.

Ric searched for a response that might lighten the mood. But implicit in Camille's conclusion lay a bare stone, bone hard promise, and any contradiction, however amusing or subtle, seemed to Ric inappropriate, so he let it go.

25

Ric waited for Manou to call, but she didn't.

After his beer with Camille, Ric had gone home and wandered about the house looking for a place to settle. Like a restless dog turning circles before lying down in its bed, he couldn't work out how to halt the whirl of his emotions. He was at odds with himself; unsure of how to go on. He seemed to get so far and then trip over painful recollections.

Also he couldn't decide whether the grey saloon had actually tried to run them off the mountain road, or whether he should put the short but uncomfortable episode down to the habits of the local highway.

And then there was the old boy at the bar sporting his blued badge of courage; that troubled Ric too. He couldn't figure out why anyone in their right mind would whack an old boy like Camille, unless Camille had properly upset his brooding waitress of course.

The sun was leaning heavily on the mountains, retreating from the day, replacing the bright light with a golden afterglow and the heavy blanket of heat with the gossamer cool of evening.

Ric stood in the kitchen, wondering whether he ought to call Manou, when he heard a car coming up the track towards the house.

He went to the front door and tried his best to lock down his relief when he saw it was her white Peugeot.

She wore a formal dark blue shirt and skirt as though she was going to or had been to a meeting. Her hair was pinned back and her shoes were heeled. They clacked on the tiled floor as she walked straight past him into the house.

"Would you...?"

"Yes," she said. "A cognac, with soda."

She flicked off her shoes as though they offended her, went out to the patio and sat down at the table, her dark cloud hurrying to keep up with her.

Not sure whether Manou wanted a long or short drink, Ric poured her a large brandy with a dash of soda water and followed her outside.

She was still more than a little agitated, he judged from her overly upright and square posture, and as she drank, as opposed to sipped, her body language was all tight angles rather than relaxed curves.

He waited until she was ready, for clearly some hyena of thought was preying on her mind.

"I'll tell you mine, if you'll tell me yours," he began, thinking a dash of humour might soften her. But, as with Camille earlier, levity was not the prescribed balm.

She turned from her thoughts, pausing long and hard to stare at him. "Would you Ric? Would you tell me what it is that bothers you? Or will you tell me where you go sometimes when I am with you; this place you go to, alone?"

Ric was not expecting a frontal assault, and was not sure what he had or had not done to deserve it. The hurt in her voice took him by surprise.

"Whoa! Hold on a minute. Why is this all about me? Looks to me like you're the one who's got a burr under your saddle! What's going on? What's the matter, Manou?"

She sighed. "Is that what they taught you in the army, Ric? Attack when you are being attacked? Meet aggression with more aggression? Go forwards before retreat? Distract from your weakness?"

"Marines," he corrected. "But you've lost me, Manou. You're the one doing the attacking."

"Yes, perhaps I am. And it is true. We all have our problems, our past to deal with, but the night before and this morning…." She was marshalling her troops. "Ric, when we are together it is like we are together but sometimes you are in a different place." Manou lifted her hands to her face. "What I mean is; this place you go to, if I cannot come to this place with you, it will be very difficult for us to go any place together." Her eyes softened from their intense stare and the tension in her face ebbed.

"We go so far and then it is like we come to a wall. You walk through this wall to the other side, but I cannot go with you. I cannot get through this wall, and this is a wall you have put up. It is like I am left outside with only half of you. So I don't understand what is going on-on the other side where you are."

"I'm not sure I know what you mean," he tried to delay her, take the sting out of her.

Manou looked up to the heavens. "Thank you Ric! You are so English. You know, sometimes at Renabianca the English come to the office to complain about something trivial; sometimes it is that the showers have stopped working, or their neighbours make a noise too late, or perhaps the weather is not good. But I have learned that most of the time it is because they have had an argument with their wife or their children, or they have a problem at work and so the holiday is not going the way they want. They don't know how to make it better, so they make it like the problem is not with them, it is with someone else. So we have to talk about the other things for a time; discuss the sport or the politics. But usually, after a while, they will tell me what the problem is; the daughter is staying out late with the boy of the neighbours; the car is broken; the wife doesn't like camping...."

Manou paused, looking at Ric with the same questioning intensity of a few moments before. "Are you one of those? Are you, Ric? Because I have as many of this person at the camp as I need."

He was on the back foot, desperate for cover, but not finding any. "I'm sorry you feel that way, Manou. It's not always so simple...."

He hesitated. To continue talking would only serve to close the door through which he felt himself passing, a door through which he knew she knew she could not follow. So he decided to retreat as gracefully as he knew how. "Another cognac?" He went to get up from his chair.

But it was Manou who stood up first. "No!" she shouted at him. "I don't want another cognac. And I don't want you to run away from me Ric...."

Ric looked round, a little self-conscious and embarrassed that the maquis should witness the flare of her frustration.

Maybe it was the very last of the day's shadows, the colour rapidly withdrawing from the light, or perhaps it was the eerie fringe of purple playing along the crest of the mountains in the west that reminded him of another place. Maybe it was that in wanting something, anything, from him, Manou was simply asking too much. He couldn't tell. But a host of harrowing images once more slipped into his mind, and he knew if he could not banish them they would all too quickly subdue him.

"What is it, Ric?" she asked, interrupting his distraction. "Why have you come here? Is it that you have a wife or a girlfriend you have you come here to escape? This would not matter," she chided. "You can tell me this because this I would understand. This would be so easy. It would not make a difference."

Ric wanted to tell her. He so desperately wanted to tell her, but he could not bring himself to reopen the wounds he had spent the last months trying to heal. So he said simply, "No. I'm not married, and I don't have a girlfriend or partner; not now, not anymore. It's like you said; it's complicated. And I'm not sure that I can give you what you want from me, Manou," he admitted, as much to himself as to her.

"Give me?" she said indignantly. "Give me? Why should I want you to 'give' something to me?" She paused, looking down at him. Then Manou leaned towards Ric. She placed her hands one on either side of his shoulders, and lowered her face towards his. She stared deep into his eyes, looking for his thoughts, pursuing them as they fled before her gaze. She looked down at the floor for a few seconds as though she'd dropped some link in the chain of her thinking, or perhaps she had captured one of his thoughts and needed time to interrogate it, to comprehend its significance.

Manou returned her gaze to him, the sapphire of her eyes mesmerising in the fading light. Vivid though they were, the harsh accusation in them was slowly replaced with a calm, almost comforting regard and the tone of her voice softened when she said, "What right do I have to ask you to give anything to me, Ric?"

And like an alcoholic bent on behaving as though he was anything but, Ric had one final crack at disputing his fractured state. A bitter, exhausted voice that he did not recognise as his own spoke up from behind a closing door. "I don't know what you want, Manou. What is it you want from me?"

"I don't want anything 'from' you, Ric," she said. "I want you." Manou looked deeper into his eyes. She no longer searched for his thoughts, she was searching for him. "This place you go to, Ric. This room where guilt lies," she said gently. "Don't go there. Come to me, Ric. Come to me."

She reached down, took hold of his arms and pulled him towards her.

Ric could taste the sweet caramel of the cognac on her tongue; her tongue which dipped slowly into his mouth, now firm and now soft, but all the time silken and smooth, and promising and offering. He wanted to touch her; cover her with his hands and know the curve of her breasts and the slender roundness of her buttocks. But he was wrapped around Manou, embracing her and at the same time preventing her from falling under his weight; holding her as though petrified that if he released her she might dissolve and be lost.

They both stood up and undressed each other urgently, consuming each other's flesh as soon as it was revealed; the high point of her shoulders and the nape of her neck; the thin scars on his arms and the shallow depression at the base of his throat.

Manou reached down and seized Ric with her right hand. She led him away from the table in a dominant and provocative fashion.

He exhaled a long, low breath; a sigh of surprise and relief and pleasure.

There was only the maquis to witness such an overtly sexual abduction and although Ric encountered a brief shiver of embarrassment at her brazen act; her combination of control and desire only served to spur him on.

Manou knelt on the warm ground and motioned Ric to lie down beside her. Then she pushed him back to lie flat and straddled him, pulling her skirt up and reaching down to grasp him.

She closed her eyes and took him very slowly. She began to rock back and forth with him and as their tempo increased so she opened her eyes a little and once more gazed deep into him, almost looking right through him away into the distance, as if trying to see some long awaited stranger appear over the horizon. The silence between her breaths grew longer and when she exhaled she made a laboured rasping sound as though she was struggling against a great weight.

Ric watched her, lost in her rhythm, hypnotised by the apparent pain and pleasure on her face, her hair now unpinned, falling about her, her small, firm breasts moving as she swayed, but he was aware most of all of that part of his body joined to hers. He wanted to both consume her and be consumed by her; to use and be used by her. He wanted so many things and he wanted nothing else but for everything to last.

And then she tightened about him. She moaned loudly and pawed at his chest. A sound as much anguish as joy escaped from her mouth as she bit down on her lower lip. She frowned in concentration, searching for his pleasure, and then she smiled as she found him. Manou gripped him between her thighs and crushed him beneath her hips. It troubled him that he might give in to his weakness, or that she might chase him out or leave him behind. And then from some sweet hidden beginning, that same burning ache he had felt before coursed through his thighs and raced into his groin, stronger this time and more concentrated than he could remember; neat ecstasy in place of blood in his veins, a lithe electricity surging through his muscles. And in the instant Ric tried to prevent the end, tried to hold on to the space between what was before and what would be afterwards, he was propelled even closer to her, thrown towards her, lifting his hips off the ground and bending his body up to her, reaching out to cling to her; each one oblivious to all but the other, uncaring of the vast world about them.

They lay in that tranquil, semi-exhausted state for an hour, perhaps two. Ric didn't care. He drifted as though on a receding tide; the confusion of his senses gradually replaced by a peace he had not experienced in longer than he cared to remember. He could hear her shallow breathing and he could feel her stomach pressing against his groin, rising and falling in time with her breathing.

In the background, the tympanic whispers of the cicadas rose and fell as the last of the heat departed with the day. Ric could smell the lavender in her hair.

Manou lay kneeling on top of him, her weight full on him but low enough that it did not impair his own breathing. He knew she was not sleeping; the eyelashes of her left eye tickled his chest as she opened and closed her eyes, but there seemed no need to speak.

26

The night air was cool, but Ric was sweating. And whereas he expected to find himself prone upon his bed with Manou sleeping beside him, he found himself standing some way from the house, in the middle of a vast swathe of maquis on a gently sloping hillside. He was naked, just as he had been when he fell asleep.

It was a dream. He knew that much and he shook his head to wake himself up. But shaking his head caused him to lose his balance, so he put one foot out to the side to steady himself. As he did so, he felt the gorse scratch against his leg.

It was bizarre! He couldn't understand why he should so clearly feel the sensation when he could not possibly be anywhere other than in his bed, where he and Manou had moved to from the patio.

Ric forced himself to think; they had become cold as the evening slipped into night so they had stood and, with the stars of the clear night sky illuminating their way, they had not needed a lamp to find their way into the bedroom. She had poured a cognac for them both and set the glasses by the bed. Manou had removed her skirt and they had lain down beneath the thin cotton sheet, her head on his chest, her breasts against his side, and her hand in the fold of his groin. After a while he had stirred and wanted to make love again, but Manou had wrapped her warm, slender fingers around him and held him until he was still. Unmoving, they had lain that way until a veil of sleep had settled over them both.

But now he was no longer lying in bed with Manou.

Ric looked up at the myriad stars. He could make out Orion's belt, the Plough, and other clusters of pin-prick lights. They seemed to be turning, revolving in slow motion around his head; they reminded him of the ceiling of a dance hall. He could smell the shrubs and bushes around his feet; the rosemary and thyme, reminding him of mealtime at home, the heather and lentisk, the arbutus and the juniper, less domestic aromas but clear on the air nevertheless. Definitely he could smell them and he could feel the hard, uneven and rocky ground beneath his unshod feet still warm from the day's unrelenting sun. He could feel the cool chill of the night on his back.

There was something weighing in his right hand.

Ric looked down and saw what at first he perceived to be the bone of animal; a large bone, perhaps even the thigh-bone of a human. It felt hard and heavy like a bone, but was dry and fibrous to touch like the semi-petrified limb of a tree. It was slim in the shaft and bulbous at each end and he found himself gripping it as though it was a weapon for his protection. He had seen such an instrument before, but the memory of where eluded him.

Though he found himself in such a strange place, he did not feel unnerved or intimidated. In some way his surroundings were familiar to him and though they were peculiar if not extraordinary, he perceived a visceral confidence coursing through his frame, as though whatever his task might be he knew he would achieve it. He was not bothered by his nakedness. Far from it, he was quite at ease without his clothes in such a natural environment.

The great luminous sky arced down to a mountain pass high to his left, and Ric began to make his way up the hillside towards it. He did not know or understand why; he just walked in that direction much as he would on a casual afternoon, strolling with no particular destination in mind.

He climbed steadily and more purposefully as the slope grew steeper. There was not much of a path, but he seemed to find his way through the maquis without having to pay too much attention. The shrubs and bushes brushed at his lower legs as he strode through, over and around them. As hard as the ground felt to him, his feet felt harder and unfeeling of the broken surface. As he worked his way up the hill his body became warmed by his exertions, impervious to the initial airy chill of the night.

Ric realised that he was not concerned with the choices of his actions; somehow he was making all the right moves. He was going exactly where he wanted to go. He was both being drawn and driven up the hillside. There was something, although he knew not what, that he needed to see;

something he needed to get hold of, something he needed to do.

As he crested the pass he saw a small house built into the rock face away to his left, a stone-built edifice with a low wooden door and high open window. The roof was formed from an extension of the rock face; a shelf that splayed out from the slope, the front face of the house made up of stone blocks fashioned from the rock. Again he recognised the place; it resembled the *oriu* that Manou had shown him at Carbini.

He carried on towards the higher ground; the maquis about him scraping and scratching him in his progress.

Ric broke into a run now; a measured, determined pace without haste.

Then he heard a disturbance somewhere in front of him; some animal spooked from the undergrowth. It squealed in alarm.

And Ric was chasing after it and the startled fugitive up ahead instantly became his quarry. He knew it; knew it as though he had understood all along that this was his reason for being out alone on the hillside in the middle of the night. His appetite for the hunt now thrust him forward and he was sprinting, charging along like an enraged Neanderthal in pursuit of prey, waving his weapon above his head, shouting, exhorting himself to greater pace.

Then in the grey light and half-shadows he made out the wild boar before him, frantic in its flight, desperate to escape, darting this way and that, careering through the scrub in its efforts to evade capture.

He knew the beast, the *sanglier*; it was familiar to him. And though he now pursued it with every sinew of his body, he was aware that he was just as afraid of the boar as it was of him. But in spite of his fear he felt compelled to go forward. He was spurred on by the very chase upon which he was embarked.

Ric could now smell and almost taste the musky scent of his prize and he gained on it rapidly. It was small by comparison to some he had seen; its back stood not as high as his knee, but it would be strong and in fear of its life, and would be frenzied and defiant when caught.

The boar hesitated and Ric threw himself down upon it, knocking it off its feet. It squealed in terror as he wrestled it onto its back. It kicked out, wriggled out of his grasp and set off again, but Ric reached out and grabbed a trailing leg, holding on tight until he had regained his feet.

The boar was heavy, and its head rested on the ground as Ric held it hanging down by his side. He drew breath and looked down at the pathetic, vulnerable creature. It sniffed and snorted and grunted, bewildered and scared, wriggling against his fierce grip.

And then, as if seeing his own actions projected upon a screen before him, Ric raised the weapon above his head and brought the thick end of it crashing down with all his might on the head of the boar; a crashing blow which rent the skull of the poor beast; a ghastly, shrill, hopeless shriek issued from its mouth in despair. Dark, warm blood sprayed out from the wound, covering the rock and earth with a black stain.

Ric hit the boar again. It twitched and flinched, and he struck once more. And even long after it had ceased to show any sign of life, Ric still beat the carcass as though he was not so much bent on killing the beast as he was on destroying it completely.

Soon afterwards there was nothing left to hold but a small limp corpse with an unrecognisable head attached to it; just a mess of black blood, grey matter and ochre tusk, shattered white bone glinting in the starlight.

But as he stared at the vile mess at his feet, the bloodied remains seemed to take shape. Like deceptive contours conjured out of light and shadow on an undulating sea bed, a face took shape before Ric.

At first he did not know the face, but as it gradually took clearer shape he saw the face belonged to the blond crewman from Petrossian's boat; the man Ric had tried so stupidly to punch. Bobo smirked and gloated back at him.

And no sooner had Ric recognised the face than it began to fade away, dissolving back into its bloodied confusion, returning to a visceral pulp with no image or shape.

Ric stood back from his completed task. He raised his arms above his head, brandishing the wet and bloody weapon, and with all his might he roared at the hills around him. A great bellowing, primeval thunder; his thirst satiated, his bloodlust satisfied, and now his strength reborn.

He roared until he had no breath left; all his raging anger and his manic pride thrust out loud and unmistakable across the hillside.

The echoes of his kill bounced away down the slope, reducing as they tumbled further away into the infinite night. Only the stars and the maquis stood witness to his depraved and degenerate act.

As Ric knelt to peer at the result of his repulsive and temporary madness, the face resumed the aspect of a boar in death; the dread panic in the drawn and bloody features, the sheer horror frozen in its wild eyes.

And just as the grey, pastel promise of the new day crept mute above the dark Tyrrhenian, it dawned on Ric that he had seen this vivid mask of terror before; a mask of death he now knew for certain he had seen in another time, in another land far away.

27

Unsure of whether he was going to wake up on a hillside, dancing around a campfire decorated in the blood of his kill, or simply wake up lying in his bed with Manou, Ric contemplated opening his eyes long and hard.

He felt warm. His forehead felt damp with perspiration. But he hoped to hell it was the temperature in his bedroom which was causing the moisture on his brow, rather than the exertions of some megalithic ritual.

He tried to feel out and check his physical systems, but they were still sleeping on the job. Which job, he wasn't sure; his lovemaking with Manou or his pursuit of the boar? He kept his eyes shut, delaying receipt of further information from his senses and so putting off his inevitable decision. What concerned him, or even alarmed him more than the bizarre and barbaric fantasy, was the creeping realisation that he had endured something similar before.

"Ric?" Manou murmured. "Ric?"

He felt her stir in the bed next to him. He was suddenly both grateful and relieved.

"I know you are awake," she said, "your eyes are moving. I have to go."

"What time is it?" he asked, blinking in an effort to focus on the white ceiling.

"It is early, but I have to go now."

Ric closed his eyes again. He was not ready for this and he did not know how to deal with her, or himself for that matter. Images of the evening flooded into view; her deft hands as she straddled him, lifting up her skirt to reveal her dark pubic hair, the frowning expression of her face as she searched for him beneath her, her breasts swaying, her hips riding. And then he remembered her cry of pleasure as she found him. He rolled onto his side and moved his hips over to her, suggesting to her that she had only found a little of him and that there was much, much more to discover.

"No, Ric. I would like to stay, but I have to go," Manou replied.

He reached behind her and drew her buttocks tight against him, pressing his groin to hers, leaving her in no doubt.

"No," she chuckled. "No, Ric. I have to go." She gripped his hand and pulled it away with enough determination to get her message across. Manou got out of bed.

Ric pulled back the sheet, taunting her that surely she must find him irresistible?

Manou turned to look down at him. She shook her head, an amused resignation in her eyes. "So now you are still the same man, but different, eh Ric? Now you are *incorrigible*." She said the word in French; the way she rolled the *r* and softened the *g* the word settled on him like a velvet glove. But she turned back, went into the bathroom and after a moment on into the living room to find the rest of her clothes.

He watched her; took in her lithe curves and the way her firm buttocks moved in rhythm with the lightness of her step.

When she came back she brought him a glass of grapefruit juice from the fridge. Her hair was a little untidy. "Believe me, I would like to stay. Please Ric, I have to go."

"*A dopu?*" he asked, trying to give the Corsu the proper inflection.

"Yes Ric, later. I will call." Manou kissed him; a demanding, reassuring and resolute kiss with just a flick of her tongue between his lips to leave him with her sharp then sweet taste in his mouth. She stroked the strawberry mark above his right eye and then was gone.

Ric closed his eyes and lay on his back, loving the way she made him feel, alive with the new-found confidence she fused into his previously distant and faintly unwilling body. He realised that Manou was more than merely something he may have needed; much more. A smile spread across his face, a smile of plain and ordinary contentment. And for the second time in recent days Ric was taken by an easy peace; a peace that permitted no intrusion.

He threw the sheet back and sat up on the edge of the bed. Ric stretched his arms up, yawned and rubbed the back of his neck. He remembered the curious dream during the night. It had been as though he had accidentally strayed onto some prehistoric landscape and assumed the role of hunter gatherer.

Then, as he put his hands down and pushed up off his knees to stand, he realised there was something terribly familiar about the dream. His head swam a little as he stood upright. He wondered whether he might be having one of those moments of déjà vu he'd heard others talk about; a flash or feeling of having been somewhere before. The impression was so sharp and intense that he experienced an alarming weakening of his knees. He looked down as if he expected them to snap beneath his weight.

"Oh, no, not again," he moaned. His shins and feet were cut and scratched, and his hands, though not grazed were stained black beneath his nails.

28

Ric showered and took extra care to clean his hands and the scratches around his ankles. His feet looked and felt as though he had run unshod through a field of barbed wire. The lacerations stung a little when he dabbed on the only disinfectant he could find in the kitchen cupboard; the bottle smelt of disinfectant, so he hoped it would have the same cleansing and protective qualities even though he could not translate the label.

Faced with the painfully tangible proof, Ric was unnerved that he could have left Manou in bed and gone out for his midnight ramble without either of them knowing about it. And he found it hard to imagine that he had been so deliberate, so premeditated in his actions that he had possessed the wherewithal to wash much of the blood off before returning to bed.

Although darkly surreal, the memory was so vivid in his mind that he began to consider it might even constitute stark reality as opposed to fantastic dream. If so, he argued, where was the weapon he had used? Had he dropped it in his trance-like state, or even concealed it somewhere out there on the hillside before returning? Had he left the bloodied remains of the boar in the same spot? And again, if so, what had been the point of the exercise? From which corner of his tortured soul had come that craven and carnal behaviour?

Ric scrolled through a menu of psychoanalysis, wondering if his lovemaking with Manou had sparked some obscure and diabolical response within him; some sort of adverse reaction to his overwhelming emotions; a sort of dialectical behaviour gone awry, a trigger to fulfil some irrational desire for base misconduct rather than post-coital tranquillity.

But whatever had triggered the bizarre episode was perhaps not so important. What was important was that he knew two things for sure:

first, the physical evidence of what he had got up to during the night was undeniable; and second, given a change in location and terrain, he had dreamt something similarly unpleasant more than once before.

He tried to avoid the reflection of his grin in the bathroom mirror. But despite his scraped and scratched legs there was one thing for certain: Ric felt a thousand times the man he had been the day before, even if in his sleep he had traded his nightmares for a grotesque animal hunt in the maquis. And whereas before, where there had been little other than pale impotence in his libido, now there was Manou.

Ric finished washing, shaved, threw on his shorts and shirt, and headed down to the village on his motorbike. He would need more than a solitary pain-au-chocolat to satisfy his appetite. And in the absence of the charitable old crone, it was the promise of a more substantial breakfast in town which seduced him out into the sunlight.

29

There wasn't much more than the usual going on in Zizula. The sky was blue, the sun bright, and as yet there was no breeze.

He checked his mailbox at the post office which was still thankfully empty, passed beneath the wandering gaze of the brunette in the doorway of the *Patisserie*, and bumped into the chef from the hotel who queried why his previously generous and regular supply of octopus had so recently dried up.

Ric could not explain it. Perhaps the octopus had decided to return home early from their summer vacation. Perhaps he wasn't such a good fisherman after all.

The thin moustachioed mouth of the chef broke into a rueful smile. Perhaps, he countered with a knowing wink and a nod of his domed head towards the *Patisserie*, Ric had found other more attractive fish to fry?

"*Petit-dejeuner?*" he asked before Ric could object to his innuendo.

"*Dejeuner?*" replied Ric, patting his stomach and so suggesting he could do with more than a single croissant and thimble-full of freshly squeezed orange juice.

The portly chef beamed. What greater compliment could Ric pay on this fine Corsican morning than to ask a chef to cook for him? He ushered Ric in through the back door to his kitchen.

After a protracted negotiation which began at blackbirds in cherries and ended at kid's tripe via sea bream baked in cheese, Ric and the chef agreed at a plate of eggs, tomatoes and *panzetta*, a pork belly similar to its more common Italian counterpart. The combination was laden with chilli and garlic. A little bold for breakfast, but, taking into account Ric's hunger, it served the purpose and, he decided, girded his loins for whatever the day might throw at him.

He sat alone on the restaurant patio, not knowing whether he was either too late or too early for the hotel residents and not really bothered one way or the other.

Ric, swept along by the rising tide of his own potential, dared to think that he might, just might, manage to address the rather thorny question of his future. He half expected the vision of that future to be clouded by his many thoughts of Manou and his new found feelings for her. Yet rather than complicate his approach to what lay ahead, it seemed that Manou had somehow reacquainted Ric with a broader horizon; a horizon that he had been denied sight of for some time. Curiously, the world seemed a bigger place washed in brighter colours and with greater possibilities than it had up until recently, and Ric was more confident of his part in it.

Then Pela, the blond Georgian woman, stepped out onto the patio. She wore a long, white cotton shirt belted at the waist, over-sized sunglasses that painted a rather alien picture, and carried a large, zebra-striped beach bag. She made a pretence of looking around the patio as though all the other tables were reserved for guests, and then acknowledged Ric in a manner which suggested that if he had a spare seat going she might join him.

"Ah Ric! Good morning," she smiled, baring her unnaturally pearl-white teeth. "Is this seat taken?" Pela didn't wait for his reply. She pulled back the chair and sat down. A waiter appeared and set a cup and coffee pot before her. Pela poured her coffee, took a cigarette from a gold case in her bag, lit the cigarette, dragged heavily on it and exhaling a long plume of grey smoke, took a sip from her cup. She closed her eyes whilst she relished the flavour of her coffee, as though it was some kind of life-giving tonic. She was ready to be spoken to.

"Nice day," Ric said, "again."

"Mmm, you think so?" Pela looked around as though she had not yet taken notice of the weather. Her English, laced with her drawling Georgian accent, held more than a heavy dose of sarcasm. "I don't think so. It's boring here. When you have the suntan, what else is there here that you cannot get in other places?"

"You can a get a suntan in plenty of places," Ric replied. "Why come here if it's not to your liking? It's not exactly a cosmopolitan Mecca. There must be more exciting venues around this part of the Mediterranean to suit a girl with your sophisticated tastes: St Tropez, Monaco, Portofino."

Pela warmed to his compliment. "Yes, Ric, it is true. There are other places I would like to be. But sometimes a girl has to go where a girl has to go, as you English say. Sometimes 'we' don't have all the choices 'we' would like." Her nose wrinkled as she sneered.

Ric noted the case form in which she referred to herself, as though she belonged to a profession. For the want of anything more profound to say, and as it was still a little early in the day for too much sagacity, he nodded in agreement. "If that isn't the case."

A breeze freshened from off shore; wisps of spray leapt from the crests of small white caps like the ricochets of sniper fire on a purple plain.

They talked for a while; she about places already visited and those she had yet to visit; he, about places he had already been to and would rather not have visited in the first place.

She flirted a little with Ric, which he played to. Having last night regained control of his previously wayward libido, Ric wondered whether he might now be more attractive to women in general; wondered whether he was now giving off a more animal scent.

He ordered tea and more coffee for Pela. He didn't find her company unpleasant, if anything her dry humour betrayed a calculating and acutely observational mind, albeit one constrained by her unhappy deference to… well, Ric wasn't absolutely sure what the fellow Kamo was to her, or she to him, but there seemed little love lost between the two. That opened the door for Ric.

The large motor yacht swung gently at anchor, head to sea. When Ric realised she was watching the boat he asked, "And Kamo? He has all the choices money can buy, right?"

"Oh, yes. He has all the choices. Money gives you so many choices."

Then remembering what Camille had said a couple of days before, Ric waded in deeper. "Kamo is Georgian, right?"

Pela turned to look very directly at Ric, her head perfectly still, her slender mouth set in a straight line, her eyes hidden by the large, dark, oval sunglasses.

Ric wondered whether he had crossed some invisible border without first offering her suitable credentials.

Then her mouth softened into a slight smile, as though having considered his question to be more for conversational purposes than for information gathering she decided there was no harm in carrying on.

"No. He is from Armenia. At least that is what he likes us to think; from Yerevan. He says that is why he likes the sea so much, because in Armenia there is no sea. But Ric, I come from Rachvelia. It is not so far away from Armenia and even I know that Lake Sevan is bigger than this ridiculous island," she scoffed, "and the mountains are bigger than the ones here."

"So, why does he come here for his vacation, if it's better at home?"

"Pah!" Pela scoffed again, throwing her head back. "This man would not call the country of his birth his home. This man has no home." She thought for a moment, stirring her coffee. "Or perhaps everywhere is his home. Who knows? He sees some place he likes; he makes the place his home. He gets tired of his home; he goes some other place, some new place. But he is not stupid, huh. He keeps the old home and adds it to his collection."

"Who needs to bother with making a new home when you have a mobile home that size," Ric nodded in the general direction of the *Kohar*.

"No, that is not his home." She was silent, thinking for a moment. "Perhaps to you and me this is a big boat. But to Kamo that is just the way he gets from one place to another; like you and me take the car, or the train, or the plane. When you and I would stay in a hotel, he does not have to; he takes his own hotel with him." Pela curled her lip in mock disgust. "This is how he finds the place he wants to make home; like the hermit crab, yes? It is his shell. He takes this with him until he finds a new place."

"And here? This is his new home?"

"Yes. Maybe? I don't know." Pela shifted her head to look away from him, fidgeting as she did so. Question time was up.

"You want to talk Ric, or play twenty questions?" she asked tartly.

Then she hesitated, and having considered for a couple of seconds decided to take a second bite out of him. "You know Ric, you seem to be a nice guy; what I have heard you English people call a 'nice' fellow." She leant forward to speak as though the deserted patio was crowded with eavesdroppers.

Ric leant forward too, expecting this to be the moment Pela might either tell him to pack his bags or make a pass at him. It had after all been his day so far.

"But this is what you get when you ask too many questions." She lifted up her oversize sunglasses to reveal an unsightly bruise that had swollen up about her left eye.

Pela stood and gathered up her big, zebra-striped beach bag. "Thank you for the coffee," she said as if she really meant 'thanks for nothing' and left, her sandals flapping against the soles of her feet, flicking up the sand.

30

Ric dropped by Camille's on his way out of Zizula, but the old boy was not in residence.

The stern-faced gypsy of a waitress encouraged him on his way with one of her withering glances, as though Ric was some kind of bad omen in search of purchase. Quite why Camille employed her, Ric could not understand. He debated stopping to have a beer merely to annoy her, but reasoned she wouldn't appreciate his mischief, and there was probably some perfectly reasonable explanation for why she glared at him so. Perhaps she held him responsible for the wind, which was now whipping the white caps into urgent foaming crests.

But it was not the *Mezzogiorno*, the warm wind driven on by the heat of the land, which blew. The new wind came from the north and was cool. Camille had told him that when the wind came from the north and was cool on the skin, it would be the *Tramontana*. And because the air was colder, the visibility was again crystal clear all the way out to the far side of the bay and beyond. The little multi-coloured sailing dinghies and Hobie-cats pitched and yawed at their moorings, and here and there rogue parasols bucked and cartwheeled away across the beach, pursued by owners anxious to avoid expensive litigation.

Seeing Pela with her black eye, and Camille the night before with the same, Ric was feeling out of sorts.

He rode back to the house, showered and changed into a pair of chinos and a shirt, and drove his old Citroen into Porti Vechju. There were easier ways to gain information, but the small internet cafe in Zizula was not sufficiently intimate to be discreet. Ric was not prepared to risk the wagging of tongues in town. Information, he knew, was best gathered on the quiet.

He parked at Ste Catalina on the road into town, sandwiching his car neatly between a couple of large floral painted vans, the summer residence of some more organic culture, he judged by the sweet agricultural perfume wafting about.

A fan of mare's tails dulled the sun as Ric strolled through the old town. Now and again small columns of dust motes whirled along the road, causing people to rub their eyes as if in disbelief that their heaven could be diverted from its balmy norm.

He walked around and up, and entered the citadel through the fortified Génoise gate, strolled past the bars and restaurants on the Rue u Borgu, and up into the Place de la Republique. Like the Génoise gate, the main square was provincial in proportion, the many tables and chairs set about the square suggesting it was pretty much the tourists who kept the town affluent. The City of Salt had long since ceased to rely for revenue on its salt pans in the south eastern corner of the bay. Now it was the marina below the town and the ferries to Marseille and Livorno that filled the local coffers.

Ric found an internet cafe in a side street off the Cours Napoleon, bought a bottle of water at the counter and sat at one of the terminals. He navigated his way to a search page and entered the name of Petrossian. There were a good number of entries; a caviar house with a string of restaurants in the kind of cities you'd expect to see caviar on the menu; one Levon Ter-Petrossian, first President of Armenia in the nineties; more on-line caviar shops; a few notable individuals, academics, media characters and medics, most of whom had dropped the 'Ter' prefix, and the inevitable Facebook registration. By the fourth page he had drawn a blank, so he preceded Petrossian with the name 'Kamo', knowing it was obviously some sort of self-styled nickname, but thinking it might be worth a look.

Without telling him who his man was, the entries gave Ric as much the information as he needed. There was and there wasn't a Kamo Petrossian. The historical figure featured in most of the entries was Simon Ter-Petrossian, a homicidal maniac, bank robber, and early known associate of prominent Georgian gangster 'Oddball Osip', aka Joseph Stalin. It was as the policeman Bosquet had told him; Kamo Petrossian was not the man's real name, he had merely borrowed it from a page in history, albeit one out of his own country's past – that is if he was the Armenian he pretended to be. But the litany of harm both wrought and endured by his historical namesake was clearly intended to garnish Kamo's reputation and promote some sort of malevolent aura.

Ric found it vaguely amusing that the fellow should have assumed the name of not only the former chief politician of Armenia, but also the country's most notable psychopath.

He entered the name of the boat: *Kohar*. That threw up a number of hits relating to a symphony orchestra and a location in the Punjab, Pakistan. He searched for yacht names and registrations, and found a list of off-shore jurisdictions and legal firms. He tried the Lloyds Register, but found he needed to register himself. A North American Coast Guard site popped up with a small hatful of vessels registered under similarly spelt names, mostly dinghies and small craft. Ric tried 'Kohar Panama' for the registration. There was the inevitable YouTube clip, a real estate mention and a few other marine related entries, but nothing that pointed anywhere until he came upon an old webpage from a yacht brokers. Ric navigated to a page listing former high profile yacht sales and right at the top was a picture of the *Kohar*. Only it was listed under a different name, *Impetus II*. But there was no doubting it was the *Kohar*, every detail of specification and livery were identical. She was, just as Petrossian had said, designed in Italy and built in Antalya, three MTU engines, range in excess of 600 miles, etc, etc, and the legend at the foot of the picture read that *Impetus II* was sold to a multi-national conglomerate called SEDA for an undisclosed sum. That was all.

He typed in SEDA. A host of press articles and business blogs defined the company as an acquisitions vehicle with interests in property and technology, but there was no official company web address. SEDA turned out to be an Armenian girl's name meaning 'echoes of the forest' and *Kohar* the Armenian for 'jewel'.

All Ric could confirm from his searching the web was that Petrossian had a sense of theatre, and a certain flash, brash, ostentatious style. Or perhaps he just wanted to be someone other than who he really was. Ric could relate to that.

He wondered whether he should check his emails, but decided they could wait. So he left the cafe and wandered up towards the Place de la Republique, dominated as it was by the tall Romanesque church.

The air was cooler and even fresher now, the sky a shade darker, and the wind hastened by as though it was running before a menace. Tourists, unprepared and ill-equipped for a change of the elements, peered up at the clouds, unsure of when the rain would arrive. Local gossips ignored the threat, shrugging and barking at each other in gravelled tones long cured by anise liqueur and dark tobacco. They knew the rain was not for today, and besides if it did rain it would just go to show….

Ric took a table under the broad red awning at the back corner of Le Glacier de la Place. He was happy for the moment to people watch. Before, surveying passers-by with a rifle in his hands had required complete concentration in observation. Now, people-watching was a trivial luxury; something he could enjoy, immerse and lose himself in. He ordered a coffee and in spite of his breakfast a plate of spicy *merguez* sausages.

Over the last couple of days he had thought a great deal about Manou, her effect upon him and where their relationship might go. But not much of that thinking had involved in any way issues concerned with his returning to the UK, and he had found in that a calming release, almost as though he was slowly being set free. He knew the best course would be to stay out of the way and just enjoy his time with Manou and how she made him feel.

And at the very moment he thought of Manou, she appeared from the southern end of the square, dressed in the same blue outfit she had worn the night before, walking briskly across in front of the facade of the church.

She was accompanied by a tall, thin man wearing a dark suit, white shirt and dark tie. He was leaning down in order to hear Manou speak as they went, his long, thinning grey hair falling over his face as he nodded in understanding. As his hair fell so he pushed it back in place with a practiced sweep of his left hand.

For a moment they halted, at which the man stood upright, making his face more visible; he had a lean, pallid face with hawkish eyes and his forearms protruded far beyond the cuff of his jacket, the elbows of which had been patched. He listened to Manou, poring over her the way a priest might pore over a confessor.

Manou, Ric was surprised to see, looked flustered and upset. She gesticulated at the man, tapping the palm of her left hand with the index finger of her right, as though to stress some crucial point. Her brow was furrowed with concern and her lips moved urgently and angrily as she denied her companion the opportunity to interrupt. Then she looked around the square, clenched her fist and shook it in frustration, not so much at the man beside her, more at the gods in general. Manou turned on her heels and strode away northward out of the square.

The elderly gent paused for a moment and then followed her, his long legs pushing out straight, like those of a marsh bird.

The episode did not last more than a sip of coffee, and had he finished his meal Ric would have gone after her. He was concerned that she looked distraught, vulnerable. For the first time he saw her as someone other than the composed and confident woman he had come to know. Manou, he decided, looked distressed.

Ric stood up to draw some money from his pocket, checking the menu for the cost of his meal as he did so. He put a note on the table and was about to leave when he saw the policeman, René Bosquet.

The chubby, moustachioed man walked casually across the square from the same direction Manou had come and left in the same direction as she had gone. He was following Manou and her companion, of that there was no doubt, and he was making a very discreet job of it. He was wearing the sort of clothes any day-tripper would; beige slacks and a brown shirt. He looked marginally less corpulent out in the daylight.

The waiter appeared; a different one from before. He asked Ric what he had ordered, and in the second Ric turned away and back, Bosquet was nowhere to be seen.

Ric swore to himself. The chance was gone. He couldn't make a hasty dash across the square without drawing attention to himself, and besides an inner voice cautioned against it.

A gust of wind rattled the awning of the cafe and a newspaper pirouetted across the square. In the face of local prediction, heavy rain began to fall. Ric ordered a *Pietra* and sat down to wait out the shower.

31

Later on, Manou called to say she would pick him up and they would go to Camille's as she needed to talk to her old friend. From her tone Ric could not gauge whether she was still upset, but when she did arrive Manou had regained her composure.

She looked stunning. Each time she appeared, Manou seemed to take a little more of his breath away. That might be, he told himself as he drank in every inch of her, because he was beginning to see her in a very different light. She was no longer someone to look at, to be seen with, or someone whose company he found pleasantly engaging or diverting; last night Manou had changed the way he saw her, and now every time he looked at her Ric felt a sweet, aching paralysis creep through his limbs closely followed by a warm, languid want.

His preoccupation must have been evident for Manou stopped in front of him as he sat at the table. "What, Ric? What's going on? Why are you looking at me like that?"

But Ric didn't really need to answer. He just sat staring at her; all of her.

She wore a loose-fitting cream shirt, patterned emerald-green in the manner of Indo-Chinese figures at prayer. Her breasts would have been clearly visible through the gossamer thin material but for her bikini style bra. Her skirt, a dark green sarong style, hugged her hips but hung looser below her knees. Manou had tied her dark hair back off her face, accentuating the depth of her brow and the rise of her cheek bones, and she had treated her blue eyes to a slender tail of mascara at the corners, completing her oriental flavour.

"What are you doing, Ric?" Manou asked, smiling nervously at him. And then, with just a hint of self-consciousness, she understood his craven indulgence and played to him, turning side-on and lowering her eyes at him.

Ric realised she was all at once demure, sexy and incredibly beguiling.

"I'm pleased you like it. I thought that perhaps it would be too... fancy?"

"No," Ric replied, knowing full well that his voice would betray his appreciation, "not at all." He hauled himself from his trance and stood to kiss her.

Manou leant towards his kiss, but turned to present her cheek to him. It seemed a shade formal, but Ric supposed she didn't want him to smudge her make-up.

"Can I get you a drink?" Ric asked. "Do we have time? I'm sorry, I'm making us late. I should have been ready." He was still wearing the same chinos and shirt he'd had on all day, and compared to the vision before him, he felt shabby. He had hoped he might persuade Manou to take up with him where they had left off the night before and not bother with going out. But, if it wasn't to be, there was no way he was going to hang out with Manou looking like that and him looking scruffy.

"Yes, something to drink would be good, thank you. We are not late. We don't have to hurry. I'd like a glass of white wine." She smiled in a relaxed and easy fashion, suggesting she was just as comfortable in his company as he was in hers. She appeared to him not to have a care in the world.

Ric was more than a little confused by this having seen her in such a state of anxiety in Porti Vechju, but then he reconciled his confusion with the logic that there was much more to Manou than he understood and therefore so much more of her to get to know. And besides, with Manou looking the way she did, he wasn't entirely sure that it mattered if he understood her only a little, if at all. He fetched a glass of wine from the kitchen. "Don't go away," Ric suggested.

Manou laughed: "And where will I go? But don't be too long, eh Ric! You know our saying: *Donna chi posa mal'pensa.*"

Ric wondered if he had read the proverb in her mother's book. Then he remembered seeing it: "A woman who does nothing thinks no good?"

"Yes," she agreed, "very good. So I will wait here and think no good." Manou arched her left eyebrow and bit her lower lip provocatively. She giggled at the pain in his face.

Ric went into his bedroom and made his bed, annoyed with himself for not having made it earlier. He threw his clothes on the chair, grabbed a towel and headed for the shower. On his way he glanced to see if Manou was still as relaxed as before, but she had gone out to the patio.

He tried his best to occupy himself with more benign thoughts; the distraction Manou caused him threatened to overwhelm his ability to think straight, or even walk straight, he noticed as he stumbled clumsily into the shower. However, try as he might while he washed, all of the paths of thought he trailed eventually led him in a roundabout fashion back to her and the vision of her looking down at him, moving her hips back and forth in rhythm. It was as though his every waking moment was governed by her and rather than be concerned by the influence she appeared to exert over him, he allowed himself to revel in his fascination for her and glory in the desires she aroused in him.

Ric left the shower, tying the towel around his waist as he went back to the bedroom. He checked to see if Manou was still outside. He couldn't see her. Maybe she was getting something from her car. But then again, maybe she wasn't. He hesitated in the doorway to the bedroom.

Manou was lying completely naked on his bed in a pose which left Ric under no illusion that she was unconcerned about being late for dinner.

She pouted at him and ran her left hand down over her bare, flat stomach towards her hips. "You took too long, Ric, and I have been thinking too much about no good."

Through the next few hours dinner went the way of all other intention and by the time the sun had fallen and the cicadas quieted, the indulgence alive in their early lovemaking had calmed like the sea after rain.

Ric found himself at the mercy of his emotions and confusions. Light feet danced feather sensations through his form and distant voices threw frivolous and trivial enquiries randomly about his breezy mind. But through all of his many and magnificent reactions to her, his manifest awareness was one of release, as though he had been tied to the ground for far too long and Manou had simply rushed in and slashed the tethers restraining him. A fine and airy buoyancy infected his senses, and a slow weightlessness he had never imagined possible assumed his every fibre.

Manou had touched him in all his most secret places; places he had considered lost to a past which seemed now to belong to someone else; someone he'd once known. She had excited his nerves and opened pathways he had long since declared dulled, constricted and off limits, and which he had not necessarily wanted to rediscover because before they had always led to disappointment or worse grief. But now, each time she touched him, the lightness of his soul increased until he felt he would float away, high above, out of reach for good.

And he would not have cared.

They lay together, their legs entwined. Manou rested her head on his chest, her fingers toying with his hair. Her eyes were open and he was certain he could hear her thinking.

He wondered at how she knew of so many ways to thrill him, and marvelled at the control of her subtle teasing; the way she instinctively knew how much to promise and exactly when the right moment came to deliver. If Ric had died right then, his only regret would have been that in dying he would be denied further access to the space in which he found himself; the fine margin between heaven and earth.

Somewhere along the way they slept the exhausted sleep of lovers who had taken without asking and given all they had to offer; a sleep of fulfilment and contentment.

Later on Ric half-woke to find her kneeling beside him stroking his legs, soothing and cooling his cuts and scratches with her gentle caresses. He could make out Manou gazing down at him, watching him; the fragile light cast by the stars glistened on her breasts and glinted in her eyes.

The thought crossed his mind that he might wake up at any time, caught up in one of the same dreamy reels of sleep's wicked designs, charging naked across the maquis or crouching, bleeding over a fallen comrade. But he did not. No spectral vision crossed his path. No ghastly carnage invaded his slumber.

Manou left silently before the dawn woke sufficiently to grey his room. And as his mind had reserved his more haphazard thoughts for the small hours, Ric wondered why she did not stay to wake up beside him in the morning and why he did not speak of seeing her in Porti Vechju the previous afternoon.

32

Light crept reluctantly into the day revealing a lukewarm mist that clung in thick, clammy patches to the coast. The threatened rains of the previous day had escalated to nothing more than a few squally showers. Someway up the coast the *Tramontana* had reached the limits of its resupply and turned for home, retreating back to the plains of the Po in northern Italy from where it had set out. Now the burning sun in all its radiant glory was needed to disperse the vapours in the same way that a varnisher's lamp drives the moisture from fresh veneer. It would happen later; most things happened later.

Ric allowed the old Citroen to free wheel down the bumpy track to the beach. For a brief moment through a break in the mist he glimpsed the flat top of the island out in the bay, but then the dense white blanket moved back in to obscure the view.

He didn't take to the idea of swimming out to the island. Though there was not much swell in the small bay, he knew only too well the dangers of swimming without solid, visual reference. But, wanting to work some of the stiffness out of his limbs, he decided a run up the beach and back would be sufficient, and although the air was far from cold he wore a loose T-shirt and shorts as the atmosphere clung to his exposed skin like a damp towel.

On his third time back down the strip he ran as far as the beach extended. He didn't intend to; he usually turned thirty or so metres from where the sandy strip finished and the rocky incline began, but being pretty much blinded by the mist he could not make out the end of the beach. So by chance Ric found himself with no further to run. As he turned to head back he noticed a path which cut right, up the slope. He had not seen it before and for the want of another run up the beach he decided to see where the path led.

A little steep in places, the path meandered up towards the saddle that led into the next bay and a couple of times he had to reach out to keep his balance as the rocky surface fell away beneath him. After a hundred metres or so he arrived at a fork in the path; one route going into the pines to the right, the other staying out in the open to the left.

Ric turned right into the wood and continued to climb.

The visibility was better amongst the tall aleppo pines, the moisture laden mist resting on top of the trees rather than penetrating down through the branches, and the floor was strewn with pine needles muffling his footfall, lending the place an eerie quiet. The scent of the highly resinous pines was so heavy he could almost taste the minty sweetness, and the stillness was only disturbed by the nuthatch that darted inquisitively about the slender trees.

He sat down on a bald crop of rock at the side of the path and watched the forest around him. Ric remembered the night before and smiled. He could not fathom why he should deserve to be rewarded with Manou. Maybe, he reconciled, it was just his turn on the swings, having seemingly been going the wrong way on the roundabouts for so long.

There was someone coming along the path.

For a couple of seconds Ric sat perfectly still, not moving his head at all, only concentrating on the shuffling sound he could hear to work out from which direction it was coming. Then he turned to his left and saw a figure descending the path as it twisted and turned down through the trees. He climbed up three metres or so above the path. From his position he could watch the figure pass below him.

He looked for the movement again and when he saw the figure he realised it was a child, perhaps ten or so years old, with a mop of very dark curly hair that bobbed about as he tripped, skipped and ambled down the path. The child was humming to himself as he stripped the leaves from a twig, and when he'd finished he proceeded to rub the bare twig against his teeth as though it was a thin toothbrush. He was completely oblivious to the possibility of any other human presence in his world and now and again he raised his head to look at the ceiling of the tall pines as though he was expecting shafts of sunlight to break through at any minute.

Ric expected the lad to see him, but the young boy was so preoccupied with his stick breaking that it was not until he was on the path immediately below Ric that he became aware of his presence. He looked up startled, turned to face Ric, staggered back a pace and, dropping his stick, toppled over down the slope. He yelped, the noise echoing loud about the wood.

Ric chuckled, jumped up and leapt down the slope to find the boy frantically trying to grab at the trunk of an adjacent fallen pine to pull himself up from his prone position.

"Steady on son," Ric said in as calm a voice as he could manage between laughing. "Where's the fire?" He reached out to lend a hand, but the boy would not take it.

Instead the youngster struggled to his feet without any help and then looked about nervously for an escape route or perhaps someone else to blame for his indignity. Apart from running off down the uneven forest floor, he soon realised he would have to get past Ric to reach the path and, after working out that Ric was far bigger than he and would catch him if he tried to get by, he calmed down. His left knee and the palm of his left hand were grazed from his forced landing; otherwise he hadn't sustained too much damage. As much as anything it was the surprise that had frightened him. His eyes had watered, but there was a feral defiance in the way he stood and fronted up to Ric.

"Okay, I'm sorry. I didn't mean to scare you," Ric said. And then, when the boy just stared at him, Ric realised his stupid mistake and repeated his apology in French.

The young lad replied in what Ric reckoned was Corsu, so he didn't understand, but from the tone it sounded as though he didn't hold Ric responsible for his fall. The only Corsu Ric understood were the translations into French in the booklet of proverbs Manou had lent him. And then he only remembered how some of the words were spelt; there was precious little chance he could parrot the phonetics.

So he asked: "Okay?"

"*Okay!*" replied the boy, leaning his head to one side and drumming up half a smile. His eyes were greenish brown, with yellow flecks, his eyebrows thick and his skin, though lighter than some of the locals, was nevertheless tanned a rich hazelnut in colour. His shirt and shorts were grubby from climbing and scrambling about on the rocks and in the maquis.

Ric was at a loss for a moment. This was the lad he had seen scurrying away over the saddle a couple of days before. The kid was also very possibly the reason why he had so often felt observed when he exercised. He pointed in a rather Neanderthal gesture at his own chest: "Ric."

The boy nodded and pointed at his own chest: "Gianfranco," he replied and smiled broadly to expose slightly uneven teeth. "Franco," he then said and smiled even more.

"Pleased to meet you, Franco," Ric offered his hand, which Franco, having licked and then rubbed his own right hand on his shorts, shook and then rather quaintly he bowed.

"Well, now that we're mates Franco, let's see what you get up to out here all on your own these mornings, shall we?" He knew the lad Franco did not understand what he was saying, but it seemed appropriate to chat to his new companion. It was, he decided, better than a wary silence.

As if reading Ric's mind, the boy then pointed at Ric and said, "*Piscatore?*" And he picked up a stick and, with both hands holding it, made as if to haul something heavy on the end of it. He then threw it like a harpoon and pointed out through the trees in the rough direction of the island in the bay.

"Yes, Franco, fishing. You've been watching me, huh." Ric tapped at the corner of one eye.

"*Si,*" he said, grinning even more broadly. "*Polpu!*" and cupping his hands together and extending his fingers, he made a flowing, wave-like, undulating motion. Then he stopped, pursed his lips, patted his stomach and hummed a hearty gastronomic approval.

"*Si,*" Ric replied, hoping a more Italianate response might work better. Trouble was Ric spoke little or no Italian. "*Vous habitez-la?*" he asked, pointing in a curving motion to suggest he meant over the hill.

Franco nodded. "*Si, culà,*" he replied, and then started walking down the track in the direction of the beach. His gait was relaxed and jaunty, and for a kid who wore no shoes he paid the path scant attention, as though he had walked it a thousand times and knew its little dips and ridges off by heart. Even when they reached the bare rock surface and had to climb down it seemed to Ric that the kid did not bother to look to place his feet on any of the ledges; he merely scaled down in a smooth, practised glide with Ric following on a little hesitantly behind. His relaxed manner suggested he was completely at ease in Ric's company out on the deserted beach. But then he realised that Franco must have been watching him for some days and probably reckoned Ric was as much of a threat to himself as he was to anyone else, maybe even the octopus.

They walked along the beach through the mist towards where Ric had parked his car, both of them content in each other's silence.

Franco turned, tapped Ric on his wrist and made a clear breaststroke motion with his arms, smiling again and then pointing out in the general direction of the tall rock in the bay. *"Nutà? Si? Nutà?"*

"Bit far for a nipper, isn't it, must be all of 400 metres there and back?" Ric looked down at Franco, who wore a sort of frowning, curled-lip, quizzical expression as though he couldn't understand why Ric was not already in the act of stripping off to dive headlong into the water. "No, not today, son. Too foggy. Too dangerous."

But the dense mist didn't seem to faze his new companion; he began to remove his shirt.

"No, Franco," Ric said sternly, and realised he sounded as though he was addressing a dog. "I mean, *non. Attention! C'est dangereux! Brouillard:* fog. *Pas aujourd'hui."* He softened his warning some. *"C'est mal aujourd'hui pour nager,"* he concluded.

Franco got the gist of Ric's verbal onslaught, and shrugged and grimaced to show he understood but that he reckoned it a shame.

Ric got the feeling that had he been up for the swim, Franco would have been off around the island and back with all the ease of a pond skipper. After all, this was Franco's patch, not his. He acted the charade of reading a book and said, *"L'école?"*

Franco frowned at him and then got it. *"Ah! Scola! Si."* And then, *"Eo nò schola, oghji sàbatu."*

Ric recognised the word for school: "No school, eh. Sure! Lucky chap! Not a bad place to spend your holidays."

Here and there warm patches of beach told a tale of the sun breaching the mantle of mist; the day was on its way.

Franco was drawing patterns with his toes in the sand. Ric stood and watched, captivated by the boy's relaxed and casual manner. There was no doubt the youngster was at one with his environment and very accustomed to spending time on his own at the beach but, whilst Ric understood the environment to be about as benign as any one he had ever come across, he was surprised any parent would leave a ten year old to go swimming alone.

They wandered up and down the beach until the sun cleaved a break in the fog and began to heat up the bay, dispersing the moisture in much the same way as liquid slowly evaporates in a heating saucepan. Franco waded about in the water and skimmed pebbles he picked up from the back of the beach. Ric joined in, but did not choose his projectiles with as much care and so lost out in the competition to see whose pebbles bounced most before sinking. Franco laughed easily and very readily at Ric's poor efforts, raising his arms triumphantly each time he won. Even though Ric wanted to know more about the boy, he saw no real need for conversation; he was just as happy as Franco seemed to be; a kid on the beach shrouded in the cloying fog one minute and basking in the blazing sun the next.

Then Ric heard the sound of a car engine somewhere up the track.

"*Ric!*" shouted Franco, pointing out towards the sea, clearly impressed with his throw. "*Magnìficu! Vincitore!*"

Ric turned back to acknowledge the boys arm, but as he did so he heard the noise of the motor come and go in the mist. "Quiet, Franco. *Attention. Silence,*" he said in as French an accent as he could manage. He waved down the boy's enthusiasm and pointed to his ear.

Franco in turn caught on, stood still and cocked his head to listen. "*Vittura? Voiture?*" he asked, his face all screwed up in concentration.

He was right. It sounded as though a car was coming down the track.

As the thick white mist rolled and drifted around them, the dull moan of an engine came and went, bouncing and echoing down the slope. The noise ceased for a moment, suffocated by the fog. The silence extended while Ric and Franco looked at each other. Then the noise returned, but this time the engine was working under load to propel its weight up rather than down the track.

"Never seen anyone down here," he said to Franco, who shrugged his shoulders. Ric wasn't sure whether the boy understood what he'd said, or whether he was suggesting he felt the same.

The fog at the back of the beach broke and lifted slowly up the slope like a curtain call at a theatre. Whoever it was that had driven down the slope was being shepherded back up it. Ric followed the fringe of white as it revealed the track scaling up out of the bay, but just as it reached the entrance at the top, it settled again, and all Ric could make out was a dark shape, probably that of a car, reversing out of sight behind the hill.

He turned back to look at Franco just as a heavy bank of fog enveloped them both.

Ric waited patiently for the dense pall of vapour to move on, but it seemed to have stalled in its progress. "Hang on, Franco," he said calmly, "it'll be gone in a minute."

The fog clung to his skin and his shirt was soon saturated as though he'd just run a couple of miles.

And when the clammy atmosphere finally coasted away, Franco was nowhere to be seen. He'd disappeared in just the same way as the morning mist was disappearing up the beach. The lad was gone in as many seconds as it took the cloud to leave. Both ends of the bay were once more shrouded in mist, but Franco was absent from where he had been standing, as though the fog had simply swallowed him up and borne him away.

Ric could see all the way out to the vast rock, *la Tozza*. There was no sign of him in the water and besides, Ric figured, he couldn't have swum far and he wasn't the type for drowning. He assumed the boy must have skipped down the beach and gone back home over the saddle into the next bay. He wondered whether he should follow the boy to see where it was that he had come from, but then Ric decided he'd probably lose his way in the mist and that once up the slope was enough for one day, even if he hadn't quite reached the top.

33

An hour later the platinum sun was occupying its rightful seat in the vast ring of blue sky, glaring and glowering down at the small bay, throwing its imperious and oppressive gaze about like a prize fighter staring down his foe. The last delicate fingers of mist were slipping up the hillside and what had been a veil of damp air was now replaced by a blaze of severe heat, as though super-heated metal plates had been scattered here and there about the beach. With that in mind and considering that unrestricted visibility had returned, Ric took to the water and swam out to the rocky outcrop in the bay. Once there he tracked the waterline around to the far side, located the rough old rope and climbed up to the top of the rock.

He felt good, revived, invigorated; the best he had felt for many months. Even though the salt stung his scratched legs, reminding him of his recent midnight excursion, Ric figured the sea water must have been doing them some good. He sat cross-legged, hands on his knees like an errant Buddha and, closing his eyes, turned his face to the sun.

Then a picture of Camille with the bruise around his left eye came to Ric, quickly followed by a similar picture of Pela sporting the same. He didn't care much for the woman, Pela. She had a body that would melt hoarfrost, but he didn't feel particularly sorry for her one way or the other. But no one, wife beater or otherwise, had the right to treat a kindly old man in such a way.

Ric needed to speak to Camille, and he remembered Manou had also needed to speak to Camille when she had pitched up the previous evening. But then the pair of them had never made it out of the house.

Even in the heat of the day the memory of the evening before sent a cool shiver down his back and made his toes curl.

At that, Ric stood up and surveyed the rocky surface around his feet.

The shreds of fishing line and lead weight were still lying in the bottom of the shallow depression. The pen knife was there too, but the curious club-shaped piece of wood was gone. Someone had been up to the top since his last visit; Franco, he decided. And as he recalled the lad, Ric looked over at the saddle of the hill expecting to see him scrambling up the path. But he was long gone; no doubt off to spend the day badgering his parents. Franco was a live wire; no sitting idly by on the beach for him. He was too busy; his parents probably wished he was back at school.

The sun was not now merely in the ascendant, it was the absolute master of all it surveyed; the world was subordinate to it. There was a very slight breeze from the south, but the air was thick and humid, almost sweltering. There was not much point in frying to a crisp on the rock, so Ric stretched his arms high above his head, reached down to touch his feet and swallow-dived off the rock. He revelled in the sublime lightness of his suspension and then the sea rushed up and hit him with a resounding thump.

Ric swam away under the surface until his lungs threatened to burst.

34

He drove back to the house and breakfasted on *prizuttu*, a plate of cold tomatoes with olive oil and salt. He drank a couple of bottles of water from the fridge; the water was very cold and streaked through his torso like the piercing thrusts of a cold blade.

The temperature was as high as he had known it since his arrival, possibly forty-five going on fifty degrees, and the ground was beyond parched; the soil breaking up and crumbling into dust under foot. There was a strange filmic quality to the atmosphere, as though the molecules in the air were fastening together to hinder his progress through it, and every now and then, somewhere to the south, a wicked concierge opened the door to his Turkish bath so releasing a fierce blast of heat towards the north.

It was too hot to be doing much, but too hot to be doing nothing; the encouraged lethargy being as unbearable as the heat.

After a lengthy counsel Ric decided the coolest spot was to be found on his motorbike, even though he had no particular place to go.

He walked round to retrieve his bike from where it was chained to the shade of the north-facing wall. A section of the lower part of the wall contained a stone block that differed from the others adjacent to it in as much as it was three times as long as the others and more yellowed in colour. The stone was of a strange type too, perhaps quartz, and polished smooth, similar to some of the pebbles he had seen at the beach, their sharper edges blunted by the constant rolling back and forth in the swell. It then occurred to Ric that he had seen the curious anomaly somewhere else; locally, not in another country, but in Corsica.

Passing from the harsh sunlight into the black hollow of the shade behind the house, Ric was temporarily blinded but kept moving forward as he knew his bike would be exactly where he'd left it.

It was. But he failed to notice too late that the long stone in the wall had a stick or something similar leaning against it, and promptly tripped over it, falling heavily against the box of the gas supply.

He swore, more at his slow reaction than his exasperation at the item being there. Ric had not left anything there. Maybe the old cleaning lady had discarded it, tossed it out rather than having to bother with taking it out with the rubbish. He regained his balance and bent down to pick up whatever it was that had felled him.

It was a stick; a stick of hard-wood, heavier than it looked, slender in the middle and knobbly at either end.

He walked out into the sunlight to examine it. The central stalk was not much thicker than his wrist and bulbous at both ends. The wood was dark and solid and about a metre in length, or maybe just a bit longer.

He studied the misshapen baton for a while and then realised he had seen it before; perhaps not this same one, but definitely a piece of wood of similar shape. It bore an uncanny resemblance to the club shaped artefact he had found in the scorched depression on top of the rock in the bay. He tried to remember: the fishing line, the weights, the penknife and the club. Ric gripped the shaft towards one end and held it out, rotating it as he scrutinised it. The stick he had seen at the rock had been missing when he'd climbed up earlier in the morning. That was when he realised someone else had been up there, and Ric had thought maybe it was the kid, Franco.

He couldn't be sure it was the same one though.

But as he turned it over and held it up, as he felt the solid strength and the inherent threat of the club, he realised where else he had seen it before.

A cold shiver of a very different kind raced up his back.

Ric had for certain seen the implement before. And the last time he'd seen it he had been wielding it above his head and raining hammer blows down against the fractured and bloody skull of a boar.

He dropped it. It made a vacant, knocking sound as it bounced several times on the ground, like a hollow bone on rock.

Ric stared at it until he could feel the white heat of the sun burning his exposed shoulders. Then he stepped over it and unlocked his bike, which he wheeled round to the front. He hurried back into the house, threw on a shirt, grabbed some money and rode down the drive, as if pursued by an unpleasant thought.

35

Camille was in residence and his snowy locks were indeed melting.

His customers, familiar with and grateful for the cabaret their patron often provided, had forsaken the beach in search of an alternative and more fluid solution to the problem of the high temperature. The main benefactor of the searing heat would be Camille's pension fund; a fund that did not extend as far as an improved wardrobe, which was self-evidently necessary, but that did stretch to the occasional libation with a client.

Ric accepted the chestnut flavoured beer from the old boy; the condensation on the brown bottle of *Pietra* ran the sweat on Ric's brow a close second.

The bruise around Camille's left eye had made the transition from red to purple, and now, though unsightly, looked more of a smudge than a welt. He sat down, creaking beside his new friend. An envious wistfulness afflicted the expressions of the Germans at whose table he had been sitting until Ric's appearance.

"Too hot?"

"For some," Ric replied without particular commitment. "Good for business though."

"*Si*," said Camille, "but when the sky is like an oven, if we do not have rain today, then we will have rain tomorrow. The sun is always good for business!" He shrugged as though there was little else he could do but accept the natural benevolence distributed by the golden orb to the many little fishes such as he.

"More sun; more drink. More drink; little eat and more drink. It goes round and round like *manège* until somebody fall off." He laughed, rolled his eyes and shook his head all at once. "But now, much heat; heat and sand. This wind, the *Siroccu*, brings much sand too, from Africa." He sighed. *"Brume matinale;* cloud in the morning, everywhere sand, very hot. The Arabs; they should keep the sand. We do not need it. We have enough."

"I guess you'd know a thing or two about Arabs, eh Camille?" Ric suggested, feigning to look at the tattoo on the old boy's shoulder.

"Oh this?" Camille said. "The Grenade? You know this?"

"The Grenade of the Legion? Sure," Ric replied, "I have seen it before. I met a couple of Belgian guys working Private Security Details in Iraq; they'd been in the Legion, had the same tattoo. Well to be more accurate they said they were Belgian and that they were working PSDs and that they had been in the Legion. At least I suppose the tattoo wasn't lying."

Camille studied Ric in much the same way as Ric had seen him study people when they asked for credit.

To break his look Ric said, "Like my father and grandfather, my great-grandfather was in the army. I have a photograph of him. Here," he pulled out his wallet, extracted the faded photograph of his great-grandfather, and handed it to the old man. "He fought at Gallipoli."

"He was in British Army?" Camille asked, blinking. He examined the photograph more closely. But his eyesight wasn't up to the mark, so he got up and fetched a large magnifying glass from behind his counter. When he inspected the photograph a second time his eyebrows rose and he turned to look at Ric in surprise. "He was a Legionnaire? He is standing by the gate at Bunifaziu!" He went back to studying the photograph again.

"Seems that way," Ric replied. "I located the gate at the garrison in the citadel soon after I got here. He was at Gallipoli with Amade's regulars; the first French troops ashore, or so some of the books say."

"He was French?"

"Not sure. Family history's a bit muddy on my father's side. My father didn't know that much about his grandfather; wouldn't be drawn on the subject. Bit of a rum cove my great-grandfather. We traced as much about him as we could a few years back. We think he left Gallipoli on a hospital ship and, more by luck than judgement, ended up in Wales. Or maybe that was what he wanted. We don't know?"

"You can't find out? I thought to find this thing out was easy these days," Camille said, as though these days all things were possible.

"Well," Ric sighed, "we know he married my great-grandmother in

Monmouth, in Wales; got that much from the parish register. But he died soon after they were married. My father remembered something about him coming from Corsica and I found a picture of him in uniform standing beside what looked like the entrance to a garrison. I sent a copy of it to the guys in Aubagne, they identified it for me. There's a mausoleum in the cemetery up in the Bosco with the name Rossi on it. Asked one of the guys sweeping up where I could find out more information; thought I might trace the name. He sent me to an office just down the road in the Place de l'Europe." Ric noticed Camille was grinning sheepishly.

When he waited for Camille to interrupt, the old boy merely waved his cigarette in small circles, by which Ric assumed he was supposed to continue.

"They weren't terribly helpful. In fact they were less than that. They pretty much shut up shop on me. Didn't get the impression they were too inclined to help." Ric shrugged. "All they would say was that the answers were to be found in the cemetery. Couldn't see how I was going to get anyone to speak to me there, so I gave up."

Camille chuckled and examined the sand at his feet. "No. The dead will not give up their secrets," he said and chuckled some more. "But they were not saying that you must ask the dead. What they were saying to you was that you must ask one of the men who attend the cemetery. The office of records is not allowed to give out this information. It is forbidden. But one of the *guardianu* would tell you, for a price. He will know who pays him to put out fresh flowers. He will know the family who own the tomb."

"Owns?" Ric asked.

"Yes," Camille nodded slowly. "You take out a... a lease? Is right? Is what you call it? For 100 years, sometimes less. Even in death you must pay to be comfortable, eh!"

"So the family pays for the upkeep of the mausoleum?"

"It is so. But your great-grandfather's name was *Rossi*, and now you are Ross?"

Ric nodded, "Looks that way."

Camille laughed and looked up to the sky.

"Yes, I know," Ric agreed, "it is a bit strange. Most people think I'm Scottish."

The old man shook his head: "No. This is not what is amusing. First of all, *Rossi* is common name in Corsica: *Casanova, Albertini, Rossi*. There are

194

many families with the name *Rossi* in the south. But that is not what is so funny." He laughed again and began to cough.

"Then what?" Ric frowned, a little irked that he could not see the joke.

When Camille's shoulders had settled he spoke. "What is amusing is, if your great-grandfather was a soldier in the Legion, why do you believe *Rossi* was his true name? Anyone who enters the Legion can have a new name. That is how it is. When you enter the Legion you leave your old life behind and you start a new one, and with a new name. You leave problems behind, whatever they are." Suddenly the humidity closed in on their conversation and Camille was lost to some very private thoughts.

Out in the bay the horizon shimmered in the heat. "The Legion was my homeland for ten long years," he said.

"What drove you into the Legion?" Ric asked, but immediately wished he hadn't, as the old boy shot him a look of the kind that suggested he should have known better than to ask. "Sorry Camille. That was stupid of me. I meant to ask when you joined up, not why?"

"Oh, '46." He paused for a moment. "When we finished with the Germans I thought I knew all there was to know about war. *Mà*, there were other things also. But chasing the Panzergrenadiers through the maquis was different to being chased by the Viet Minh through the jungle of Indochine. When I saw how those little men move those big guns across the mountains…." He shook his head: "Then I understood that the jungle was to them what the maquis is to us, and it was their jungle; it belonged to them, not us. Diên Biên Phu was the end for me. Too much blood! Too much blood for nothing!" Camille quieted once more, no doubt recalling names and places he would rather have forgotten.

They drank a few more beers and gradually common interests and the uncomfortable silence of remembering encouraged them to conversation. The gypsy of a barmaid flashed her eyes menacingly at Ric whenever he looked over to order, but even she seemed vaguely subdued by the oppressive heat. It was as though the world was in slow motion and only a fool would hurry.

"Your waitress?" Ric asked.

"Seraphina."

"She glares at me all the time. Have I done something to upset her?"

Camille chuckled again, a sort of amused, stuttering wheeze that mutated into an uncontrollable and consuming cough. When the old boy had his lungs back under his command, he dabbed at the corners of his watery eyes with a serviette and said, "You were born a man. For her that is enough. It is better that men don't go so close to Seraphina. She is exactly as her name says she will be: much fire. But also she comes from Olmeto. You know it is where *vindetta* was born. So the combination is what you would call unpredictable, perhaps *combustible*." And with that Camille's lungs erupted once more.

In order to placate his volcano he ordered more cold beer, which the misandrist duly begrudged them.

"What do you do in the winter, Camille?" Ric asked.

The old man shrugged: "Oh, I have a sailing boat. It is in the marina at Porti Vechju; not big, but enough for going to Grèce, Crète, sometimes Espagne. It is enough for me. I don't need to go too far to find little peace. All summer I have many people here, they want me to be…."

"The life and soul of the party?"

"*Si. Esattamente!*" Camille nodded slowly, almost philosophically. "Everybody want something."

So they sat and thought for a while; the pair of them considering the demands made upon them by others, others who had no right to expect anything of them.

Then Camille said, "You," with a hint of accusation. "You want to ask about Manou."

Ric gagged on his beer. He turned to Camille who just stared out to sea.

After he'd cleared his throat Ric said, "Yes, I do. I saw her in Porti Vechju yesterday, in the afternoon. She was with a man; a tall, thin man. She was upset."

Camille glanced at him and then reached a hand over his head, as though wiping an imaginary flop of hair away from his face.

"Yes. That'll be him."

"*Notaire,*" said Camille. "Lawyer."

But Ric noticed Camille was now staring out to sea with a different intensity, staring as if he were expecting a squadron of Corsairs to round the headland at any moment.

"Only…," Ric hesitated, searching for the right words. "What I mean is… if there was a problem I could help with, with Manou, I'd like to know about it." His offer provoked no response from the older man. "I mean, perhaps you would tell me if you knew Manou needed some sort of help."

Camille sighed, took another swig of his beer, and continued to fix his gaze on the horizon. "Help?" he repeated with a shrug. "Help, eh! You think you come here to help? I told you before; everybody come here to help: Greek, Roman, Christian, Moors, Italian, French, German, and Russian. *Oh Si*, and you English." There was no malice evident in his tone; he might as well have been reading his weekly shopping list.

"Come to help, or help themselves?" Ric asked.

The old man glanced at him and wiped his moustache again on a paper serviette. "You think you are different? You are young, Ric. I say this for you; you have imagination and good intention. And for you perhaps a little love, yes, eh? Perhaps?" His eyes twinkled mischievously. "You think you are in control of your destiny. You think you have the power over providence?" Camille paused even though he was clearly not waiting for a reply.

"But also, I think Ric, you are not so young. I know you have seen some things; some things people do not need to see." He turned to face Ric, so that the younger man would not mistake the sincerity in his intention.

Crammed in the small space between Camille's bushy moustache and eyebrows, his eyes were a piercing jet black. He looked hard at Ric.

"This I can see in your face. I know this because I have seen it in my own face, many years ago. I think maybe this is why you come here; to find out if you can live with such a thing. You want to know if you have enough room in your soul to 'receive', *mà*, to accommodate, yes, it is better, to accommodate this bad thing. *Mà, Un ghjudicà a vita Fin à l'òpara finita.* Do not judge your life until it is finished."

A lecture in philosophy Ric had not expected. "Sorry Camille, I'm not much of a one for God."

"*Le bon Dieu?*" Camille disdained, turning his attention back to the vacant horizon. "No, I'm not talking about the 'good God'. He makes us believe if we worship Him, He will look after us. The Pisans and the Genoese promised everybody the same. When the sky is blue, everyone is happy. When the sky is black, what happens? I make *un cacà* in my neighbour's field, or you think someone from Genoa do it? Pah!" He waved

197

his hand as if to swot away a bothersome fly. "It does not matter who makes the bad things happen, the sky will be blue or it will be black. And the Pisans and the Genoese they go home; like everyone who comes here; like the tourists, the French, the German, the English. They think they stay forever, but they do not. They always go home. You will go also," Camille pronounced with absolute and unarguable certainty. "It is true."

"Thanks for the vote of confidence, Camille. But what about Manou?"

Camille swigged his beer, put the bottle on the table and stretched his arms above his head, signalling that the conversation was now moving into unwelcome territory and that he would soon be drawing it to a close. The white-haired old man turned to his face Ric: "You know, my friend, Manou is my child, but she is not my daughter. Her father was a difficult man to know. Her mother? She was very beautiful." Camille wallowed in his reminiscence for a moment.

"Manou can be... like her father. Her father was... well, he was... *multu risulutu; très résolu*, a hard man; tough, you would say; perhaps too tough for his good and the good of others. Sometimes I think I know Manou, my child, this daughter of my friend, and sometimes I am absolutely certain I do not. She is *Signadori*," he tapped his temple by his right eye, "they know all there is to know."

And with that enigmatic conclusion, Camille hauled his reluctant, calcified form upright. He looked down at Ric, his eyes wide, but at the same time frowning as if in some discomfiting warning. He hitched his grubby shorts around his ample waist and lurched off back behind the safety of his counter and the forbidding scowl of his sentinel.

36

The blue helicopter zipped overhead in the opposite direction as Ric rode his motorcycle up out of Zizula. He ducked as it passed a few metres above him. But as he accelerated over the next brow of a sweeping curve in the road, he came face to face with the chopper, nose-down, hovering above the tarmac. It didn't scare him as much as frighten the living daylights out of him. He felt as though he was going to ride right into it.

He hit the brakes too hard as he crested the rise and both wheels locked up. The tail of the bike slipped round, but he managed to catch the slide, turning the front wheel into the road, allowing his weight to fall back, leaning his shoulders forward over the centre of gravity to maintain balance. He skidded pretty much sideways down the road beneath the irritating blue wasp that buzzed above.

There had been no time to swear.

Ric got the bike back under control and slowed to look round for the helicopter. He was aware of the screeching whine nearby. As he did so he saw it flying parallel to him in the same direction on the seaward side of the road. He could not see the occupants because of the darkened glass of the cockpit windows, although he had a pretty good idea who might be inside. He could almost hear the Armenian laughing above the sound of the engine and rotors, and he considered giving him the appropriate salute. But just as he took his left hand off the handlebar, the noisy blue machine pulled up and shied away in a great screaming, banking arc towards the sea, and then disappeared from view back in the direction of the town.

Now there was time, Ric swore and then broke into a laugh that was as much a reaction to his relief as his amusement.

Kamo possessed some unpleasant habits, but he had a distinctive style; Ric had to give him that.

Back at the house Ric showered, respectfully grateful to the plumbing for granting him the necessary water.

The heat of the afternoon was, if anything, more intense than at midday. Even the passage of his bike through the air had provided no relief. At times Ric had felt as though he were speeding towards a great wall of fire around the next bend.

As he showered he thought of Camille's strange reply to his questions about Manou. His response had been so veiled, so enigmatic that Ric wasn't sure from which angle to approach it.

Was it a warning that Manou was going to metamorphose into some many-headed Hydra? If so, she hadn't so far, but then he remembered that she did have the habit of leaving his bed before dawn.

Was she a descendant of the Laestrygonians he had heard about; the giants who'd destroyed Odysseus' fleet at Bunifaziu? Ric grinned a little lasciviously. If she was, depending on how big her cousins were, he could put up with their association in return for Manou's many charms.

Was it an excuse for some personal characteristic he hadn't picked up on; some physical disability? He grinned again; he hadn't witnessed any part of her body missing, or being impaired, and he had seen just about as much of her as there was to see.

And, what was a *Signadori*? And if they knew everything, was her crystal ball large enough to sort out the next few weeks of his life? Ric realised, taking into account the way she made him feel, there was certainly a considerable benefit in Manou knowing all there was to know, as Camille had put it.

Ric drew the curtain halfway across the glass door onto the patio, lay down on the sofa and soon fell deeply asleep.

37

His phone woke him. It chirped loudly, signifying the arrival of a text. It was Manou; she would meet him at Camille's after eight. She didn't say when after eight; just after eight. He felt a little summoned, but then reckoned she was probably reluctant to come to the house in case they once again found better ways of taking up each other's time. Whatever the reason, he had not much time to shower, if there was any water left, and make himself presentable; he'd been dead to the world for a couple of hours.

Ric walked outside to stretch his aches out and try to invite some life back into his frame. He noticed the curious club-shaped object lying where he had dropped it earlier in the day. For a moment he thought about picking it up. Then he decided he'd had enough confusion for one day, so he left it where it was and went back inside to freshen up.

Later, faced with the choice of riding his bike into town or taking the car, he took the bike. The sky was still a rich blue, and the wicked sultan to the south had left the door to his Turkish bath open and gone home, thus releasing a now continuous blast of stultifying air up the coast. The heavy climate suggested shorts but, considering the scratched and unsightly condition of his legs, Ric went for jeans. He put on the only clean colourful shirt he had left.

Down at the beach the visibility was no longer clear to the points of the bay, and only the most veteran sunbathers were out catching the last rays.

When he arrived at Camille's the venerable host was not in residence, but the party-throwing Armenian was, flanked this time not by his monkey, but by two women Ric had not seen before; one very dark skinned with oriental eyes and short, cropped black hair, and the other a voluptuous blond, somewhat fuller where it counted than the Rachvelian Pela who was notably absent. A gaunt, pinch-faced individual sat with them; he had the grey complexion of the habitual smoker, a vice to which he was pandering. The women were very much not with him. The man had been present at the bar the first time Ric had met Kamo.

Ric saw them as he walked along the beach towards the bar and considered walking away, but in the same way that his thoughts of earlier had suggested it would be in his better interests to give Kamo a wide berth, he now found himself drawn towards the intriguing Armenian.

Anyway, Ric owed him one for frightening the daylights out of him with the helicopter.

Kamo had more eye-catching candy to look at than Ric, so he did not notice Ric until he had walked right up to the collection of tables at the front of the bar.

"Ric Ross," he said, rising from his chair, his teeth gleaming below his graded sunglasses.

"Don't get up," Ric said.

"A beer or something more exciting?" Kamo offered.

"A beer'll do. I may have had enough excitement for one day," he replied, trying to hold a straight face. But it cracked into a broad smile when he thought back to the way he had held the bike in the long glorious slide as he had passed beneath the chopper.

"Ah, Ric. Forgive me my little amusement; a little joke. It was naughty of me. Is that the correct English expression; naughty?" Kamo feigned contrition. "I am sorry. Sometimes my games are not to everybody's liking. Come, Ric, join us please. Ami will be nice and make apologies on my behalf."

Ami didn't look to be bothered either way, but Ric sat at the table in the only available seat, which just happened to be next to the dark-skinned Oriental. She shifted in her seat to accommodate his presence and pay him her bidden attention. She was wearing the shortest black shorts that money could buy and a matching cap-sleeved shirt. The blond, Ava, wore blue, but not much of it. In spite of the temperature, which early in the evening lingered in the low thirties, Kamo wore white jeans and a crewman's shirt, unbuttoned to show off the matt of dark hair on his chest and the gold medallion nesting in it. Yuri didn't matter.

The waitress appeared and set a bottle of *Pietra* down on the table in front of Ric with a clumsy thump.

"So, Ric, you have been behaving while I have been away?"

"That depends on how long you've been gone?"

"Yes, I know what you mean, Ric. The days here appear to come together two or three at a time; my memory escapes me. It is so easy to forget. I think," he paused for effect, counting to himself, "Thursday morning, a couple of days; the morning after our little party. Tell me: you left without saying goodbye. What happened? My hospitality not good enough?" Kamo laughed so that no one in his audience would reasonably entertain the ridiculous notion that his hospitality might be sub-standard.

"No, Kamo. There was nothing lacking in your hospitality. If anything the problem was I was too full of it." Ric pulled the backgammon counter he had found in his shorts out of his pocket and passed it over.

"Thank you," said Kamo graciously. "And yes, it's true. I can be too generous. It is one of my many failings. We all have failings, eh, Ric. But I heard a rumour that you were not wet enough on the inside and that you needed to be wet on the outside also. It's true?"

"I heard that rumour too. But then as you so rightly say, the memory gets a little fuzzy after a while, and it's not always useful to believe in rumours."

Kamo nodded in agreement. "Well, let us hope you didn't forget all of our little party. It is better to remember when you have had a good time, so that you know how to do it again. Hah!" He laughed loud enough for the few others in the bar to look round. The two women either side of him laughed too. "And the rumour is; we may have another little party tonight; perhaps a game or two." He playfully slapped the knees of the women. "What do you say girls? What about you, Ric? Shall we have some fun?"

The gentle reminder regarding the debt of the favour was not lost on Ric. "Sounds good to me," he replied to let the other man know he had not forgotten, "but I have plans."

"Oh yes! I remember." He pointed a finger at Ric, which he then waggled in some cheeky measure. "Pela said you had a girlfriend. I didn't believe her, but of course it would be true. She would know. She can be very... perceptive."

"Where is the lovely Pela?" The other women showed not the slightest reaction to Ric's inquiry.

"Oh," he said, waving a hand as though dismissing an irrelevance, "she was having a problem with her relations. It was better for her to leave for a while. She will be back when she has sorted it out."

Ric wondered what kind of problem, and what sort of relations. But then he realised that if Kamo had been gone since… was it Thursday, two days; he couldn't have been the one to beat up on Camille, or Pela. "Sorry to hear that."

"Oh, it's nothing," Kamo said. "You know girls. Sometimes they listen to their mothers too much, and sometimes not enough." He playfully pinched the chin of the blond who smiled on cue. Then Kamo looked briefly towards the diminutive Yuri, who was in the process of lighting yet another cigarette even though he had one going in the ashtray. Gauging Kamo's expression, his eyes hidden as they were by the large graded sunglasses, was difficult. He inflected his words in much the same way as his moustache extended along his lip and bent drooping around his mouth. He gave the impression that his mouth was the stage from which the oral play was performed and his moustache the side-curtain decorating it. At times it opened to reveal broad comedy; at other times the stage grew thin and unwelcoming. His eyes were not for display.

Yuri fidgeted and then came to some sort of attention: "Excuse me," he mumbled. "I… go."

Ric went to stand, but Yuri leapt up so fast he was gone before there was much point.

The girls looked nonplussed.

"Forgive Yuri," Kamo suggested more than asked. "He's not at home on the beach. And he is nervous in the company of beautiful women. That's right girls, mmm?"

Now that Yuri was gone the two women did come to life. The blond draped herself on Kamo's shoulder and the darker one, Ami, smiled and began to pay Ric more attention.

They ordered drinks. Kamo was murdering *Pernod* at an alarming rate, the blond vodka tonic, and Ami the local sweet 'vin de myrte'. Ric took another *Pietra*; the chestnut flavoured beer was beginning to grow on him, which, he noted, was not a good sign.

Turning to Ric to get his full attention, Ami asked: "It's a beautiful island, isn't it. What made you decide to come here, Ric?" The whites of her eyes shone against the darkness of her skin, and her face was rounded with the subtle oblique lines of her origin. Her accent gave away her French roots, but her looks suggested she was a colonial; Indo-Chinese perhaps, with some Afro-Caribbean thrown in. She was strikingly beautiful rather than conventionally so, and once she had fixed her ebony eyes on Ric he found it hard to break her gaze.

Ric, rather than answer her question posed her another. "You know the island well?"

"Oh, yes," she replied. "I know most of France well."

Their conversation came and went in much the same way as people drifted in and out of the bar. Everything moved in slow motion; the temperature refusing to fall in conjunction with the daylight. The humid breeze from the south persisted. Few of the customers ate, and none of the more usual young crowd appeared even though it was *le weekend*. Camille was nowhere to be seen, which in itself was unusual, as he was a crucial ingredient of the ambience. There would be no cabaret this Saturday evening, but the gaily dressed patrons of the various nationalities around the bar seemed unconcerned; they were worn down by the sultry heat, they'd been too long in the oven to entertain more energetic amusements.

Ami was practised in the art of gentle chat; she was also aware which of her equally gentle mannerisms would appeal to the man before her, whether it was a slight lowering of her head as if to accentuate her attention, or simply a raised eyebrow and a knowing flexing of her lips, or the very delicate way she flared her nostrils. She smiled much.

Ric, for his part, steered their dialogue away from the inquiring line he had adopted with Pela. Although he was still keen to know more about the man opposite, he was aware that if he began to pry too openly, he could not count on Ami's discretion. Also, he did not want to know how long Ami had known Kamo, or how they had met; they weren't the kind of questions he needed the answers to. So general international gossip and media scandal flowed along like leaves on a lazy river.

All of a sudden Kamo seemed to tire of the blond; his attention span for her had run its course. He grinned at Ric, a grin that suggested he was extremely pleased with himself, or that he was privy to some information he thought Ric might be interested to know.

He interrupted Ami as she was in the act of draping her arm around Ric's shoulder; a lightly provocative act in response to a joke he had made, nothing more.

"So, my friend," Kamo began, "is the moon at the right angle, the breeze from the right direction, and is your chair facing the right way this evening? Can a man ask for anything more than to be in the company of a very beautiful woman on a night like this?" He lent forward, pointing at Ric and in an alcohol amplified whisper said, "I told you; money can buy many things, heh?"

It wasn't so much what Kamo said, it was more the way he said it; as though he was the sole pimp through whom all the world's desires could be purchased, and as though nothing stood outside the spectrum of his procurement.

Ric stiffened at the idea he might be bought in the same way as the woman who rested her hand on his shoulder.

The heavy breeze faltered for a few seconds, and although it was only Ric's impression, the hubbub of the bar seemed to tail off. He wondered if others around him had heard Kamo's suggestion and had drawn a similar conclusion. But quickly he realised the pleasure seekers seated around him had fallen quiet because they were, every one of them, looking behind him.

Ric turned in his seat, and out of the dark blue evening Manou appeared.

She was wearing her trademark green camisole top and skirt. Her hair was curled and hung loose about her face. There was a burning blue ice to her eyes and a shocking thunder in her scowl.

For a moment Ric believed he was hallucinating, so he shook his head, hoping the vision of Manou might disperse.

It didn't. She remained right in front of him, staring at the four of them around the table as though they were engaged in some appalling sexual recreation. She looked hard at each one in turn; the women for less time, Kamo and Ric for longer.

By now the bar had fallen deafeningly quiet; as though Manou's sudden presence commanded the attention of the whole audience. The ebony-eyed Ami removed her arm from around Ric's shoulder, realising by Manou's reaction that she had her hand on someone else's property, but she didn't rush it.

Manou looked from Ric to Kamo and from Kamo back to Ric. The whole incident lasted only a few seconds, but seemed to Ric to go on for minutes.

Kamo was, for once, lost for words.

"Manou," said Ric, but the sound of her name was lost somewhere

between his sharp surprise and his hesitant welcome. "Manou, may I...?
Would you...?"

She cut him off before he could recover.

"No, Ric," she said with a resolve that left no room for doubt. "Right
now I don't think I will." And with that Manou turned around and walked
back into the shadows. Manou had spoken to Ric, but she had been
looking at Petrossian.

Ric looked at Kamo, who was clearly spellbound, in exactly the way
Ric had been the first time he saw Manou. The women knew better than
to speak.

"Excuse me," Ric said, and got up without waiting for permission.

All the same Kamo said: "Yes, I will, of course, naturally."

And Ric noticed as he left that Kamo had taken off his sunglasses and
was rubbing his eyes as if they had deceived him.

38

"Manou," he called when he picked up her profile against the street lights. "Manou wait, please," he called again, a little out of breath.

But she was not waiting and she was not out of breath. She did not want to speak to Ric.

He caught her up before she made it to her car, but he had to hurry. There was a real and deliberate purpose to the way she walked, like she was an irresistible force and would brook no deviation.

A voice in his head told Ric that she was behaving in an unreasonable fashion; that there was no issue with the other woman; that if she didn't stop he would turn back and let her go on alone; as if it mattered to him? Yet he ignored the voice of complacency from within and walked beside her as she carried on. He wasn't going to let her go without an explanation. "Come on Manou." Ric softened his approach. "Stop for a minute. Wait up, please."

Her pace slowed, but only because they had arrived at the back of the beach, and she had to step over the pavement to get to her car.

It crossed Ric's mind that Manou's anxiety of the day before might just have spilled over. But, he countered, she had been more than alright by the end of the evening.

Manou unlocked her car.

Without hesitating, Ric got into the passenger side.

The sultry atmosphere of the beach paled by comparison to the blue funk in the car.

"How did you come to Zizula, Ric?"

"I brought the bike," he replied. "But I can leave it here."

Manou sulked, staring at the steering wheel of her Peugeot as if it was responsible for all the ills of the world.

"No!" she shouted and banged her fists against the wheel. "That is not what I meant. I meant why did you choose to come to Zizula in the first place, in the beginning? Why here? Why come to this place?" She demanded to know as though there was some clandestine premeditation behind his choice.

Of course there was, but none of the reasons were remotely related to Manou. He had mentioned to Camille why he had chosen to come specifically to Corsica, but ending up in Zizula rather than any one of the other tranquil villages along the coast, was down to chance, nothing more.

"I don't know. I suppose I just ended up in Zizula. I came to Corsica because my great-grandfather, whose name by the way was Rossi, was in the Legion. I have a photograph of him at the garrison in Bunifaziu. I knew the place had been deserted for years, but I thought I might find out a bit more about him. I didn't really understand that the only Legionnaires still in residence live in the cemetery." Ric fell silent as he remembered wandering around the cemetery; the tombs all huddled together on the high promontory.

Manou scoffed, clearly believing he had made the tale up on the spot.

"Yes, I know. It does sound a little daft when I say it out loud. Funny; it didn't sound so stupid in my head. All I found was a tomb belonging to a family by the name of *Rossi* about the time of the Crimea." Ric struggled to remove his wallet so that he could show her the photograph.

"Is that it, Ric? Have you finished?"

"Well," he began, trying to remember whether there had been a reason for his choosing to finish up in Zizula, "I…."

"Enough, Ric!" Manou shouted again. "Half of Corsica lives in a tomb, and every other person is called *Rossi*. Enough!" She started the car, and then looked across at him. Even in the dark he could feel her eyes burning into him. "Do you want to get out, because I am leaving?"

"No, I don't want to get out. I don't understand, Manou. If you think I was flirting with that woman at Camille's then say so. I admit it didn't look great, but give me a chance to explain."

She was silent for a few seconds.

Manou backed her car out of its parking place and drove in a controlled, but far from sedate, fashion south out of town. The further out of town they got, the longer her silence extended.

Ric decided from her reticence that she wanted him to continue with his explanation. "Listen Manou, the people I was with; the guy was from the motor yacht in the bay. He was the guy I had too much to drink with a couple of nights ago. He's not such a bad guy."

"Yes?" was all she said.

"I arrived at Camille's a little early and it would have been rude of me not to have joined them. When I arrived there was another chap there; some fellow called Yuri, from the boat. He left which meant we were four at the table. I know it looked a bit like a set up, but that was how it happened. Can we not just go back to my place and talk about this?"

There was no response from Manou, and Ric felt he was digging a bigger hole for himself by talking. The tyres squealed as she got too deep into a bend.

"For Christ's sake Manou, will you slow down," he said in a tone that only just masked his exasperation.

She jerked the car round another bend.

"Perhaps, Ric," she shot him a quick flashing glare before looking back at the road, "you are the one who needs to slow down. Perhaps you are the one who needs your own home." Manou stood on the brakes and the Peugeot screeched to a halt at the side of the road. "Get out Ric. Please get out!" she screamed. Then she fell silent again and stared at the road out front.

"Hang on a minute; I've no idea where we are."

"I did not ask you to come, Ric."

Even in the dim light thrown by the car's instruments he could see that her eyes were glassy and unseeing, the tips of her knuckles white on the steering wheel. "Come on Manou, please don't do this."

"Ric," she turned her face to his, "I did not do this. You did." There were lines of tears running down her cheeks; the fire in her eyes melting the ice of her thoughts. "Get out, Ric. For me, please get out."

He lent towards her, but she shied away. He said: "I know it didn't look good, but...,"

"No, Ric," she interrupted, wiping her face with the back of her hand. "Right now it does not look so good. So please, get out! Go home!" she screamed. "Now!"

39

The white Peugeot started away up the hill, bucking like a horse encouraged by sharp spurs and a rough hand at the bridle.

Ric had a pretty good idea of where he was in relation to his house and decided it was shorter to walk home than to trek all the way back down into town and pick up his bike. His decision was arrived at more in anger than with a level head. Having just experienced such an unpleasant time in town, he reckoned he might be better off out of the water than dipping his toe back in it.

He sighed. The stars were out. The breeze was hot and humid. He was wearing a Hawaiian shirt and jeans; what on earth could happen next? He wondered about the odds of being hit by an asteroid? Ric vented his frustration at the twinkling firmament and trudged off in the same direction as that in which Manou's car had just left.

He followed the painted line at the verge, trotting across the road at the sweeping curves to stay on the more open seaward side.

A cavalcade of cars crammed full of young party goers lurched out of the night; horns and music blaring, their lights flashing, gaily painted kids cheering, breasts and chests bared, hanging out of sunroofs and windows waving bottles, offering wild and open invitations; singing, shrieking youth in hedonistic pursuit, the aroma of eastern herbs and spices and the echoes of their enthusiasm the only evidence of their passing. No sooner had they appeared out of the night than they were swallowed up by it.

"Perhaps that's what I came to Corsica for," he muttered to the maquis as he spurred himself on up a rise.

But that wasn't what he'd got. In the space of the same breath Ric realised how undeserving he was of all the unnecessary flak coming his way, of how none of it was of his making, and of how tired he was of it all following him around like a trail of spent cartridges. Then, as much as he liked to think the predicament he now found himself in was not of his making, he realised that without his presence his predicament could not have occurred in the first place, and therefore logic dictated that he must have played some integral part in its construction.

He walked on a little uncaring and dejected, but each time a car full of revellers passed, he smiled, waved in recognition and shook his head. Whatever the situation, he was still living, breathing and walking home along the country lane much as he had done a hundred times before after raising a little hell back home.

And Manou wouldn't be the first girl he'd upset; he'd upset a few along the way. Then again, apart from one other none of them could have held a candle to Manou.

The road took a couple of tight turns and Ric recognised them as the last bends before the road crested by the track up to the house. He was relieved it wasn't much further. Although he had maintained his fitness with his swimming out to the island and his running along the beach, he found walking up the road hard on his knees.

By the light of the many stars Ric made out the pale walls of the tomb at the side of the road. The bushes and scrub of the maquis, the tarmac road, the rocks and boulders off the verge were all bathed with a tincture of silver, as though some celestial old master had reached down and soft-brushed the top surfaces with white argent.

Ric heard a sudden scraping, brushing sound behind him, like a body pushing through the undergrowth.

"Who's there?"

A voice from the dark on the other side of the road rumbled in a deep *basso Corsu*.

"I'm sorry," Ric replied. "I don't speak Corsu; a little Français, but not Corsu."

"It's okay," said a figure that appeared out of the shadows of the maquis across the road, "you are English. I speak little English." The voice, French accented, was smoked and dry; hollow like the inside of a tree trunk split by lightening.

The man wore a dark hat, flat-topped with a wide brim which kept his face concealed, and a dark waistcoat and ill-fitting trousers of a similar shade. His shirt was loose like his trousers, but lighter, shining almost white in the silvery light. In his right hand he held a walking stick, as long as the man was tall; a gnarled, gargoyle-like carving to the haft at the top. He was old; his movements betrayed a slim torso and he was unsteady on his feet, reliant on the stick for balance.

Ric turned to face the figure.

"Stay where you are," growled the old man. "I have my dogs."

There were no dogs to be seen, and in Ric's experience it was more usual for dogs to appear before their owner, but then he heard a rustling sound coming from behind the man; a sound like that of animals foraging in the undergrowth. And yet they did not bark at Ric's presence.

"You are lost?" inquired the figure.

Ric began to reply, but curiously he found his voice had temporarily deserted him. He wanted to speak, but no words came.

"Ah, you stay in the house," the man said indicating up the track with his stick. "It was my house, since many years my house." Now he walked forward with the aid of the tall staff. As he came closer to Ric the man's height became more apparent; he was shorter than Ric and slender in build. He used the stick because of some infirmity with his right leg which caused him to limp, but he used it as though he was familiar with the help it provided him, as though he had used it for a long time.

"You have seen the paladin?" he asked, as though Ric could not have missed it.

Paladin? Ric had not seen any paladin. Maybe the old man meant some constellation above, but though Ric could recognise some of the stars linked together as they were, he had not heard of such a group. He went to reply, but his voice was still missing.

"It lies there in the north wall. You will have seen it," said the fellow. He hobbled over the road with all the awkwardness of a beggar after too many nights slept on hard pavements, and stood before Ric.

"Show me your hands!" he growled. "Come on, show me your hands."

For some inexplicable reason Ric found himself holding out his hands, palm down, showing them to the man.

In the stark light the man leant forward to examine them. He looked them over then stepped back and, although he didn't relax, his countenance altered as though he was now not so tense in Ric's company. "I am sorry. You are not the man I am looking for."

The shadow cast by the wide brim of the man's hat concealed his eyes, but Ric felt transfixed by them, as though they prevented him from moving. They also drove the power of speech from his throat and replaced it with a light weakness, like slack muscle.

But as he watched the fellow, Ric could see that his right leg hung crookedly from his hip and his foot pointed outwards, not straight. His trousers were tied at the waist with string and his shirt was open at his neck. He looked much like Ric imagined a shepherd would look; perhaps one of those who slept in the *oriu* that Manou had shown him. There was something about his neck that suggested the man was aggravated by it; he scratched and pawed at it as he stood.

"You will know the man I am looking for. He wears my stone; the *Catochitis*. They are few. It is rare." He paused for a few seconds. The act of speaking appeared to sap his energy; the words he searched for required his complete concentration. He rubbed at his neck again the way another might scratch his head in thought. There was more rustling and brushing from the maquis behind him.

"When you see the man I am looking for, tell him I want it back."

Ric heard the distant moan of a car approaching up the hill from the south. He started towards the man, but his limbs were curiously heavy and refused to respond. He needed to warn the man to move back from the road. Ric tried to speak, but found he could not.

"When you see this man, tell him I will not rest until I have it," the old man said, raising his voice against the sound of the oncoming car. "Tell him...." He extended his arms, imploring Ric to convey his message.

Ric could now see the beams of the car's headlights arcing up into the sky, forewarning them of its arrival as it rounded the curves and raced up the slope, nearer and nearer.

"Tell him, I cannot rest...." he implored. "I cannot...."

Then the car was cresting the rise and upon them; the driver blind to the two men talking in the middle of the road.

The old man's words were now lost to the noise of the rapidly approaching vehicle.

Ric moved towards the man to push him back from the path of the car, but realised he had moved too late and that if he moved further forwards he would leave himself at too great a risk.

The old man stood exposed in the glaring head lights, but strangely unmoved by the threat of the car. He seemed either inured to the danger or uncomprehending of the coming accident.

In the final moment of terror, Ric's voice returned and he yelled at the man to move out of the way.

Ric threw himself back, landing on his hands and knees.

The last thing he saw as he leapt backwards was the car tearing right through the old man; no blaring of horn in warning, no last minute change of direction or hopeless braking, no squealing of tyres and crashing of metal on stone as the car left the road to avoid the accident. The car drove on, plain and straight through the old man, just as though he was not there.

40

Sleep had, at best, been fitful. The old man had seen to that.

Of course Ric had known it even before it had happened. He had realised the old man was a figment of his imagination. He knew it because the fellow's dogs had not appeared as they ought to; knew it because his own voice had deserted him for which there was no logical explanation; knew it because there had been no stain of any accident and no corpse; and he knew it because he believed it, down in his core, in the pit of his stomach, down where every thought is born; he believed it. The old man had not been real.

Picking himself up off the tarmac Ric had watched as the car did not deviate from its natural path or speed. The dark blue saloon continued on its way as though it had neither seen nor hit any obstacle in the middle of the road, its passage smooth and continuous. And afterwards there had been no evidence of any collision: no broken body, no blood, no moaning in pain from the dark.

He had searched the undergrowth at the verge in the dark, but had found nothing to suggest there had been any kind of accident at all.

Ric got up when his room became too hot. The same hot breeze was still prowling up from the south, and when he went outside to his car he noticed the horizontal surfaces of it were dusted with a fine yellow powder that stayed on his fingers when he wiped it from the windscreen. It was as though the sands of the Sahara were in the midst of some great distribution.

He ambled, stretching as he went, round the outside of the house to the north facing wall where his bike would normally have been chained. The smooth, yellow stone lay beside the box that contained the gas canister. It was the only remarkable part of the wall, standing out as it did amidst the other stones. Ric stood, arching his back to stretch the sleep out of it. His recollection of paladins was dim and distant. He remembered them as being knights of Charlemagne's court, but otherwise his memory was too sketchy to be of much use. What association they might have with this sandy stone, Ric could not imagine.

Ric drove to the beach where he swam and ran, but not for long; the heat sapped his energy.

There was no sign of the lad. In fact there was no sign of much; even the fish had sought cooler waters deep down, far away from the baking atmosphere above. The exercise felt good though. In spite of the clutter in his head, his body reacted well to the demands he placed upon it and when he returned to the house he felt refreshed and capable.

He showered and changed and drove over to Renabianca to see Manou. Ric figured that the pig's ear he had made of trying to explain the situation she'd found him in at the bar the previous evening, was as much responsible for their argument as was her intransigent attitude towards his explanation. That state of affairs needed to be addressed sooner than later; if left it would only fester. And as Ric was now more inclined to sort out whatever problems he perceived he had, rather than letting them take care of themselves as he had up until recently, he decided to grasp the nettle no matter how painful it might prove and go to see Manou at the campsite.

In fact there now appeared before Ric an entire bed of nettles that required grasping but, he reasoned, he would deal with them one at a time rather than by the fistful.

At Renabianca he noticed a new sign at the entrance which prohibited and warned against the use of campfires; bold red lettering on a white back ground proclaimed the message in no uncertain terms; a garish picture of a pine being consumed by flames was painted next to the lettering lest anyone be in any doubt.

There was no question the maquis was anything other than tinder dry. Even the darker green hue of the holm oaks and aleppo pines seemed pale and parched, each one plastered in the arid tones of the Saharan sand that had settled upon it overnight.

Ric parked his Citroen in the dustbowl of a car park and strolled to the office. Manou's Peugeot was absent.

His attempt at sartorial elegance had come unstuck. The heat seemed greater at the campsite than up at the house; his shirt stuck to his back and his feet were covered in dust. He stopped in the shade of a plane tree and brushed himself down.

Manou was absent. A smiley girl in her late teens, wearing the cream blouse of the camp uniform, occupied the office.

"No," she replied to his enquiry, picking his nationality. "She is in Porti Vechju. Later she returns. You want leave message for her?"

"No. Thank you," Ric said, but then pretended to have made a mistake. "I am sorry. Maybe I was supposed to meet her in Porti Vechju. I thought she wanted me to pick her up. She is at the *notaire* right?" He spoke quickly, hoping the girl would pick up his intention rather than see the lie behind his words. He patted his pockets as though he had mislaid something.

The girl watched him, still smiling, parading a balustrade of heavy ironwork across her upper teeth. "*Oui, notaire,*" she agreed. "*Monsieur Grua,*" she laughed behind her raised hand.

"It's funny?" Ric asked.

She leaned forward across the counter towards Ric and looked around the vacant office. "Yes, of course. Grua; like bird." She stood up and with her hands acted out the shape of a long beak and long neck, and proceeded to strut about the office on tip-toe like a long-legged marsh bird.

"Yes. Monsieur Grua. Like pelican," Ric agreed.

"No, not *pélican*, but like *pélican*. In French it is *grue*, like bird. But this word it can also mean 'prostitute', eh. Not so nice." The girl grinned, very pleased with her knowledge of all the wrong English and very pleased to have Ric break the monotony of her morning.

"Okay, thanks," said Ric as he turned to leave.

But the girl wasn't finished. "Moment: you know where is the office of Monsieur Grua?"

Ric pretended to think, taking his time over it. It wouldn't be much trouble to go into town and trawl through a phone book, but the enthusiastic young secretary had an easier solution for him. She pulled the solicitor's address up on her computer screen and wrote it down on a notepad. She hesitated, frowning. At the last minute it very obviously crossed her mind that perhaps she shouldn't be dishing out Monsieur Grua's address to strangers. Then after a quick study of Ric, probably to tease him, she handed it over and reverted to her smiley face again.

Not wanting to risk his luck turning sour, Ric checked that he could read her scrawl, but refrained from asking her to draw him a map as well. He thanked the girl again and left to the light birdsong of her farewell.

With the aid of a street map, Ric located the solicitor's office in a small courtyard behind the Rue Géneral Leclerc, just over the road from the post office. The building was old, but lacked the character of its years because its occupants had removed the wooden doors and windows, and replaced the frugal erudition of age with the lavish sterility of smoked glass and chrome plate.

Grua was out, his office vacant and shut, so Ric went for a stroll in the vain hope he might catch sight of Manou and her solicitor at one of the many restaurants dotted about the walled town.

It was not until he arrived at the entrance to the restaurant L'Antigu, on the very colourful Rue u Borgu, and found it closed that he realised it was Sunday.

Of course Grua's office would be shut.

41

He drove back to the house as fast as the car would allow. There was no point in hurrying in the Citroen; the harder Ric pushed it through the corners, the more likely his haste would result in disaster. The lurching assemblage of tin protested at his encouragement by trying to leave the road at every bend, and he was certain it was only the thin tyres sticking to the tacky, melting tarmac that kept him upright.

As he drove up the track to the house all looked normal, but when he walked in through the door nothing did.

The place was an absolute shambles. The one item of furniture not up or overturned was the heavy table in the main room. Everything else was out of place, scattered about the way a fox scatters the contents of a rubbish bin. Even the meagre contents of the fridge had been removed and thrown on the floor, the morsels of food being devoured by the grateful ants. His bedroom was a complete mess; the mattress was on the floor, ripped down the centre as if disembowelled, and his clothes were lying about and some of them torn to shreds. The bathroom was not much better. His modest music system was smashed and broken. As far as Ric could make out the only missing ingredient was the lack of graffiti scribbled on the walls and the odour of excrement, otherwise it would have passed for a Military Police holding cell on a Saturday night.

Amongst the debris in the kitchen Ric found a bottle of beer that was, despite the orgy of vandalism, still intact.

He stood dazed and more than a little incredulous at the wanton destruction. There was nothing stolen; nothing he could see that was missing from when he had left earlier. They had left the music station, albeit smashed to bits. But everything else that had been there was now wrecked; the debris told its own story. Ric was no policeman, but he knew the difference between a house that had been robbed and one that had been ransacked. And this fell right in the middle of the latter category.

He walked outside to the garden and found the earth by the small plump cactus where he had buried his passport and papers undisturbed. At least he had that to be grateful for.

In fact the patio seemed undisturbed, as though whoever it was had just been hell bent on destroying the inside of the house.

The lively young thing behind the counter at Renabianca had given him the run around. He'd bought her story about Manou being in Porti Vechju, and as the sweat began to trickle down the back of his shirt, Ric tried to convince himself that Manou would not have put the girl up to getting him out of the way.

But if she had wanted him out of the way, what was the reason? There was nothing in the house worth stealing. So whoever it was that was responsible, had done it to send him a message.

He sipped from the bottle of warm beer as he surveyed the chaos.

So what message was he supposed to read into the picture of confusion before him? Surely there were only two conclusions to be drawn. Either it was a less than subtle way of suggesting it was time for Ric to leave, or whoever it was that had been in the house had been looking for something – something Ric did not know he had, if indeed he did have it, whatever 'it' was.

The merry-go-round of reason revolved too fast for him to make any sense of it. What was it the old man had said he was looking for the night before? Ric tried to remember; the *Catochitis*, the stone, he had said. But then if that had been a dream, this was something of a waking nightmare.

Logic suggested he should report the ransacking of the villa to the local *Gendarmes*. But logic also suggested he would have to deal with the curious policeman René Bosquet, and that he would avoid if at all possible.

The afternoon was pretty much spent by the time he'd got the place straight and finished clearing up. There was still a considerable rip in the mattress and the music system was beyond repair, but otherwise he'd returned the house to a habitable state. The only item he could not lay his hands on was the old leather-bound notebook of proverbs that Manou had given him. He could not imagine it was of value to any other person than either Manou or himself, so he hoped he'd just mislaid it and that it would turn up later.

Even though it was Sunday the small supermarket in Zizula would be open, so Ric drove down into town to restock his fridge and buy a couple of new light bulbs.

With so much occupying his mind he had all but forgotten his motorbike until he saw it where he had abandoned it the evening before. It was still chained to the lamp post like a faithful dog waiting on its owner, but it was no longer in the condition in which he'd left it.

Both tyres had been slashed.

Far from a picture of cool, the bike now looked, with the dusting of airborne sand, more like a tired film prop; a remnant of better times.

Ric guessed the responsibility for the vandalism probably lay with whoever had turned over his house. Whoever it was, the message they were sending was more to do with his presence than anything he possessed, though the curious irony followed that a bike with deflated tyres was less easy for him to leave town on. He was glad he had taken the Citroen into town, not that he had any alternative transport left; the old crate would not stand up to much abuse, however maltreated it might look in its natural state. Nevertheless, Ric was careful to park it in plain sight when he went into the store over the road.

When he came out, a paper sack of provisions in each arm, he saw René Bosquet loitering over the road in the shade of a shop front awning, eating a pastry.

The day may have been uncommonly hot for most of the tourists and even some of the locals, but for a pale skinned, overweight, glutton like Bosquet, a man better suited to an air-conditioned office, it was abject hell, and the dark stains about his armpits and collar did little to conceal his discomfort.

Ric ignored him, even though he had made eye contact, and strolled towards his Citroen.

Sadly, Bosquet heaved over to meet him at the car. "Mister Ross, how are you on this warm day?"

Ric balanced the sacks of shopping on the sloping bonnet of his car, which was so hot he wondered if the eggs would fry in their box. "I'll do, thank you."

Bosquet threw the last half of his pastry into the revolving machine that was his mouth, chewed it for a moment and then consigned it below to aid in the expansion of his girth. "Is that the right way to thank a kind

stranger for giving you a lift home and saving you from a night in the...
what is it the Americans call it-the 'drunk tank'? And there would have
been a big fine, *n'est ce pas?*"

"Know what? You're quite right Mister Bosquet," Ric admitted.
"Thanks for the lift home. I appreciated it. My manners desert me
sometimes. Must be the heat." For the second time Ric took an instant
dislike to the owlish face, proving that drunk or sober the policeman
provoked a common reaction in him.

"It is true. It is very hot. But it is unusual for an Englishman to forget
his manners I would say," continued Bosquet. The pencil line moustache
above his plump lips looked lonely without cause for movement, but, like
the skilled magician his stomach demanded him to be, he produced from
the thin air another pastry with which he could satisfy his interminable
appetite. His hands were pale and liver spotted, like the baggy flesh around
his devious eyes.

Ric chose the opportunity to load his sacs into the car and get in. He
wondered about telling the policeman about the trashing of his house, but
for all he knew it might have been the policeman's work. He did seem to be
well informed, as most of the policemen who'd ever crossed Ric's path
seemed to be. He slid back the fabric roof and hooked open the window
flaps to allow the temperature inside the car to reduce to a manageable
level.

Bosquet continued, "I would say also that you are not taking my
advice regarding Monsieur Petrossian. That is a pity. Perhaps you were not
listening to me? Maybe I have to repeat what I have already said?" Bosquet
raised his voice at the end of his question, introducing a hint on menace.

"No," replied Ric. "I heard you the first time." Then he found himself
saying: "I've got no interest in him, Bosquet. We don't sing from the same
hymn sheet. I ran into him last night by accident, not by design." Ric also
realised as he said it that every time he bumped into Petrossian his world
seemed to get turned upside down.

"I see your motorcycle has suffered an accident too." He paused to
allow Ric time to appreciate his powers of observation. "Are you making
enemies or friends here, Mister Ross? I am not certain that you know the
difference between the two."

Ric nodded in agreement. "Maybe I don't. Which one are you,
Bosquet?"

"I should have thought that would be very obvious to a man of your knowledge and judgement. We have something in common, you and me."

"How'd you work that out?"

"You are a soldier, are you not Mister Ross? And I am a policeman. We both attend to the *désordre*, the disorder of life that some people make. For you it is the disorder produced by politicians; for me it is the disorder produced by criminals. I do not think we are very different, you and me."

Ric disagreed again. "Marine, not soldier. Were, not are. And, like it or not, I don't think we do have much in common, Bosquet," he said testily. "Other than that, you got it about right." He was reluctant to interrupt the policeman's eloquence, however banal he found it, but clearly the man had been doing his homework and wanted Ric to know it.

"And I think you should call me René. After all, if we are going to be friends I think first names are appropriate, don't you, Ric?"

Ric pulled on as straight a smile as he could summon from his locker. "Sure, René." They shook hands as though the symbolic gesture implied the sealing of some fraternal covenant. "Why not?" added Ric, retrieving his hand with the distinct impression he'd put it somewhere unhygienic.

"Now that we are friends and we have shaken hands; the word of an officer and a gentleman," Bosquet preened, "I will be generous. First, here is my card." He handed Ric a business card. A quick glance revealed it had only his name and a mobile phone number printed on it. "Please call me if I can be of service. And second, I want you to take this advice in the way I give it, from one friend to another. It will be in your better interest, I think it is the right expression, to return to your home before your life here becomes more difficult. I think this would be the intelligent thing to do as it would be stupid, perhaps even ridiculous to ignore so many – what is the English word – ah yes, *blatant* encouragements to be somewhere other than here in Zizula, *n'est ce pas?*" Bosquet stood back from the car as though by allowing Ric more room between them he might see the sense in the advice just given him. "What do you think, Ric?"

Ric looked at the pale, fleshy policeman standing beside his car. He wanted to tell the fellow his gratuitous obesity would be the death of him, that his prolific sweating and his body odour would condemn him to a life void of anything but loneliness, and that his limp sycophancy was so obviously full of dishonesty that it made Ric's skin crawl.

He also wanted to tell Bosquet that he had no intention of taking his advice, but instead he said, "Sure! You're right, René! You know sometimes I just don't see what is right in front of me." He smiled at Bosquet and was about to reverse out of his parking space when a thought came to him. "You didn't by any chance drop by my place this morning, did you?"

"Why no, Ric. Why would I come looking for you? It would appear that you have the habit of finding me whenever I need to speak to you."

Leaving Bosquet at the side of the road, Ric waved goodbye thinking how lucky he was to have so many friends, and how wonderful it was that so many of them were so eager to offer him the benefit of their advice.

There was not much to be done for his motorbike. It wasn't going anywhere fast; it would have to wait until he felt a little more inclined to deal with it. When that would be, he hadn't the faintest idea.

42

The curious irony of what had occupied his waking thought before the beginning of the week and what had occupied it in the last couple of days, intrigued Ric, as he sat outside on the small patio watching a dizzying sun melt into the rim of the mountains. Before, there had only been room for doubts about his past. Now much, if not most, of his thoughts were taken up with his future.

Manou was, he knew, responsible. She had restored his flagging libido and underpinned what had been, until recently, his fragile ego. She had replaced his pliant core with something altogether more inflexible, as if by the heating and cooling of his emotions she had tempered some metal into him. Even her rejection of the evening before had not reduced him to the low state it would have if she had rejected him in such a manner a few days before.

Rejection, Ric grumbled; he was no stranger to it. Usually it made him more determined to succeed, and the warm knot in his stomach told him in no uncertain terms how much he wanted to succeed this time.

He fixed a plate of bread, *prizuttu* and *ricotta*, and ate. He drank water to combat the incredible heat. The air was so thick it possessed weight and was so hot it assaulted the skin as though he was locked in an equatorial jail. He felt as though he could hold the air in his palm and draw patterns in it with his fingers. There was no escaping it, no hiding from it; it was enveloping, stultifying. The breeze from the south was strengthening and sitting outside in the face of it was becoming less than pleasant. Someone needed to shut the door to the fan oven, and soon, otherwise the world outside would be roasted before nightfall.

There was no mileage in going to see Manou again. He decided she would call if she wanted to. He had made his intentions clear by his visit to Renabianca. She had made hers clear by having the girl get rid of him. Still, Ric didn't quite understand why she should have reacted so the night before, but he also understood, by how much he had come to know Manou already, that there was no point in his committing too much energy to talking if she was for the moment deaf to him.

Ric scratched his head to arrest his thoughts, went inside and lay on the sofa.

He soon fell into a deep and resounding sleep. He lay there as the darkness came and the stars began their glittering and shimmering.

For once he did not begin to dream straight away, but slept well below the surface at which dreams take on their luminescence; down in the darkness where the mind is dormant and the body maintains a comprehensive lethargy; down where strangers can enter the room and move about without fear of disturbing the sleeper.

At one point Ric flicked open his eyes, dragged from the depths of his slumber by a familiar noise in the distance. He could hear the sounds of an aeroplane, but he couldn't place the type. The deep hum of piston engines, a straining, droning thrum, bounced off a hillside far away; a murmur that faltered and then faded into the night.

Sometime later, although he had no way of knowing how much later because sleep had employed its trans-dimensional deceit and abridged time, he was convinced he could smell the scent of lavender and heather, but the scent was sweeter and more pungent than he remembered. The perfume lingered in and tickled his nostrils and caused him to sneeze; an act in his sleep that piqued his senses and fired rockets of light into his eyes.

He dreamt of Manou, of her blue eyes, her dark eyebrows and her dark hair, of the way she drew her teeth over her lower lip in concentration while she stared at him, watching for his reactions to her carnal pleasures. They were lying beside a log fire beneath the stars and as she leaned over him he could see the reflection of the fire in her eyes. He could smell the wood-smoke, and the herbs of the maquis. The odour was strong and felt close. It swelled and took on a texture that lay on him; a perfumed pleasure that was thickening into an overwhelming vapour, and then too late he realised it had become noxious and suffocating; hot fingers were scoring his lungs and the pain urged him to react.

Ric woke up. It was not some fragrant dream he had been enjoying.

There was smoke in the atmosphere; smoke from a fire born on the breeze. He got up and went outside.

There was smoke and a glow of paprika light to the south, like the promise of fair-weather at dusk; a golden-orange on the horizon that reflected brick-red higher up in the sky.

Ric could just make out the raw flames, and judging by the radiance thrown up by the fire it burned over several acres and covered a broad front. He stood mesmerised by the differing hues of yellow; bright ginger and turmeric at the centre, sombre saffron and cayenne at the edges; a great crescent of dazzling colour thrown up against the black of the night. The stars were extinguished by the ambient glare, snuffed out in the face of a wicked blaze. There was a disturbing hostility to the scene, as though an army of burnished shields was approaching from over the skyline; an army dispatched with one purpose; to consume and lay waste. His eyes were drawn to the eerie glow the way those of a child are drawn to a terror.

The bush-fire burned away to the south; maybe two or three miles, he reckoned; maybe somewhere down near the turning to Renabianca.

He ran back inside, fished his shoes out from underneath the bed, grabbed his jacket and a shirt, and ran to his car. He drove down the track as fast as the lumbering vehicle would allow. He wondered whether the fire would leave the road south clear. With the stiff breeze at its back, it was unlikely.

Ric could measure his proximity to the fire by its growing brightness. Each time he lurched around a bend in the road the yellow of the fire ahead increased in intensity; each time brighter until he could feel the heat of it on his forehead and taste the wood-smoke in his mouth. And then he was forced to cough against the presence of the smoke. He rounded a tight right-hand curve that crested on the shoulder of the hill and stamped in over-reaction on the brakes.

The Citroen threatened to topple over, but held on and slewed to a halt sideways on in the middle of the road.

Below him, some 200 hundred metres away on the coastal side, the maquis was ablaze. It was as if the Stygian hordes had risen from their graves, each one brandishing a flaming torch, marching forward both in huge disciplined phalanxes and smaller darting cohorts. Wherever a gap in the line appeared a fresh detachment of flame bearers marched forward from behind to fill it.

The road in front followed the contours of the hill, descending on a serpentine course towards the landward extremity of the fire, at times disappearing in the dense eddies of smoke that billowed about. It was impossible to make out the exact edge of the fire, but Ric hoped he might be able to get round the side of it.

He drove on with the road in full view before him one moment, the next in suffocating darkness through which fell a sporadic rain of fluorescent cinders and flyash. The further down the hill he guided the car, the more uneasy he felt about his progress and the hasty decision he had made to continue. Ric knew that if the fire, racing as it was northward into the hill and in his direction, flared up a gully and got in behind him he would have to abandon the car and take to the maquis on foot. He also knew that however fit he was the fire would climb through the heated air of the hillside much faster than he could run.

As spurred on as he was by the potential disaster faced by those beyond the wall of advancing flames, he now understood the lack of wisdom in his decision to go on.

He hauled the Citroen round into the hill, blind to the width of the road as the smoke chose at that particular second to close in on him.

When he backed up, his rear wheels dropped with a thump beyond the lip of the road and the car grounded.

Ric opened the door and a blast of scorching heat roared at him from the outside. He put his shoulder to the roof arch and heaved the car up. Nothing happened. He needed another foot to depress the throttle as he could not heave up and reach the pedal at the same time.

He tried to lift the back of the car, but all that accomplished was to raise the body an inch or two whilst the wheels stayed in place. Ric got in, pushed the clutch out, grabbed the gearlever and pushed it in to first gear. He kept his right foot on the throttle, let the clutch in, dropped his left out of the open car door and tried again to heave the car upwards.

The tarmac beneath him was melting and the searing heat charged through the sole of his shoe. The smoke threatened to choke him.

Again, the body of the car rose a few inches, but the wheels stayed put. He swore and fell into the car, accidentally treading down on the throttle in an effort to maintain his balance.

The act of his weight transferring down onto the car's suspension caused the vehicle to bounce and, with the aid of the increased revs from his foot on the throttle pedal and the added grip supplied by the tyres beginning to melt into the sticky surface, the battered old Citroen gave a great jump like the releasing of a compressed spring and leapt forward, dragging its rear wheels back onto the surface of the road.

As it leapt upwards Ric was thrown almost into the back seat. The car stuttered and jerked up the hill and he had to clamber back into the front seat, like a rodeo rider trying to maintain his hold on a bucking steer.

But at least he was going back up, away from the danger.

Nearer the top of the hill the flames had reached the verge and as he drove past them the engine of the car gasped for oxygen. The glass of the window and the metal of the door at his side became too hot to touch.

Ric drove with the fire in his mirrors back to the bungalow and carried straight on past to take the turning down to the bay at *la Tozza*. His only chance of getting into Renabianca would be from the north.

He leapt and bounded down the track, and drove straight onto the beach, parking as near to the water's edge as he could trust the surface of the sand to remain firm. He hurried out of the car, but made sure to turn off the lights and remove the keys from the ignition, throwing them on the floor and grabbing his jacket.

He ran fast to the southern end of the beach. He could see exactly where he was going; his path was lit by the peculiar red glow from the fire on the other side of the saddle he was about to climb.

He made good progress, slipping only a couple of times when his footholds deserted him or when the rock crumbled. Ric kept out of the woods and took the steeper, shorter path up to the left. As he approached the top of the saddle, the heat grew more torrid and the night took on a devilish crackle. The gradient levelled out and, stumbling upright and wiping the sweat from his eyes, Ric arrived at the top.

The view that met him was a canvas from hell; an uncontrolled, erratic, flaming battle; bright orange light interspersed with unfathomable darkness. The flaming hordes were forming into more concentrated bands; one diverted by its mission to consume, whilst another sprung forward, leap-frogging its busy fellow to rush on and claim trees not yet ablaze. The fire was a hundred yards or so back from the beach. Ric was again mesmerised by the flames; routed to the spot by the awful and awesome beauty of their natural energy.

Through the enormous belches of smoke Ric could make out several small groups of people on the beach; dark figures running back and forth between the scrub and the waterline.

Some of the campers were loading their families and what possessions they could carry into small speedboats close in. Others stood in the water trying to hold Hobie-cats and windsurfers still as children climbed on board out of the water. Clearly there were not enough rafts to accommodate the seventy to eighty figures still milling about on the smoky, sandy strip.

Ric wondered whether adding his number to those already marooned on the beach was wise. They looked to him to be too tied up with their own safety than to be bothered with his help. Yet he knew the path which he had just climbed up from the bay behind him. If he could find the path down – the path up which the young lad Franco must have come-then surely he could hope to spirit some of those on the beach away from the fire.

Just then an incredible whooshing, booming sound assaulted him from behind; an unanticipated, thrumming, blast that knocked him, unsuspecting, off his feet. A huge aeroplane, which even in the dark he could see was a similar orange to the flames of the fire, buzzed so low over him he thought it had shaved his head.

The Canadair flew in at a hundred feet from north to south, parallel with the raised ground to the east. Just before it arrived above the flames it released a vast, misty, ghostly-white, sail-shaped torrent of water; a deluge of sea water cascading down over the advancing fire, providing vital time and relief to those running before it's sucking heat.

The path down twisted and turned, vanished across the barren rock a few times, and ended with a considerable leap down onto the rocks at the end. The jump was a good five metres down, and to attempt it in the dark would have been stupid. Much as he could see some of his landing area, he wasn't inclined to make a leap of faith.

He searched for another route down, but could not find one. He looked back at the beach some 300 yards away. People were silhouetted against the fire; figures running onto the beach, shouting above the rush of the flames, distressed parents in search of missing children; children, who knew no better, transfixed by the irrepressible and beguiling advance of the fire before them, the voracious beast that was devouring their holiday. Some, in a futile attempt to discourage the fire, ran with sandcastle buckets and plastic kitchen containers down to the water, filled them and ran back to throw them on the, as yet, untouched bushes. There was little else they could do but attempt to control their panic as much as control the fire.

There had to be a way down. Even the kid Franco, as athletic and able as he seemed to be, could not have scaled the rocks without some kind of aid.

Then Ric realised he was looking for the wrong solution. Of course there would be another way. The boy Franco would have had to use a rope to get up in exactly the same way he used the old rope to scale *la Tozza*.

There was then a huge explosion some distance back from the beach; a great detonation and at the same moment a massive sheet of white flame which soared up into the night; the gas tanks at the camp compound. For a few seconds the whole beach and surrounding area was illuminated as though in daylight. As luck would have it for Ric, the blast provided sufficient light for him to locate the rope.

He found it coiled and tucked into a crevice, secured by a piece of hardwood that was jammed into the top of the crack in the rock. The whole of the rope was at the top of the incline rather than hanging straight down it, which bothered Ric in as much as he had to hope the rope was long enough to reach the bottom.

He tossed it over the side and climbed down as a second Canadair thundered over him.

When he reached the base he set off across the rocks and up the beach towards the groups of campers huddled together. He did not know what to say to the people he might encounter. True, he had found a way out, but it would only be of use to those capable of climbing five or six metres up a rope.

Fortunately the breeze was driving the smoke north, keeping the beach clear.

The first group of ten or so elderly campers were standing together, talking in loud voices as if each were trying to assert their authority over the others. They were an incongruous sight, all standing round in an orderly circle, lit bronze by the angry fire, wearing their swimming costumes. Ric picked the tall one doing most of the talking and, striding into their midst, spoke as loudly and firmly as his gasps for air would permit, "Does anybody here speak English?"

"Naturally," the tall, grey haired man said in rounded, judicial English.

"Then listen to me." Ric addressed all of them, but particularly the man who had just replied. "There is a rope up the rocks at the far end of the beach. It's not an easy climb up, but it will get you off the beach and over into the next bay."

In the harsh yellow light of the flames the man stood erect and towered over Ric displaying a *sang froid* more suited to the deck of the Titanic. "My dear boy," he said, "do any of us look as though we're up for mountaineering? Some of us have just managed to escape from this wretched inferno without serious injury, we're not about to go risking our necks rock climbing in the dark. One life at a time, if you don't mind?" He turned to address his group and ignored Ric, so Ric set off up the beach again.

He came to another gathering, some of whom carried young children in their arms.

A hysterical woman in a gaudy swimsuit on the periphery of the gathering grabbed hold of him. "I can't find Tommy!" she shouted at him in panic, "Or his bloody father. Have you seen them? The bloody fools went back to the caravan."

"Sorry, I haven't. I just got here," Ric apologised, shaking the woman off. He passed on his information about the rope climb at the northern end and, seeing that Manou was not in the group, moved on. As he looked back he saw that a couple of the younger members had taken his advice.

There was a larger body of people gathered ahead. Some of them were gibbering into their mobile phones. As he reached the edge of the group, a bush just beyond burst into flames as though it had been drenched in petrol. As it did so a flaming gas canister flew, like a rocket propelled grenade, past Ric's head and landed hissing in the sea. There was some screaming and a swaying of the huddle in reaction. The campers, he judged by their raised conversation to be French, were a little less together than some of the others, but they were at least discussing their options, which were few and reducing.

Ric explained in his own makeshift French about the way out up the beach, but stressed that the rope climb would not be easy for the not so strong. They thanked him; some of them seemed to regard him as though he was some kind of spectral figure, a prophet from the dark. Even in the heat and smoke from the bushfire this amused Ric, particularly after the curious apparition he had met by the tomb the evening before.

"Where is Manou, Manou Pietri?" he asked dispensing with his French. "Pietri, Manou, Directrice?"

A short, stringy fellow, his body grey-streaked where the sweat had run down his blackened torso, pointed up the beach. "*Là,*" he said. "*Elle est là!*" then he turned his back to rejoin the conversation.

Ric ran on up the beach, the fire threatening to cut it into two distinct halves, separating those at the southern end from the escape route he had found for them.

Random clouds of ash and cinders floated over the sand causing him to duck and crouch as he ran. His body itched and irritated, the salt of his sweat leaked into his eyes and the smoke stung them, and he felt as though the inside of his nose was lined with steaming hot grit. Bodies rushed by him in either direction, but he was no longer in a mood to divert valuable time to people who were not interested in his help.

Then he saw Manou, in filthy T-shirt and jeans, running between the smaller congregations. By her body language Ric realised she was searching for someone; perhaps she was conducting a body count? He ran to her as fast as those in his path would permit.

"Manou!" he called, but somewhere off the beach a vehicle exploded with an enormous thump.

"Manou!" he shouted louder. She was splashing her way towards a small group of campers standing in the shallows, staring bemused at the pyrotechnics at the back of the beach. As she strode through the water, Ric reached out and caught her arm. "Manou?"

She reacted violently to his touch, rearing at him as he pulled her round to face him. She did not seem to recognise him. Her eyes were wild and unfocused, and her face was dirty with flyash.

"Manou!" he shouted at her. "It's me, Ric."

"Ric," she replied just loud enough for him to hear. "Ric, what are you doing here?" She was astonished at his presence. Then she came out of her daze and her face softened. "What are you doing here? How did you get here, Ric?"

"I came to help, Manou, from over the hill. Tell me what I can do to help?"

She looked at him as though he was mad. "Help? In this?" Manou wrenched her arm out of his; her eyes now wild again, shining with the reflection of the fire, her chin thrust out defiantly. "I tell you what you can do to help, Ric." She paused, wiping her forehead with the back of her hand. "You can help me to find Gianfranco. That is what you can do."

"Gianfranco?" Ric repeated in surprise.

"Yes. Gianfranco, Franco, my son."

43

"What do you mean?" he shouted at her as if she'd spoken to him in an alien tongue.

"Gianfranco, my son, *mon fils, u miò figliolu*, Franco, my son." Manou was saying it in as many ways as she knew how in order to drive the confusion from Ric's face.

As his senses returned to him, Ric saw Manou come to realise what in her panic she had forgotten, namely that she had not told Ric she had a son – not until now. And as she had not told him, how could she expect him to understand this secret preserved for so long in the muscle of her frantic heart. Manou lowered her head, searching the black water around her for a way to explain this secret she had kept from him.

"Franco," Ric repeated, grabbing her by the arm and shaking her. "He is about this tall?" he said, putting his hand up to his chest, "dark brown curly hair, green-brown eyes? Is that him?"

She nodded twice, astonished by his accurate description of her boy.

"Come on, Manou. We don't have much time. We must get these people off the beach."

She raised her head and wiped away the tears welling in her eyes. "But they don't all swim the way you swim, Ric."

"You mean they don't all swim the way Franco swims," Ric replied. He remembered seeing the rope coiled at the top of the rocks and now he understood why it had bothered him. Of course the rope was at the top; Franco had climbed up it and pulled it up afterwards. That way the rope would be easier for the boy to reach when he wanted to climb back down.

"What are you saying, Ric? I don't understand. Where is Franco?"

"Franco's alright. Believe me. He'll be okay. I know where he is. He's safe." Ric tried to sound as convincing as possible.

Although he did not know it for a fact as he had not seen the boy safe with his own eyes, he was pretty damn sure he knew where Franco would be. "Trust me, Manou. I know he's okay." He watched her eyes; wide blue staring, questioning, hoping eyes that shone in the reflection of the flames; eyes that did not want to believe him or trust him, and yet eyes that were at the same time desperate to do both.

"You want me to trust you?" she said in a forlorn and reluctant voice. "You want me to believe in you?" She repeated her question without lifting her head to look at him, as though hers was a damning and pitiful accusation.

A shower of cinders spiralled down around them like fine golden rain, and a great barrage of dry heat beat at them with all the force of a blacksmith's hammer.

He knew she had little choice other than to believe him, but to make it easier for her he said, "Look, Manou, it doesn't much matter whether you believe in me or not right now. What matters is that I," he pointed at his own chest so she was in no doubt, "wouldn't tell you if I didn't think Franco was safe." Ric waited for some reaction, but saw none. "And we have to get these people off the beach now or some of them are going to die."

The very mention of death seemed to bring Manou back to life. She looked up and wiped her face with hands as soiled as her cheeks.

"Okay, Ric," she said in a voice that left him in no doubt she was prepared to believe him only for as long as she wanted to.

Given the incredible heat thrown at them from the fire, which was now being fanned in their direction by the strengthening breeze, he could not understand why she still stared at him so. Her eyes flickered at him, but not with the reflection of the flames, rather her brief look was charged with a bitter coldness and an iron purpose; an unqualified promise of retribution should harm come to her boy.

Ric shuddered under her gaze. He knew somehow that hers was a look he would see again; knew it with all the certainty that comes with knowing the sun would rise and the fire would burn itself out, and he perceived a faint sadness within him, like a gentle falling away of hope.

"What can we do?" she said, dragging him from his moment of reverie.

They were standing ankle deep in very warm sea water, as though the ocean had taken on some under-floor heating. The airborne cinders and flyash were now driving people towards the sea, and the flames, having broken through in two places, were close to the line of the scrub that backed the sand. The breeze had prospered into a wind that was veering towards the east, encouraging the fire onto the sand.

"There is a way up the rocks at the far end." He pointed to the north. "But whoever goes that way will have to climb a rope to the top of the rocks; otherwise they will have to swim round the point. Is there no way at the southern end?"

"No," she shouted back, "the maquis is too thick that way, and if the fire goes there the people will have to jump off the rocks into shallow water. It is too much risk, too dangerous."

Right at that moment a cloud of the hot cinders fell on them, some settling in Manou's hair. She did not appear to notice the danger, but Ric at once cupped his hands and threw seawater at her head.

She moved back, startled, and fell into the dark water with a scream as she realised her hair was burning.

When she got back to her feet her hair was plastered wet and the water had cleaned her face. With the profile of her head against the bright yellow flames, Ric grew even more aware of how beautiful she was; how beautiful and yet....

Ric looked up and down the strip. There were four groups of campers banded together, he supposed, by their nationality.

"We have to get these people up to the northern end of the beach. Go and tell them we will be able to get most of them up the rocks somehow. Tell them there is no other way. At least if they are doing something positive it will keep their minds off the alternative. But hurry," he encouraged, raising his voice. "Tell them to walk in the water where the fire has come down to the beach. Better a few urchin splinters than burns. Explain to them what you told me about the southern route being too dangerous. Don't run. Try to walk. It will calm them. You are the director of the camp. Make sure they understand that."

Out in the water the speedboats and other makeshift rafts had moved further out, away from the danger. People clung to the sides of the boats and the boards rather than stay on the beach; a bewildered audience ranged round blazing footlights.

Ric and Manou waded out of the water.

237

Although he had his running shoes on Ric could feel the heat in the sand, so he ran by the water's edge up to the first group. He spoke slowly and concisely, as though he was in the possession of some authoritative mandate. They were reticent to begin with, but after much translation and with the bubble of their hysteria pricked by others about them, they began to migrate up the beach in the direction of the north point.

Ric turned and was relieved to see Manou had drawn the same response from the other sorry groups down the beach.

Progress was slow, but steady. Feet were unsure and unused to wading through the shallows in the dark.

In daylight the waters were clean and transparent; the sea bed beneath visible to the bathers as they observed the small fishes and the dune-like undulations in the sand. By night, the paranoia engendered by what lay unseen in the dark water curbed the stragglers progress. They hesitated whenever they were beset by the rain of cinders, and every now and then a frightened child was plucked from the water.

Ric encouraged them as often as he could without panicking them. At the point where the trees and scrub were at their thickest, the beach narrowed and it was, Ric realised, the only section of the back of the beach that was not ablaze. Once the fire broke through to there, they would all have to take to the water, young or old alike, swimmers or otherwise.

It was as though they waded away through a vast iron foundry or smelting factory, the sparks and cinders and embers whirling around them, like angry fireflies dancing a menacing jig on the breeze.

A Canadair boomed in from the north and disappeared behind them. They gained a light relief in the misty vapours of the brief shower. Some paused for a few seconds, welcoming the change in atmosphere. But the let-up in the formidable onslaught of the fire did not last long.

Then the very thing that Ric was afraid of, happened.

Instead of the fire running along the floor of the scrub to the far northern end of the beach, it jumped across the tops of the tress. A vast sheet of flame, like a bright golden gossamer fabric propelled by the wind, lifted up, sailed high, tumbling and turning, and settled on the pines and the maquis before them. All at once the whole section of foliage where it pushed out to meet the water was on fire. It had been the only area left unassailed by the voracious conflagration.

The limbs of the tall pines and the curling sweeping branches of the smaller oaks caught alight as though fire was sprayed on them. A lone Eucalyptus tree crackled and flamed like a magnificent firework; a tall, princely tree hundreds of years old incinerated in an instant, a blinding flare of yellow-white flame, a brief blazing funeral pyre from which there would be no return.

People screamed in shock and confusion. Many of them looked at Ric as though they expected him to rectify the situation with some miraculous intervention. But now they were cut off. They would have to swim; even those who couldn't swim would have to.

Manou splashed through the breakwater to him, eyes wide, horrified.

"Oh Ric, what are we going to do now?"

Ric looked beyond her out to sea. A gust of wind propelled a shower of cinders wheeling into the night air. And, as they dropped down and died in the water, Ric thought he saw some of them stay strangely alight.

The heat was getting to him. He had to think straight. He rubbed his eyes with his sandy, charcoal encrusted fingers. When he opened them again some of the lights were still there, burning on the water.

Then two things happened at once; two things the refugees from Renabianca would dine out on for weeks, months, and some even for years.

The lights on the surface transformed out of the darkness of the northern point into a vessel of some kind. As their eyes focused through the stinging smoke, a large motor-yacht lit up like a Christmas tree cruised swiftly towards them. And at that very same moment the klaxon of the ship shrieked out a riotous blast of tuneful notes causing some to cheer and others to cry, but all with the same tremendous, uplift of joy and relief.

None of them saw the smile creep onto Ric's face as it dawned on him that it was Kamo, the glorious and cavalier Armenian, who was to be their salvation.

44

Through no great sense of responsibility but, he supposed, through some misguided inclination to superintend, Ric made certain that he was the last off the beach.

A few of the speedboat owners, those with enough fuel and spirit, acted as ferrymen conveying the last of the stragglers to the *Kohar* on their makeshift packet-boats. And between those who could bear the intense heat long enough to make certain no one was left behind, there was considerable back slapping and mutual appreciation during the final evacuation. A grand feeling of collective endeavour and resilience was assumed by all to have prevailed over nature's precocious and destructive energies; the name 'Dunkirk' tripped off many a tongue. Some of the more veteran campers, those who had experienced the vagaries of bushfires in the south of France and Greece, exchanged long knowing looks and shook their heads in disbelief. They knew they had been lucky to escape such a fast moving, all-consuming inferno. And, as if they needed reminding of their minor significance in the scheme of things, an enormous bright-orange Canadair appeared like a ghost out of the black night and thundered shoreward to deliver yet another cargo of salty water into the jaws of the fire.

When they arrived at the motor-yacht they were treated to a sight that was as surreal as it was risible: Kamo Petrossian dressed in whites and sporting a captain's hat complete with gold braid and embroidered badge, strutting about the sun deck, clutching a champagne flute. Between issuing orders left, right and centre, he casually sipped. Every single man in the boat with Ric laughed; a nervous relieved chuckle that rippled like a refreshingly cool line squall across the balmy water.

The Armenian noticed their levity, raised his glass and grinned.

Once on board, Kamo slipped Ric a cold bottle of beer as though he was smuggling him a state secret.

"For you," he whispered and clinked his champagne glass against Ric's bottle. "What shall we drink to?" he added, pretending to search his mind for an appropriate toast: "How about 'Per Mare, Per Terram'?"

Ric studied Petrossian, wondering for a moment whether the coincidence of his quoting the motto of the Royal Marines was carefully contrived.

"How about," Ric replied, "'your generosity knows no bounds'."

"It's true," replied Kamo, with a liberal dose of self-effacement. "Tell me Ric. Be straight with me. Was I too early? Or was I, as you English say, in the nick of time?" He grinned. Even though it was well after midnight Kamo still persisted with his graded sunglasses; his eyes may have been concealed, but his amusement was unmistakable.

Ric drank from the cold bottle and then said, "Oh, I bet you always made it into school just before the bell."

Kamo frowned. "School?" He turned the word over in his mind. "What a coincidence, I was thinking of school only a few minutes ago."

"Happy times?" Ric asked.

"Oh, yes," he shrugged. He arched an eyebrow and his mouth turned down just enough at the corners to suggest he wasn't sure, and added, "in some ways."

Sizeable though the *Kohar* was, she wasn't the largest jewel in the ocean, and with eighty extra guests on board, all of whom were soiled and grubby, Ric decided she had the air of the tender to a mud wrestling competition, a cart waiting in the wings to collect more mud-spattered contestants from the ring.

None of the would-be contestants however, looked as though they had much fight left in them. Most stood about in shocked silence. Some perched on the pristine, pastel-shaded leather seats, far too conscious of their own filthy state to relax in such plush surroundings. It wasn't that they didn't appreciate what Kamo had done for them; it was more that they considered it would be unreasonable to repay him his kindness by contaminating his immaculate boat with their soot-covered and ash-encrusted forms.

The tall, elderly, hawk-nosed patrician who had balked at Ric's offer of the rock climb off the beach, stood, still lecturing his patient devotees as though nothing out of the ordinary had taken place; he was draped in a blanket in the manner of toga, his fine grey hair swept back from his imperious temples lending him a senatorial air; albeit that of a senator somewhat perturbed that his city should have burnt down while he wasn't paying attention. Those in a huddle about him clasped each other's hands and clucked like broiling hens saved from the pot. Ric was aware that the man was prone to glance at him now and then; an inquisitive look that suggested he was building up to broach some inquiry.

Close by, the middle-aged woman in the gaudy swimsuit was berating an astonished older man and a puzzled younger boy about some item of crockery, no doubt a family heirloom, they had both, stupidly, failed to preserve from the fire.

Ami, the Oriental girl Ric had met at Camille's the night before, was going about the throng offering glasses of water and wet towels, making jokes with the children and commiserating with those mothers for whom it was all too much. She was possessed of the sympathetic nature Ric had seen before, a nature usually only present in permanent exiles.

Ava, the blond still wearing not much more than her little blue number, busied herself doing nothing in particular bar providing some distracting eye-candy for the dazed men folk.

A couple of the crew, including the white coated young Asian steward, were applying first aid dressings to the unlucky few who had received burns. The flat-top of a bodyguard, the one known as Bobo, and at whom Ric had thrown his fist four nights before, was nowhere to be seen.

Manou was trying to commit some kind of headcount; reuniting the separated and reassuring the anxious. She wasn't avoiding Ric; at least he didn't think so. Those she sought to reassure appeared to show as much if not more concern for her, desperate to convince her that they did not hold her responsible for the wind that had fanned the flames or the spark that must have ignited them. But then some who had known her for many years burst into tears at her comforting and hugged her the way they once would have hugged their mothers after an argument. Manou's brow was furrowed in concern as she listened to their litany of disaster. Now and again she wiped away a tear as they recounted their individual and miraculous escapes into the night; how they only noticed the presence of the fire when the flames began to lick the guy ropes of their tents and the cinders from the pines began to fall upon their fly-sheets. And at one point Manou broke down as she apologised for the lack of warning given to the campers; but, she told them, the blazing heat, the incredibly hot wind, the parched vegetation, the speed at which the fire spread and the ferocity of the flames....

Ric and Kamo stood side by side watching her progress as though she was an angel gliding amongst her flock. They were transfixed by the change in her composure from dealing with one couple to another; she seemed to know how to address each individual in some personal and idiosyncratic manner; a pet name, an intimate greeting, and more appropriately just the right amount of sympathy relative to the demands or otherwise of each unlucky camper with whom she spoke.

Even Kamo seemed to appreciate her gifts. Though his eyes were concealed by his sunglasses, the look on his face suggested to Ric that perhaps he was not the only man who appreciated and understood the woman before them. There was no doubting the fact that Kamo pandered to his libido at every opportunity; Pela, Ami and Ava were testament to that. But Ric found himself now in the unusual position of resenting the way he felt the Lothario beside him was observing Manou; as though there was something unclean and unhealthy about the manner of his appraisal, something more than familiar.

Then Ric remembered Franco, and how he was probably at the very moment Ric was sipping cold beer, sitting all by himself on top of the tall rock over the saddle, a wide eyed spectator to the fiery picture show on shore.

"Kamo, there's a big rock in the next bay; the locals call it *la Tozza*. It is slap bang in the middle of the bay a couple of hundred metres from the shoreline. Can you drop me off somewhere near it on your way back to Zizula?"

"Sure," said Kamo, not taking his eyes off Manou. Then realising the absurdity of the request he turned to Ric and asked, "Excuse me? Did you say you wanted to be dropped off in the next bay on a big rock-in the middle of the night?"

"Yes. Something like that. Sounds strange I know, but if I'm right, which I hope to God I am, there'll be a young lad perched on top of the rock and we need to pick him up."

"You mean there is another one to rescue?" Kamo pondered this for a moment. "What is he doing on top of a rock in the darkness, Ric?

243

"Oh, he doesn't need rescuing really. Not this lad. He'd be more likely to rescue you. But I think it would be for the best if we collected him as soon as."

Kamo rubbed his chin with his empty champagne glass. "This I have to see. I will go and make arrangements. Besides it looks like it is time to go." With that he walked away forward, acknowledging the sincere thanks of the crowd as he went.

As soon as he had gone, Manou came over to where Ric stood. Her face had assumed the same anguished look he'd seen when he'd first taken hold of her earlier that evening during the fire.

"Yes," Ric answered, "right now. We're going to find him right now."

Her expression softened, but only for a second or two. Then the hard look he had seen earlier returned; the look that suggested that Franco had better be safe otherwise Ric would not be.

Ric didn't much appreciate her reaction, but then, he reminded himself, he was not a parent, so he decided it was probably the depth of her emotional response that he could not comprehend. Maybe it was the unique bond between parent and child that provoked such raw and intense emotion in adversity; a bond he didn't know.

"I'm sure he'll be there," he murmured. But as he went to put his arms around her, Manou pulled away from him, rejecting his comfort as though it was neither appropriate given the company nor warranted given the circumstances.

Kamo appeared, grinning. "I have seen to it." And as he spoke so the large motor-yacht shuddered as it came about.

Ric wondered whether it might have been Manou's very overt rejection of him in front of the Armenian that jolted him, or maybe he was feeling somewhat sensitive after the way he had seen Kamo watching Manou. Whatever it was, he was aware that there passed between the two of them some brief communication; some mutual recognition of each other's presence. And then he realised that although they had met at the bar the previous evening they had not yet been introduced.

"Manou," he said turning to face her, "this is Kamo Petrossian, your knight in shining armour. Kamo," he said turning to him, "this is Miss Pietri. Miss Pietri is the director of Renabianca."

"Miss Pietri?" Kamo asked, smiling and raising an eyebrow. "I think perhaps I have earned the right to first name terms, have I not?"

Manou shook herself a little defiantly and, for Ric's money, a little ungraciously, but she replied: "Yes, of course, Mister Petrossian. Please call me Manou, everybody does."

Kamo preened like a cock pheasant in season. "Ah, Manou, but we have already met, have we not?"

"Yes," she agreed and added quickly, "we have – last night." Then Manou smiled, her white teeth shining out from her rather grimy face. "Mister Petrossian…."

"Kamo, please," he insisted.

"Yes, Kamo," she went on without raising her voice, but apart from the drumming noise of the engines and a gentle slapping of wash from the stern, the deck had fallen remarkably silent. Now those present were watching and waiting on her every word. She coughed and cleared her throat. "On behalf of all of the people, not just our guests at Renabianca, but also all the staff…, I think we, I mean you, have managed to help us get everyone off the beach. May I say how very grateful we are that you have come to our rescue this evening? Without you and your boat it is very possible that some people may have been more seriously injured tonight. And I must apologise for the terrible state we will be leaving your boat in. I am not sure how I, or we, can repay you for what you have done. Thank you." Manou bowed. And as if to emphasise her gratitude another Canadair thundered low overhead.

There was a good deal of clapping and some heartfelt cheering, and many gazed at the shore to witness the devouring flames continue along the side of the hill in the direction of the rocks where, everyone hoped, the fire would burn itself out. The campers knew all too well that they had, at the very least, to be grateful to Kamo for helping them escape with their lives, but many sat in silent reflection, no doubt counting up the various costs of the devastation: their cars, their camping paraphernalia, their clothes, food, personal documents, their holiday, and for some, worst of all, their composure.

Kamo was keen to make the most of his moment in the sun. He smiled and replied to Manou's appreciation.

"I can assure you that sad though your misfortune is; it is my very great pleasure to be of service to you all. And, if I have enough champagne in my fridge, I will try to arrange a glass for everyone to toast our very good fortune." Kamo bowed as if at a curtain call and there was more applause and more smiling.

"Before that, I believe we have one more rescue to perform," he announced. "For now please make yourselves as comfortable as possible," he added, as though everyone found doing so a hardship. "And don't worry about the cleaning; the girls will sort it out tomorrow. Won't you girls?" Ava grimaced, not understanding. Ami smiled and shrugged.

Kamo disappeared forwards to supervise the execution of his hubris.

"See what I mean," Ric said to Manou. "It's difficult to avoid drinking in his company. Must be some traditional hospitality, I suppose."

Manou glowered at Ric, her eyes now distrusting and a colder blue than was imaginable after the burning of the fire.

"Yes, I suppose," was all she said.

Ric felt a shade disconsolate at Manou's attitude towards him. He wasn't sure that he deserved such off-hand treatment.

"Glad I turned up," he grumbled just loud enough for her to hear.

"I did not ask you to come," she snapped.

The woman with the gaudy swimsuit distracted Manou and she moved away.

As soon as she did, the tall Englishman from the beach detached himself from his acolytes and made his way over. Apart from Ric throwing himself overboard, there was no other avenue of escape.

"I say!" He towered over Ric, using every inch of his great height to dominate him the way a swan spreads her wings to engulf a potential threat. "Aren't you that Johnny from the Marines the tabloids were cackling about a while back?"

"Shouldn't think so, pop. Must be some other Johnny. Sorry."

The man looked crestfallen at Ric's reply, but came back for another go. "Well, I suppose I could be mistaken. Have you been at Renabianca long?"

"No, I'm not staying at Renabianca. I came to help out because I happened to know the way off the beach at the north end." He paused, expecting the fellow to leave, however he stayed put.

"Look," Ric said trying to divert him, "you were right. Getting this lot up the rocks was probably asking a bit much, but there were no other options available until Mister Petrossian pitched up." He turned to try and duck under the man's shoulder and give him the slip.

"Can't for the life of me remember his name," he went on ignoring Ric's diversion. "Dare say there is some resemblance between you and that Johnny in the papers though."

"Dare to say all you like, pop. Must be someone else," replied Ric, too exhausted for pleasantries. He barged past the tall man and walked up to the galley to see how Kamo was getting on.

When Ric put his head round the door, Kamo was engaged in a gruff but controlled argument with his steward. "Problem?" asked Ric.

The Armenian grinned at him: "In some ways yes, but in other ways no. We have enough champagne, but not enough glasses. We have enough champagne, but for the wrong palates, I think."

"Good thing I'm drinking beer then," said Ric with a chuckle.

Kamo nodded at the steward, who reached into a fridge behind him and passed back a bottle of beer.

"Thanks!" Ric left them to it and went to the bridge to watch their approach to *la Tozza* on the radar screen. The fellow Bobo was not, he was relieved to find, present on the bridge either; a couple of white-uniformed, clean-cut, efficient types were in charge and bathed in the sinister pink light more suited to a photographic dark room. Neither acknowledged Ric's presence. As the *Kohar* rounded the north point, he saw on the screen a three-dimensional image of the shore, their perceived distance from it and the relief both above and below the waterline; an image not in terms of a human's eye view, but more in terms of contours and colours and the progression of the motor-yacht in relation to those contours, almost like a flight simulator. A bank of dials measuring artificial horizon, swell and current, gave constant readings, whilst another bank appeared to adjust the boat's attitude in concert with the information supplied. It struck Ric as being even more sophisticated than he had thought when Kamo explained it to him.

They left the flaming shore behind them as the north point obscured it from view, but the foreboding glow still lit the sky for miles.

The *Kohar* rolled and yawed a little on the turn into the adjacent bay. She was built to carve her way through open water from one ritzy berth to another, not to pick her way through shallow coastal waters like a fisherman's dory. From studying the screen Ric reckoned the boat drew about four metres, which was why she wallowed some at slow speed, but that would allow them to approach *la Tozza* safely to within shouting distance as the sea bed around the rock sat about ten metres down.

He wondered what the lad Franco would be thinking all alone on the rock, watching the glowing sky and the curious collection of illuminations advancing towards him through the dark; the boat must have resembled some kind of spaceship intent on his abduction. Yet Ric was of the impression that Franco was not the kind of lad to lack for common sense. In the short time he had spent with him, Ric had seen him as a down-to-earth sort of kid; one who saw the difficulties that were presented to him in simplistic terms, probably in as much as they existed merely to be overcome. Ric reasoned that any kid of his age who could swim 200 metres through open water and rope-climb up a ten metre sheer face, let alone one who had to be restrained from doing so in a blinding mist, would qualify as determined and confident. It was evident that Franco's spirit was at home in the woods, the maquis, the rocks and the water, and that spirit was a fundamental element of his youthful enthusiasm. He wasn't the sort to be spooked by the appearance out of the night of a lean greyhound of the sea got up like a fairground harlot.

But, he wondered, how could he not have seen that Manou was Franco's mother? He kicked himself that he could have been so dumb. And yet Manou had none of the physical signs of motherhood that he had met in other women who had born children; her hips were slim and taught and....

Kamo appeared on the bridge.

"I think we will do this from upstairs. It will be easier," he said, and one of the two uniforms in the room nodded and disappeared out of the door. "Like what you see?" he asked Ric.

"It's a lot of flash."

"Yes. It is impressive, huh. Come, let us go upstairs. Our audience is waiting." Kamo spoke briefly, in what Ric assumed to be Armenian to the crewman on the helm and they picked their way between the passengers crammed about the deck. As they climbed the steps up to the flying bridge, Kamo asked: "So, tell me, this young boy we are going to collect; this young boy who stays on a rock in the middle of the bay in the middle of the night? What is he doing there?"

"Fishing I guess, or just hiding out like any other sensible creature running before the fire," Ric said, as much to himself as his companion.

Up on the flying bridge there were screens similar to those in the control room below, only fewer and smaller. The crewman who had left the bridge before them was now controlling the passage of the boat with gentle and deft touches to a more standard helm and throttle levers. Kamo spoke to him in low but authoritative tones and the man nodded his understanding. "I have asked him to stop thirty metres short of the rock. We can use the spotlight from here, but I think it would be best if you and I took the jetski in close. How old is this boy?" Kamo asked.

"Ten years old, give or take."

"Ten!" Kamo exclaimed in astonishment. "How tall is the rock?"

"About ten metres or so from the waterline."

"About the same height as this bridge," Kamo mused. "We can pick him straight off the rock on to the bridge."

"No, the sides of the rock are too sheer," Ric replied.

"Okay. We will go with the jetski. You don't mind swimming in the dark, Ric?" Kamo asked. But before Ric could reply Kamo's face broke into a broad, mischievous grin and he answered for him. "Stupid of me! How could I forget? You like to swim in the night, huh, Ric."

"Save it. Let's just hope the boy is there."

Away over the saddle the bushfire was exacting a heavy toll on the wildlife. The smoke blown their way by the southerly wind clouded the air with the odour of the burning heather, rosemary and pine. And the reflection of the flames from beyond the hill touched every south face with an eerie crimson hue.

A Canadair thundered over them causing some of the passengers still a little traumatised from their experience to duck and gasp.

The rock materialised out of the gloom of the smoke like a tall ghost on sentry duty.

Kamo spoke to the crewman at the controls, who in turn spoke into an intercom.

"Come," said Kamo. "Showtime! Our audience is waiting."

He switched on the spotlight that was attached via a swivel to a circular rail at the side of the bridge. A pencil of blue-white light glowed for a few seconds then grew into the light of a thousand candles. Kamo adjusted the beam to give the light a broader spread and targeted it on the top surface of the rock. He produced a megaphone from beneath the helm controls, which he switched on. It chirped, screeched and whistled all at once, and then he blew into the mouth piece to test it. "What is the boy's name?" he asked Ric, broadcasting the first part of his question to the company assembled below.

"Gianfranco, but try Franco, I'm sure he'll answer to that."

Manou joined them on the bridge. Her face was clean. The skin around her cheeks and chin was drawn tight, and her forehead was furrowed in so much concern that it seemed her eyes would disappear beneath her brow. She was oblivious to any presence beside her, concentrating all her will on seeing Franco alive and in one piece.

"Here," Kamo said, handing the megaphone to Ric. "You talk. You know this kid."

Ric glanced at Manou, but she ignored his offer. "Well, I've met him the just the once," Ric replied, accepting the responsibility only because Manou would not.

A gust of smoke then obscured the rock from view just as Ric spoke into the device.

"Franco?" he called. "Franco, it's Ric. Franco, are you there?"

By now all of the passengers had crowded on to the sundeck and lined the stairs, all peering into the fog in the direction of *la Tozza*, all waiting to see the extraordinary boy who was rumoured to be hiding on top of the tall rock shrouded in the white smoke of the fire.

"Franco?" called Ric again. But it was as if the rock had moved from its last position as the clouds of smoke billowed and swirled before them.

Then, in much the same way as a bank of fog will drift by to reveal a coastline alarmingly close, there appeared again on the bow the great rock, seemingly much nearer and taller and whiter this time. And the glaring beam of the spotlight picked out, standing on top of it, the young, curly-haired Franco, wearing nothing but a pair of grubby grey shorts and a shirt, and grinning and waving in exhilarated welcome.

"*Hey, Ric!*" he shouted. "*Ric!*" he repeated with all the casual ease of a young student recognising a classmate on the way home from school. As incredible as his predicament was to those that did not know him, he might as well have been just another kid in the playground. "*Bona sera, Ric!*"

The passengers below and about them began to cheer at this apparition. Ric was under the distinct impression that had they been wearing hats they would have, to a man, thrown them up into the night air.

"*Hey, Ric!*" shouted Franco, shielding his eyes from the blinding light.

Kamo was confounded. "So this kid walks all the way to this bay, swims out here and climbs up this fantastic rock using a rope? And all of this in the dark?"

Ric lowered the megaphone. "Yes," he replied, smiling as though he had some natural paternal fund invested in the boy. "Quite a kid, huh?"

"Unbelievable!" Kamo declared, not able to conceal his astonishment.

"It is," Ric agreed.

Kamo fidgeted on his feet. "So this is Franco. Tell me, Ric," he demanded perhaps with a hint of annoyance, "where are this boy's parents that they allow him to be here in the middle of the night?"

"Well his mother is here, Kamo," Ric said before the Armenian went off from the hip.

"His mother?" he asked. "Where?"

"Right here," Ric replied. As he did so Ric found himself pointing away at the still waving Franco. "That is Gianfranco Pietri. Miss Pietri here," he said turning to Manou, "is his mother."

Manou was staring at the boy, listening to neither of them. She was trying to remain unmoved by her emotion, trying to prevent the dam of her control from breaching. But overwhelmed by her fatigue and the tow of her own maternal nature, Manou gave up the fight. She raised her hands up to her face to support the weight of her relief and catch the cascade of tears that she was no longer capable of holding back.

Ric glanced at Kamo. His mouth was open as if in shock and his face had taken on a grey pallor. Clearly as taken aback as Ric had been when told by Manou that she was the boy's mother, Kamo could not conceal his reaction. But what surprised Ric more was the way both he and Kamo moved to comfort Manou at exactly the same moment.

45

The elation that followed on the heels of finding Franco on top of *la Tozza* did not extend much into the actual mechanics of his rescue.

Naturally the many refugees from Renabianca filled the decks eager to observe the intrepid Ric and Kamo scale the great rock and retrieve the boy. The entrée to their efforts was met with enthusiastic applause and much cheering. But there were too many eyes focused on the rescue for either of the two heroes to feel anything other than intimidated as they set out on the jetski; one slip or misjudgement of the swell and their heroism would literally have been dashed against the rocks, plain for all to see. The consequent anti-climax was not helped by the ease with which the cheerful Franco, displaying all the gymnastic dexterity of a circus acrobat, rappelled down the sheer face of the rock and leapt onto the waiting jetski without getting his feet wet. The scene proved mildly perverse and was, considering the heat thrown over the hill by the still raging fire, something of a damp squib.

Nevertheless, the irrepressible Franco was reunited with his tearful mother and it was decided that in spite of all the material possessions that had been lost, none were as important as he who had just been saved. All, though still black and blue from the evening's very unpleasant trials and tribulations, were exhausted as much by the great relief garnered from rescuing Franco, as from anything else life in all its eccentric humour had seen fit to throw at them.

Ric, his position as saviour to the masses now well and truly usurped by Kamo, found himself peculiarly excess to requirements and felt rather spare.

Manou, whilst outwardly grateful in the company of others, was casually obtuse with him, even when he managed to manoeuvre her into a quiet corner. He was very aware that Manou's natural preoccupation would lie with the many sorry, inconvenienced and displaced tourists, but Ric's natural instinct compelled him to offer her as much help and sympathy as he knew how. For sure he felt inclined to do everything he could, but he also assumed that having seen to the safe return of Franco and indirectly to the safe return of many of the campers as well, Manou would drop her antipathy towards him.

"Would you and Franco like to stay up at my place while you sort this out?" he asked.

She blanked him and shrugged her shoulders in an offhand manner. "If it is convenient?"

That told Ric nothing, as he guessed it was intended to. And whilst his patience had rediscovered some of its former breadth and depth, he had endured about as much of her recalcitrant manner as he thought he deserved, so he replied, "In your own time then," and left her to talk to herself.

Before the gin palace departed back to Zizula, Ric asked Kamo to run him ashore to pick up his car, which he hoped was still cooling where he'd left it.

The bushfire had by now reached the top of the saddle between the two bays, the tongues of flame licking high into the night sky, and to leave the car where it was would risk losing it. Without the services of his bike, still sad and deflated and attached to the lamp post in town, he decided he would be better off to collect the Citroen when he could.

Kamo took him back to the beach on the noisy jetski while his own larger boat made slow passage out of the bay.

"Thanks," said Ric, dismounting and putting his hand on the Armenian's arm to let him know he meant what he said. "I owe you."

In the eerie crimson glow of the burning hillside, Kamo beamed his trademark cocky smile. "I know, my friend. I know you do. But this night you tried to do something for these people that they did not understand, and especially you did something for Miss Pietri and for her boy. So we will discuss favours some other time, not now. You need to go home and I need to get these filthy people off my nice clean boat." He laughed a broad generous laugh, turned the jetski round and sped off into the night, howling at the sky as he went.

The battered old Citroen started first time and he was grateful, patting the dashboard as the breathy engine spluttered into life.

At the top of the hill he was confronted by a road block set out by the *Sapeurs Pompiers*. The firemen, mooching about in their heavy dark blue uniforms with their reflective chest and side strips, had decided to surrender the small bay to the fire should it spread over the saddle and were amazed when Ric appeared galloping up the hill.

Although tired he felt rather public spirited about his part in the rescue of the campers and felt obliged to fill the rather surly and indifferent bombardiers in on a few of the details. He reckoned it better that they should know there were no other refugees from Renabianca down at the beach.

They listened, nodded much and finally shrugged: *heh, the world could end tomorrow, what could they do about it?* They trudged away as though Ric's was little more than everyday tale of Corsican life: *besides, why had he come to the island if he found it an inconvenience to have to rescue a few campers from a brushfire every now and again?*

He began to wonder why he had bothered, when a lithe fatigue, similar to the languor exhibited by the firemen, spread through his limbs and weighed at his temples.

As he turned onto the track that led up to the *villa*, he smiled a grudging and inevitable surrender; the reaction of an overtired, overworked, underpaid, and without doubt under-appreciated individual. He toyed with the idea of parking up by the tomb and waiting to see which revenant figure might approach him out of the darkness; whose turn it might be to set his mind adrift. But then Ric reckoned that even the spirits had got enough on their plate, what with the forest fires threatening the haunted gorse and young lads playing ghosts on granite chimneys.

Once at home Ric showered the traces of the fire and his evening's exertions from his weary form, but, due to the weakened water pressure from the many hoses of the firemen away over the hill, the flow was interrupted just as he had lathered his hair.

It was the last straw! He finished washing in the pool, towelled himself down and collected a bottle of whisky, a glass and a bottle of cold water from the fridge; a fridge which was, he noticed with some appreciation, still working.

Ric retired to the patio to watch the pyrotechnics in the distance, accompanied as they were by the distant droning of the fire-fighting aircraft and the occasional wailing of a siren.

He poured himself a righteous measure of the whisky. Finally he could exert some kind of control over what little was left of his night.

It was then that he heard the car coming up the track.

He chucked back the glass of whisky and walked out the front just as a maroon taxi was pulling to a standstill in a cloud of dust. Out of it stepped a very weary Manou and an almost comatose Franco.

For a split second Ric wondered whether he should be at all indignant, but then the voice of reason counselled that whatever he had been through during the evening, Manou had been through a lot more.

She held Franco to her side. "You said...?" she began in a feeble tone.

"I did," he replied and moved towards her.

Whilst Franco's eyes were open, there was little going on behind them, and Manou was on the point of collapse. Ric helped them both inside and sat them down on the sofa.

Manou put her head in her hands trying, he guessed, to shut the world out.

He shepherded the boy into the kitchen, where he gave him a cup of water and then put him to bed, dressed as he was in his shirt and shorts; hair matted with sand, fingers and feet blackened and dirty. As he pulled the sheet up to his chin the boy spoke, "*Ric?*"

"Yes, Franco?" he whispered.

"*U miò amicu, Ric?*" The boy frowned.

"For sure, Franco! For sure we're mates. You go to sleep, son."

And with that the boy's eyes closed and he slept.

In the living room Manou had stretched herself out. She faced away from him, lying on her side, and she too appeared to be asleep.

He perched on the edge of the sofa, trying not to disturb her, and put his hand against her shoulder as much to comfort her as to reassure her that he held no disaffection for her in spite of her treatment of him.

Manou was in no better shape than her son; her legs were filthy, her arms grimy, and she seemed to be coated with some emulsified lotion of perspiration and black-ash. She smelt of burnt wood and cheap soap of the kind you find in a public washroom. "I did not know you knew Franco. I am sorry, Ric."

"It's okay, Manou." He was about to say that she could not have known, but the fact was obvious that she did not know for the simple reason that she had not told Ric she had a son. So he said, "He's a good lad; strong for his age."

Manou sniffed and Ric fetched a kitchen towel, but she didn't turn to face him when he passed it to her. She wiped her face and blew her nose and gave it back to him as though he were her handmaid.

Ric took it and dropped it on the floor in case she needed it later. "I'm sorry," he said, "there is no water here. It has run out."

She sniffed and coughed once again, trying to clear the residue of smoke and tears from her congested airways. Then she reached for him with her free hand and grasped his forearm.

"Ric, there is no water in Zizula either." She paused for a while, leaving her hand on his arm, breathing in broken and uneven rhythm. "Ric, I am sorry. I did not believe in you. I am sorry."

"Save it, Manou," he replied. "Save it for tomorrow. You're going to need all your strength in the morning."

Ric got up and fetched a sheet from the bedroom which he draped over her. "Sleep," he ordered, and as he said it she drifted off to join her son in the quiet of a forest untouched by flame.

He went outside and filled his glass. Ric drank the whisky, moving the warm flavours around his mouth, washing the evening's acrid tastes away. He was not only out of a place to sleep, but also fast awake.

In the distance of the crimson horizon the fire surrendered to its craven desires, but close by, deep within his chest, Ric's heart burned with a greater longing. He would trade all the fires in hell for Manou and the boy.

46

The dawn found Ric sprawled on his sofa. When the whisky had slowed the carousel of his mind sufficiently for him to dismount without risk of injury, he had moved Manou to the bed alongside Franco, lain down on the sofa and fallen into a deep and dreamless sleep; a sleep of absolute and perfect fatigue. However, the whisky bottle, which now stood upright and accusing on the patio table, or more accurately what little was left of the contents of the bottle which now stood on the table, suggested his head was well within its rights to complain about his overindulgence. He blamed the fire. It was that simple.

Thankful that the water was back on, he showered, found a pair of clean shorts and tidied up the patio as best he could. The *Sirocco* that had fanned up from the south for the last two days was blown out and the bushfire had either surrendered to the Canadairs or had plain satisfied its appetite. But the silken sand from the Sahara had mingled with the fly-ash from the blaze, so the world was paved in two colours: a faint porcelain blue above and an overlay of dirty beige beneath. All Ric achieved in trying to sweep up was to redistribute the fine, dirty, speckled dust from one place to another.

When he went back inside, Manou was in the shower. She was washing her hair and treading on her trousers and shirt in the shower tray beneath her feet as though they were the first grapes of the harvest. She watched him as he stood in the doorway watching her.

Ric saw the thin scar from her caesarean. He had not noticed it before now. Perhaps, he wondered, it was why she had left him before dawn on both occasions when they had made love, or even perhaps why she had worn her one-piece bathing suit that day at the beach. But, he also wondered, why she should have wanted to conceal the existence of her son from him?

He found the sight of her in the shower captivating, even arresting, and then he remembered the boy was asleep next door. It would not have done for Franco to find him observing his mother so. Still, had Franco not been there he would have been even more tempted to get into the shower with her. It was as Kamo had said the night before, all a matter of timing.

He made a pot coffee and after a while she came out to the patio, his white towel wrapped about her torso, her sodden jeans and shirt over her arm. They wrung them out and he pegged them on the clothesline out the back. Ric wanted to remove the towel and interfere with her the way she had interfered with him two nights before, but her brow was heavy with the burden of a thousand unanswered questions; the offer of making love was not one of them.

They sat at the table and he poured her coffee. She drank without looking at him, staring into her cup, breathing in the familiar empowering hot scent; a rousing contrast to the cool of the morning.

"You want to know why I did not tell you about Franco?" she asked, knowing his mind.

"Not really," he replied. He reckoned that if she thought he ought to know why, he wasn't going to give her the pleasure of finding out he had not the faintest clue.

"So you tell me why you don't want to know and I will tell you why I did not tell you." Manou had woken up on the offensive and following on from her rather wilful rejection of him the previous evening, he found her aggression more than a little unnecessary and very definitely misplaced.

She was obstinate, possibly even obdurate, and Ric remembered what it was that Camille had said of her father; 'resolute' was what he had said, that was how he had described him. Well she was certainly that, he decided; that and some more considering the events of the night before. So, much against his better sense of judgement he volunteered some reasoning, choosing his words with care: "I suppose you thought you might not be so attractive to me if I found out you had a son. I suppose you thought some men don't want the complications of a relationship involving someone else's child but that you were going to tell me when the time was right."

"You suppose, eh?" she mocked; her eyes were hard and hostile for what seemed like an eternity. Then, probably at the urbane honesty of his answer, she softened and the lines at her mouth and her brow eased with some vague amusement.

"You suppose I would care about this, Ric? You think perhaps I have trouble getting to know men? You think you are so special that I would worry if you did not like me because I have a son? *Merda!* You English can be so conceited. You come here looking for summer romance, and when you find it you think no one else in the world is capable of such love; love in the sunshine, in the sea and on the sand. Making love is better when the bed is not so cold, heh?"

"Sorry. I haven't got to that page in your mother's book yet," he bridled.

"But," she ignored him and continued, "summer romances grow like olives in the groves of the Balagne. I can choose to pick this fruit when I want. But a son I cannot choose. He chooses to come to me."

"Hail Mary, full of grace," he replied with a touch too much sarcasm.

"No," Manou dismissed, clearly riled by what she considered to be his mistaken assessment of her belief: "Not Catholic. It is not about being Catholic, or Christian. I told you what happened to the *Giovannali* at Carbini. That is what happens to people when religion is confused with life."

"So why did you not tell me about Franco?"

"I am telling you, but you are not listening to me." She paused for a moment, sipping her coffee, again choosing her words with care. "We don't believe in God as most people understand. We believe there is a higher power; something up there, something beyond the horizon. It has no real identity, but it decides what happens for us. We have to live our lives knowing we can do as much as we can do, but sometimes what we do, what we can do, is not enough. Sometimes it is out of our hands."

"Camille," he interrupted, "tried to tell me some of this; providence and destiny were the words he used." Ric was about to explain to her how fatalism had never been itemised in any of his training manuals, but then decided it wasn't the right moment for his brand of boot leather philosophy.

"Yes, it is true," Manou went on, looking at him only in brief glances to gauge his appreciation. "We say it is *qualcosa* – something, or *quallo quasso* – *là-haut, là-bas*, something up there." She pointed towards the horizon. "It is how we have survived. It is what has helped us get through all the difficult times; believing that it is not our fault but without having any other person we can blame." She poured more coffee, sipped and began again. "I was no different to most of the kids who grow up in Corsica. My father was strict. My life was to be like his life, but it was not for me. Who would want that kind of life at eighteen years? Naturally, I wanted to live like the other young people of France, like the pictures in the magazines; Paris, the Côte d'Azur. My aspirations," she checked his face to make sure she had chosen the correct word, "my aspirations were the same, yes?"

Ric nodded, immediately wondering what his post-school aspirations had amounted to.

"So I worked hard at school and I was lucky to be offered a place at the Université Paris-Sorbonne. My father did not want me to go. His aspirations were what we call *paroissial*. If this place was good enough for him, then it was good enough for me. It is important to remember that my mother came from Paris; it is one of the reasons I wanted to go there and also one of the reasons why he did not want me to go there. He thought everything bad comes from Paris. I have told you of the corruption too. So he did not want me to go. If I wanted to go to university, why not go here in Corsica, to Corte. But I thought I was too big for this island, so I make a big fight. My father would not help me with money, so Camille made it possible for me to go. By this time I was twenty and I was old enough to make my own decisions. Well, that is what I hoped.

But after six months of living in Paris, I had to come home to my father and explain to him that I was pregnant. As you can imagine, it was not easy. But it was not just the anger of the shame I put on my family name, it was also because when I was born my mother was taken from him and this made him frightened as well as angry; maybe he was worried he would lose me too. It is a bad combination when men are both these things; frightened and angry."

Ric recognised both the menace and sadness in her tone.

She went on talking as though she was not only unburdening herself, but also asking for his understanding.

"So he made me tell him who the father was. I did not want to, but he was so angry I imagined he would kill me and the baby if I did not. I have never experienced so much terror. He said he would go to Paris to see the father. Perhaps he would kill him. I did not know what he would do. He got as far as Calvi to take the boat to Nice, then the rest I have told you; the boat was cancelled because of the storms."

"So your father didn't go to Paris at all," Ric offered.

"No." Now she looked about the maquis, no doubt looking for

answers to questions she had asked a thousand times. "No. He did not go to Paris. The police said he did not get on the boat the next day and he did not come home from Calvi.

"At first I thought maybe he went another way; another boat from Bastia or Proprianu, or by aeroplane from Figari. The police said he did not. Besides, my father did not trust aeroplanes. So my father disappeared into the very same air of the aeroplanes he did not trust; into the very same sky in which our future is written. He never came home. We never found him."

She paused and lifted her watery blue eyes to look at Ric. Her voice cracked a little as she spoke: "So, because of me Franco has no grandfathers or grandmothers, and because of me I have lost my mother and my father. So I will not lose Franco because of something I do. And this is why I have to be sure of you, Ric. This is why I had to be certain that you were not just some stupid summer romance before I could let you meet Franco."

He reached over and took her hands in his, looked into her tearful eyes and said, "But if this is all meant to happen; if this is what providence or destiny has designed for us, what can we do about it?"

Manou shook her head very deliberately and, staring intently at their entwined hands, she replied, "Oh, Ric. We have to fight. We have to fight until the end. But what happens in the end; that is what is written in the sky."

Ric let go of her hands and moved towards her, putting his arms around her. He felt the stresses and strains of recent months fall away from his thoughts as he set himself free to think of her and what he could do for her if only she would let him. He wondered what, perhaps, they might achieve together.

After a while of sitting holding each other, Manou wiped her eyes and tried to laugh and smile all at once. The result was an apologetic, stuttering assessment of her pretty hopeless situation. "Now I don't even have any clothes for us to wear. Can you lend me a pair of your jeans and a shirt for now, and can you look after Franco for the day? I have much to do and it will be a difficult day."

"Not a problem. Leave him with me," he replied with as much reassurance as he knew how. But then he remembered it was Monday. "But what about school?"

"Franco doesn't go to school. I teach him at home, and there are other teachers for the subjects I cannot teach; except that now I have nowhere for him to learn so he will have to stay with you. Okay?" She wrote a note for the still sleeping Franco.

Then they drove back to Renabianca through the swathes of razed and blackened vegetation. In some places the maquis still smouldered and smoked with a noxious clammy mist, and here and there small patches of green persisted in spite of the cruel assault from the flames. Much of the terrain was a post apocalyptic wilderness of dwarfish stumps danced upon by sporadic, ashen dust devils.

At the camp a handful of grubby campers, *Sapeurs Pompiers* and *Gendarmes* were sifting through the rubble of the buildings trying to salvage any unaffected items of furniture or food. Four burnt out cars stood in a row in the car park, like the token vestiges of a battle fought in a century gone by. The roofs had fallen in on the shop and the restaurant, and the beautiful and hardy plane trees were leafless, scorched and scarred. There was a news van parked off to the side with a reporter talking into a camera. Both the reporter and the cameraman were smartly dressed in comparison to those others present.

Ric wished her luck as she got out of the Citroen. She smiled and shrugged as though providence would decide how the day went and that it was as much out of her hands as it was in them. She cut a solemn and pathetic figure walking away wearing his oversize blue jeans and his baggy cheque shirt. Manou was barefoot too, as if her plight needed greater emphasis.

The news crew made towards her, allowing Ric to slip by unnoticed.

47

Franco was up and about by the time Ric got back to the *Paviglione* and, as any boy of his age would, he was making himself busy by being nosey. He was out examining the long sandy coloured stone set in the north wall. In one hand he held the strange club-like stick which he tapped against the stone, and in the other he held a sprig of lentisk from the maquis which he had stripped of its leaves. This he was working assiduously around his teeth, as if it doubled for a toothbrush.

Ric fixed them up some grapefruit juice and some *figatellu* and buffalo tomatoes for breakfast. They ate in silence at the patio table. The boy raced through his plate of food, displaying all the appetite of a trencherman, and nodded his cheerful approval when he'd finished. Although there had been something of a language barrier between the two of them before, on the way to Renabianca Manou had assured Ric that Franco's French was as good as his Corsu and that he was not to be strung along by the boy's playful humour when pretending not to understand what was being said to him. It was a facility, Manou said, he had learned when deciding whether or not he wanted to talk to the campers.

So now they had at least a channel of communication open to each other; although that assumed in the first place that Ric's French was comprehensible to Franco.

Whether it was down to Providence or the meteorological gods Ric did not know, but whoever was responsible for the weather had decided that two days of the *Siroccu* was enough punishment for whatever sins the coastal dwellers had committed.

The morning air was clear and refreshing, even though every now and then it was overlaid with the odour of dewy charcoal. The sky was light blue, the sea a deep purple and the sun seemed to be withholding its withering glare. After the rigours of the evening before, a day of cool and sharp air would be welcomed by many.

As they cleared the plates the boy still toyed with the hard stick in his right hand. "*Qu'est-ce que c'est ça*, Franco?" Ric asked him, enunciating so there would be no confusion.

"*C'est une branche. Un rameau*," he replied. Then he added, "*Mais c'est aussi une mazza.*"

Ric understood the first two, which both meant branch, but he didn't think he'd heard the word *mazza* before. "*Mazza? C'est quoi ça?*"

"*C'est l'asphodèle, pour tuer les animaux, pour combat.*" Franco held it high above his head and brought it down as if to beat an imaginary animal.

This play-act caused a light, cold sweat to break out around Ric's cheeks and neck.

"Asphodel, huh! A stick for killing animals." Although he had already known it, the boy confirmed it was a similar weapon to the one Ric had wielded in his dream; the dream after which he had woken up with his legs all scraped and scratched. He watched as the boy proscribed great arcs in the sky with the knobbly head.

"*C'est pour les Mazzere*," Franco said as if to himself. "*Mazzere*," he repeated.

"*Mazzere?*" Ric replied, uncertain of the correct pronunciation. He'd heard the word before, Manou had mentioned them. But there was no way Ric was going to explain to the boy he had seen this club-like instrument in a dream, so he asked, "What shall we do today, my young friend? *Qu'est-ce qu'on fait aujourdhui, Franco?*"

Franco put his finger to his lips in mock deliberation, looked skyward and said: "*Nager? Nutà?*" He made a breast-stroking motion with his arms.

"Yep, figured so," Ric agreed. After all, he had no clothes to fit Franco, and the boy would be just as well off washing his shorts and shirt in the sea water as anywhere else. So they finished clearing up, made the bed, and went down to their own private beach to swim out to the great rock that was *la Tozza*.

They spoke little; happy in their shared silence in much the same way Ric found he was with Manou.

Occasionally, when Franco spotted something of note he told Ric the French name; *sitelle*, in the case of the friendly nuthatch which flitted out of the trees as they got out of the car. Though nervous, the small dark-headed bird seemed to be at ease in Franco's company and followed him about the beach as he ran up and down, no doubt amused at watching the boy imitate Ric at his early morning exercise.

Ric shook his fist at the boy to let him know that he understood when he was the source of the youngster's mirth. This caused Franco to collapse in a fit of hysterics on the sand.

They swam out to the rock. In deference to what he perceived would be the boy's disadvantage, Ric did not wear his flippers or take his mask. However, the boy turned out to be just the pond-skipper Ric had guessed he might be, and Ric had to work hard to keep up with him. The lad climbed up first, causing Ric further embarrassment as he dragged his own sorry weight rather more slowly up the vertical face.

Once on top of the great rock, Franco pointed out where the fire had crept up over the saddle and lost its momentum and so had not fallen upon the small bay.

There was some relief between them that their secret strip of beach was untouched. They danced a jig in celebration and clapped each other's hands high in the American style. Then they sat down, their legs dangling into the small depression in the rock which held the fishing line and the old rusted penknife. They watched as a sailboat laboured along the horizon; a three-masted schooner bound south to Sardinia or Sicily, its white canvas sails filled with the northerly breeze at its back.

As they sat and surveyed the great porcelain-blue sky that bowed down to meet the purple sea, Ric noticed the black stripe that ran through the rock beneath them.

There were small seams of the dark rock that ran through and along the granite surface, like blood vessels standing proud on muscle. In the bottom corner of the hide-away, a point at which he had earlier assumed the rock to be blackened by a fire, Ric noticed a thicker seam of the darker rock, about the width of his hand, colouring the surface. It reminded him of a zebra stripe, the way it ran straight across the rock. He bent down to feel the texture of the rock, and as he rubbed at it with his fingers some of it broke up into small, round fragments like soft gravel. He studied the small bits of rock. If squeezed between his fingers the rock was malleable, almost like some kind of stiff or heavy clay.

Franco saw him examining it.

"*Catochitis,*" he said in a manner that suggested everyone should recognise it when they saw it. *"Insòlitu, heh? Bizarru. Sulamente la Tozza, heh!"*

Ric looked hard at the boy, wondering whether the boy was playing some kind of trick on him; wondering if the boy was in league with the old man he had seen by the tomb, or whether it was simply that he knew the names of the stone in his own backyard.

"Only at *la Tozza*?"

Franco nodded.

'The *Catochitis*' was what the old man had said to Ric; the old man who was nothing but an apparition to Ric on a night when his fertile imagination had run riot with him. But he found it a curious and uncomfortable coincidence that he should be told what this stone was out here in the middle of the bay by a ten year old lad, when the last person to mention it had been an extraordinary phantasm who had materialised out of the night. He worked the black stones in his hands. They left a dull smudge mark on his palms; the same kind of mark one is left with after writing with charcoal.

"*Catochitis*, huh!" And then he remembered to ask about the ring the grey figure had mentioned. *"Pour une bague?* A ring?" He pointed to his finger.

Franco looked up from his daydreaming: *"Si, une bague; anellu. Comme la bague de Camille."*

"*Si*," Ric agreed as though he knew it all along. "Just like Camille's." He tried to recall seeing a ring on Camille's finger, but he could not remember one. He screwed up his face in concentration, an act that was to Franco's great delight. Then it came to him; that day he had been abducted from the beach bar by Kamo on his jetski, when Camille had handed him the cold beer he wore a signet ring on one of the fingers of his left hand.

"Good lad, Franco! Well done!"

Franco grinned, aware that Ric was paying him a compliment and unfazed that he didn't understand what the compliment was for.

Ric watched Franco kick his heels against the hard rock and screwed up his face as he looked up at the sun. He envied the boy his innocence, his blissful, youthful ignorance and his aspirations. But in the same moment Ric pitied his future, his inevitable disillusion, and the burdens life would heap on him when the boy realised life was not always to be lived in the clean, sharp air of dawn.

They sat or lay about on the warm surface of *la Tozza* in the sunshine.

Seagulls wheeled about them in great spirals and banking turns, shrieking their frustration at the two invaders, like children screaming in a school yard. With his eyes closed, Ric lost himself in the harsh, erratic and unmelodic calling of the birds.

Before too long the skin on his back began to feel tight, "Come on son," he said to Franco, "time to go. If we stay any longer, we'll fry up here. *Il fait chaud, huh?*"

The boy shrugged his shoulders as if to suggest it was always hot up here on the rock, but not so hot that one should be concerned by it. He grinned.

Ric walked over to the seaward side of the rock from where the rope hung down. He knelt and reached to pull a length of it up for Franco to begin his descent. But, as he did so, the boy walked round him and jumped clean over the edge, all ten metres straight down into the water.

48

They drove by Zizula on the way back and Ric dropped into the small general store for a few supplies; a football T-shirt for Franco and some washing kit for him and his mother. As much as he felt like a surrogate father, he'd never imagined it might happen. It felt good and curiously natural, and as though he'd waited too long to step into such shoes. He felt as though he belonged to the role, a sensation that was new to him, as new as the company of his young charge.

Kamo's motor-yacht was still moored in the bay. There were a group of garishly dressed individuals gathered on the sun-deck.

Press, Ric guessed. He could imagine the Armenian soaking up the attention as he regaled the reporters with his timely intervention and subsequent rescue of the campers from the deadly conflagration. His timing had been perfect, almost as though he had been waiting in the wings for a cue.

There was quite a gathering at the beach bar, but Ric could not see Camille; he was absent from the throng of tourists no doubt stimulated by their relief in the change of atmosphere. But Ric was not about to take the boy for afternoon cocktails, particularly as it would seem that Camille was very much an integral part of Manou's family. He remembered how Camille had referred to her as 'his child'.

Fortunately he was not waylaid by the obsequious Bosquet; not questioned as to why he had not yet 'gone home'.

They drove back to the house, Franco bouncing up and down in his seat in time to the lurches of the vehicle. He appeared to smile and laugh permanently.

During the afternoon they lay about the house, played cards in the living room and fooled around outside. Ric watched the young boy. He could see Manou in his physical movements, in his facial expressions and in the way he asked and suggested, acted and reacted. There was a softness to him, as Ric guessed there would be to many a ten year old boy happy in fresh company, but there was also a defiant separateness to him; something that marked him apart from other kids Ric had met, like an abiding potential barely concealed in the layers beneath his exuberant and blithe exterior.

Manou arrived at the house not long before sunset. She was dressed to impress in a dark blue business suit and had rented a white hatchback. She had been to Porti Vechju to see Monsieur Grua, her lawyer, and meet with a representative of her insurers. She had procured alternative accommodation for some of the displaced campers, the rest having decided to return to their respective homes away from the island. She had bought new clothes for Franco, and food and wine for their evening meal.

Franco threw his arms about his mother's waist the moment she walked through the door, and he did not release her until she had lifted him off his feet and hugged him as though she had not seen him for a hundred years. And before she had the opportunity to acknowledge Ric in a more familiar way, she was forced to run the gauntlet of Franco's descriptions of his day's activities; a great stream of rolling Corsu, not so much a flash flood as a fast flowing river in full spate. Manou went about her food preparation and the only time she wrested her concentration from her son's elaborate account was when the boy referred to Ric as the butt of some humorous happening. At these moments Manou raised her eyes to glance at Ric with a look of such lambent warmth that he felt his insides turn to a pool of sweet oil.

She poured him a glass of wine, a full bodied red from the north of the island, and she set out a bowl of dark-green olives, the fruity flavour of which added to the already lively confusions in his mouth.

Ric sat out on the patio to watch the evening colours, wondering if his contentment was common to those who looked forward to another's home coming as much as he had looked forward to seeing Manou.

A short time later the three of them ate a simple dish of pasta with tomatoes and chilli, accompanied by a salad of local wild chard, garnished with raisins and walnuts and the wild sorrel that grew in profusion about the island. With the aid of the heavy wine the meal removed any of the smoky after taste still lingering from the night before.

Franco went to bed, as far as Ric could make out, in union with the sun. He appeared, to Ric, to know when his time had come, but before he went he thanked Ric formally for his company, and flashed him a smile so bright it was as though all the lights in the world had been turned on for an instant. His mother oversaw his showering before bed.

"I could not stop him talking," Manou said when she reappeared. "Do you have this affect on all children?" She had undone the top buttons of her blouse and the bottom buttons of her skirt.

Ric could not help but notice and wondered for whose benefit she had relaxed her clothing. "He spends much of the time on his own?"

"Mmm, yes. He plays sometimes with the other children at Renabianca, but I think perhaps he is a little too adventurous for them."

"I'll say! He's a little too brave and adventurous for me at times. You didn't know he had been spending time on top of *la Tozza* on his own?"

"No," she denied. "He would make himself busy and sometimes I would not see him for a couple of hours. Most of the time he was helping the campers carry water, or running errands for people – they used to pay him. I had to tell him to stop bothering them. Maybe that was when he started going to the bay. But I did not think he would swim out to the rock. And you can imagine I did not expect he would climb up."

"Never mind climb up the rock," Ric replied chuckling and shaking his head, "you should have seen him jump off the top. Frightened the life out of me! I expected to find him at the bottom of the sea, but, no, he popped straight up like a cork; incredible. Strange place though, *la Tozza*."

"Strange? In what way is it strange?" Manou asked.

"Don't know really. I get a strange peace sitting up there, like every time I climb up it's as though…, I don't know. It feels sort of safe. I guess that's why Franco went there during the fire. He was telling me about the black layer of rock that runs through *la Tozza*; the *Catochitis*. He said Camille had a chunk of it in his signet ring."

Manou raised an eyebrow and poured Ric another glass of wine. She sipped her cognac.

"Yes he has. It is very rare this rock. I have never seen this stone anywhere else. They say it has special qualities; qualities like people say some crystals have. But I'm not sure if it is true. My father also had a signet ring; the same as Camille has. There was a jeweller in Porti Vechju; he made the rings for them. I think they used to fish together from *la Tozza*.

270

When they were young they were like blood brothers; they were inseparable, I think that is the word, is it?"

Ric nodded. He did not need any more wine; he felt light headed as it was, but he was happy to listen to her talk, sitting out as they were under the great canopy of stars.

"You said Camille helped you get to Paris?"

"Yes," she replied staring into her glass, swirling the amber liquid round and round. "That was the end of the friendship between my father and Camille. Or maybe I should say I was the end of their friendship." She paused, considering her part in their quarrel. "You see, because my father did not want me to go, he did not help me with any money for going to the university in Paris; money for a room, or clothes, or even for food. So I asked Camille to help. I was naïf. I did not understand the problem this would make for Camille. He made me promise I would never tell my father where I got the money. But, when I came home pregnant and my father was so angry with me, I was stupid; I told him that it was Camille who had given me the money." Manou recounted the story as though she was speaking about some person other than herself, but she glanced at Ric as though looking to him for some absolution from her weakness. Her blue eyes, so normally brilliant and lively were now dulled with a distant sadness. "My father said he would kill Camille for giving me the money. He said he would kill the man who made me pregnant. My father was so angry that I think at that time he could have killed anybody. But, he didn't kill anyone. What happened was perhaps that someone killed him and that is why he did not come back from Calvi. But, you see, Camille thought he was doing the right thing for me. He thought he was helping me. Perhaps it was a good thing my father disappeared. Perhaps it was better that it was my father who disappeared; better that than my father kill Camille who only meant well for me. You see this is why I was not so 'fond', as you called it, of my father."

Ric now understood why her bond with the old man was so strong and why Camille had referred to Manou as 'his child'. He thought of her; pregnant, without a father for her child, without parents she could fall back on; of how determined she must have been and of what she had achieved. Then he realised how all that she had achieved in the ten years since the death of her father had been taken away from her in one wretched night of flames; all of it except of course for Franco. It was then

271

that he grasped why she had been so overly-protective of the boy; why he was so sacred to her. For the time being Franco and Camille were all she had left. She had bared her soul to Ric and he was certain, in that way one is certain when one is told a secret which has been kept for many years, that he was as close to her in that moment as he would ever be.

Manou cleared their plates and took them inside, leaving Ric to contemplate his empty bottle of wine.

When she returned, Manou still wore her blouse, only now it was completely unbuttoned and she had removed her bra. She hooked her leg over him and sat down on his lap facing him. "Franco is asleep," she said.

49

"Ric?" Her soft calling of his name was followed by a lengthy silence. Then she repeated it again, but even more softly as if not to wake others close by: "Ric?"

"Yes," he replied without opening his eyes; his mind was too busy trying to place the voice than to wrestle with the task of lifting his eyelids. Her gentle hand shook his shoulder; there was something more important than his sleep.

"Ric?" she asked again from the dark, her voice accompanied by a more urgent shaking of her hand.

"Manou," Ric said, as though recognising her voice at the other end of an echoic telephone line. "Manou, what do you want?" He could just make out the contours of her face; a pale light shimmered off her proud, firm cheek bones.

"They want you to come," she said, her gleaming teeth now showing bright in the darkness. "Come on, Ric. You must get up."

Ric felt himself rising, felt the sweat in his hair underneath his helmet, felt the ache in his knees and hips and the protestations in his lower back at manoeuvring his collective weight upright. Some parts of the jigsaw presented to him did not ring true to the overall puzzle of what was happening; his eyes were open for he could see the stars twinkling above, and his senses were charged. He could hear the irregular shuffling of many feet on parched earth and taste the dull, alkaline musk of sleep in his mouth.

Some way off in the distance, as if to confirm the confusion of his whereabouts, an owl hooted a long and eerie summons to Tartarus.

Still, there was the persistent drumming and brushing of footsteps all around him. But neither were they timed as though square drilled, nor erratic as though in disorderly retreat; there was just the steady rustle and hum of a vanguard marching through the vastness of the dark. It was as if Hades was marching the armies of the underworld down through the Elysian Fields and the Asphodel Meadows of Tartarus, readying skeletal troops to invade the slumbers of those across the river who sought respite from the calamities of their nightmares; those sleepers whose dreams were but an extension of their troubled minds and whose dreams only alcohol and pills can extinguish. And yet the phantom hordes remained hidden in the hissing shadows; elusive and amorphous.

"Ric," said Manou, her teeth shining white and sharp, like those of the tiger in the poem of his youth. "Everything will be okay."

They waited for a break in the audible mass that passed in the darkness beyond. Ric could not understand how such a supernatural force could make such a deafening row; how it was that feet not in contact with the ground could produce such a din? It was as though each phalanx that passed by trod heavier than the one preceding it. The thumping, scuffling, brushing rhythm reached a crescendo in his head; the noise swelling his brain to press against the inside of his skull. Ric held his hands over his ears lest they burst.

And then the noise of the marching faded and grew distant, the murmuring drifting away like chaff on a mellow breeze. And with the dwindling noise so went the darkness and Ric was confronted by a procession of white-robed and hooded penitents carrying lighted tapers; a server at their head bearing a tall staff. They filed by, swaying in rhythm as though pulling a heavy cart behind them, not one of them looking up or paying attention to their surroundings. Their faces, indistinguishable within their hoods, seemed to flicker with a pallid and unhealthy light. There was no heavy cart to their rear; at the back of the long procession, eight of the figures bore a coffin hewn from light wood and on top of the coffin rested a soldier's hard hat. But he drew no recognition from the pallbearers; they shuffled past in hopeless and mute congregation like condemned heretics, denied proper representation, resigned to their inevitable fate, plodding towards their execution.

"Who are they, Manou?"

"They are the *Squadra d'Arrozza*," she whispered.

"Where are they going?"

"They go to slaughter the first born, the innocents."

Ric watched the continuing file of robed spectral figures and wondered if it was he they were in search of. "The innocents?" he whispered in a frightened, almost childlike voice.

"Yes Ric, those who cannot know the coming of their death."

"Are they coming for you and me, Manou?" he asked, as much afraid for her as for himself.

"Me?" she replied, turning from the macabre procession to look at him. "How could they be after me? I am not innocent; for me it is too late. But you, Ric, are you innocent? That is the question you will have to answer when they find you. Are you innocent?" And with that, Manou, wearing a white robe similar to those worn by the ranks of the slaughterers, slipped away from him and ghosted amongst them, like a silent assassin in pursuit of prey.

Ric's feet were glued to the hard ground beneath him; his knees, bent in crouching, resisted his commands to unbend. He felt somehow held at a traffic light, as though a great power was forcing him to watch as the last of the slaughterers passed by. They were either oblivious of his presence, or plain bent on less suspecting victims, but whichever it was they left Ric behind as they trailed off into the darkness.

A presence materialised before him, questioning.

Ric could not make the features of the presence, for it was shrouded in a mist that rose up around him. The more he concentrated on the face the more difficult it became to make out the form it possessed. He felt the presence might be Manou and he drew comfort from knowing he was not alone. He was sure Manou was nearby and he heard her asking him a question, over and over. The sound of her soft voice calmed and soothed him. It came from all around him as he floated through a vast, dark and grey panorama. She was summoning him from somewhere far off in the mist, "Ric, talk to me. Ric, can you hear me? Tell me, Ric, what you know? Ric, you must tell me what you know."

Her commands were as confusing to him as his dislocated predicament. "I can hear you," he replied. "But know? Know about what?"

"About love, Ric," she replied. "Tell me about love."

"I love you," he said, hoping his admission would satisfy her.

Manou's face appeared close to his now; her blue eyes shining, alive with a cold fire that beguiled and disturbed.

"All of you Ric? Is it all of you that loves me, or is there some part of you that cannot love me?"

He saw her face so close to his, her eyes tight shut, teasing her lower lip the way she did when she knew she was about to take what she wanted from him. But somehow he sensed she wanted more than just physical pleasure. There was something more she wanted from him; not simply all the love he had to give, but something more.

"You have my heart," he said, surrendering. He raised his face to hers. If he kissed her he might silence her demands, might chase her interrogation from his dream, or even replace her inquisition with his own inconstant passion. "What more do you want?"

But she refused his offer and pressed him back down. Manou rested her full weight against him and he was incapable of resisting her. There was a manic desperation in her expression now, as though she could not understand his reluctance to commit to her.

"Your soul, Ric? I want your soul."

"I have no soul," he replied. "I have no soul to share. How can I share with you a soul I no longer have." Ric felt his body begin to spin gradually away from her; his form began to turn even though he could still see her face. It was as though her face, those blue eyes, that perfect shape, were the sky all about him and he was orbiting in her sky.

"Give me your soul, Ric," she continued from above, her voice emanating from all the dimensions through which he now revolved. "You can give me your soul, Ric. You must give your soul to me," she repeated. "If you give it to me I will make it live again, for both of us."

"But I have no soul. There is nothing left. There is nothing more that you or I can do." He stared down into the well of his soul. It was deep, and he could not see the bottom.

But for all that, he knew the well was dry.

When he looked up again her face was so close to his that Ric could make out the fine down of her top lip and the tiny lines at the corners of her mouth, the curl of her eyelashes and the whiteness that surrounded her blue, blue eyes. He tried to kiss her again, but she slipped away from him.

When she returned she suggested, "Yes, there is something you can do for me, something you can do for us."

"Tell me, Manou. Tell me what I can do," he ordered, the anger of frustration seeping into his reply. "I will do anything you ask, but how can I know what it is that you want from me if you will not tell me?" He was afraid he might lose her because he did not know what it was that she seemed to expect him to know. But as he asked the question her face began to melt away, as though she was sinking into dark shadows.

"What must I do?" he demanded as she disappeared.

"You know what to do, Ric." Her voice grew fainter now as though she was shouting at him from the bottom of a great cave. "You know what you must do," she said again, and just before she vanished she left him with no choice: "You must do this for me, Ric; for us, for me."

He called out to her as her image faded from his sight: "What, Manou? What must I do?"

"You will know what to do, Ric. Do it for me, Ric, and for us."

And she was gone.

He was drifting again now in the great expanse of grey that seemed to know no end. Ric could not touch any surface or control his passage through this enormous chasm. He was out of control and yet unconcerned because he was so comfortable drifting on the tranquil sea of cloud that bore him aloft.

But the demand she had made of him fractured the seabed beneath his memory. A singular bubble ascended from the fissure, like a silver dome of oxygen released from the aqualung of a diver. The bubble rose smoothly up through the deep, still water until it broke upon the surface of his thought and he could no longer ignore the truth it released.

Now again, someone was asking him to prove his affection, to demonstrate his commitment, to stake his claim in some overt and masculine way, like a gaily decorated bird of paradise fanning its tail-feathers. But this time was no different from the last, except that the last time he had known what to do. He saw the face of another once more; a soft, innocent face pleading, begging and crying for him to stay with her and not to leave her. She had asked him to prove his love by staying with her; the one course he could not take. And when he had returned, it was she who had gone out of his life instead.

Ric had not proved his love for her, so she had left.

He floated once again in the opaque universe and Manou was once more around him. He no longer perceived any need to post his colours, or any threat from any other suitor to his love for Manou; he could see no reason for choosing between fight and flight. And as if by the very mention of the word flight, as if by some surreal autosuggestion, his body suddenly relinquished its belief in its capacity to stay aloft and he began to fall; to fall slowly at first, and then faster and faster, gaining pace until he reached a great speed. As he fell he saw the faces of people from the last few days. Like a passenger in a glass elevator that descends through the many levels of a building and at each level one catches a snapshot of someone they once knew, Ric saw the impish grin of the boy Franco, the avuncular beam of the bar owner Camille and the iron frown of Seraphina his waitress; the self-absorbed smirk of the enigmatic Armenian Kamo and the menacing sneer of his sidekick Bobo; the insidious leer of the policeman Bosquet, the amiable, doughy features of the old cleaning lady, the stern expression of the old man in search of his signet ring, and the wickedly suggestive smile of the woman who always stood in the doorway of the *Patisserie*. Their faces flashed before him one by one. He wanted to show them that he had seen them, acknowledge them and see in their expressions how disposed they were towards him, but they were gone away, above him, too fast for him to react to their leaving.

He felt certain the ground, though invisible below, was now rushing up to meet him. The bottom of the chasm was looming through a hard darkness that now appeared beneath him. His muscles tensed ready for the impact, his nerves tingled in anticipation and his face strained in preparation. And, just as he relaxed and decided there would be no end to his effortless flight, he hit the hard ground with such force that his teeth banged against each other, his head bucked as if struck by the butt of a gun, his arms tried to wrest themselves loose from his shoulders and his legs splayed out either side of him, as though they belonged to some abused or insanely deconstructed mannequin.

He lay that way for... how long he didn't know.

When Ric came to, he was lying in the maquis. He was dazed from the fall and much as he tried to think clearly, his thoughts came in stroboscopic images that dimmed before he had the chance to latch onto them. In effort to save itself from the rough treatment of the fall, his body reacted; his bruised bones cajoled his muscles into levering his body upright in a succession of awkward jerking movements.

He saw a length of wood on the ground beside him. He bent and picked it up to use it as a staff, and in doing so, stumbled in the direction he was facing. Soon his stumbling and staggering joined together to allow him a shambling, lurching trot, which in turn progressed quicker until Ric was running and running fast.

His clothes dropped from his frame, falling away from him the way dust flies off an old dog. He was naked and in his hands he held no longer a piece of wood, but the asphodel club the lad Franco had referred to as the *mazza*.

Ric understood that he was once more hunting in his dream; charging through the maquis after the wild boar which he could hear squealing in terror, desperate in its flight for life.

His feet knew no pain. He hurdled bushes and vaulted dry stream beds, and understood he ought to have been appalled at and arrested for what he was about to do. But none of that mattered. What mattered was to catch the boar. What mattered was to catch the boar and dispatch it, to kill it and to see whose face the carnage of his destruction would reveal.

Almost at the same time as Ric understood the mission upon which he was hell bent, the boar slowed giving him time to take hold of it. He grasped the frenzied, shrieking animal by its hind quarter, saw the yellowed tusks and felt its harsh breath against his face, and dragged it beneath him. He knelt on its ribs, raised the *mazza* above his head and brought the hard head of the heavy club down onto the awful fury of the boar's mad, terrified eyes. He thumped and crashed and splintered and smashed until there was nothing more left of the boar than a bloody pulp of skin and bones and brains and brawn.

And sure enough, through the confusion of viscera on the ground at his feet, a face slowly took shape; a face he had only recently come to know and one that he recognised all too well.

It gazed back at Ric from the hot, muddled mess that had once been the boar.

Ric raised the club up again, ready to launch one final shattering assault on the image before him. He could not bear to look at it any longer. He had no reason to hate this face and yet he felt compelled to drive it from his sight.

Then a sudden stinging slap hit him in the face which caused him to hesitate. At first he thought the stinging was from fragments of thrashing boar splashing up against his face, and yet he knew it was not so. The wild boar was destroyed. How could it have moved? Surely it was now dead?

A second slap hit him in the other side of his face, and on the back of the pain the image of the face before him began to fade. In the water of his sight the image of both the boar and the features of the person began slowly to dissolve.

A voice was calling urgently to him: "Ric. Ric, it is me, Manou. Ric, wake up."

He tried to ignore the voice and tensed to strike once more with the *mazza*, but a third stinging blow landed on the side of his face and the fight left him.

Suddenly there was no face and no animal at his feet. There was only Manou, and he was straddling her on the floor of the living room and he was about to bludgeon her with the *mazza*.

"Ric," she whispered, aware from his gradually relaxing form that he was no longer a threat to her. "Ric, it's alright. It's me, Manou. You are safe now. I am here, Ric."

He threw the *mazza* away, collapsed on top of her and sought to escape the nightmare of his sleep in the warm and enveloping consolation of her body.

50

Ric woke up with the kind of thick head that told him he ought to give up wine, or at the very least corked wine. He wondered how it was possible that he should have such realistic and graphic adventures in his sleep and why they should make him act so. If Manou had not woken him, he was in no doubt he would have killed her in much the same way he had dreamt of killing the boar. Waking up bathed in cold sweat was, for Ric, nothing out of the ordinary, but waking up in the act of clubbing the woman to whom he had but a couple of hours before made love, was….

"You have a very vivid imagination, Ric," she said, "even when you are sleeping." Manou was dressed in her camp uniform of blue skirt and cream blouse.

They stood in the kitchen, wary of each other. Like two lovers the morning after an inebriated one night stand, neither was confident of the others appreciation. But then, he reasoned, it was only natural that she should be wary of him after his hallucinations; they frightened the hell out of him.

"You want to tell me about this," she hesitated, "this thing that makes you do this in your sleep; this madness?"

'Temporary madness', or was it a madness that having happened twice, he could no longer regard as temporary? "No, not really," he replied. "I'm not so sure I understand it myself."

She stepped towards him, laid her hands on his shoulders and her head on his chest, and was quiet for a minute.

He could smell the lavender in her hair and feel the heat of her cheek upon his chest. Her tenderness weakened him and yet at the same time it relieved him.

Then her face, as it had been in his dream, materialised before his eyes and he could hear her say there was something he must do for her; that was what she had told him, he was sure; something he must do for her. Was that what she had said to him? He searched for her face in his mind, but it was melting away again, back into the shadows of his sleep.

Manou lifted her head from his chest and looked at him: "What is it, Ric? Something you are not sure of?" She withdrew from him, still watching him but with an expression that suggested a sudden mistrust of him. Or perhaps it was the way she turned her face so slightly down and to the left, obscuring the side of her face so that she looked up at him around the veil of her hair, as though questioning him, as though she was expecting some response from him.

But Ric did not know what she expected of him or what more he should tell her. Should he tell her he had endured the same dream before? Should he tell her that the first time the bizarre hunt had invaded his sleep he had been on patrol deep in the Hindu Kush, and in his dream hunt he had seen the face of his wife, and the next day they had informed him of her appalling accident? Was there any point in telling Manou that he had not made it home before his wife had died and that much of him had died with her? And should he tell Manou that at last he felt he was coming back to life because of her, as if she had dragged him from his interminable hell?

Just at that moment Franco walked in; grinning as usual, his brown hair an unruly mass of curls.

Manou turned from Ric and began to peel a bowl of fruit for Franco's breakfast. She ignored Ric as she did so, but when she had finished what she was doing she said, "I must go. I have to go to Porti Vechju this morning," and began to gather up her jacket and handbag.

"Going to see Monsieur Grua?" Ric asked. He feigned innocence, though he knew she would recognise his words as anything but. Ric wanted her to know and take comfort from knowing that he was aware all was not simple in her world either.

But she took his question in her stride and carried on checking the contents of her new bag.

"Yes," she replied, without lifting her head or showing any other visible reaction. "Today I have some decisions to make, Ric. Maybe I will tell you about them when I get back this evening." She turned to him and smiled and rolled her eyes, suggesting to him that there was much she would rather do than go into town and meet with the vulturine Grua.

"But for now," she walked to him and kissed him on each cheek, as though any more public a display of affection would have been inappropriate in front of her boy, then she ruffled Franco's hair into an even more untidy mop, kissed him on top of his head and said: "I must go. You are happy to be with Ric for the day?"

Franco mumbled a rather bored acknowledgement of his fate without looking up. He would put up with Ric for one more day if there was absolutely no possibility of any alternative. And besides, he was used to being deserted by his mother. It was all the same to him.

"Then, goodbye, I will see you two later. Take care of my boy, huh?"

As soon as she was gone, Franco turned and fastened Ric with a wide-eyed, conspiratorial grin. "*Miraculatu,*" he said. His mother was gone, the day was theirs.

51

To divert his thoughts from more serious matters, Ric turned his attention to an easier task at hand; the recovery of his bike from the front at Zizula. There was no easy way for him to remove it with flat tyres, so he would have to remove the wheels before he could get new tyres fitted at the tyre shop in Porti Vechju.

Franco was happy to be his grease monkey and even happier to chat as they bowled along in the old Citroen on the ride into town.

The atmosphere was tepid. An agreeable though cooling breeze glided down from the north as if to remind the lotus eaters that summer really did have to come to an end sometime; not that any of them cared as long as the weather held until it was time to leave.

By the time they got back to Zizula and reattached the wheels with their smart new tyres, the cafés and bars were filling up with their late lunchtime clientele.

With the same curious ability possessed by his mother, Franco knew what Ric was thinking before he had the chance to say it.

"*Manghjà? Manger?*" the boy suggested, nodding with considerable enthusiasm. Then he added: "*Ziu Camille, mon oncle?*"

"Sure! Why not? I could do with a word with Uncle Mosca myself," Ric replied. "You go," he nodded in the direction of the beach bar, "and I'll follow as soon as I've checked the bike works okay."

And with the permission of his elder, the boy tore off down the beach in search of his uncle's affection and generosity.

Ric put his tools away, unchained the bike, kicked it into life and gunned it down the strip out of town. As he did so he caught a glimpse of the young boy racing up the beach. At the town sign Ric slowed, squeezed the front brake, opened the throttle and slid the back of the bike round in a standing turn. The bike was no worse for wear from its couple of nights abandoned in town. He rode casually back to the beach and parked up next to his car. He chained the bike up to the lamppost and locked the car, grabbed his phone and set off without any particular hurry towards Camille's beach bar.

Away in the bay nothing stood out of the ordinary; the dinghies and Hobie-cats jostled on their moorings, the flags along the beach swung and flapped in the lazy breeze. Out in the bay a few of the waves tried their best to whip up a white-cap here and there, but even the purple sea was unable to foster any great enthusiasm. The cooler breeze of morning was being chased away by the warmer *Mezzogiorno*, released as it was by the heating up of the land through the day. Though every day must have seemed the same to everyone else, each one blending in similar fashion into the next, to Ric even yesterday seemed a lifetime away; to him each of them seemed very different and intensely precious, as though there was slim chance they would ever be repeated.

"*Salutu Ric,*" said Camille, his broad smile suggesting he was pleased to see Franco's chaperone. He handed Ric a *Pietra*.

This morning even Seraphina wasn't glowering at him. "Thanks Camille," he said, pulling out a chair.

"No," said Camille. "It is for me to thank you for you bring Franco to see his uncle. I wish that he comes here many times, but he has to study, eh."

"Where is he?"

"Oh, he is talking to people on the beach. He is artist, eh; master of the art to get ice cream without paying." He paused and they turned to watch the boy in animated conversation with a family fifty metres up the beach. Then Camille sat round to face Ric, his face a little serious, the bruising above his left eye now no more than a dull discolouration: "They say you went to the beach when there was fire at Renabianca. You went there by *la Tozza*, no?"

"Yes," Ric replied. "I tried to get by on the road, but the fire was too strong. I knew I could get into the campsite from the bay, because I had met Franco there a couple of days ago and he had shown me the path."

"Very dangerous," Camille remarked. "The fire, it move very fast; very dangerous. You are brave man. I knew this before, but now I know for certain it is true." The old man pursed his lips to the side, an act designed to inform Ric that he had dedicated some considerable time in reaching his conclusion.

"Thanks, Camille. That beer was just what I needed."

Camille turned to the counter and mouthed something at Seraphina. She broke her daydreaming and came to the table with two fresh bottles of beer. She even managed something approaching a smile for Ric, which, he decided, she should not have for her face was not given to smiling.

They sat and surveyed the scene. The large blue yacht, the *Kohar*, still dwarfed the other lesser craft that had slipped into the bay for lunch. There was a pale brown sloop Ric had not noticed before moored just beyond the buoys marking the swimming area. She was ten or twelve metres at the water, wooden hulled and old, judging by the ornate joinery, but sturdy like she would not be intimidated by the average squall. They both watched her ride on the gentle swell.

Camille said: "My boat, eh! I bring it yesterday from Porti Vechju. This winter maybe I go to Turquie."

"Beautiful, Camille," replied Ric: "She is very beautiful." The pale tawny colour of her hull was distinctive; very different among the more ubiquitous, sterile white.

"Yes," Camille agreed, nodding with all the confidence that there was not another sailboat in the whole Tyrrhenian to match her.

"*Cèdre du Liban*," he said as though the boat was carved from some mythical medium. "In the war we use the boat for…," Camille rubbed his fingers together as though the friction between them might bring the words to him.

"Smuggling?" suggested Ric.

"*Si. Esattamente!*" the old boy beamed. "In the war, we smuggle guns into the bay at *la Tozza*. Many great adventures!" His eyes twinkling with mischief. Then he shook his right hand as though he was trying to flick water off it. "Dangerous too, eh!"

"What's she called?"

"*Mara*," Camille replied and then repeated the name as though he hadn't heard it in a long time, "*Mara!*" The M was deep and warm, the first *a* was long, and the *ra* at the end was short. His eyes took on a lost and dreamy glaze.

Ric thought to ask him what the name meant, but he was unwilling to interrupt the old man's recollections. He found himself looking at Camille's hands, trying to catch sight of the signet ring he wore on one of the fingers of his left hand.

"Manou told me you and her father used to fish from *la Tozza* when you were children. I guess that's why Franco goes there."

Camille raised his right eyebrow. "Oh, yes. We were fishing at the rock when we were very young, before the Italians and the Germans come. For Gianfranco and me it was a special place."

So the boy had inherited his grandfather's name and his mother's smile. "You go fishing there with young Franco too."

At this Camille shrugged; a 'so what, who cares' kind of expression on his face, as though this was something over which he could exert no control and therefore something for which he could not be held responsible. He wore the face of a kid who'd pocketed an apple after it had fallen from the fruit stall. He coughed a muted reply; a noise that was as affirmative as it was non-committal.

"Good for you," Ric said. "I would have done the same."

The reassurance helped Camille. He sat up a little straighter, his pride restored.

"Manou told me you and her father had two rings made, each one set with a stone taken from the *Catochitis* that runs through *la Tozza*." Ric asked: "Is that right?"

He didn't want to dredge up painful memories for the old boy, but a couple of pieces of the jigsaw from the last few days were, as far as he was concerned, not yet on the table.

"It is true," said Camille, turning and offering his left hand.

The signet ring was, like the finger it adorned, old and weathered, and larger than one had the right to expect of a man of Camille's modest size. It was plain in both design and make up; unpretentious and even rather unremarkable in an ordinary and traditional way. The goldsmith had not tried to fashion an item of exquisite jewellery. It was a simple and unsophisticated gold ring, dulled with age and with a protruding lump of smooth black stone set in the round head. If there was anything extraordinary about Camille's signet ring it was that the inset stone was as dark and dull a shade of black as Ric had ever seen. It reflected no light and had no lustrous shine to it whatsoever. It reminded Ric of the dark eyes of a corpse.

"*Attinzioni*," Camille said. He took hold of Ric's right hand with his large free hand, twisted it, and ran the top surface of his signet ring across the open palm, then he let go.

Ric examined his palm. The stone of the ring had left a dull, dark streak, like a thick, but faint charcoal line. A diagonal line that was very much in evidence one minute and virtually invisible the next; almost holographic in the way the image was present on the palm when viewed from one angle and then gone the moment he altered the angle of his hand. Ric also noticed that the marks left by his rubbing of the rock in his hands from the day before when he was sitting on top of *la Tozza* with Franco, were still faintly visible, like the last vestiges of an old bruise, but again only when he viewed his palm from an offset angle. "Manou said people think it has some strange powers; the *Catochitis*."

But Camille was acknowledging some of his customers who were leaving the bar.

Ric looked round to see where Franco had got to. Seraphina was busy serving and the boy was no longer to be seen with the family down the beach.

"It is true." There was a rascally twinkle to Camille's eyes. "They say if you touch the *Catochitis* you cannot be," he mimicked wide and mesmerised eyes, and waved the blunted fingers of his right hand around in front of them, "you cannot be...,"

"Hypnotised?" Ric offered.

"*Sì. Ipnotizà. Esattamente. Hypnotisé.*" He rolled his eyes as though suffering from a sudden dementia. But then Camille ceased his play acting and fixed Ric with a stern and serious scrutiny. "*Mà*, perhaps it is true, eh? Most things we understand; some things we do not." He tapped his forehead.

"Like women, eh, Camille," Ric chuckled and his host burst into a deep and guttural laugh that ended in an explosive fit of coughing. "It's a special ring, Camille; unique?"

When Camille had finished rearranging the carpet of his chest, he nodded. "*Sì*; one for Gianfranco and one for me."

"But Gianfranco disappeared, didn't he, Camille? Manou told me about when he went to Calvi and never came back. So that means your signet ring is unique."

The old fellow stared at the sand beneath his feet and Ric wondered if the disappearance of Manou's father was still too unpleasant a memory for him.

"I'm sorry Camille, I don't mean to pry."

But that was exactly what Ric was doing, prying, and if his host realised it, which Ric reasoned he probably did, Camille didn't appear to feel the need to deter him from doing so as he had done a few days before when asking about Manou.

"It's okay. It was long time, long time ago," he muttered in a manner that suggested he believed unpleasant acts or happenings, if not called to mind every so often, would naturally pass on into the foggy province of history.

"Manou described him as a 'man of the maquis'."

"*Oh, si,*" he shrugged again. "It is true. He was," he hesitated, "hard man, just as I have said. He could be hard; not so forgiving, you would say. It was very difficult for Manou." Then he laughed in a resigned and bitter manner. "And me. Oh si, he could be difficult for me too. And I was his friend. His father also was same; very hard – *granitu*, eh. You know, like *la Tozza*, hard like rock and *feroce*, fierce, like paladin. You know what it is; a paladin?"

"I think I do," Ric replied, and as the old boy was obviously waiting for him to carry on, "They were warriors; Knights of the Court of Charlemagne. We call them the twelve Peers; a bit like the Knights of the Round Table I suppose. They fought the Moors, didn't they?"

"*Ghjustu!* Yes; but in Spain, not here in Corsica. But here our ancestors fought also the Moors." Camille smiled evidently pleased with his history lesson. "We have the stone warriors here. You can see them at Filitosa. They are carved from stone. But I think they are from before the time of Charlemagne. People like *mitologia*. Always. They like history. History and sun together make people feel *intellettuale*. You can see these stones in strange places. Where you are living, the house, *Paviglione*, where Gianfranco lived when we were young; there is a stone Paladin. It is fixed in the wall."

Ric nodded; he had seen the strange long stone. But then the implications of what Camille had just told him sunk in. He felt the blood drain from his face and a frisson of electricity ran up his back. Ric suddenly felt as though he was being watched.

"In the house where I am staying?"

"Yes," Camille confirmed. "It is in the wall; a big stone. Like this." He outlined a rectangle with his hands that was roughly the same size as the block of stone Ric knew from the north wall of his house. "It brings luck, eh."

Ric felt a little dizzy. "It is where Manou's father lived?"

"*Si*," Camille confirmed again, "in the house where you are living. You have seen it?"

"Yes, Camille. I have seen it," he said, then added; "and a lot more besides."

They sat, comfortable in their own meditations. The old boy sipped his beer while his now well informed protégé tried to fathom the depth of the information he had just received.

After a few minutes of juggling the skittles of thought flying around in his head, Ric arrived at the only conclusion open to him; the curious apparition he had met two nights before by the tomb was Manou's father. Naturally such a conclusion troubled him. For if indeed it was Manou's father, or more accurately the spirit of Manou's father, then what might happen to the other faces he had glimpsed in his more recent nocturnal fantasies.

Ric felt nervous and a little separate from those about him. Even sitting in the bright afternoon sun on the sandy strip, surrounded by the convivial beachcombers and cheerful sun-worshippers, eating and drinking, talking and laughing in the bar of his most affable old host, even when immersed in the warm hubbub of their reassuring conversations, he perceived an edgy, fretful, uncertainty about his own existence. For a brief moment he wondered whether or not all those about him were alive, or whether the whole scene was one great transcendental joke being played on him; some droll payback for a crime or affront he could not recall committing. Or could he?

Then he remembered Franco.

He turned in his seat, expecting to see the boy seated behind him making a meal of an ice cream, but he was not there. "Where is Franco?" he asked Camille.

The old boy turned his head, his white hair catching the breeze and standing up straight for a moment. He growled at Seraphina in Corsu; a similar enquiry to Ric's. She shook her head and then went behind the counter to see if the boy was hiding there. He wasn't. She went behind the shack. He wasn't there either.

Both he and Camille stood and looked around the tables at the beach bar to see if Franco was sitting with some of the other customers. He was not. They looked up and down the beach, but neither was he sitting with any of the sunbathers. They checked the water in case he was swimming. There was no sign of Franco anywhere. He was nowhere to be seen.

A small, but shrill voice whined in Ric's ear, and he began to be concerned. Very soon his concern swelled into a weakening and disturbing worry, and the longer Franco did not appear the faster his worry magnified into frantic alarm. After a few minutes frenzied search, Ric recognised the distress and terror that now raced unchecked through his own form.

Franco was gone.

52

Panic was a by-product of fear, Ric reassured himself as he hurried along. At least that was what he always told himself whenever he perceived the chill bubbles of calamity quickening through his body.

He asked at the dinghy hire hut and the sun-bed rental if they had seen Franco. He asked the car park attendant, the sand sculptor, the souvenir seller, the café waiter, the pharmacist, the young girl on the check-out at the general store and even the wizened, old gnome at the tabac booth. He continued past the spiny buckthorn tree, the Jujube from which Zizula derived its name, along the promenade of stalls and shops, most of them now open again after their late lunchtime closing, and in his halting French he asked if any of the young, docile and rather disinterested staff had noticed a young lad, so high with much curly brown hair, pass by.

But no one had seen the boy.

Ric felt a hollow well of worry fathom within his chest. The more Ric asked the same question and the more he received the same negative answer, the higher up the well the bitter frost of alarm rose.

Camille was busy surveying the beach, yet Ric was sure they would have seen Franco sooner if he had been there.

He hoped that the young boy would appear at any moment and kept telling himself that that would be the most likely outcome. Franco was as mischievous as any ten year old and had probably run into some friend from Renabianca or a school chum. They were probably hiding somewhere, giggling as they observed Ric dashing about like a headless chicken. But then Ric remembered Franco didn't go to school; his mother educated him at home. The boy spent most of his time dawdling about the bay at *la Tozza*; maybe he didn't have too many friends.

Ric tried to think straight. He paced back up the road. He was trying to contain his physical self as much as control his muddled mind. His pulse raced and the sweat that collected at his hairline irritated him. He began to feel sick at his own inability to influence what was happening.

The brunette from the bakery came out of a shop and he nearly ran her down as he looked in every other direction except the one in which he was hurrying. She flirted with her eyes and mouth, and pretended to be sad when he mentioned Manou's name. But her face tightened in concern when Ric explained the situation to her and she soon sensed his apparent anxiety.

She would help him of course. Naturally she knew Manou and Franco, and Camille. Who did not? She was sure he would turn up. You know children, she said, and after all this was Zizula. Who would take a child from this quiet cul-de-sac? But there was a *Gendarme* she knew. She would go.

As he strode back towards the beach he realised the woman had been right. Zizula was a cul-de-sac. There was pretty much only one road into Zizula, granted there was the small road up towards his house and Cirindino, but that was a slow and winding route out. If someone came into the town to abduct a child they would know there was only the one suitable exit – the same way they had come in. Besides, Corsica was an island; abduction would be difficult and extraction even harder.

Ric went to the kitchen door of the hotel. It would not open from the outside. He marched round the front. He wasn't exactly dressed for the hotel, but he wasn't bothered. The reception desk was deserted so he went into the kitchen. There was no one there either, but then he heard someone talking around the far corner. The portly chef was in conversation with himself, poring over a large tureen of *bouillabaisse*. He was embarrassed when he realised Ric had caught him arguing with his own recipe. But, no, he had not seen the boy. Of course he would keep a look-out for him. However he didn't see much back here in the kitchen; you see it is the fate of the chef never to see....

As Ric turned on his heels the chef asked if he wanted to come for dinner; this particular *bouillabaisse* he was addressing would be *eccezziunale?*

Ric in his increasing frustration shoved open the door to the patio and it banged loudly against its backstop. A handful of hotel guests turned from their coffee at his interruption.

Alone at a table, a table that had recently been occupied by others judging by the spread of used cups and saucers, sat the policeman Bosquet.

For perhaps the first time Ric was pleased to see him. He was wearing a rather formal dark suit, tie and white short-sleeved shirt. His jacket was hung over the back of his chair. He was polishing off a plate of cheese and biscuits.

Ric pulled out a chair opposite him and sat down without waiting to be asked. He sat with his back to the sea so that Bosquet had nowhere else to look other than directly at him.

"René, my friend," Ric began as casually as his enervated state would permit, "I see you are having another demanding day in paradise."

René Bosquet chewed his mouthful with patient concentration; a cow ruminating in a field of silage. When he had reached a stage at which he was confident none of his food would be lost if he opened his mouth, he wiped his lips with a serviette and fixed Ric with a disapproving gaze.

"You did not take my advice, Mister Ross."

"Your powers of observation serve you well, René," Ric began, "and it is your powers of observation that can be of service to the local community right now. Have you by any chance seen…?"

Bosquet interrupted him. "Why have you not taken my advice and returned home?"

"And I thought we were on first name terms, René? Does this mean we are no longer friends? And just when I'd grown to like your beautiful island." Ric flavoured his levity with a pinch of sarcasm.

"It is no more my island than it is yours," Bosquet replied. "I am not from Corsica and I would prefer not to be here. I would prefer it if the island belonged to Italy; it would be less trouble. But, you know, even the Genoese gave it away. But this is however not the issue as I see it. The issue, Mister Ross, is that you are trouble. This, all my information suggests; trouble which could be avoided if you took the simple step of leaving Corsica. And I would like you to go home." Bosquet's face changed in line with the hardening of his tone. The flaccid jowls that hung about his chin seemed to draw up like the undergarments of a Can-Can dancer and his cheeks and forehead took on a hard-baked consistency that suggested insult and injury were anathema to his features.

"So I tell you for the last time, the very last time, go home, go anywhere, but go before you leave me no alternative but to find a way of having you removed." The effort of his threat was as much as his system could take and, having summoned all the serious intention he could manage whilst at the agreeable harmony of his lunch table, Bosquet exhaled, his frame deflating like a punctured dirigible.

"Haven't got time for all that now, René, I need your help." Ric wondered what it would take to get Bosquet back on side; that was if he had ever been on it in the first place. "Tell you what, René, you're a straight fellow. If you help me with my little problem, I promise to go home as soon as my little problem is solved. That sound fair?"

Bosquet shovelled another hunk of cheese into his mouth and tossed a biscuit in after it for good measure. The idea obviously bore consideration as he made Ric wait while he chewed it over.

However, before he swallowed the contents of his contemplation he asked: "Okay, Ric. You tell me what your problem is and if I can help you to solve it, then you promise me you will leave Corsica. Is that a deal, Ric? I think it is a good deal for you, because the local police have already been informed that you are here and," he waved his left hand like a monarch waving to his subjects, "I can request them to detain you on whatever charge comes. So I don't care whatever you do; for my part I have other business that is more urgent and important than repatriating an unwanted visitor, which is without doubt the correct term for you, is it not?"

It occurred to Ric that Bosquet had agreed to his offer too readily, but now that they were back on first name terms again and the policeman had cleared his plate and would therefore be more relaxed, he hoped a status quo might be achieved. So Ric threw his hand in: "I was here on the beach today with a young lad; son of a young lady I have met. The boy's name is Franco, Franco Pietri. He about this tall," Ric lifted his hand, "has curly brown hair, greenish-brown eyes, local lad, about ten years old."

"Yes," René Bosquet encouraged. "So what is your problem with his young boy, Ric?"

"My problem is, René, I've lost him."

"Very careless of you."

"Yes, I agree, René. First time I've lost someone else's kid. Can't say I like the feeling very much."

"But," Bosquet interrupted, "people, even children, are rarely lost. You would be surprised. Usually it is because they are not where people expect them to be. But, everybody is somewhere. Is it not so?" He shrugged his shoulders. "Although sadly in my business some of them are not always in the best condition when we find them, if you understand what I mean? However, I am absolutely certain that in this case this is not so."

Ric suddenly got a nasty feeling he was being played along by the obsequious policeman. He felt a warm, crimson embarrassment rise in his cheeks and the muscles of his throat tensed in reaction. "What do you mean, Bosquet?"

He smiled; basking in the power granted him by his knowing something the young man opposite him clearly did not.

"You know where Franco is, Bosquet, don't you." It was very much an accusation and not a question. Ric stood up without moving his chair back and in doing so upset the table in Bosquet's direction; the crockery slid into the man's lap. The other guests around the patio fell quiet; they were all very suddenly distracted and absorbed by the commotion and by the intriguing possibility of a fracas.

Ric spread his feet and clenched his fists. "Where is Franco? Come on Bosquet. Shape up or so help me I'll...."

"Calm down, Ric. Remember we have a deal; I help you and you go home." Bosquet stifled a chuckle and waved Ric to sit back down. "Your promise of violence will not help your situation. It will only serve to provide me with an excuse for removing you from what is a very delicate and difficult situation. And do not concern yourself with this boy. Young Franco is perfectly safe. He is with his father."

"His father? Where?"

Bosquet inclined his head to look beyond Ric, out into the bay; he nodded in the general direction of the sea. "He is with his father on his father's very beautiful yacht. Oh, I see they are going for a cruise."

Ric turned as he stood and looked for a yacht heading out of the bay. For a moment he wondered whether Bosquet meant Camille, but the little wooden yacht was moored just as it had been a few minutes before. Besides, there was precious little wind; not really enough for a sailboat. The only boat on the move was the big, blue-hulled *Kohar*, gliding serenely towards the southern point.

He turned back to look at Bosquet. "You mean Petrossian?"

"Certainly, Ric; I mean Monsieur Petrossian. Monsieur Petrossian is the boy's father. And now, Lieutenant Ross," he snarled as he pushed the table away, "I believe it is time for you to be leaving us. Good day."

53

Much as Ric wanted to, there was no profit to be had from allowing his frustration and guilt to get the better of him. And rather than cause any greater disturbance in front of the other guests on the terrace of the hotel, he decided to try and plug the policeman for some more information; at least that way he might come away with some slight gain.

Unfortunately Bosquet had not only finished with his meal, he was done with talking to Ric as well. He would not make eye contact with him.

"If I didn't know you better, René, I might be tempted to think you were on Petrossian's payroll."

But at this Bosquet simply got up from the table, wiped his moustache and his mouth with all the attendant detail of an actor removing his make-up, and left muttering, "You think what you like, but think carefully." He left the patio door open behind him.

Ric sat down at the empty table, oblivious of the attention he had attracted. His mouth was dry and a hollow pit opened in his stomach, into which ridiculous and useless ideas cascaded. If Bosquet was the policeman he claimed to be then surely he was supervising, or overseeing in some way, Franco's curious abduction, and surely, therefore, Petrossian must have the question of his parental rights over Franco under some form of legal review.

Ric imagined the locals racing to light beacons on the string of Martello towers that lined the coast. The Corsica he had come to know had not shrugged off its mantle of very individual and enchanting parochialism. Camille had mentioned the 'Vindetta' when Ric had asked him about the glowering Seraphina. He couldn't imagine the community would give up one of its own lightly.

Logic and nature decreed that Manou must have known Petrossian ten or so years before and he wondered whether that was why she had reacted so when she found Ric in his company at Camille's bar. He also wondered whether that was the reason why she had asked Ric what had brought him to Zizula in the first place? Clearly she had decided he was in league with Petrossian?

The idea that she had taken him for some kind of lackey of Petrossians, or a paid bit-part player in a peculiar charade, gnawed away at Ric like needle teeth in his skull. He wasn't sure whether he was angry at being made a patsy of by the Armenian or by the very obvious fact that Manou had thought his intentions with her dishonest. Whichever of them it was, he was now caught up in someone else's domestic.

Ric turned to watch the *Kohar* cruise effortlessly out round the point and couldn't believe neither he nor Camille had seen the boy leave. He wondered whether young Franco had resisted his abduction, or whether the excitement of being on the boat persuaded him away without any reluctance. It didn't make a difference really; the plain fact was that it was he, Ric, who had allowed the situation to develop in the first place and now Manou would think he was part of a larger 'fait accompli'.

Ric decided not to think about it any longer; thinking would only heap yet more pressure on him, and lately he'd had a surfeit of the stuff; whichever form it took.

He left the hotel, the chef pursuing him from out of the kitchen as he walked swiftly through the reception. Once outside he ran in a fast but controlled fashion back to the beach bar where Camille was deep in conversation with Seraphina. She jerked her head in Ric's direction as he entered the bar area and glared at him as though it was her child he had mislaid.

"Camille, I know where he is," Ric said.

"Tell me," the old man commanded.

"You're not going to believe this," he paused, even before he had delivered his rather implausible explanation, "but Franco is on the big motor-yacht belonging to that Armenian, Petrossian. I've just had words with a policeman, name of Bosquet, who rather coincidentally turned up about the same time as Petrossian did. He swears the man is Franco's father."

If Camille was surprised he didn't show it. He met the information with all the steady composure of an *Imperial Guard* standing to in the musket smoke. "Tell me again," he asked, and then he looked down at the ground as though it was the sand that was about to speak to him.

So Ric repeated what he had said, this time more slowly so that the full and astonishing weight of his information could settle on the old man's shoulders.

Camille raised his head. "Where is the boat going? Do you know?"

"No," replied Ric. "Back to Armenia if he's got any sense. Let's hope he hasn't."

Camille stilled, deep in thought. Like the veteran guardsman he resembled, he was peering into the distance in an attempt to predict his enemy's progress. His waitress stood over him, waiting for her orders to break camp.

After a lengthy pause, during which time Camille teased at his bottom lip with the fingertips of his right hand, he found some conclusion. "I think this man has come here for more than his child – if it is so that Franco is his child. I think we must talk with Manou. There is much we do not know that she must know. We don't have a telephone here." He looked to Ric to solve his dilemma.

"I have my phone in the car," he said and with that Ric turned and ran back to the Citroen. By the time he had retrieved his mobile phone from beneath the mat and pressed the relevant buttons, the old boy had caught him up.

Ric switched his phone to loud speaker and held it up. It rang. They both stood and tried to catch their breath as they listened to the buzzing monotone.

"Come on, Manou," Ric urged impatiently. "Come on."

Camille turned away, still searching the ground for clues to a puzzle he did not yet understand.

The tones ceased and Manou came on the line. Her voice was muted and perhaps a shade childlike. She was crying. "Ric?"

"Manou," he replied, trying to smother his alarm with as much calm authority as he could muster. "Manou, I'm so sorry. I am at the beach with Camille. We were sitting in the bar talking when we noticed Franco had gone missing. He was on the beach one minute and he was gone the next." As he spoke Ric steeled himself for her response; losing Franco was one thing, explaining that loss to his mother, something else entirely. But he knew that unless there was a corpse involved, bad news was best delivered in segments, otherwise too much information given out too quickly often led to the glaze of rejection and denial. "We can't have taken our eyes off him for more than a couple of minutes and…."

"Ric," Manou moaned down the phone to interrupt him. "I know what you are saying. He has taken Franco? He has gone with Kamo, yes?"

It wasn't the fact she already knew Franco was gone that loosened the surface of the pavement beneath Ric's feet; he was beginning to get used to more than one surprise in each day. It was more the way she referred to the Armenian by his first name. There was a vague tenderness, perhaps even an intimacy to the way she spoke his name which provided Ric with all the confirmation he needed that what Bosquet had told him was undoubtedly true – Manou had indeed known the Armenian and that he was Franco's father.

"Yes Manou," Ric said, "he has taken him. He is on the boat. But we don't know where they are going. Where are you?"

Manou didn't reply. She was fighting to contain her emotions. Then she sobbed and tried to speak through her tears. For a moment she fell back from the phone. When she came back on the line she said, "I am with Grua in Porti Vechju. I did not think this thing was possible until it was too late." She fell silent again and they could hear her choking back more tears.

Ric looked at Camille. The old boy had a stern and thoughtful expression, listening harder to the silence the longer it extended, as though he was straining to hear a voice from far away. His eyes had turned an impenetrable black. There was a readiness and seriousness about the way he rested his hands on his hips and studied the ground around him, like a wrestler rehearsing his next throw.

"We have to find out where they are going," Ric proposed. "We have to plan what to do next."

Manou spoke, this time her voice was a little clearer on the line. She'd regained her composure. "Yes," she agreed. "I am not sure but I think I know where they will go next. They will go to Renabianca. Kamo wants to take more from me than only my son. He wants to take Renabianca as well."

"He what?" Ric shouted at the phone, surprised at his own raw anger. "Why does he want the campsite too? Surely he has his son back; isn't that enough for him?"

"No, Ric. I believe it is the camp that he was after in the first place. He did not know Renabianca belonged to me until he came here. I am certain of that. I will tell you, explain it to you later. Meet me at the campsite when you can," she said, more by way of command than invitation, and then added, "Tell Camille I will meet him later this evening."

At this Camille ceased his inspection of the sandy pavement beneath his feet. He looked up at Ric and nodded. Ric sensed some greater communication between Manou and Camille, as though by his passing on of her message he, Ric, was nothing more than a link in their chain of preparation towards an action that required no open dialogue or discussion, just some quiet and hard intent that was implicit in their very personal understanding of each other. He realised Manou had failed to mention where or when she would meet Camille, as if she was leaving Ric out of the loop on purpose, as if she did not want him to know. That perplexed him, but it irked him more than it intrigued him. He felt compelled to offer her some words of encouragement, some gentle platitudes about how they would get through this dreadful confusion. But he realised by the metal in her voice and the way she had just told him to meet her at the campsite that Manou, in that moment, needed neither encouragement nor sympathy, rather it was his deference that she wanted, or, perhaps, even his consent.

54

Ric left his car where it was and rode back to his house on the motor bike. If he should he have to evade any nuisance and get across the open country the bike would be sharper and much faster than the galloping dustbin of a Citroen. Besides, the more he opened the throttle of the trials bike, the greater the rush of air blew through his mind, and through the late afternoon the air had turned cool and refreshing. He used the buffeting, blasting draught to sweep from his mind the less important details of Manou's predicament, allowing him to focus on those that troubled him.

He had no real plan, but that didn't really bother him either. He believed from Manou's instruction that she had some idea of what to do next, though what that might be he couldn't imagine.

He wondered as he approached the turn up to the house whether, after threatening Bosquet, the policeman would try to remove him from the scene. Clearly Bosquet viewed Ric as some kind of fly in his ointment. He half expected to find a couple of the local *Gendarmes* standing sentry outside the house and his trials bike was far from quiet, so he pulled off the road a few yards short of the turning and hid the bike in the maquis.

He skirted the track to the north and on up around to the east, coming towards the house from the mountain side. If there were unwelcome visitors they would be expecting him to arrive from the road and would doubtless be watching that way.

Sure enough, when the bungalow came into view, parked outside was a blue and white police car, the inhabitants of which he could not see. He cut further round to come up from the south east.

The maquis provided about as good a cover for approach as he could ask. It grew like uneven stubble on an uneven chin; the cistus and thorny brooms, the tall tree heather and the occasional cork oak provided such depth of shadow that he could have marched a patrol through it unobserved.

The nearer he got up the shallow rise, the louder voices grew. The cooler atmosphere allowed the sound of their conversation to travel easily across the hillside and the clear air provided good, sharp visibility. His approach must have taken him the better part of fifteen minutes, but he had to be careful. He knew the policemen would have a broad view over the surrounding countryside.

Then he saw them; two blue-uniformed officers sitting on his patio, chatting. Fortunately they seemed more interested in their own conversation than watching the road up to the house or the countryside around them. And even more fortunately, what Ric was after was not in the house, but buried between the two cacti on the eastern slope roughly fifty metres from the house.

He crouched in the shade of a cork oak and considered his options; a diversion, to distract the *Gendarme's* attention away from the garden, or get to where his valuables were hidden, pick them up and slip away. He had enough time and for the moment there was nothing in the house that he needed, so he chose the latter.

Another fifteen minutes passed before he was close to his stash. Ric concentrated on finding the quietest path through the undergrowth and listening to the voices; any variation in their pitch or tone would alert him to a change in their position. Unfortunately he would be directly in their line of sight when he unearthed the plastic bag. He had to hope they would be looking seaward but he would not be able to see their attitude until he was out in the open.

Then just as he was about to move out of his cover, he heard the radio in their car crackle into life with a hissing crash of static and a shrill digital signal.

One of them got up; Ric heard his chair grate on the stone as he slid it backwards. The tall *Gendarme* came into view as he walked into the house and out the back to the car. He opened the door and got into the driver's seat. The policeman sat and spoke on the radio; through his reflective sunglasses he was looking straight at where Ric was crouched in the shade of the maquis.

Ric realised that owing to the contrast of the bright sunlight against the black shadow thrown by the shrubs and small trees around him, the policeman, though staring directly at him, could not see him. He might as well have been painted white for all it mattered; as long as he stayed motionless in the shadow he was invisible. The tricky bit, though, was that whilst the policeman maintained his position, Ric would not be able to move much, if at all.

A few minutes later, Ric's knees began to grumble at his squatting. The *Gendarme* was evidently dictating a report.

Ten minutes later the report was still not finished and Ric's ankles and lower back had joined in the chorus of disapproval from his legs.

And just as Ric was considering revealing his position to save his legs from giving up, the fellow replaced his microphone and called to his companion. He also got out of the car and went inside, allowing Ric to stand up, move back and stretch his aching limbs.

From behind the trunk of the tree and concealed in the deep shadow, Ric watched them come out of the house, get into their car and drive off down the track.

That gave Ric all the time he needed. He stretched and flexed his legs and moved swiftly to locate the spot between the small, bald cactus and the taller, flat-eared spiny cactus. He knelt and pushed a couple of handfuls of earth aside. The soil was parched and loose and soon revealed the small plastic bag in which he had stowed his passport, credit cards and the 5,000 or so Euros he had left from the wad he'd arrived with. He then went into the house and changed his white shirt and blue jeans for a green T-shirt and brown shorts, and swopped his espadrilles for a pair of running shoes. There was not much else that he could think of that he might need. He didn't have much of a clue as to what he was expecting to be told when he met Manou, and he had absolutely no idea what the next twenty-four hours might bring, but he wondered what else, if anything, he ought to take with him. After all there was not much that was of any use; he had not brought much with him. A few clothes lay about his bed, and the dishes from breakfast were being cleaned by a host of large, black and extremely diligent ants.

Perhaps it was the act of retrieving his passport, cards and cash that imbued him with a sense of departure, he wasn't sure. But he perceived a curious finality to his actions. For sure he was taking them with him in case he had to make tracks in a hurry, but there was nothing to say he would not be returning. Maybe it was the presence of the *Gendarmes*. He didn't know. But he took a look around, wishing he could find the notebook of proverbs Manou had given him. He felt guilty that it should have gone missing whilst it had been in his care.

Ric kept to the side of the dusty drive on his way back down. He remained screened by the maquis until he had reached the road and located his bike. As he walked through the maquis his ankles and calves were tickled and scratched by the vegetation, reminding him of the marks left over from his hunting the boar. He still hadn't worked out quite how he had received the cuts and scratches whilst he was asleep, but guessed there were more pressing issues to deal with.

There was no one in evidence at the road, so he hauled the bike out from its hiding place, encouraged it into life with a hefty kick and roared off down the road in the direction of Renabianca. Down the hill where he had turned his old Citroen round amid the raging inferno two nights before, the maquis was blackened and shrivelled. There were all the signs of the bushfire: grey and black ash and yellow sand lay like patches of carpet tossed upon the surface of the road; here and there a charred rodent gave note of the speed of the fire; and in places the tarmac had melted into viscous, lava-like pools.

Ric pulled off the road up a track that led into the maquis. There was no sign to suggest he would find a house at the end of it; it just led up the hill to the east. He was very aware that if Bosquet had tipped the local police to keep a look-out for him, they might have sent a car to cover the entrance to the campsite as well.

Again his instincts proved correct. From his vantage point above the turn-off for Renabianca, he saw the police car parked just off the road and from where it sat the occupants had clear sight of the entrance.

He didn't feel the need or see the point in advertising his presence to the *Gendarmes*, so he wheeled the bike round and set off back towards his house and the bay at *la Tozza*; the front drive was not the only entrance to Renabianca.

He met no traffic on the way even though he was very prepared to have to leave the road and take to the maquis.

The view out to the horizon was vivid and clear as he idled down the slope into the secluded bay. There was a curious chill to the breeze which cooled the back of his head as he rode, and before him the sea lay dark purple, an imperial toga fringed with pale aquamarine at the hem. The impressive column of rock that was *la Tozza* rose out of the middle of the bay, like the granite focus of a vast roulette wheel.

Ric stowed the bike out of the way at the back of the beach, depositing his bag of personal effects and the car keys in the branches of a holm oak, and set off south to the path that Franco had shown him. He hurried, but measured his pace so that he had time to study his surroundings as he went. When he entered the woods, he noticed the nuthatch darting from branch to branch, keeping track of his progress.

He reached the higher edge of the wood, slowed from his jogging to a walk and crept up the final part of the rise to the lowest point of the saddle that opened into the adjoining bay.

He was glad he had taken his time, for when he looked over the crest he was confronted by the *Kohar*, basking like a great blue shark in the bay a hundred metres or so off shore. A couple of the crew moved about on deck, but they were at least 400 hundred metres from him and didn't appear to be on any kind of watch. They would need to be looking for him to see him.

The beach itself was deserted, and nothing moved in the desolate wasteland that had once been the shady environs of the many pine trees and tents.

Stopping every few metres to check the boat for any further or unusual movement, Ric slipped down to where he had left Franco's old rope hanging. He wasted a couple of minutes trying to locate it without taking his eyes off the boat, but once in his hands, he swiftly lowered himself down. He kept his path to the rocks at the back of the sandy beach and soon made his way into the charred and scorched vegetation.

He trotted up the clearway between the blackened stumps and fallen trunks. The eucalyptus tree he had seen flare like an enormous, sparkling torch two nights before, still stood in place, but now its bare and scorched limbs were bereft of any leaves or secondary branches; it resembled a wizened arm reaching out of the ashes of its own funeral pyre, its sinuous wrist supporting twisted, thin, black fingers pointing as if petrified in pleading to a pitiless sky. At irregular intervals on the denuded forest floor, Ric came across the incinerated tokens and sad detritus of the bushfire: stained and singed canvasses suspended from the skeletal frames of tents, camp beds with grotesque, naked spines that stood upright, begrimed pots, smudged cutlery, singed sleeping bags, wire clotheslines dotted with pegs that in the enormous heat had fused in place, and all manner of beach-shoe left where they had slipped from fleeing feet. What had been a great orchard of light and laughter was now a barren acre of mortified trees and ash covered sand; the dreams of vacation reduced to cloying soot and abandoned refuse.

By the time he reached the edge of the camp clearing, where the shop, restaurant and offices had stood, the cool wind from the north had gained sufficiently in strength to whisk up small clouds of grainy mist, part ash, part dust and sand, which, when wafted by the breeze, lazed on the air like thick cigar smoke.

A large, square, blue tent had been erected in the clearing beside the blackened plane trees. The buildings had not fared well; not one of them was intact. The central restaurant had been more or less demolished when the gas tanks to the rear of the building had exploded. The roof had fallen in and the rear wall had collapsed. Where the office had been, there now lay not much more than a pile of bricks and charred wood. A substantial and old fashioned half-height safe stood in the middle of the mound of rubble, its heavy door hanging open to reveal its vacant interior.

Ric stood back from the clearing and watched. He could not see anyone moving about, but he could see Manou's white rental hatchback parked just beyond the plane trees beside the hulks of several other burnt out vehicles.

Then Manou came out of the tent and walked to the back of the restaurant ruins out of sight.

When Ric was satisfied there was no one else around, he emerged from the cover of the trees and edged over to the tent.

Manou reappeared from behind the dilapidated walls. She was carrying a small wooden box, which she very nearly dropped with surprise when she saw Ric in the tent.

"Sorry," he began as he moved towards her, "I didn't mean to startle you. I wasn't sure who else was here." In truth he was more than a little nervous as to what her reaction towards him might be, considering he had just lost her son, but her face held little, if any expression.

"Ric," she replied, "where is your car?" She walked over to a trestle table and put the box she had been carrying down amongst the files and papers that were arranged on it. Then she turned and waited for him to come to her as though it was his movement to make, not hers.

So Ric did go to her; encouraged to do so as much by his guilt at losing Franco as by his desire to comfort her. But when he put his arms around her she was coolly unresponsive.

She did not shrink from him, but neither did she give him any physical indication that his sympathy, or warmth of heart, was necessary to her.

"I didn't bring the car," he told her. "I left the bike at *la Tozza*. There's a police car at the end of your drive. I don't know whether they're waiting for me or watching you. There were a couple at the house when I went back just now."

Manou pulled back from him at the information. Her blue eyes so normally bright and lively were heavy and veiled, and her complexion so pallid it looked rice powdered. There was an air of removal about her. She was reserved and restrained.

She said, "There is no point in them being there for me or for the business. Perhaps they are looking for you. Why would they do this?" Her hair was uncombed. It hung in uneven curls, and her blouse and skirt were dusty and charcoal marked; Manou had been reclaiming as much of the paperwork from the rubble as was still legible. There were inventories, invoice files, cash books, safety deposit boxes, cheque books and passports all laid out in neat stacks. She saw him studying them. "The campers thought they had lost their papers, in the fire. But I kept them in the safe. It was fireproof. They have all left without them. How did they do that?" she scoffed. "Who needs a passport these days, heh?"

He put his hand on her arm and without squeezing her too hard he pulled her round to face him. "Talk to me, Manou. Please talk to me. Tell me what is going on."

"I am talking to you, Ric. What makes you think I am not?" She looked up at him without seeing him; her eyes focused on his mouth, not on his eyes.

"No, you're not Manou. You're talking at me, not to me. I need," he put his other hand on her chin and raised her head so that she could not avoid his look, "I need you to tell me what is going on, or what has been going on from the start. Because if you don't tell me there is no point in me trusting you, in much the same way as you did not trust me when you saw me with Kamo. And if I can't trust you, then I might as well leave as you told me to."

But Manou lowered her eyes as he raised her chin, so that she did not have to meet his stare.

"Trust?" she mocked. She rolled her eyes and bit her lower lip, but when she had finished her hopeless ridicule she looked straight at Ric; her blue eyes now vivid and clear as her anger rose like a sudden squall.

The brief intensity in her eyes caught him off guard.

"Trust?" she repeated. "You want me to trust you when I cannot trust myself to look after my own child." She swore in Corsu; her anger and frustration unmistakable.

"Explain to me, Manou," he asked. "Does Kamo have a legal right to Franco?"

At this she tensed and stepped back out of his reach, the squall in her eyes swelling into a furious and hostile storm. Manou bunched her fists and raised them to her forehead.

"Of course he has a legal right!" she yelled at Ric. "Or he will have. He will have all the legal right and I will have none. If we go to court I have none and Franco will have less." She turned away from him and leant on the table. Her head dropped; the effort involved in summoning the storm was too tiring for her to maintain.

"We all have rights, Manou."

"Not if we don't exist," she replied calmly. "If you don't officially exist you don't have the same rights as people who do exist." She paused. Her shoulders shook and then she banged her hands down on the table before her. But she did not turn to look at Ric as she spoke.

"When Franco was born I was alone. I was ashamed. Having a child outside of marriage is still tabou here, even today. Men can behave like men, but for women – you have to be engaged before you sleep with a man. So when my father disappeared I was alone. There was no one to tell me what was right and what was wrong; Camille tried to be a new father to me, but I did not want to listen to him and I was full of so much anger for the world." Manou paused again, pulling the stitches from old wounds; going over in her mind the mistakes she had made and the rough hand she had been dealt.

"Franco was born at home. You know Mariucca, the woman who comes to clean at the house for you? She helped me. She is a good person. It was Mariucca who nursed my mother when I was born. But I made a simple mistake. I did not go to the *Mairie* to register Franco. I was ashamed; I did not want people to know. I was frightened for him too. It is understandable after what happened to his grandfather, eh? I knew 'if' his father was looking for him, he would find out about the children born the same time here. Pah!" she scoffed: "So many reasons; all of them wrong." She turned back to look at Ric, gauging his reaction.

But he would not judge her. He wondered if she was waiting for his confirmation of her stupidity, or whether she was saying to him that she knew she was not the only one to live with guilt. What she wanted was his absolution. But Ric felt there was more to come. "And now?"

Manou tried to smile a hopeless, abandoned smile; the smile of someone left ashore after the boat has sailed. "And now I have lost him. His father's lawyers will be big lawyers. Because I had not registered Franco in the correct way, the courts will say that I am not fit to keep him and they will for sure give custody to his father. There will be nothing I can do. When Kamo saw me at Camille's with you, he knew he had found me and it did not take him long to find out about Franco; it was just bad luck."

Ric wasn't sold on the idea that Kamo relied on luck, but he could see no point in suggesting it and it didn't matter either way. The boy was gone-for the moment. "But you said on the phone that he was after Renabianca?"

"Yes," she nodded. "To begin with Grua, my notary, my solicitor, was approached by another company of lawyers in Paris. They had a client who was interested in buying Renabianca. It was maybe three or four weeks ago. We told them we are not interested in selling. They offered a great deal of money. We told them we are still not interested. Then they start to play games. They question everything to do with the land; the deeds and my right to the land. They made life difficult with my suppliers, they spread rumours. Soon I have the Préfecture visit every week; they came to inspect the food in my kitchens, my safety procedures, my inventory, records of the campers who have been staying... it goes on. They asked for documents from so many years ago that I could not hope to find. They tell me they will close down Renabianca; tell me I have no right to the land. But I think someone is paying someone more money than I can pay. So perhaps I am finished. These people who want the campsite, they are very clever and very rich." Manou clapped her hands as if to applaud the pressures they had forced upon her.

"Kamo!" she spoke his name, and again she spoke it with that curious mixture of tenderness and regret. "Yes, he is not like most people. He is not the kind to allow other people to stand in his way."

Ric stood and waited for her to continue.

310

She studied him, as if she was contemplating whether or not he needed to know any more of her history. Manou pursed her lips and then sucked on the end of her thumb for a second. "You understand, Ric, that I had not even one boyfriend before I went to Paris; my father would not allow me to have a boyfriend. And in the university I met Kamo. He was very confident. All the time and in all situations, he was always full of a *perpétuel* confidence. He made Paris look like it was a small town. I was studying; I had no money. He was studying; he had money. I was a naïf and I thought I was his only girl. But I was not and then I was pregnant." Manou paused, waiting for Ric to show some reaction, perhaps even some disapproval of her naivety. "So I ran home, as you would say, with my tail between my legs," she laughed at herself. "No," she added, "with my baby between my hips, eh?"

"Did Kamo try to find you?"

"What would he have done with a simple girl from Corsica and her illegitimate child? He wasn't the kind of man who cares for this kind of problem. For all I know he probably has many children that he does not know about; for certain he had many girls. I was not sophisticated when I was young; not even sophisticated enough to understand that it is the girls who need contraception, not the men. That was pretty stupid, huh? But a girl does not learn of such things from her father; especially the kind that was my father."

"But your father...?" Ric asked. He understood all of what she had told him, some of which was not so unusual, but he was still uneasy at the coincidence that her father should disappear when he was on his way to confront the father of her coming child; the man Ric now knew to be Kamo.

"I told you...," she began, but there was a noise from outside the tent; a car was approaching down the drive.

Ric stood still and Manou moved to the entrance of the tent.

"*Gendarmes*," she said, "from Porti Vechju." She moved to the table, picked up some sheaves of paper and laid them over the wooden box she had brought into the tent. Then she picked up a couple of files and walked outside.

As she went out under the awning she said: "Don't worry. I know them. If I cannot make them go away, get out of the tent and come back later."

Ric heard Manou greet the *Gendarmes*. The sun was now low in the sky on the far side of the police car, so there was no possibility of them seeing his shadow in the tent. He listened for the opening of the doors as the car pulled up beyond the plane trees, but there was no such sound. As he listened to Manou chat with them he looked over the papers on the trestle table. Much of it was accounts paperwork, entries in columns, and reconciliations. There were cheque book stubs, bank statements, cash balances, profit and loss sheets, and all the everyday records of a small business. Ric moved the sheaves of paper she had laid over the top of the wooden box. He picked it up; it was not much bigger than the kind of box used for storing chess pieces, but it was heavy enough to contain something more solid than carved lumps of wood, even hardwood. It was old and weathered; the wood was pine or something like it, yellowed and rough edged, and thin like plywood. He imagined he could break it open with his hands, but the lid was latched and a small padlock hung from the hook of the latch. Something about the mass that lay inside the box was familiar to him; a weight he recognised, perhaps a kilo, perhaps more. He replaced it and put the papers on top.

Outside she was still talking with the policemen. The driver had turned the engine off. Judging by her light and familiar tone she was flirting with them.

He looked through the different passports bundled together; the navy blue British, the deep ruby German, the brighter red Italian, and the crimson Dutch; some biometric, some European Union, some old, some more recent. Ric looked at the different mug-shots. Amongst the British passports he found the one belonging to the tall, grey-haired Englishman who had bothered him on the night of the fire; he was a titled gentleman Ric was unsurprised to see. That explained the fellow's right to authority he supposed. Mostly the passports belonged to people of older years, but a few did not.

Then Ric heard the car start up again, and a raft of goodbyes were exchanged. Manou was laughing.

She walked back in and dumped the files back on the table. "They were looking for you. They say they have been asked to detain you if they see you, but they are not too serious. You are not going to keep them from their families." Manou checked her watch, and then added, "I have to go to meet Camille. Will you wait for me here?"

She walked over to him, put her arms around his neck, and pulled him to her. Manou kissed him in that way she had of slipping her tongue out from between her mouth to flick at his lips, an act he had decided that lay somewhere between a taunt and a promise.

"I don't think I have any particular place to go right now," he replied when she stepped back. And as he said it, the truth of what he had said dawned on him; it was true, only more so. He didn't have any place to go, particular didn't come into it.

Manou looked into his eyes. She mesmerised him.

"And I'm not sure I'd go if I did," he added and kissed her again, but with more force and no little passion.

When they felt the moment pass and they softened to each other, he let her go.

"Take this," she said, offering him the box. "I have lost the key. You will have to break it open. I'm sure you can find something to open it with." Manou moved back to him. He could not touch her; he had the box in his hands. She kissed him once more. "A dopu," she said. And then she was gone.

Ric watched her drive away, trailing a cloud of dust and ash behind her. She was going to meet Camille at the place they had not mentioned and at a time he had not heard them agree.

He knew for certain that he was not wanted for now. He also knew for certain that there was little he would not do for her and that though common sense suggested he was better off away from her, he did not feel inclined to desert her.

He found a piece of angle iron lying amongst the rubble of the office behind the tent and, inserting it under the latch, he prized the lock off the box. In doing so the old desiccated wood of the box cracked, the lid came adrift from its hinges and a waxed paper parcel fell out.

55

Ric picked up the brown parcel and the broken box, and took them inside. That the wax paper contained a gun was obvious; the outline was unmistakable. It was a little shorter than his splayed hand and was flat sided like an automatic pistol rather than cylindrical like a revolver.

The string securing the wrapping was neatly knotted, but old and greasy and untied easily. Unfolding and laying the greasy paper to one side, Ric lifted the gun up and examined it.

The semi-automatic weighed perhaps a little more than his electric razor. He checked the safety catch on the left side was pushed round into the locking position and pulled back the slider to check there was no round in the chamber. There wasn't. Ric studied the circled 'PB' etched on the grip; an Italian Beretta. He remembered an American telling him they had been prized souvenirs amongst the troops in Europe during the Second World War.

He pressed back the switch at the base and dropped the clip out of the grip; it was full. Someone clearly wanted it to work when he, or she, he corrected himself, needed it. He pulled back the slider engaging the safety-catch, pushed back on the barrel freeing it from its locking recess, pulled the barrel back up and out, and laid it next to the magazine on the table. Then he pushed the slide, recoil spring and guide straight off the front. He checked the spring and guide in their seats and the safety locking nut. Everything moved as it should; there was no apparent degeneration in the condition, no visible corrosion. It was plain to see why the Americans liked it; it was neat and tidy, and stripped easily. The gun had the dun, blued-black finish in common with all of its type, like a blade that had been left overnight in the embers of a fire. He wrapped it in the wax paper and put it back in the now lidless box.

There was nothing else in the box; no additional rounds, no cleaning equipment, no spare magazine; just a blow-back, semi-automatic pistol with seven rounds ready to go.

Now at least he understood a good deal more about Manou's intentions. She might have laced Kamo's name with a distant affection when she spoke it, but she wasn't about to confuse sentiment with objective.

Ric stood beneath the awning of the tent and looked up at the sky for some inspiration. A fantail of ultra-high clouds was spreading down from the north and the atmosphere seemed off-balance; cool and dry down from above one minute and warm and moist up from the ground the next. In the west the amber sun was being squeezed between the rising granite and the lowering clouds, as though the blue sky, like Ric, was being compressed into a narrow margin.

In the distance Ric could hear the nasal whining of a motor. He walked away from the tent and out beyond the shield of the charred plane trees in order to work out from which direction the noise was coming. At first it sounded like a motorbike out on the road, but then he realised the noise came from the direction of the beach.

He went back into the tent. There was a tray of small, plastic St George's water bottles under the trestle table and seeing them reminded Ric how thirsty he was. There was a full one on the table, so he drank most of it, collected the box containing the pistol, rearranged the passports into a pile to look as though they had not been touched, and walked out from the ruined edifices of the camp down towards the beach.

The burned trees and stumps stood about like anxious reserves waiting to be ordered into battle, their shadows long and slender across the sandy road. Here and there a bird pecked about amongst the blackened detritus hoping to find one uncooked grub, and the ants were slowly emerging to reclaim their territory. Otherwise, except for the intermittent angry buzzing of the motor, all was still and quiet.

At the derelict shower block just back from the beach, Ric stopped and placed the box carefully beneath a basin in the open washroom. Where before men and women had rested their mirrors, no doubt grooming themselves in preparation for their evening of dancing in the circle of plane trees outside the restaurant, now there stood grimy taps drooping over dirty basins and the melted plastic of wash kits cast about in haste; everything coated in the dark soot and grey ash of the bushfire. Around the block the sand was littered with fragments of charcoal, black cinders and the larger shards of cremated wood, a couple of which he placed over the box. Ric counted his steps from the block back to the dust covered tarmac road.

By the time he got to the beach the light from the advancing dusk was pale and clear. First he saw the large motor-yacht dominating the view out towards the open sea, and then he saw the jetski bombing up and down, throwing great curtains of spray as it careered from one end of the bay to the other.

Although it was a good hundred metres or so away, Ric could see that it was Kamo driving. And in spite of the fading light he could make out Franco sitting behind his father, holding on to him for dear life.

Ric looked to the north from where the irregular *Terrana* seemed to blow. There was a larger weather system assembling up the coast and he wondered if the higher clouds might bring a change in the weather.

He saw the pillion rider attract the attention of his chauffeur and the jetski slowed down. Both faces turned his way and then the machine stood on its heels and leapt towards Ric, like an arrow loosed from a bow.

Kamo still wore his dark glasses and the same Grateful Dead T-shirt. He reined the jetski in ten or so metres off the beach, and broad-sided it opposite from where Ric was standing.

Franco's enjoyment was self-evident. "Hey, Ric," he called out, waving with both hands as though it was some kind of clever trick to let go.

"Franco," acknowledged Ric. "Looks like you're having fun."

"*Si*," the boy shouted, exhilaration and entertainment writ large over his beaming face. "*Fantàsticu! Splèndidu!*" he shouted. "*Jetski u meddu.*"

Kamo's mouth was set in the half smile of a confident poker player. He just sat in the saddle and watched Ric's face; showing off his new-found son and showing Ric that the boy was not being held against his will.

At the exact moment Ric went to speak, Kamo pulled back on the handlebars, steered the jetski around in a steep turn and hared off back towards the *Kohar*, his young passenger grabbing him around his middle to prevent himself from falling off backwards. Once comfortable, Franco twisted in his seat to wave farewell.

Ric waited to see what the Armenian would do next.

The beach was deserted; nothing moved except for a few restless waves a fair way down where a sand bar had built up in the shallows.

When the jetski arrived at the transom of the boat, Kamo offloaded Franco into the care of a crew member, pushed off and turned back in the direction of Ric and the beach. This time he didn't cream the jetski towards Ric, he motored in calm and measured.

He was either gathering his wits or cruising purely for effect, like the general of an overwhelming force advancing to demand his enemy's surrender. Ric chuckled at the man's bravado and then sighed at what havoc it might wreak.

Kamo rode the jetski right on to the beach, much the way a man might park his car when arriving at his office.

"Ric," he acknowledged as he dismounted. He offered Ric his hand.

Ric hesitated at this.

"Come on Ric," Kamo suggested smiling, exposing his over-white, fabricated teeth, "for sure things may not be how they were, but we are gentlemen, don't you think?"

Ric shook his hand. He noticed that whereas before, when Ric had first met him, Kamo's hand had promised a hard, bone-strong and uncompromising character on the end of it, now his hand, though cool from the water thrown up by the jetski, was less firm and less testing, and he held on to Ric's hand for a moment longer than was necessary.

"Well Kamo," Ric replied, "maybe that's for others to define." He withdrew his hand and folded his arms across his chest.

Kamo raised his hands up to the sky in appeal. "Ah, then permit me to define it on your behalf. You have worthy ideals. You are respectable. You are courteous. But you are a man of honour and integrity as well. It's true," he confirmed when Ric rolled his eyes in dismay at the Armenian's need to explain the way he saw it. "Come," he said, "we have much to discuss. Let us walk a little. I always find thinking and talking are easier when one is taking a little gentle exercise."

"Where did you learn English, Kamo?" Ric asked as they turned to stroll south down the beach. They could have been mistaken for two friends shooting the breeze after a long lunch.

He sighed and weighed up his answer. "I was lucky." His tone suggested his luck was of the kind that was thrust upon reluctant shoulders. "I lived in England for a while. I attended a course at the London School of Economics. I lived in France for a while and attended a course in sociology at the Sorbonne."

"Where you met Manou," Ric interrupted.

"Yes. I was coming to this. But first it is important for you to understand that I also studied at Berkeley in California and in Hong Kong. I was very lucky. My sponsor; he wanted me to understand how the world is not so big today as it was when he was young and that we can no longer fight over the small scraps our country gives us; our appetites need to be satisfied. If you remember, I told you that the world is no longer big enough to have borders and that the borders most countries have are not strong enough to keep their people in."

"I was under the impression borders were meant to keep people out," Ric offered, "not in."

Kamo bridled at this: "Not so. You think the Berlin Wall was built to keep people out? No. You think the Americans and you British are in Afghanistan to keep people out of your country? No. You want to keep all the bad people in one place; they are easier to deal with that way; much like a disease that must not spread. But what is important is that the world has become a small place. In the beginning of the last century people used to live in their own backyard; there they were safe and the world outside was this great, foreign, unknown and dangerous place. In this century the world has become just an extension of that backyard; it is no longer so foreign, so unknown or so dangerous. So my sponsor wanted me to understand the world for what it is, not what it was. He made sure I was educated in many different places, so that I would be at home in all of them; think perhaps further than the bourgeois confines of my own country. Also, if you like, to understand how other people define what it is to be a 'gentleman'." He fell silent, allowing his companion time for his educational edict to sink in.

"You're such a Mensch, Kamo," Ric carped.

"Perhaps," he said, stroking his moustache. "Perhaps it is true, but I don't think you see what I am meaning." He paused as he summoned and assembled the words. "I met Manou when I was at the Sorbonne. You think she is a great looking woman now; well you should have seen her then. At nineteen she was even more beautiful; like a new dawn that no one on earth had ever seen."

"You mean 'ever touched', I think."

"Yes, that also. But I don't mean just a physical beauty; I mean her mind as well as her body. She was enchanting; perhaps you would say she was hypnotising or maybe even bewitching. She was not like the other girls;

318

rich girls who wanted to try everything, bourgeois girls who wanted everything, or poor girls who would take anything they could get. She had no ideals, no preconceptions; her mind was not confined like all the other girls. There was something about her. She possessed this inner presence that would shine out like a great light." He laughed out loud as though he was remembering some amusing anecdote. "Manou had a presence just like she still has. I saw it when she came to the restaurant. She saw me, and she saw you too. Her face was like a very beautiful storm; a storm that doesn't die, it only falls quiet until the next time it breaks."

"Some storm," Ric agreed. He was aware of his companion's ongoing charm offensive. "So?"

"So, one day she disappears, just like that; as you would say 'into the blue'." He snapped his fingers like a magician. "Gone, I did not know where."

"That's 'out of the blue', not into it, Kamo."

"Out–in, you know what I am talking about," he said, a hint of frustration creeping into his tone. "It was true she was not the only girl at that time. But she was incredible. And I did not know where she came from, except that she came from Corsica. It's not a big island, but it's big enough to hide in if you don't want to be found."

"And the next time you saw her was when she walked into Camille's the other night?"

"As I stand here with you, it is the truth," Kamo stated, putting his hand up to his chest as though he was happy for his heart to depend on it.

Ric scoffed: "So you roll in here on your ship of dreams, your flags flying and your whores on display, and happen to be in the process of buying the land that belongs to a girl you slept with at university ten years ago?"

They turned to look at each other.

Kamo's back was to the sea; the low sun was reflecting off his glasses. Neither of them had made a threat towards the other, but Ric had decided that enough of Kamo's history lesson was enough. It didn't matter. It was irrelevant.

"I don't mind the occasional coincidence Kamo, but when too many come along at the same time, I get nervous. And I've got to tell you, you make me nervous."

Kamo stroked his moustache again at this. "I did not know that this

319

place belonged to Manou until I arrived here and I saw her name on the deeds to the property. This you have to believe because it is the truth. There is someone I mentioned before; a 'sponsor'. He made many things possible for me that otherwise would not have been possible. You understand what I am saying, Ric? My parents have no money; my father works in Baku, in the oil fields. It is not his fault, but he is not a man of great intellect and he could not afford to send me to a proper school. My sponsor; he is a man of great intellect."

"And this 'great intellect' decides that he wants to buy himself a piece of land in Corsica. And because he paid for you to go distributing your youthful seed about the world, you have to repay him by setting fire to camp sites in quiet backwaters of the Mediterranean; doing his dirty work for him when he doesn't want to be associated with it?"

"Dirty work?" Kamo seemed offended. "This is not dirty work. This is just business."

"You could have killed a lot of people in that fire, Kamo."

Kamo feigned indignation at Ric's accusation. He turned and moved into Ric's space: "And you never consider the collateral damage your country causes when you invade Iraq or Afghanistan? Look me in the eyes, Ric, and tell me you don't take into account the casualties who have nothing to do with your wars." He paused, not expecting a reply, and then turned to carry on walking. "At least I came to rescue them. You know, Ric, I could have left them for you to rescue all on your own. Or perhaps it is that I did not let you be the hero for Manou; perhaps it is this that has upset you? Did I steal your thunder?"

"Don't try selling me that bullshit, Kamo. You already knew Manou owned Renabianca. Or did you forget that you told me that just now with your hand on your bleeding heart?"

It was now Ric's turn to be indignant and box his way back into the centre of the ring. "So when did you find out about Franco, eh? When did you find out you had a son?" The Armenian's lack of reaction to the question gave Ric all the answer he needed; he closed Kamo up. "So you found out about Franco sometime on Sunday evening and decided you'd better cruise on over here pretty damn quick in case you were told the next day that your son had died in a fire which you had started. And you call that business?"

There followed a protracted silence between the two of them as they both wrestled with their own individual and precarious rationales.

But though Kamo was not to deny or excuse the truth, he wasn't about to give up justifying his way of getting things done either. So when the weight of implication had been allowed sufficient pause to settle, he carried on: "This land is like any other, Ric. You think that because this land belongs to a woman you fall in love with it makes it different to any other land? No." He tapped his palm with his index finger to drive home the point. "This land is like any other; the sun comes up, the sun goes down. The Corsicans think it is their own sacred island and that no one else is entitled to make life in it? Well," he concluded, "they have to learn like everyone learns that the world is no longer the same way it used to be. And it is a lesson they need to learn sooner than later."

"And Franco?" Ric asked. "Where does he fit into all this?"

Kamo reached up with his left hand and removed his large sunglasses. It was the first time he had done so in Ric's company, and in the clear evening light the sun reflected off the yellow flecks in his green-brown eyes, like gold flakes on an autumn leaf. There was no doubt Kamo was Franco's father. "So you see, Ric; Franco is my son. I did not know he existed until I came here, in the same way that I did not know until I came here that Manou owned this place. You think I wanted this to be so complicated?"

Ric was still recovering from the shock of seeing the similarity in Kamo and Franco's eyes. He wasn't sure which way to fall now.

Listening to Manou explain to him that Kamo was her son's father as she had done just one hour before was remarkable in itself; hearing the same thing again from Kamo was equally extraordinary. But witnessing the apparent genetic proof for the first time was for some reason bewildering, as though he had not been prepared to believe it was possible unless he was presented with the undeniable truth.

Ric felt, and he could not remotely recognise or understand the logic in his feeling, cheated. It was as though Manou had cheated on him; as though she had cheated on him in that instant, when in reality she had slept with Kamo ten years before; ten years before he had met her. It was ridiculous and nonsensical and he tried to shrug the puerile, jealous and wounding notion aside.

"I see," began Kamo, "that you are beginning to understand that this situation is not so simple."

Ric's frustration turned to anger; an anger born because he wanted his life to be some other way and not the way it was right now, wanted it to be easier and without so many crowding and wretched decisions.

Ric wanted to drop the man beside him on the spot; hurt him the way Ric now felt the hurt deep within. But there was little point. He knew his violence would lead them nowhere.

They walked back up the sandy margin in silence.

As they neared the beached jetski Kamo said: "I tell you again, Ric; this situation is complex, as much for me as it is for you and Manou and Franco. I have many obligations that I have to honour; Franco is one of them. But I have also said to you before; when all the other people have gone from your life, all those people who tell you they care for you for whatever their reasons, when they are gone, all you are left with is your family. And Franco is my family. I will not let him be brought up in this pathetic backyard; this poor backwater of the Mediterranean."

Ric stopped by the green jetski. "Kamo, hasn't anyone told you that green is an unlucky colour for a boat?"

Kamo smiled a self-deprecating smile and shook his head to let Ric know he wasn't taking him too seriously. "Didn't I tell you, Ric; I don't believe in luck. You have to believe you will throw the double six before you roll the dice, otherwise you will never win the game, eh! And as you mentioned luck; let us speak of backgammon; I remember a game we had together; one particular game at the end of many games; games we played for a bet."

Somehow Ric had known throughout their long promenade that the other man had every intention of calling in his marker. "Keep going," he said.

"Ric, I am going to ask you to honour your favour to me. I will ask you to honour this not specifically for me and Franco, but also for you, because I think it is going to be just as much to your advantage as it will be to mine." Kamo looked at Ric very seriously, squared his chest and held out his hand for the other man to shake. "All I ask you to do is to leave now while there is still time. Do yourself a service and honour the favour that you owe to me. Go. Leave. If you do this now I will consider us quits. I think that is the correct expression; quits. Please leave and let us remember how it is between us now; how both of us have been fortunate enough to appreciate the same beauty."

"That seems to be the way of things," Ric grumbled, more to himself than to Kamo, "people asking me to leave."

They shook hands and Ric helped Kamo push the jetski into the water. The Armenian slipped the dead man's cord over his wrist, pressed the starter button and pulled the throttle lever; the jetski growled into life. Kamo waved farewell and set off towards his floating hotel, now lit up in all its vain and vulgar glory, like a whore glowing in the shadows.

56

Ric stood in the cover of the charred trees at the back of the beach and watched as Kamo drove up to the stern of the motor-yacht. A crew member held the jetski steady for his boss to dismount, and then tied the machine off to one side.

At the top of the steps up to the sundeck, Franco was waiting for his father. They greeted each other in excited and exuberant fashion and turned away to go inside.

He wondered how Kamo had explained to Franco the sudden change in his fortune; how Kamo had, if he had, made the lad aware that he was the father who had been absent since before Franco's birth. And that unless there was some kind of remarkable rapprochement between his parents, he was likely to be spending much of his time away from his mother but playing with his father's rather extravagant toys.

But Ric also wondered how Manou had explained the absence of his father to Franco over the years.

As the Armenian had said: 'it was complex', but for whom? There was no doubt Kamo was obligated to his master, the father figure who had seen fit to invest so much time and money in his *protégé*. From their conversation Ric understood that Kamo was under considerable duress to do his master's bidding.

The real reason for Kamo's presence, or so he professed, was his procurement of the property on behalf of his master. Ric curiously didn't doubt that; there was too much evidence pointing towards it; even Manou had said that she had been fighting the unwelcome advances of an anonymous suitor for a few weeks.

The other succession of coincidences; the property belonging to Manou, Manou having the son Kamo never knew existed, Kamo having first met Manou ten years before and not since, and all of them finding each other in such an idyllic hideaway: they were all too difficult to balance.

The intriguing thought popped into Ric's head that Kamo might just be nothing more than a puppet in someone else's theatre. But did that mean his intentions for Franco conflicted with his other obligations?

Kamo may have had a rather convenient and cold hearted view of the world, but he appeared to value his family in a completely different currency. When they had played backgammon he had mentioned it, and he had mentioned it again as they had strolled up the beach: 'family'. If that was the case, and Ric believed it to be so, Kamo would want for his son all the education that he could offer him; all the education that his father had been unable to offer Kamo at the same age. It would be natural that he would want to atone for the shortcomings of his own father, and neither would he want Franco to grow up thinking of his father in the same vein as Kamo had grown up thinking of his, as someone incapable of providing for his son. And after Kamo's rather eloquent diatribe expounding the virtues of a global education, Ric could see that it would be difficult, if not impossible, for Kamo to leave his son in what he perceived to be a regressive and insular community.

Manou, on the other hand, would do what any mother would do to keep her son; she would not let him go without a fight. For her, there was nothing elaborate or confusing about the situation. It was plain and simple. For her, extravagant toys, a global education and glorious horizons boasted no useful purpose. She had glimpsed those horizons ten years before. She had been blinded by them and her sight had never recovered from the harsh light. But now the flames from those glorious horizons had found her once more. They had destroyed the many years of hard work she had given up to Renabianca, and now they threatened to destroy her only son.

Ric understood that a rapprochement of any nature was unlikely; perhaps for all the reasons he had just appreciated impossible. He turned through the emaciated trees and brush and strolled through the lengthening shadows back to the centre of the camp. He hoped he might find Manou in some kind of conciliatory mood, but knew in his heart of hearts he would not. The moment he had opened the box and felt the weight of the gun inside, he had known there would be no amicable solution, but he left the Beretta where he had hidden it all the same; that way at least he would be the one person using it, if using it became unavoidable.

There was, he judged, less than an hour of daylight left.

He debated going to collect his bike and just disappearing like Manou's father had. But then, he decided, Manou didn't deserve being abandoned twice in her life, even if it was the more sensible of his two options, so he carried on walking to the camp centre where she had left him earlier.

He approached the buildings, waiting longer between each move from cover the closer he got. Manou's car was back, and a hurricane lamp glowed in the tent, throwing her shadow against the back screen. She was looking through the papers on the trestle table, and as far as he could make out there was no one else about.

Manou said nothing when he first appeared in the doorway of the tent. She didn't acknowledge his presence.

So he watched her sort the papers into piles, stopping as she did every now and then to read one. She had changed into blue jeans and a shirt, the sleeves of which she had rolled up above her elbows. Manou looked ready for work as opposed to ready for an evening out.

"The box I gave you?" she asked without looking up.

"The Beretta," he confirmed. "I put it out of the way. Better off where it is." He stood and lent lightly against the door pole, his arms folded as though their's was a casual conversation. "I've got to ask, but I don't suppose there's any way this can be settled without having to start a shooting war, is there?"

"No, Ric. There isn't," she said, turning to face him. There were a couple of bottles of *Pietra* on the table. They were cold judging by the condensation on the outside. Manou walked over and handed one to him, then retreated back to her table out of his range. Her face was impassive, and she tilted her head forward so that she had to look up at him, like an animal readying for some kind of challenge. She picked up her bottle and drank from it, watching him.

"Well, I wouldn't put it past Kamo to know how to defend himself either. I don't think he plays by our rules," he added.

"And whose rules are you talking about, Ric?" she snapped. "Yours?" She took a couple of paces towards him, an aggression that caught him off guard. "You think we care whose rules we play by. You think we care how you see our rules?" Manou raised her voice to emphasise her rejection. "We do things the way we have to. We have always done things this way. We don't ask for permission from Paris, or Brussels, or whoever is our master this year. We are not interested in how this looks to anyone else. We do what we have to do to survive." She paused, waiting for his challenge.

Ric drank from his bottle. The liquid was light and fizzy in his mouth; the taste of the chestnut bitter and curiously alkaline on his tongue and in his cheeks. He had the feeling Manou was not finished, but hoped that if he allowed her to continue her storm might blow through and then she might just start listening to some common sense.

"You should know Kamo works for a very dangerous company. This company buys land around the world and builds its own exclusive communities; gangster towns where it is easier for them to grow their influence in which ever country they want." At this Manou walked about the middle of the tent and raised her arms in frustration. "They already have these communities in Spain, in Morocco, in the West Indies, and in Malaysia. They are like an infection; once they have taken hold in one place it is just a matter of time before they take over the whole area. At first they are silent and keep themselves away from the local people, but then they start to use their influence and in the end they will work their way into the communities, and by then it is too late to throw them out. They will change our society to meet their needs. We cannot let them do this here. They will wipe out first our heritage and then our people."

Ric sipped at his drink. "I'm not sure the Fifth Republic will stand idly by and let that happen."

"Paris doesn't give a shit what happens in our little island," she dismissed. "We are nothing more than an inconvenience to them. They continue to play their *chienlits*, their great masquerades. They pacify us, tell us we will have the reforms we ask for, and then they forget about us. Every government has been the same; one unfulfilled promise after another. No, Ric, this island is too much trouble and too little benefit for anyone. That is why we have to make sure this new kind of people cannot make their new kind of home here. We, by ourselves, we have to do this without any help. We didn't want the Greeks, the Romans, the Pisans, the Genoese, the Germans or the French in the first place. But there's no point in replacing the French with some other master. At least the French have learned they cannot change us. At least they leave us alone, most of the time."

"You're beginning to sound like Camille."

Manou glared at him: "With good reason. He has been here long enough to see many come and go."

"And what about Franco?" he asked, remembering he had asked the boy's father the same question a few minutes before. "What did you tell him about his father? I suppose Franco makes this that bit more personal; gives you all the justification you need to send these guys packing in whatever manner you think is either appropriate or necessary." Ric drank some more of his *Pietra*. He noticed that the drink seemed to accelerate his thirst rather than diminish it. The contents of the cold, brown bottle left him with a strange, bitter aftertaste; an unpleasant flavour which he felt an increasing desire to rinse away by drinking more.

Manou lowered her head again so that she looked up at Ric from beneath her brow. She stared at him with an intensity he could not disregard; her eyes the cold blue of flame.

She spoke to his eyes rather than to his face when she said, in a deep snarl almost as though hers was the voice of the animal she concealed within: "When he involves Franco it becomes a different matter. It becomes no longer a matter of business, or what we have to do to maintain our heritage, or even what we have to do to survive. It becomes something I must walk towards and not something I can walk away from."

"Another of your convenient proverbs?"

She ignored his taunt. "But Ric, I must ask you one more time why you have come here to Renabianca? Why do you come to this place at the same time Kamo comes here?"

"I already told you why I came here, and I told you I'd never met Kamo before coming here. If it makes a difference, I also came here to try to understand why it is that four generations of my family made the military their home. I wanted to understand why I was fighting to save strangers a thousand miles away when the one place I truly needed to be was at home, fighting to save the one person who needed me. I wanted to know why I wasn't there when I should have been." Ric knew his voice betrayed his great hurt, but he was powerless to restrain it. He stared at the flames in Manou's eyes and wanted to burn himself in them.

"Is that the truth, Ric? And if that is the truth, has my *cavalieru curaghjosu*, my brave knight – found what he was looking for?"

Then, in spite of his anger, Ric chuckled at the ridiculous idea that he might have been searching for some sort of personal grail. "Yes," he replied. "No. Maybe. I'm not sure. I was beginning to think I'd found something else."

It suddenly dawned on Ric that he felt light headed, as though his confession had knocked him off balance. And, if he wasn't mistaken, just at the moment when he wanted to speak again, the ground beneath his feet seemed to shift. It pitched as though he was standing on the deck of a ship in heavy weather, and he bent his knees and flexed his legs to adjust to the change and to stay upright.

Manou was still talking to him. He could hear her one moment, and then not the next, like she was speaking to him from beyond a heaving deck, her voice being taken by the rise and fall of the wind.

"But this is something for us, Ric; not for you," she was saying. "This is our fight... and not for you... you should have gone when you had the chance...."

Trying to keep his feet flat upon the ground was now a considerable effort; one matched only by him trying to keep his head still. Ric was again aware of the bitter, alkaline taste in his mouth. It attacked the sensitive corners of his cheeks, drawing beads of saliva into the furrows behind his teeth and below his tongue, forcing him to swallow to keep from filling up. He concentrated on her eyes; they looked up at him, but seemed to have exchanged the vivid blue of the flame for the impenetrable black of night.

"You could have walked away...," was all he heard her say.

He reached out to hold onto the guy rope beside him, but felt himself stumble and fall sideways. Ric grabbed for the tent pole on the other side, but noticed it leant him little or no support as he began to slide down towards the ground. He wished he could walk away and wished he had walked away when he'd had the chance. He knew that he should have, just as she and all the others had advised him. For now it was too late. Now he no longer possessed the strength to sit upright let alone make it back to his feet.

Manou had laced his drink. It was the last articulate and complete thought he managed to string together before he was no longer lucid enough to summon and assemble words. And in the brief moment before he lay back and the drug turned his lights out, he saw the son of Hypnos, the god of sleep, charge at him out of the gloom; Hypnos and his son Phobetor the boar with his huge yellowed tusks, bristling hairs and foaming breath. And the boar had come to pursue Ric in just the manner he had pursued it in the dark underworld of his dreams.

57

When Ric came round he found he was lying flat on his back in the entrance to the tent. It would have been dark had it not been for a pale-silver light thrown out by the birth of a new moon. And apart from the constant washboard whir of the crickets, there was no sound.

His mouth tasted of stale, rancid glue and, like his eyelids, seemed unwilling to open. When he moved his head it banged like rifle fire on an empty drum, and the continuous percussion made him nauseous.

Something, an ant he hoped, was crawling up his calf inside his trousers. He got up and shook his leg. A small, almost translucent scorpion fell out onto his foot. He flicked it off and shivered as he watched it scuttle like a mechanical toy into the shadows.

Ric understood that she had laced his beer with some form of narcotic. He looked around the inside of the tent for the bottle Manou had been drinking from; guessing hers would not have been doped. It wasn't on the trestle table, but he located the tray of water bottles underneath and broke one open to wash his mouth out; the aftertaste and noisy head the drug left behind reminded him of the headache he had woken up with in the morning, and Ric wondered as he rubbed the dullness from his eyes whether it was the first time she had plied him with it. Whatever she had fed him, it had done the trick. It had served Manou's purpose. As far as he could make out he was an inconvenience to her. She had wanted him out of the way, and dead to the world was about as far out of the way as she could have got him.

If it proved anything, it was that there was nothing further to be gained by hanging on. The message that his presence was no longer required was written in such bold and brilliant letters across the night sky that Ric, even in his doped and dopey state, could not ignore it. It was time to leave. And yet when bathed in the reflection of those letters, Ric still felt himself physically drawn towards Manou. Like an unwanted and irrelevant planet banished from the physical orbit of a blinding sun, he still felt reluctant to take his own newly prescribed route out into the darkness away from her.

Then the litany of confusing events from the last few days came to the rescue and beat his more carnal desires into submission. There was either little or no point in staying. It was that simple.

Ric walked out of the tent into the cool night air. He did not need a torch to find his way; the light from the thin moon dressed by the curtain of stars cast an ethereal glow about Renabianca. It was as though one half of the world lay dead and the other half alive. There existed no common ground between the two, only a clearly defined border of light and dark, without amalgamation, subtle or otherwise. The charred pines threw long dark shadows across the open ground before him, like black notes on a white keyboard, and the scorched remains of the maquis watched without comment as he passed by. The world did not possess the scales of grey which so often painted his sleep. There was either pure light – a straightforward and honest light that provided a stark clarity in which all was revealed and made plain – or there was the dark contamination of shadow; devious and dishonest shadow which concealed and obscured.

He made his way down the tarmac road towards the beach, turning left before the dunes rose to follow the track north. To the left of him lay the swampy lake and to the right amongst the denuded trees lay the sad wreckage of the immolated tents and caravans.

Walking in silence along the track, Ric was wondering how long it would take the vegetation to recover when he perceived an obstruction up ahead of him on the track: a black mound sat in his path. It was not as tall as Ric, but it was wider, and it was still.

He halted ten paces short of it, trying to make out the shape. There were odd curves to the surface at the top and the sides.

Ric was very suddenly aware of how exposed he was out on the track. The obstacle had not been there when he had walked back from the beach earlier. He stood still and slowed his breathing so that he might sharpen his hearing, but above the slight tinnitus left him by the narcotic and the murmur of the crickets and frogs, there was no uncommon noise. He waited a minute, maybe two, then, when he was satisfied there was no other movement from the shadows, he moved to the side of the track and approached.

His movement to the side exposed the object as a trailer and on it, he realised as he got closer, was a jetski. In the contrast of light and dark it was difficult to make out the livery of the machine, but when he arrived at the trailer and stopped and examined it, he recognised it as the jetski that he had himself ridden a couple of days before, and the same one that he had seen Kamo and Franco riding earlier that evening out in the bay.

Ric wondered why it would be sitting on a trailer in the middle of the track, and wondered where the vehicle was that had towed it out of the water. He looked in the pale light for tracks leading away from the tow hitch, but he could make nothing of them. There was a lot of disturbed sand, as though many feet had twisted and turned upon it. Whoever it was had pulled the trailer and its contents from the beach up to the track; there had been many of them.

Twenty metres ahead and to the right was the shower block in which he had hidden the Beretta. He was of a mind to take the gun with him and toss it into the sea off the rocks. He figured that if he stripped it and threw its component parts into the water at different points it would be of no further use or harm to anybody. And he figured it might salvage a little of his conscience when it came to his inability to influence the inevitable mayhem that Kamo and Manou were going to cause. It was a plan. He felt better for it.

But as he neared the shower block he became aware of figures moving through the trees towards him. There were several of them; three maybe four, their uneven shapes ghosting through the black pines.

The hairs on the back of Ric's neck began to stiffen, and he sensed the cool essence of adrenalin seeping through his frame. Tired and slack muscle tensed as he recognised by their vigilance that these figures were wary of his presence in the same way he was wary of theirs.

Ric counted off his steps from the road to the shower block, careful not to make any sound that might give away his position. The box containing the gun was beneath one of the basins in the open wash area. He knelt quietly and felt for the box, but it was not where he had left it. He moved on to the next basin, but it was not there either. Then his hand hit upon a hard object at the spot where he expected the box to be. He ignored it thinking it to be a fragment of charred wood, but as he passed his hand over it the curved and elongated shape was vaguely familiar to him. He ignored it however and carried on until he got to the end of the wall. The box was not there. He tracked back along the hard ground towards the piece of wood. Here in the wash area there was little or no ambient light and he had to feel to identify the different shapes.

Ric came to the piece of wood. It was, as far as he could remember, below the basin right at the place where he had put the box. But the box was gone and in its place was a strange stick of hard wood, bulbous at both ends, but heavier at one. It was the small limb of Asphodel that Franco had called the *mazza*. It felt like the same club he had first seen on the top of *la Tozza* and similar to the one he had found later at the house. It also felt like the very club that had appeared in his hand during his dreams of hunting the wild boar at night in the maquis.

Someone had replaced the gun with the *mazza*.

The cold hardness of the *mazza* was stark against the warmth of his right hand. If nothing else, it was a weapon with which he could defend himself.

He slipped out of the shower block. The figures he had seen a few moments ago had disappeared, for now there was no movement other than his own and he knew that made his situation precarious. He knew it would be impossible to conceal his motion through the light and shade.

Ric had taken but five paces towards the track when a figure stepped out of the darkness into his path.

The moonlight shone down from behind the man. He was medium height and muscular, but his flat haircut was unmistakable, and when he spoke Ric immediately knew him.

"You steal my jetski!" It was not a question that Bobo asked; it was an accusation that cared nothing for validity. There would be no denial.

Ric remembered the fellow from the first time he had seen him walking along the beach to Camille's bar. He was well built and he carried himself with the rolling athletic gait that suggested he would be fast as well as strong.

"You steal my jetski," Bobo repeated a little louder for the benefit of his companions.

"Sure," replied Ric with easy sarcasm. "Simple. I swam over to the boat, unhitched your jetski, towed it back here, lifted all half a ton of it straight out of the water, dropped it onto the trailer, and pulled the trailer a hundred metres up the beach." Ric needed to know how outnumbered he was, and he knew his chances of catching the man off balance were better if he could rile him.

"Typical Englishman," he said, "always make joke when things look bad."

"Wrong," replied Ric, watching for the movement. "I only make jokes when things amuse me." Four, he counted, including the guy in front of him. Too many. If they were armed, they didn't show it. He stepped towards the man. He knew it would allow one of the others to get in behind him, but he had to demonstrate his confidence and his intention, and he knew he had to get further away from the shower block if he was to make a run for it north into the shadows. "Besides, your boss, Petrossian, said I could borrow it anytime. Ask him," Ric offered, buying time. As he got to within a couple of paces, he kicked up a little sand at the man who had crouched in readiness.

"Petrossian not my boss," Bobo sneered, wiping the back of his right hand across his mouth. "He does not tell me what to do. My boss, he gives orders."

It came to Ric, in working out that the man before him was right handed, that Kamo, being left-handed, was not the man who had assaulted Camille and the woman Pela. The man in front of him was most likely responsible; right hooks gave left black eyes, not left hooks. "Does he tell you to beat up on women and old men too, Bobo?" he chided.

Ric was as close as he needed to be. He stared not at the man's face but at his waist. If there was any movement, he would notice it in its beginning.

"They are all the same," Bobo scoffed, straightening in his bravado. "You f-."

Ric struck as fast as he could, swinging the *mazza* in his right hand in an arc from below the inside of his knee, up and out to the right. The fellow was not expecting the club to come up at him from such an angle, and it caught him high on the right of his forehead as he tried to step back out of the way. It was an opening jab; no more.

Ric followed the momentum of the *mazza* and rolled out to his right, separating the two of them either side of a dead pine. He felt the others move towards him and, not wanting to lose any advantage he might have gained, Ric advanced around the tree, edging nearer to his objective. He needed to be closer to the trees on the other side of the track. As he lunged forward again, his adversary gave ground, but his cronies moved with him.

The Russian barked at the other men and they seemed to drop back, as though he had told them they would not be needed.

That unsettled Ric even though he already knew his opponent had the measure of him.

And with that unspoken concession, Bobo darted forward directly at Ric, who swung the *mazza* hard at the onrushing man. The blow caught Bobo on the side of the shoulder as he tried to duck inside the arc. His hands grabbed at Ric's arms as he attempted to restrain the blows raining on him from the club.

Ric managed to get in two good hits which solicited grunts of acknowledgement and pain, but his rival kept coming, oblivious to the weight of the blows. Ric stumbled back, losing his footing, and in an attempt to lever his arm holding the *mazza* away from the man's grip, he let go of the club and it flew out of his grasp into the darkness.

They flailed at one another, punching with clenched fists; wide hooks and straight jabs and solid uppercuts through guarded arms. And now and then they threw open handed grabs at each other's clothing, trying to gain position to pull or push the other off balance. Yet both stayed on their feet. They boxed and kicked, took hits and gave them. They grew tired and heaved great breaths, broke away and stepped off each other to compose themselves for the next hit.

Ric tasted blood, raw, thin and alkaline. As he and his opponent circled, Ric got closer to the track. He trusted he would have sufficient strength left in reserve to bolt into the trees, but he knew his legs were growing weary.

Bobo lunged towards him again, but Ric stepped to his left and back out of the way as fast as he could, only to find one of the other men standing behind him. He moved towards the man, but he did not give way. Ric moved right, away from his objective, but none of the others moved.

The Russian barked at his companions and they began to move in towards Ric.

The end was coming; he knew it. So he set his feet and leapt in towards his opponent, hoping it would be the last thing he was expecting. Ric crashed into the wall of dense meat that was Bobo's torso and tried to blast through the man's arms as they closed around him. He pumped his knees up into the man's groin and midriff, trying to knock him over.

Bobo was caught off balance and fell over backwards. And in the moment Ric knew he was no longer held, he burst through and over the man, planting his feet not only squarely so that he could push through the man, but also so that he would exact as much pain and hurt upon the guy as he could. But as he pulled his trailing leg away from the man's clutches, the Russian swung his arms up and tripped Ric over.

He staggered headlong for a couple of paces, trying all the time to drag his legs up beneath his body to support it.

In a frantic effort to stay upright Ric reached out, hoping to find a tree to which he might cling and arrest his downward progress long enough for him to regain his balance. But he had reached the track and there were no trees close by.

The game of catch-up his legs were playing was over. He lurched forwards and crashed onto the sandy ground about the same time as the three other men landed on top of him. The racket of their feral exertions filled the night.

Ric struggled against their holds, but knew deep down he had lost any position worth fighting to maintain. He slackened a moment.

They pulled him up and forced him to kneel, two of them then holding his arms straight out behind him, whilst the third took hold of him by his hair and yanked his head back. Ric gasped for breath as the Russian got back to his feet.

Ric felt appalling; his body ached and the abrasions to his face and hands stung. But he knew it was nothing compared to how he was about to feel. He steeled himself for the beating to come.

Bobo wobbled as he got to his feet, lending Ric a little warmth in the knowledge that he had given perhaps better than he had received.

Without a word the dishevelled bundle of muscle rose to his full height, dusted his shirt and trousers down as if to suggest he had not suffered any bother of note, then strode in a businesslike fashion over to where Ric was kneeling and kicked him in the stomach.

It knocked all the wind out of Ric.

For a couple of seconds there was no sound, no breath, no nothing; just a sickening paralysis, and then all at once he retched and breathed. He fought to get some air back into his lungs, but the compressed muscles in his abdomen rebelled at every request. He gulped and gasped, and dry retched again and coughed. "Just like I said," Ric began when his breath eventually returned, "women and old m-."

Bobo kicked Ric in the stomach again; the pain this time was far more intense and stung as though he had been stabbed by a blunt blade.

Ric retched and heaved again.

Then a hand clutched his face with such force he felt his head would separate from his jaw. Though his cheeks were squashed together in the man's grip, he opened his eyes not wanting to give the Russian the benefit of knowing he was defeated.

Bobo bent down to face Ric. "Yes. Old men too! Young men, old men; it makes no difference to me if a man is old. If his time has come, then it has come." He held up his right hand so that Ric could see his fingers, and more importantly the ring on his little finger. It was a small gold signet ring, too small for the thick finger that wore it. The gold had long lost its shine. In any other circumstances it would have been unremarkable, and maybe even gone unnoticed, but now brandished in Ric's face so that he could look nowhere else other than straight at it, it became obvious that it was no ordinary ring, for in the centre of it, where a coat of arms would be inscribed or a family jewel lie, was set a small, smooth black stone, one identical to the lump of stone set in the head of the signet ring worn by Camille; a pebble of the *Catochitis* from *la Tozza*. The ring glinted a little in the light, but the dull, inset stone threw no reflection.

Ric looked into the abyss that was the stone.

At first he was afraid it was Camille's ring and that the wretched bastard must have taken it from Camille. But then he reasoned the ape would never have got Camille's ring onto his thick finger. So it wasn't the same one. And if it wasn't the same one, then whose was it? Camille had said two rings had been made and the second was lost when Manou's father disappeared.

And so it dawned on Ric whose ring it must be.

His eyes must have given him away.

"I see," said Bobo, his face cut and bleeding. "I see you know this ring." He paused for effect. "So you must know who it belonged to." He paused. "Yes," Bobo preened, "It was the old man; the father of your pretty lady-friend."

Ric recalled the old man beside the road; the old man searching for the one who had taken what was his. And he realised and, curiously, quickly accepted that it was the spirit of Manou's father who had shown himself from the shadows that night, and that for the last few weeks he

337

had been staying in the house that had once been home to Manou and her family. And he also understood that he had failed them all by surrendering to this assassin who smirked and sneered in his face.

"He was a problem," Bobo continued. "The old man was going to be difficult. He was going to shout and make a noise. So I made sure he could not make any more noise. It was not difficult. He was strong for an old man. But he was not strong enough, and his neck was thin."

Ric remembered how Manou's father had pawed at his neck.

But the ruthless figure now before him wasn't finished with his bragging. "He was a problem that I had to deal with. Petrossian, he is not enough of a man to deal with his own problems. So it was left for me to clean up; perhaps like I have to clean up you?"

He let go of Ric's jaw with his left, but brought his right hand in towards Ric's face, and putting the head of the ring against his forehead, he drew two lines in the shape of a cross in the centre above Ric's nose, sniggering as he did so.

"There," he concluded. "Now you are ready to join the father of your lady-friend. Please, when you see him, give him my best regards." Bobo stood back away from the penitent figure at his feet.

Ric closed his eyes. He knew the blow was coming at his face, and knew it would come at great speed and with huge force. But when he shut his eyes he saw before him the putrid remains of the boar; the boar he had beaten to a bloody pulp in the hunt of his dream. And through the carnage of what was left of the boar's face, Ric made out the vicious leer of the killer before him and very suddenly he understood the purpose of the dream.

He calmed. He smiled to himself and looked up.

Bobo sneered, his teeth blackened by the blood in his mouth. "You want, I kick you to sleep? Or perhaps like the old man, I squeeze the last breath out of you?"

"Makes no difference to me, Bobo," Ric said. "It's not my time."

And, instead of the blow landing with its full weight right in the front and centre of his face, the silence of the night was broken by two large and sharp reports.

As if in slow motion, Bobo's foot pulled up from the progress of its long arc. It lifted short and just grazed Ric's cheek.

Bobo, the sadistic, brawny, flat-topped clown, jerked and then swayed backwards away from Ric. He clutched his chest at his breastbone with both hands, stood a couple of seconds, as though tottering on the edge of a cliff, and then staggered back as if trying to put some distance between himself and the edge of the drop. He frowned in misunderstanding as he looked down at the dark stain spreading across his chest.

His eyes glazed over. Bobo toppled over backwards.

Ric felt the hands tight about his arms and head soften and release him. He slumped down. He was aware of the figures about him taking flight into the night, of hasty feet rushing by, flicking sand at him as they went.

He rolled over onto his back and looked up at the stars. There were so many and they were so bright and so still and so peaceful, and he was so very, very tired.

And then into this canopy of twinkling gems appeared the face and form of the frowning Seraphina, all long curly hair and bandanna, the whites of her eyes shining out like the stars behind her. She peered down at Ric to see whether there was any life left in him, and when she had decided there was, she stood back and waited for him to get up.

As was her way, the tall woman scowled at Ric. And in her right hand she carried the Beretta which she pointed straight at him.

58

Ric was not wholly surprised to see Seraphina pointing the Beretta at him. A harping voice suggested to him that just because she had delivered him from one evil, there was no reason to suggest why she shouldn't deliver him into another. He was however, more than a little offended that the scowling woman should feel the need to view him even in his battered state as a threat. But that was the way things were going and he could see no reason why he should expect them to change.

"Thank you," he said, more because he thought he ought to. But, judging by the complete lack of any teeth gleaming in the dark, Ric guessed his gratitude was wasted. He wondered how long she had been watching the action, and whether she'd only pulled the trigger after she'd seen him get a decent kicking. He turned round expecting to see the other three mugs lying prone on the track, but only the dead Bobo lay where he had fallen. The other three men had bolted. He could hear the commotion of a struggle being played out not far away in the darkness; a muted grunting and groaning of men straining to lift weight, closely followed by the sound of wood snapping or bones breaking?

Then there was silence again. Seraphina was not alone.

"Where to now?" he asked, wiping warm blood from his left eye.

She gestured with the gun down the track, away from the beach.

Ric considered rushing her. On the track, in the half-light, if he could get close enough to her, he fancied he might get the better of her. But when he stretched himself to assess his damaged torso, small rockets of electric pain streaked from his midriff in all directions. And Seraphina was not shy of using the gun, he had seen that, and he didn't fancy his chances of getting into the shadows without her shooting him first. And that was to ignore whoever it was that had just dealt with Bobo's companions.

He held up his hands and started to walk up the track. He turned left when she indicated and skirted the jetski lying like a sleeping Sumo on the track. They walked back up the road to the main camp area. The incessant whispering of the crickets and the croaking of the frogs deadened the sound of their feet upon the tarmac road, the pungent aroma of decaying pine-needles and stagnant water lay heavy on the air, and the stars just hung about blinking in observation, shepherding their progress.

At times his sight deceived him as the world seemed to lose all dimension; the ambient light glowed almost bright upon the ground, as though all about was illuminated by radiant yet invisible lamps. But upon the scorched stumps, the slender charred trunks and the blackened bushes, the light seemed to die, as though each immolated fragment presented a fathomless void from which all light gave up any hope of reflection, much like the *Catochitis*. The world was in contrast; there was either plain sight in which he could not hope to hide, or the very flat black of blindness in the shadows, hiding only god knew what, or whom.

As they approached the tent, Ric could see the lighted hurricane lamp hanging from the ceiling. It threw the shadows of two occupants against the tent sides. By the presence of his guard, logic proposed the shorter of the two was Camille, but, unless there was some trick of the light, the other was not Manou as both shapes were too corpulent.

He steeled himself against who they might be, hesitating at the doorway to the tent.

Camille turned from looking through the papers on the trestle table.

"Ric! *Va bè!* It's good that you are here. We were troubled by your absence," he said, his tone planted halfway between casual indifference and due concern.

Ric wondered whether his absence had been an inconvenience to Camille's sentimental anxiety, rather than the cause of it. But the brief twinkle in the old boy's eyes suggested there was just a slim chance it might be the latter. He wore dark blue trousers tied with rope and a dark blue T-shirt in the manner of a fisherman.

The other man was René Bosquet. He was more smartly dressed though equally drab in colour. He was sitting on a canvas chair, his arms folded across his chest, like a diner impatient for his next course.

"Mister Ross," he pronounced, as though he liked the way the words rolled off his tongue, "I see you now understand what happens when you don't take my advice: bad for your health, eh?" He did not attempt to decorate his opinion with any humour, and as if to confirm the situation warranted none, there lay on the trestle table a couple of short, hammerless shotguns. Each one had a short sculpted grip and double barrels that extended just beyond the wood of the fore-end. Beside them lay a prehistoric pistol that resembled a German Luger; all grip and not much barrel.

"But," Bosquet chuckled, pointing to his head, "I see you now have *Le Bon Dieu* to help you."

Ric had forgotten the thin black cross smudged in the centre of his forehead; it had been the least of his worries at the time Bobo had drawn it. And given his mauled and disfigured state Ric was surprised he had the energy to summon so much animosity for the loathsome Bosquet. But, as much as he felt inclined to take out his frustrations on the toad of a policeman, he decided he would be better to conserve what little energy he had left for whatever was next. So he said, "If it wasn't for the Angel of Mercy, here," he pointed his thumb at Seraphina behind him, "you'd be permanently troubled by my absence. Remarkable sense of timing she has; her and her *Squadra d'Arrozza*, if I've got that right?"

"Oh, you should not put your faith too much in Corsican mythology," Bosquet mocked, "the tales of old women are not in the habit of coming to one's aid when one needs them most."

Camille shot the unbeliever a withering glance, then turned his attention back to Ric. He frowned at the woman and drew back his lips in disapproval. She lowered the gun, went to put it on the table, thought better of it, pocketed it and left the tent. "My apologies, Ric," he volunteered, "Seraphina knows only one law, and she does not see fit to share it with us."

"A law unto herself, you mean," Ric corrected.

"It is so," Camille replied. He approached Ric and examined his cut and grazed face. When he was satisfied that the damage was superficial he stepped back, poured a glass of Châtaignier from a bottle on the table and handed it to Ric.

He contemplated the light brown liquid in the glass. With his head still groggy from the last narcotic, he was a little shy of drinks being handed to him by people he trusted.

Camille raised his bushy grey eyebrows, then hunched and shrugged in the caricature of a helpless vassal.

"Sure! I know," replied Ric, "Manou is a law unto herself too, huh." He drank and swilled the chestnut liqueur around the inside of his mouth hoping it would mask the thin, metallic taste of his own blood. It did, but it stung the raw flesh on the inside of his cheeks.

"Okay," pronounced Camille as though he were bringing the meeting to order, "now we have to decide what we do about Franco and his father."

Ric looked from one man to the other and then back again. "We?"

"Yes, my friend, we…," the policeman began.

"Less of the pleasantries Bosquet," Ric growled. "Friends like you I can do without."

"Alright, Ric," Bosquet agreed, "we have to decide what 'we' are going to do with the problem of Mr Petrossian before he realises his own militia are of no further help to him and that he no longer has the authority he perceives."

Ric shook his head, half in disagreement and half in disbelief. He chuckled both at the mistake he had made in shaking his head because it caused him so much pain and that he could not believe what he was hearing above the ringing in his ears.

"Would you two hang on a minute? There are a couple of things I can't get straight here." He looked at Camille. "Since when did you get into bed with the Paris?"

Bosquet broke in: "I'm not from Paris, Ric. I work for *Renseignement Intérieur*, in case you are concerned that I do not have the proper credentials for this situation."

"That's a grand name for an intelligence agency, and personally I was never very trusting of you grey types. But you're still from Paris all the same."

"Not quite," Bosquet replied, at which Camille raised a cynical eyebrow. "But what I mean to say is that sometimes our designs coincide. Shall we say they are of mutual interest to each other? Would that make it easier for you to swallow?"

"Not much," Ric replied. "I suppose I'm having difficulty stomaching the fact that the powers that be will condone murder when it suits them. The laws I'm used to haven't worked that way for a while."

Bosquet sighed as he got up off his chair. "Maybe it does not in other parts of the European Community, Ric. But this is Corsica. You would do well to remember where you are and the company you keep. I think I have said this to you before." He yawned and stretched. "Besides we are all working to the same end. And I am not so sure there is a problem with this end justifying our means, *n'est ce pas?*"

Camille maintained his silence and his expression. He stood back and watched Ric as though he was trying to make his mind up about something.

Ric shook his head again. "Oh, come off it, Bosquet. I don't believe for one moment you stand back and let the locals practise their own brand of medieval law enforcement. I think that's taking the preservation of their customs a shade too far."

"Maybe not, Ric, but, perhaps let us say that certain people in power are no longer immune to the idea that some customs are best left alone; that perhaps if we take away the control people have over their lives, if we remove their belief in what has made it possible for them to survive for so long, then we have to replace it with something. Let us say, that there are certain people in government who have come to the conclusion that there is nothing that they can substitute for this belief; that there is nothing of a great enough substance that can replace whatever it is that some people believe in." René Bosquet finished his sermon.

"Or let's," Ric protested, "stop trying to dress this charade up as anything other than what it is. You're getting these guys to deal with a problem you don't know how to deal with. You've passed all your laws to keep yourself tucked up safe in bed at night, but you haven't got anything in your warrant book that tells you how to deal with this kind of situation, so you're employing the local muscle to help you out."

"Just like you and your government have been doing in Iraq and Afghan."

"Tread lightly, Bosquet," Ric warned, feeling colour rise in his cheeks. "There's plenty of French coffins come out of the desert around Sangin lately. Anyway, this place is a million miles from that war."

"Maybe so, Ric. Maybe so. But in return for a little help, these people," he deferred to Camille when he spoke, "are allowed to get on with their lives without further interference from a government they do not care for."

Ric looked at Camille, for the old boy had dropped his gaze and was now staring at his shoes, like a schoolboy who'd been let off detention. But Ric wasn't ready to settle: "I don't buy it, Bosquet. Sounds too much like Machiavelli in a fancy overcoat."

"I am not," Bosquet bridled, "how you would say, bothered whether you believe it or not, Ric. You were given sufficient opportunity to stay out of this business and you chose to ignore my advice." Now it was the policeman's turn to raise his voice: "*Qui craint le danger ne doit pas aller en mer, Ric.* You know what this means?"

"Oh spare me the bloody aphorisms, Bosquet," Ric shouted back, squaring up. "I've stood as much heat in the kitchen as the next man."

"Gentlemen, gentlemen," Camille interrupted with a resigned and gentle authority, "we are forgetting about Franco, which is why we are here, are we not?" But he allowed the two in front of him to stare each other out for a few seconds and when they'd pandered to their machismo for long enough, he carried on. "We don't have the luxury of time in this situation. Very soon Monsieur Petrossian will be expecting his men to be returning with his toy. If someone does not return to the boat soon, he will grow suspicious and leave with Franco. Then we have a very different situation. So, what is the best for us to do?"

Ric knew Camille well enough to know he would already have a plan; the wily old fox was being polite in waiting and giving him and Bosquet their opportunity to speak before he did.

And Bosquet wasn't about to offer any great solution to the problem; he wasn't on his home patch. And besides, he seemed to show an almost unhealthy willingness to pay out enough line for the local boys to hang themselves.

Then, considering the rough and tumble he had recently indulged in, it came to Ric that the reason he was being included in this parley was because of what would be his part in Camille's plan. Of course, he realised, he was the one among them who had the best chance of getting to Petrossian without being injured, and if he did get injured, or worse, it would be of little or no consequence to either of the men standing opposite him.

"And Manou?" he asked.

Camille straightened up at his question: "She is somewhere where afterwards there will be no questions asked about her part in this. Manou is having dinner at the *Mairie* in Porto Vecchio with the Minister of Culture and other Department of Tourism officials from Paris. It is in many ways the best place for her to be this evening. It is a convenient coincidence, if you like?"

"Well, I guess even you couldn't organise that kind of coincidence, eh?"

Camille looked up at him, winked and said, "So it is up to us to retrieve Franco from this man."

"This 'man' just happens to be his father. And have you considered that maybe young Franco doesn't want to be retrieved."

Camille nodded thoughtfully. "Yes. It is possible." But that was the end of that.

"So," Ric concluded, "you'd like me to skip over to the boat, sweet talk Petrossian into letting me return Franco to his mother, and in the process tell him he's overstayed his welcome."

"*Esattamente!*" the old boy confirmed; happy in the knowledge that he had elicited from his young friend the desired conclusion.

"And what makes you think I would be willing to do this when Manou's just slipped me a knock-out cocktail, the by-product of which was that I nearly got myself put to sleep permanently?"

Bosquet sneered at Camille: "I told you Monsieur Giovananngeli; there is no reason why this *léger* should do this purely for a summer romance."

"Lightweight?" Ric took a purposeful step towards him. "Go look in the mirror, Bosquet."

"Enough," Camille said. He shrugged, pursed his lips and rubbed at his ear as though considering a menu: "But I have told Inspecteur Bosquet that you will do this; if not for Manou, then for Franco. And I think it is so, that you will do this for Franco unless I am very much mistaken, Ric?"

"I'd rather hear the whole thing had been settled by a paternity suit, if you don't mind. The court system may be long and drawn out, but murder tends to complicate custody actions, Camille, not settle them." He nodded at the collection of firearms. "Besides, I'm a student of field craft and overwhelming force, not domestic disagreement."

The old boy stood up from leaning his weary frame against the trestle table.

"Yes, Ric, I am sure you are. But like the time we are wasting talking, we don't have the luxury of appealing to the courts. It is not our way; I thought you would have realised this by now." He turned away from Ric and busied himself with one of the shotguns and a box of cartridges. Without turning back to face Ric he spoke again: "Of course you can leave it to us and we will settle this our own way. Sometimes our ways can be…," Camille searched for the words, "perhaps a little amateur."

The silence that ensued was brief, but into it Ric crammed a barrage of disordered logic. All he could hear was the deafening and relentless chirping of the crickets, interspersed by the occasional harsh ratchet-croak of a bullfrog. And like the incessant obbligato, his doubts deafened his thinking.

He could walk away. It would be the right thing to do. And yet he knew he couldn't. He tried to think of what might happen in the next moments, of the possible consequences, and of where on earth he would go and what he would do afterwards. And when he understood that all of that meant nothing, that he, like the consequences, meant nothing, he realised he didn't care, for he knew that through all of his own fear and uncertainty, it was not he who mattered, it was Franco. "How much time do we have?" he asked Camille.

The old man tugged at his moustache in contemplation, then handed Bosquet one of the small shotguns, offered Ric the antiquated Luger, which he refused, took the other shotgun for himself, and the three of them set off for the beach. "Half an hour," he said to Ric as they walked down the sandy road, "but if we see the motor-yacht is leaving we will come. *Capisci?*"

"Sure," Ric replied. "How many men do you have?"

"As many as I need," answered Camille in a cryptic way that implied he either had a legion of special forces in reserve at the back of the beach, or that it was just him, Seraphina and Bosquet, and they would have to be sufficient in number.

But when they got to the shower block, the trailer stood empty. There were other beings in the shadows. Ric could feel their presence. A little further on the corpse of the Russian Bobo had been dragged to the side of the track.

As they passed Ric spoke softly to Camille: "He has the ring that belongs to Manou's father."

"It is so," the old man replied without breaking step.

And when they approached the beach Ric could see that the jetski was now beached at the water's edge, adjacent to the tender that Bobo and his henchmen had come in on. The three men waited in the protection of the shadows at the back of the beach for five or so minutes in case any more of the crew had come ashore. When they were satisfied nothing had changed,

347

they walked slowly down to the sea. On the jetski were laid a white shirt and a pair of shorts such as the crewmen had worn. "No thanks," Ric said to Camille when the older man picked them up and offered them to him, "never fancied someone else's uniform."

The glitzy motor-yacht lay beam-on a couple of hundred metres off shore. It stood out alone in the bay with all the glittering, but illusory promise of a Ferris wheel in a cemetery. The wind of earlier had dropped, the temperature was cool, and the thin sickle of the new moon was now low in the south-eastern night sky. Ric would have preferred the cover of at least a tempest for what he was about to do, but unfortunately the water was smooth, flat and black like polished obsidian. He kicked off his running shoes and sat astride the mechanical steed.

Camille offered him the reassurance of the gun once more, but Ric shook his head. They both knew that in the scheme of things Petrossian would not allow him on the boat whilst he carried it. Bosquet, on the other hand, clutched his shotgun to his chest as though his heart would not beat without its proximity.

"I don't have a watch," Ric said.

"I will fire the shotgun five minutes before it is time for you to leave. When you hear it make sure you have Franco with you," Camille insisted, and then he added: "How many will be on the boat?"

Ric tried to remember the number of crew: "Maybe four or five others, apart from Petrossian. He told me she carried a crew of five. Three you've taken care of, excepting the one Seraphina did for, which leaves the steward and engineer, plus maybe Petrossian's creepy friend, if he is still on board. If there are any others, let's hope they're no hopers. Leave it to me," he said, with as much confidence as he could muster. Ric slipped the dead man's cord over his wrist and pressed the starter button. The machine burst alive and then settled to idle, burbling beneath him.

"Good...," began Camille.

"Save it," Ric interrupted; luck, he had always believed, was for people who liked the idea of it. He glanced in the direction of where Bosquet stood a few yards back up the beach. Ric didn't trust him, and he wanted Camille to know it.

"Okay," Camille said, patting him on his back, "but remember a good journey is one that you return from." He winked in such an exaggerated fashion Ric could see it even in the dark.

Ric pushed off the sandy bottom with his right foot and pulled the throttle lever open just enough for him to steer the jetski out into the open water.

He cruised over towards the motor-yacht. There was no point in raising any alarm by charging over with all the fanfare of a sea-born assault. They would be expecting the jetski to return, but not with Ric at the helm. The water was calm and the air so still that even with the jetski just ticking over to make way the noise seemed loud.

The beam of the *Kohar* was square before him. The coloured lights, strung from the bow up to the flying bridge and down to the stern, diverted his eyes from what might be happening on deck. What was going on inside, Ric could not see because of the reflective windows, and the aft and sun decks were unlit. He steered the jetski to port to come at her stern from the south. He expected to find at least one crewman on watch, but he could see no movement on board.

Still no one appeared, even when he got to within shouting distance. But, as he was about to park the machine side on to the transom, a figure stepped out of the shadows and moved towards him.

Ric reckoned by the broader but slender physique and the angular movement that he was a man, but the shadows of the steps and rail distorted his silhouette. Though dressed in dark colours, something reflected on the figure's chest; a brief glinting in the glow of the low moon.

A hand reached out for his line.

"Ric, my friend," Kamo said, "About time! I was afraid something unfortunate had happened to you."

59

"Ric, I see you have found religion," Kamo said with dry amusement, indicating the cross Bobo had drawn on Ric's forehead. "Is it that 'X' marks the spot? Is this where the real treasure is buried; in your head? No. Somehow I do not think you are a man who takes easily to religion." He looked Ric up and down, appreciating his rather abused state: "You look terrible; that is not good. But you look to me as though you are unarmed; that is better. I must apologise for Bobo; sometimes he takes a strange delight in his work."

"I wouldn't bother," Ric muttered. "Bobo's probably busy apologising for a life full of strange delights right about now."

"Yes," Kamo agreed, "of course I mean he 'took' a strange pleasure in his work." His expression suggested that his minder's demise was no loss to society or more particularly to him personally. "I heard the shots. And he was always much too confident to take his own gun. Expensive misjudgement on his part, but then he was always too fond of using his hands."

"The same hands he used to strangle Manou's father?"

At this accusation Kamo went quiet. It was evidently something that still troubled him. He turned and raised his head and fronted up to Ric, his face waxen and serious.

"This I did not find out about until after it had happened. It was difficult for me to deal with; a difficult lesson to learn." He dragged his gaze away from Ric and picked up two tumblers from the bar. He dashed a generous measure of whisky into each and handed one to Ric. "Perhaps it is better you understand that I did not know Bobo had killed Manou's father until sometime afterwards. He acted without my authority and the whole episode was a great sadness to me. I found out by chance. He boasted of it to me when he was drunk one night. He showed me the ring with the strange stone. It was bizarre; I knew when I saw the ring it would bring him his end. It is not like a diamond or other precious stone that promises to reveal the light of life. This stone is like the eye of a dead man; it sees everything, but shows nothing. As though when you look into it you expect to see something wonderful, but you find nothing but emptiness."

Ric waited for Kamo to drink, and when he was happy that the whisky was real he threw back his glass of amber liquid. It didn't mix with the others he'd drunk during the evening, but it soothed his aching muscles.

He remembered the ring and in doing so raised his hand to trace the still tender mark of its cross on his forehead. He now knew where he had seen the lustreless void of that signet stone before. It was as Kamo said; the ring saw everything and showed nothing.

He examined his empty tumbler, and glanced at the ornate clock hanging behind the bar. "So you didn't know about Manou's father?"

Kamo ignored the question: "How long have they given you, Ric?"

"Not long enough to listen to your confession," he replied. "Where is Franco?"

Kamo shrugged his shoulders as if the answer to the question should have been obvious. "Like the dutiful father I have so very suddenly become, my son is where he should be; asleep in the master bedroom. And," he pointed a slender finger at Ric, "that is precisely where he will stay until the sun comes up."

Ric handed his glass over for a refill, and as the other man took it from him, he hit Kamo as hard and as fast as he could in the side of his head with his right hand, knocking him to the ground in the space between the bar and the partition.

"Wait, Ric," Kamo stuttered from his prone position. "This is not the best way forward for us."

Still lying down he raised his hands in defence. "I'm not going to fight with you, Ric. You have spent your life learning to fight, and this is not just about you and me."

When Ric was certain that the other man had no weapon within reach, he allowed him to get back to his feet. "So help me Kamo, I'll break every bone in your body…."

"Wait, Ric," Kamo started again massaging his jaw. "There must be a more civilised way to settle this."

"No, Kamo, sometimes there isn't. If I don't return with Franco in a few minutes this thing is going to get a whole lot uglier," he said in a tone so unforgiving he did not recognise it as his own.

Then Ric became aware of a presence from behind. He didn't hear any specific noise, but he perceived a slight change in atmosphere as though a door had been opened and new air allowed into the room. He turned to see the young Asian steward standing behind him, pointing what looked like a small semi-automatic pistol at him. The young steward, dressed in his white jacket and trousers, held the gun as though it was a glass overfilled with wine.

"Tell the lad to put the gun down, Kamo."

"You tell him, Ric. Nobody wants to listen to me this evening; not even you it would seem."

Ric glanced at the clock and turned back to the steward. He still had ten or so minutes.

Then they heard the hollow percussion of a shotgun from somewhere outside, and in the split second Kamo and the steward were distracted, Ric rotated, whipped the bottle of whisky off the counter with his right hand and hit the steward with it. The gun in his hand did not fire even though the young man pulled frantically at the trigger. He fell backwards under the blow of the bottle and bounced off the window behind him back within range. Ric followed his initial strike with a second blow to the steward's head and watched as he collapsed unconscious to the floor. He feared he had killed the young man, but then saw the blood pumping from his nose and the wound at his forehead, and figured that although unconscious, if he was bleeding he was probably alive.

Still trying to assume a confident and untroubled air Kamo said: "No wonder Bobo came off second best to you, Ric."

"He didn't, Kamo. That's what I'm trying to tell. I had the right kind of help. Let me take Franco and go so no one else gets hurt. The longer this plays out, the worse it'll get."

"I can't do that, Ric," he pleaded. "You know that. Neither of us can back down." He paused. "Okay, maybe for different reasons. You, because it is a matter of honour. Although I am not so sure your honour is more than a flag of convenience. If you remember you are the one who owes me a favour. And me, because if I leave here without what I came for, I will not be able to show my face to my, to my... let us call him my boss. I am not sure that the concept of what you would call honour will sit so easily with him."

Now it was Ric's turn to sigh. He took the small pistol from the stewards limp hand and pocketed it. He took no delight in hurting a young man who knew so little about guns that he hadn't even released the safety catch. He supposed the rest of Kamo's muscle was now either lying dead on the beach or fleeing for their lives through the maquis; Seraphina and her chums had seen to them.

"Face it, Kamo. You're out of options. If you've got to resort to young men who don't know one end of the gun from the other it's time for you to find another occupation and leave this lot in peace."

But the Armenian was still unfazed by his predicament; he picked up the bottle of whisky and poured two more generous measures.

Ric heard the noise of the tender drawing up to the stern of the motor-yacht. He felt a slight relief that Camille, Seraphina and, if he was honest, even Bosquet were coming to put an end to what was turning into an unpleasant charade. He glanced at the clock and wondered why Camille had sounded his advance before the half hour was up.

One of the French doors to the aft deck opened and in stepped a very nervous Bosquet. He carried the shotgun Camille had given him and was sweating as though he had sprinted across the water from the beach.

Ric expected Camille and Seraphina to follow close behind. When neither did, his stomach sank and he was unsure of what to do next. "Where is Camille?"

Bosquet walked through the stateroom up to the two men, giving the inert steward nothing more than a cursory glance as though he were a pile of dirty laundry. He clutched the small double-barrelled shotgun so tight that his knuckles shone white, and his mouth twitched. He stopped a couple of paces away from Ric and levelled the shotgun at him.

"Monsieur Giovananngeli went to the back of the beach saying something about a ring. The old fool decided for some reason, a reason I do not understand, to fire his gun at the corpse of Monsieur Petrossian's man, as if the corpse was not dead enough already. I considered it better to leave him to his own special, home-grown madness."

"If you've done for that old man...," Ric began, clenching his fists.

"Oh, come now, Ric, you are hardly in a position to issue threats," Bosquet dismissed, nodding towards the pile of laundry, "and I am not so naive." He paused to let his statement sink in.

"The woman, Seraphina, is a different matter. She was nowhere to be seen. One can only hope she has met with a justice that was more suited to her own unsympathetic attitude. If that is so, then one family in Olmeto will rest when they find out her debt of blood has at last been paid."

"Talking of blood; yours is pretty cheap, Bosquet?" Ric spat.

"Oh, Ric! Such a parochial view of values," the fat man chided. "That is so very 'last century'."

"All that garbage about preserving customs and coincidental interests, Bosquet; was that for my benefit or Camille's?"

"Not bad some of that, eh? Quite eloquent," he congratulated himself. "A shame I had to waste it on such an old fool, but it was what he wanted to hear. Ric, enough of this! Both Monsieur Petrossian and I have tried our best to get you to leave, and it is clear from your continued presence that you are not going to help the one person who needs it most."

"Listen Bosquet, just because you've got the better of one old man and a young woman, it doesn't follow that Manou will roll over for you. She'll have the local mob all over you like a cheap suit when they find out what you're up to."

Bosquet sucked his teeth as though he was having difficulty with an obstinate fish bone. "You continue to disappoint, Ric; really you do. Monsieur Petrossian, on behalf of his partners, is already in," he hesitated, searching for the words, "advanced negotiations with our troublesome friends at the FLNC. Since their foolishness in shooting the prefect in '98, they have found themselves to be very isolated; found it more and more difficult to make friends in the international community. So, they have been looking for new partners for a long time, and fortunately Monsieur Petrossian and his people will oblige us in return for certain favours of an economic nature. They will become suitable partners for these foolish separatists. Sadly Monsieur Giovananngeli and Miss Pietri are, or were, one part of the FLNC council who were not well-disposed to these negotiations with our new partners, and so they represent a barrier that needs to be overcome."

"Manou?" Ric asked in genuine amazement.

Kamo held out his hands, as if to show there was no blood on them. Then he said as though he was addressing a pupil who had failed to make the grade, "Manou, her father and Camille; these are island people, Ric. Their views are passed on from one generation to the next in the same way some people cling to their religion. Here their heritage runs very deep through them, like a layer of precious stone through granite. But now," he shrugged his shoulders as though he was unable to prevent the march of time, "they are out of date; prehistoric, like paper money, or quaint patois, or, as you suggest, some sort of small-town mafia. They want the world to recognise them, subsidise them, respect and preserve them, and at the same time pass them by like they are some kind of unique and fascinating tribe with their own mysterious customs, their sanctity of the dead and their precious Megalithic stones."

"Don't get all deep and meaningful on me, Kamo," Ric grumbled. "You'll have me believing you care what happens to Manou." He paused for thought and then turned back to the policeman. "But you guys are only playing partners with them so that you can control them from the inside, because over the years you've made such a dog's breakfast of trying to control them from the outside?"

"There you have it, Ric," Bosquet said with sarcastic elation. "I knew you were an intelligent man. So why don't you prove your intelligence and leave us alone to take care of our own business; a business I must say that has little or even perhaps nothing at all to do with you. Leave us to attend to our own." He stuck the barrel of his shotgun straight out at Ric.

Kamo was standing beyond Ric from the policeman, and whilst Ric was in no doubt that Bosquet would use the gun if Ric went for him, it was clear he would also catch the Armenian in the blast.

The longer the silence extended, the more Bosquet grew nervous; his finger fidgeted around the trigger guard of the shotgun.

Kamo was trying to edge out from behind the bar where he was cornered.

And that was the moment Franco appeared at the forward entrance to the stateroom.

He rubbed the sleep out of his eyes, stared at Bosquet and his shotgun, and then realised Ric was in the room. "Ric," said the boy, "*comu và?*"

"Okay, Franco. Okay," Ric replied as though there was no gun present. He did not need to turn to look at Kamo to witness the disappointment on his face when the boy had not spoken to his father first; he could feel it. It was like a rapid electrical discharge, a sudden draining of Kamo's energy.

"Franco," Ric said, knowing he had to make as much use as he could

355

out of the moment. "Time to go home. *Nous allons maintenant.*" He beckoned the lad to his side.

"*Maman?*" he asked Ric, frowning in concern.

"She's okay, Franco," he replied. "She's okay."

"Stay where you are, boy," Bosquet barked. Then realising that the boy would not necessarily understand him in English he repeated his command in French: "*Restez-la, Franco.* And you, Ric, don't talk anymore. The boy stays here. You and I are going to leave." He stared at Ric, not taking his eyes off him for a second.

Ric still had Kamo boxed in behind the bar. He weighed up the odds of Bosquet shooting him with the Armenian close by. He knew the spread of shot from such a short barrelled gun would be wide even at close range and he had to hope Bosquet would not risk hitting the man behind him. Ric also had the pistol from the steward in his pocket, but he didn't want to pin his hopes on the gun being loaded after the way the steward had misused it; besides he would need to cock it and that would waste too much time. "Franco, go to your father; *allez a ton père,*" Ric ordered.

"Shut up, Ric," Bosquet barked, keeping his eyes fixed on his target.

Franco did not move though. He just looked at Ric as though his friend had said something incomprehensible to him. He tilted his head the way a dog does when he hears an unusual sound.

"Go to your father," Ric repeated, but the boy just looked from one man to the other, not connecting the words with the picture before him.

"Silence, Ric," Bosquet shouted, the discordance of his words and his tone adding to the confusion.

Ric moved back towards Kamo. He knew that if he could get to within striking distance he might be able to pull the Armenian across in front of his own body to shield himself from the blast; either that or Bosquet might think twice before firing. "Franco," he said, getting the boy's attention once more, "your father, *cet homme ici, ton père.*" He pointed at Kamo.

But it was all too evident from Franco's perplexed expression that Kamo had not yet told the boy the truth.

Franco looked at Kamo, still uncomprehending of what Ric was suggesting the man might mean to him.

"Ric, shut up," Bosquet bellowed, brandishing his gun. The temperature in the room must have increased, because the policeman was now sweating profusely.

"Franco," Ric said, "*u schjoppu pìcculu, l'omu grassu, sò a vargogna di a casa.*" He prayed he had got his pronunciation of the Corsu somewhere near correct enough for the boy to understand him.

Franco looked at Ric as though he'd just addressed him in Aramaic.

"*U schjoppu pìcculu, l'omu grassu, sò a vargogna di a casa,*" Ric repeated, inclining his head towards Bosquet.

And the second time round it must have sounded better, because Franco's impassive face cracked like a dam under pressure and he let loose a great torrent of hysterical laughter.

And at last Bosquet took his eyes off Ric. Even though he didn't understand the meaning of the bastardised proverb, Bosquet couldn't resist a glance at the boy's reaction. And that was all the time Ric needed. He launched himself at Kamo as the Armenian screamed out; knowing he would be caught in the policeman's line of fire.

Bosquet's face ran the gamut of his emotions as he realised he had to shoot or back off; his mouth twitched and the dark scowling menace of his expression turned to stark terror as he realised what he had to do. Then his mouth twitched a second time. Like the cold shiver that comes to the backgammon player, Bosquet realised he had to decide whether to stay put or run like hell for home.

But it was Ric's turn to roll the dice. On the first rested the hope that Bosquet would not pull the trigger and risk injuring Kamo. And on the second, one of the six sides needed to show Bosquet's face; the face Ric had seen in the remains of the boar from his most recent dream hunt, and he could only guess at its significance.

When he rolled, the first of the dice deserted him.

The policeman pulled the trigger; he tensed in anticipation of the recoil, but the small shotgun did not erupt. There was no deafening blast, no deadly outward rush of shot, and no tearing invasion into either Ric or Kamo's body. There was nothing but the dull and impotent click of the firing pins striking.

The cartridges were dud.

Bosquet looked down in bewilderment.

Ric struck out. He shoved Kamo to the floor, stood back up and launched himself towards Bosquet, extending his right arm to try and catch the fleshy throat of the heavier man as he broke the gun open to check the cartridges.

Whatever he saw, he did not like. "*Salaud!*" he swore as he stumbled back out of reach. He hurled the shotgun at Ric in a vain attempt to halt his progress and reached into the pocket of his jacket for another weapon.

Ric landed short and staggered forward and into the man as his hands struggled to extract whatever it was he sought. As he twisted and tugged at his pocket Ric hit Bosquet with as much weight as he could summon whilst he was off balance. His right shoulder slammed into Bosquet's midriff.

But the policeman was lighter on his feet than his heavy frame suggested, and he rotated as Ric connected, turning away and deflecting the full force of the blow. They grasped and struck at each other and toppled over, the heavier man falling on top of Ric, crushing and winding them both.

Straining as he tried to ease out from underneath Bosquet, Ric felt valuable time slipping away; he knew he had to subdue the man soon or risk him drawing another weapon from his pocket.

He grabbed up at the man's face with his right hand; his fingers slipping into Bosquet's open mouth as he gasped for air. Ric's thumb found the soft underside of the man's chin and he squeezed his thumb and fingers together with all the strength in his hand. Bosquet flinched and screamed; a high-pitched wail that came from the back of his throat. In compressing the nerve beneath the man's tongue, Bosquet's entire system was instantly paralysed by the acute and shocking pain.

And in the time it took for the big man to scream – completely unable to respond in any other way, even to close his mouth down upon the fingers inside it – Ric pushed up with his hand against the man's mouth, shifted just enough of his weight to one side, and slid out from beneath. As Ric rolled away and got to his feet however, Bosquet freed the gun from his pocket. He didn't bother to take any kind of aim; he just fired at Ric as Ric slammed back into him.

The gun went off and both men fell to the deck.

As Ric fought for control of the gun in Bosquet's hand, he could feel the cylindrical barrel of the revolver against his stomach as the man tried to pull the trigger. The heavier man was strong, much stronger than Ric thought he had a right to be. His fingers, like the gun they held, were short and stubby. They were not long enough for Ric to grasp, as though they were welded tight about the revolver. The two men had both their hands around the gun. Ric could feel the hammer moving back and the cylinder begin to turn as Bosquet snatched at the trigger for a second time. As the revolver cocked, Ric jammed his thumb down between the hammer and the firing pin.

Bosquet pulled at the trigger for all he was worth.

But Ric, knowing that his thumb prevented the hammer from striking down onto the firing pin, concentrated his energy on turning the barrel away from his stomach to point back towards Bosquet.

Their faces were no more than a breath apart, and Ric stared as hard as he could into the policeman's dark eyes. They were wide and his pupils were dilated and filled with fear; they looked as though they would pop out of their sockets, as though he was going to explode under the pressure of his efforts.

And as Bosquet squirmed and struggled against him, Ric recognised once more the face of fear and desperation from his last dream hunt. Just as Ric had seen it materialise from among the broken remains of the boar, so Bosquet's face twisted and contorted, his mouth stretched thin, and his heavy cheeks strained tight in his efforts.

"There's no point to this," Ric said quietly. "I've seen your face, Bosquet. Believe me. Give it up, man. There's no point."

Gradually it dawned on Bosquet that he could feel the round end of the barrel pressing against his own stomach. It was no longer pointing at Ric because Ric had forced it in between the folds of heavy flesh that lay slack around his middle. Bosquet's expression hardened as he realised he no longer controlled the direction in which the next round would be fired. He strained one final time to turn the gun away from his stomach.

But as Bosquet knew his effort was in vain and his grip began to slacken, Ric withdrew his thumb from between the hammer and the pin, and the gun went off.

Bosquet's scream was drowned out by the blast of the revolver.

He clutched his stomach with both hands. His shirt smoked from the flash of the blast, and while he struggled to come to terms with the absurdity of dying by his own hand, he did just that. The light dulled in his eyes and he lay still.

Ric slowly clambered upright and turned towards Kamo.

He shielded his right hand as he drew the small pistol he had wrested from the young steward and pulled back the slider. He faced the Armenian, pointing the cocked pistol directly at him.

The scene Ric was faced with was the last one he could have imagined. What he expected to see was Kamo pointing Bosquet's gun at him.

Instead, Kamo was standing behind his very puzzled son, pointing the revolver at the boy's head.

It was a curious, if not bizarre sight; a father pointing a gun at his son. And at first Ric did not believe what he was seeing. But when he shook his head, hoping the screen before his eyes might change to reveal a completely alternative and more rational vision, the scene remained the same.

"Well," Ric said with considerable resignation, "at least we know that gun works."

He paused. Something wasn't quite right. He could both feel his own body and yet not feel it; it ached, but at the same time the tingling pain seemed to be too distant to belong to him.

Ric sighed: "Put the gun down, you idiot. My memory may not be up to scratch, but unless it's folded on me completely you were the guy who said you hated everyone but your own family. Wasn't that it? 'All that is important now, all that is left, family'? Isn't that what you said?"

He looked at Kamo's yellow-flecked eyes as hard as the distance between them allowed and repeated himself, "Isn't that what you said? Or was that just another pale dimension of your sterile personality? You see, Kamo," Ric began, but his concentration was interrupted by a stinging pain that shot up into his chest from somewhere down near his hip. He began again, his mind muting the sudden instance of pain. "You see, Kamo, if you spend all of your time looking for the bigger picture, you forget that it's the smaller ones that make up the bigger one, and without the smaller pictures like Franco here, there is no bigger picture. So put the gun down, or leastways point it at me. Doesn't anything or anyone matter to you more than your worthless and insignificant part in the great scheme of things, Kamo? Or has your worldly and sophisticated education left your soul so barren of emotion that you can't see the difference between what you want and what your son means to you?"

With that Kamo lifted his gun from his son's head and raised it to aim at Ric. He did not, though, shift his eyes from Ric as with his free right hand he shepherded Franco to one side.

"Pardon, Ric. That was a mistake; a stupid and very unnecessary reaction. I apologise both to you and to Franco."

"Your flunky, Bobo said you weren't man enough to deal with the mess you create, Kamo," Ric goaded. "Not man enough, were the exact words he used." He would shoot Kamo, he knew he had no real alternative, but Ric was reluctant to do so in front of the boy; as reluctant, he hoped, as Kamo would be to return the compliment.

"And you?" the Armenian replied, grinning again. "You think because you have found in this irrelevant backwater of an island some kind of salvation for your soul, some kind of soothing balm to pour on your tortured conscience, that it is worth risking your life for people who do not care whether you live or die; people who would waste your precious life so that they can be left to exercise their own insignificant authority over one another? Are they really worth the price? Is that how you measure the value of your soul?"

Ric stared back at Kamo, and knew in that moment that it was not how he measured the value of his soul that mattered. It was that his soul still existed even after all the injustice life had thrown at him.

"Right now I can't think of any other way of measuring it," he replied.

He took a step towards Kamo, and as he did so another searing pain leapt up at his chest from below. He noticed Kamo glance down, and Ric perceived a cold wetness increasing about the outside of his right thigh.

Kamo lowered his gun and put it down on the bar.

Ric did the same, and as he did so Kamo went for him. He delivered a left hook to the side of Ric's head that would have floored him had he not half expected it. Nevertheless he fell back under the blow. His movement took him back into the middle of the stateroom where there was more room for them to fight.

As the Armenian came forward into the space, Ric struck him hard with his right hand in the stomach. He was trying to knock the wind out of his opponent, but his strike lacked his full strength, as when he moved off his right leg it felt numb and he could not tell whether it was in the right position to push off from.

Kamo came again; he boxed with a hands-high conventional style, but he also kicked out as though he had been trained that way. He deflected well and counterpunched hard.

Ric protected his right side and lead with his left. It was not his stronger side, but he had no choice as he could not allow Kamo to get a kick in at his right leg as he knew the pain would be too disabling.

They punched hard and kicked out at each other whenever a gap appeared or an opportunity presented itself. They both defended when they saw the blows coming and counter-attacked when they could. They grunted when they hurt and they gasped for air in between, for the longer and the harder they fought the quicker they grew tired.

Within a few minutes both heaved and stood off between hits, neither allowing the other to get close enough to take a hold.

"It does not leave you, Ric," Kamo shouted, panting.

"What?" Ric gasped.

"Your training," he replied, covering up with his hands as Ric moved in with a short left and a heavy right. Kamo puffed. "What you have learned stays with you; it serves you well. Bosquet told me you train most days; swimming out to the big rock in the bay. He used to watch you. I think he was envious of you, but then perhaps he was envious of everyone. He had...," Kamo feinted right and then pushed off his right foot fast and kicked Ric hard on his right thigh, "not many redeeming features and he did not care for himself. Perhaps it was a good thing you did; killing him. The world can do without his kind."

Ric stood off for a second: "I didn't kill him. He managed that all by himself. Why should he have been watching me?" He wondered if his opponent was trying to buy time in which to recover.

But Kamo advanced again, drew Ric left and hit him with his right beneath his ribs.

"Oh," Kamo gasped with the effort of the punch, "once he saw you with Manou, he knew you would become involved. She is not to be underestimated, my friend. I would have thought you would have learned that by now." And in spite of addressing Ric as his friend, he landed a combination of blows that culminated in a hook to Ric's ear that made his head ring with the deep reverberating chime of a heavy bell in a tall tower.

Ric was growing weaker. His right leg was beginning to rebel against his instructions.

And yet, as soon as Ric heard Kamo mention her name, an image of Manou's face materialised before his eyes. "What do you mean?" he asked no one in particular, as for the moment his sight deserted him and all he could see was not his opponent but the calm image of Manou's face before him; her dark almond skin and her bright blue eyes burning with a flaming and vivid intensity. He could not tell whether he was looking at her form in front of him or whether he was looking at her as though she was within him. He was suddenly confused and uncertain. He noticed again the feeling of trying to maintain his balance whilst the floor heaved. And then Manou spoke to him: "You must do this for me, Ric," she said, "for us, Ric. Do this for me – for us." And as he struggled to ignore her voice, he raised his right hand and rubbed at the front of his own face, hoping he might erase her image and that she might leave him to fight.

But she would not leave him; she would not go. "For us," she urged, as though they were the only two people left in the world: "For us, Ric. Do this for us."

"Come, Ric," Kamo said in mock surprise, in between gasping for air. "Don't tell me you do not recognise the witch for what she is. Does your lack of education leave you so much in the dark?" But then Kamo lowered his arms as he spoke, as though he was all of a sudden aware that the man he was fighting had lost his sight and was for the moment no longer dangerous.

"She is *Signadori*, Ric, and you are her Mazzeru. You even have the evil eye; the eye they call *l'occhiu*." Kamo stepped forward, shoved his finger onto Ric's forehead above his right eye and stepped back out of range.

"There, my friend. It is there; the blood mark above your eye; your birthmark. In this superstitious backwater they call this the 'evil eye'. It tells them you are mazzeru. You can see death before it comes to the living, and you can communicate with the dead."

They had both forgotten Franco was standing in the doorway, watching them fight.

Ric glanced at him and realised that the boy, though looking back at him, was staring at the blood mark above his eye.

Kamo noticed Ric's glance. "It means you are a dream hunter," he went on, mocking and goading. "Yes. You! You are the one who can find death in your dreams by hunting the wild animals. And Manou is *Signadori*. She has the power over you. Sure the *Signadori* can help you, but they are also the only ones who can control you. And this is what she has done, Ric. Are you stupid enough to think she does not know about the death of your wife? The story was in the English newspapers. I am sure you know this. And if I can find this out, do you not see that she could also? Do you not see how she has used you?"

Ric saw Manou's face again, but beside her he saw the face of his wife; one beautiful and calculating, the other beautiful and innocent. 'Signadori', wasn't that what Camille had said about Manou? The old boy had said that to him when they had talked at the beach bar. Camille had said she was *Signadori*.

In place of Manou's face he now saw the faces of the dead. He saw the ghostly flickering faces of the penitents as they passed by the gates on their way to bury the innocents. He saw the old, white-bearded man who had confronted him by the tomb and who could not rest until his murder was avenged. He saw the charging beast of his nightmares and the faces of the leering Bobo and the petrified Bosquet staring back at him from the bloodied remains. And in his hands he held the *mazza* he had found out on the rock; the rock from which was taken the stone of the signet ring that marked the cross on his forehead. And as he remembered the black cross of the *Catochitis* upon his forehead, the vision of Manou and the sound of her words left him, and she was gone, drifting away down to where all light was absorbed in the chasm, down where all dimension is lost deep within the darkness.

He rushed forwards, oblivious of where Kamo might be, but knowing he did not possess the strength to stand and fight the man much longer. He knew he had to advance into contact and finish it very soon, or it would be the end of him.

In a final, wild and desperate charge, like that of the great boar that plagued his sleep, he caught the unsuspecting Kamo in the stomach with his shoulder and knocked him back into the wall.

The wall shook so violently Ric thought for a moment they had gone through it. But it held, and Ric pushed on upwards, lifting and sliding his enemy up the wall high above him. And then, at the very instant he felt his strength begin to fail him, Ric pulled Kamo crashing back down onto the floor.

The deck beneath his feet shuddered with all the force of Kamo's frame landing as if it had been thrown down from a high window.

Ric staggered backwards, drawing as much air as possible into his chest. He knew it was not yet over. He knew Kamo, though broken, would not concede. And as he thought it, Kamo tried to get back to his feet. But he had made it up only as far as his knees when Ric, fists clenched together as if in prayer, delivered one last, paralysing blow to the side of Kamo's head.

The blow slammed Kamo over onto his back and he went down for good, unconscious to the world in which the three of them still lived.

60

Ric sank to the floor. The round from Bosquet's gun had caught him in the right thigh a couple of inches below and on the outside of his hip. It was more than a nick or a slight graze, but it had passed clean through his leg. He pressed his hand against the wound to try and stop the bleeding.

Franco watched him, wide-eyed in amazement. "*Comu và?*" he asked, moving hesitantly towards Ric.

"Yes, Franco, I'm okay; stings a bit, but I'll manage." Ric struggled to his feet with the aid of a chair on one side and Franco's shoulder on the other. When he stood his leg hurt less than it had a right to, but he knew his senses were cushioned by the shock. He was cold but he was sweating. He knew the greater pain would come later.

Ric limped to the bar, grabbed some paper serviettes and shoved them inside his shorts; it would have to do for now, he decided; he had to find out how many other crew were on board.

The steward still lay in a crumpled heap to the side. He would not present a threat, even if he stirred. Bosquet was very dead; his head lay at an insane angle and his stomach was covered with blood. Petrossian wasn't going to wake up for a minute or two and probably not without the aid of a bottle of smelling salts.

"Come with me, Franco. *Avec moi, Franco.*"

Franco nodded, although by now he stared alternately between the guns on the bar next to Bosquet's corpse.

Ric picked the guns up, dropped the clip out of the semi-automatic and put the revolver in his left pocket. He limped over to the forward door of the stateroom, opened it and threw the pistol over the side out into the darkness. The clips he threw on the deck. Leaning on the wall for support and dragging his right leg as fast as he could through each step so as to keep the weight off it, he staggered to the bridge. There he found one of the men he recognised from the night of the fire; the older, slimmer of the two who had been on the bridge that night. He had short grey hair and wore the customary crew whites. The man blinked and rubbed his hands on his shirt as though they were oily or sweaty.

Ric pulled the revolver from his pocket and held it in his left hand, but pointing down at the floor by his side.

"What's your name?" He was polite, but only as polite as the growing pain in his thigh permitted.

The fellow shrugged; either he didn't understand the question, or he'd forgotten what his own name was.

Ric pointed the gun at him and asked again: "Oh, give me a break, commodore. What's your name?" he asked again. This time he asked with a resigned indifference, as though it mattered little to him whether he got an answer or whether he shot the man.

"Alex."

"Okay, Alex; how many souls on board?"

"Three: chef, steward and me. I am engineer."

"Yuri?" Ric asked.

"Yuri not here," he replied. "Yuri gone away, thank you." At this Alex smiled revealing yellowed, uneven teeth.

Ric figured the scrawny Yuri would not have posed a threat even if he had been on board. "Ava, Ami, any other women on board?"

"All gone with Yuri. Yesterday! No one here: boss, chef, steward and me. All other people gone," he replied. He was nervous, but not so nervous that his reply lacked any conviction.

"Get the chef," he said. "Now!"

When the chef appeared he ushered them back to the stateroom.

They both balked when they saw the bodies on the floor, so Ric had to encourage them with the gun. He could only think so far ahead and besides, he reckoned Bosquet's corpse would have to find its own resting place, even though the easy option would have been to chuck it over the side, consigning it to a watery grave. He would let Kamo explain away the wretched man's demise later.

While Ric stood guard, the chef and engineer lifted the still unconscious steward, carried him aft and laid him out in the tender Bosquet had used to get over from the beach.

They returned to the stateroom, Franco as though on a short leash followed close behind. The engineer clearly expected to pick up the unconscious Petrossian and take him aft to the tender too, so he was surprised when, instead of instructing him to do so, Ric ordered him to carry their boss down to one of the guest cabins and lay him out on a bed.

Ric banged on the open door with the butt of the pistol and addressed the crewman whose name was Alex, "Keys?" he asked. "For the door? Keys to lock it? In here?" he gestured around the room with the gun.

The grey haired Alex shook his head and pointed back up the stairs.

"Get them. Now," Ric ordered and then waved his gun in unspoken threat towards the chef and engineer.

The engineer left, his hurried footfall up the steps loud in the quiet night. He was not gone long. He handed over two cross-cut keys; the four sided type, the locks of which are nigh on impossible to pick.

"Don't move," Ric commanded. Then he limped into the adjoining bathroom and looked around for anything that could be used to open the cabin door; there was nothing except for cosmetics and towels; the cabin was not in use. He picked up a plastic cup and removed it from its sterile wrapping. He filled it with water. Once back in the bedroom he ordered the men topside, but waved the gun at them in case they should get any bold or stupid ideas.

When they had gone, taking Franco with them, Ric threw the water in Petrossian's face.

Kamo stirred, but did not come right round, so Ric repeated the dose with two more cups of water. At the third time of asking, Kamo blinked his eyes open and slowly raised his hands to his bruised and swelling face. Without looking at Ric, he spoke, "What did you hit me with, Ric?"

"Everything I had, Kamo. And all I had, I'm afraid. I'm relieved you went down; my locker was just about bare," Ric said. "Are you alright?"

Judging by the time it took Kamo to answer, his question deserved some consideration. "Not yet," he said and then paused, clearly taking stock of his abused form. "Give me a minute, please. I don't remember that last move of yours in my self-defence class, Ric. Where did you learn that, in the Marines?"

"School playing field, I think." Ric smiled and the corner of his mouth stung as it split open.

"Tough school," Kamo said. He was willing to make conversation, but that was as far as any physical effort extended for him; prostrate on the bed was where he was happy to stay for the moment.

"How is your leg, Ric? Bosquet shot you?" he asked. Kamo coughed and groaned; the kind of groan that comes with broken ribs, much like a hesitant breath or a stupid thought.

"He did," Ric sighed, a long and drawn out exhalation of the tired, stale air in his lungs. And with it, he felt, went the residue of malice he felt towards the figure lying prone before him. "It'll do for the moment."

"What was that you said to Franco?"

"To Franco?"

"Yes," Kamo coughed again. "Just now; something about *schjoppu* and *grassu* and *casa*. You certainly made him laugh."

"Oh that; *u schjoppu pìcculu, l'omu grassu, sò a vargogna di a casa*."

"Yes. That." Kamo coughed again.

"Oh, just a phrase I cooked up from a book of old proverbs Manou leant me. It seemed funny at the time; what with Bosquet being such a glutton: 'a little gun and a fat man are the shame of a household'. It should be a thin cat, not a little gun, but it was the best I could come up with."

They paused again. Both men considered laughing, but they were tired in themselves and at the same time naturally awkward in each other's company. There was not much left to be said.

"You owe me a favour, Ric," Kamo muttered, not inclined to expand his lungs. "Strange way you British people have of meeting your obligations. Remind me to set the rules out more clearly next time."

Ric's leg streaked pain up into his groin and his back. He winced. "It's true Kamo, I do owe you. So here's where I settle up. Where do you want to go next?"

"Do I have to leave?"

"You want to stay? They'll kill you if you do."

"It would be bad for them if they did," Kamo argued, but as he said it he recognised the ridiculous irony in his threat. His tone relaxed and his words fell away into a mild laugh, a light, nasal snigger not large enough to upset the tender disorder of his ribs.

Ric chuckled at the ridiculous contradiction in the threat. "So, where do you want to go?"

"Ah," replied Kamo, considering, "perhaps Capri will still be warm enough. I have seen it many times from the sea, but I have never had the opportunity to stay there. I have always imagined Capri as a very beautiful woman who one passes in a crowded street and you know that whatever happens, one day you will introduce yourself and exchange pleasantries with her; discuss the weather, compliment her dress, ask after her mother, and who knows…. Or perhaps I read about it in a book sometime. I don't remember…."

As he left, Ric locked the door from the outside, and once he'd struggled topside, he tossed the keys over the rail and staggered back into the stateroom.

Franco stood, watching; taking in every detail and studying the unquestionable authority which Ric and his gun exerted over the engineer and chef.

"Franco," Ric said, bending towards the boy so that he would be in no doubt he was being given an order, "Take the boat back to Camille at the beach." He motioned with the gun at the boat, and then at the beach: "*A Camille, okay. Le bateau a Camille; comprenez? A la plage, a Camille. Okay?*"

At this Franco nodded again. "Okay, Ric. No problem," he said in straight English.

Ric got the engineer to start the tender up for the boy and show him how the throttle lever worked. And once Franco was happy he knew what he was doing, they cast him off. He grinned and gave the thumbs up as he stood at the wheel and set off for the beach. Franco disappeared with his dumb cargo into the darkness; the happy master of a shiny new boat.

Once the tender was out of sight, Ric pointed the gun at the chef. "Into the water," he ordered.

"I no swim," the chef said, imploring, hunching his shoulders and showing his palms.

"Learn," Ric said, shoving him off the aft platform.

Ric sat back on the steps up from the transom, waiting. He was confident the chef would make it ashore before the young steward came round, and the chef was indeed learning to swim.

When he was satisfied Franco was far enough off the stern, he ushered the engineer Alex up the steps and prodded him forward to the bridge. Halfway along the deck he had to rest for a few seconds. He could feel the cool blood from his wound down around his ankle, and a wave of nausea washed over and threatened to overwhelm him. Ric drew deep breaths and rubbed at his forehead.

Once at the bridge he asked Alex, who seemed quite at ease with his new elevated position of ship's executive officer, if the motor-yacht had sufficient fuel to make it to Capri.

Alex pressed the green button by the display panel. He typed in Capri when asked for a destination. The coordinates 40-33-0 degrees north,14-14-0 degrees east blinked back; Marina Grande, Capri. The destination was within the equated fuel range. "You want fast journey or slow?" asked Alex.

"Twenty knots ought to do it," Ric replied.

Alex nodded and busied himself setting the instruments. He hesitated as he typed the instructions on the keyboard. "I stay here, or I come with you?"

"As you wish, Alex," Ric replied, watching him, trying to assess just how far his loyalty to Petrossian might stretch.

"I get passport from cabin," he said with considerable and evident relief, and disappeared out of the room like a rat scurrying from a flooding sewer.

Ric moved away from the control desk and leant against the bulkhead aft of the bridge. He took aim at the doorway, expecting the crewman to reappear with his own pistol.

But when the grey haired Alex reappeared he held no gun, only his passport in a plastic bag which he waved at Ric, grinning. Then he frowned when he saw the gun in Ric's hand, as though he would have liked his new boss to have had more faith in him. "I make boat ready now?" he asked.

"Sure," Ric replied slipping the pistol into the pocket of his shorts.

Alex pressed a number of buttons on the control panel. The many screens lit up like ultra-violet lights in a nightclub; the view below the waterline, the relief above, maps of the departure and arrival, angles of thrust, more and more screens. "We must go," Alex directed.

Ric felt the boat vibrate and he saw the curiously shaped helm turn of its own accord. The overhead lights changed from their previous soft white to give off that peculiar red glow Ric remembered from the oil fires in Iraq. He felt dizzy and cold, as though someone had opened the door to the cold store.

"We go, now," the engineer urged. He began to pull Ric by his shirt towards the door. His face was close up; it was strained with impatience. "Come," he beckoned. "Now. Hurry."

The floor heaved a little as the large motor-yacht went about. The change in attitude increased Ric's nausea and he lurched through the open door out onto the deck. He could feel wind in his hair. It felt good. It dried the cool sweat at his brow. With his left hand on the rail and his right clutching at his leg, he hobbled aft. He stumbled and fell hard against the deck, but the engineer helped get him back to his feet and Ric mumbled how grateful he was.

The man was trying to force some kind of extra clothing on him. Ric didn't need it. After all, the air was so warm.

Ric looked up. The stars seemed to be fleeing west and the moon was nowhere to be seen; it had long since passed on to cast its pale light in some other world. Ashore the impenetrable darkness of the island moved swiftly on by.

61

During the rest of the night Ric was aware of flashed images and vague sensations. He floated in an unfathomable sea whose short waves crested in fluorescent crowns and whose amniotic warmth he found reassuring. He bore perpetual witness to the myriad stars in whose presence he also found comfort and relief, and he understood that the waters about him, though dark, still flowed in the land of light and not through the narrow straights that divide the two worlds of the living and the dead.

Faces came in and out of his view: the engineer Alex, his teeth glowing gold in the night, Camille, his curly hair framed in silver against the glittering dome above, and young Franco, the whites of his eyes shining out from the hollow shadows of his face.

At times Ric walked, but with great pain, and at times he knew he was being supported. The various segments of his odyssey grew confused; there was a passage spent laid out on the back seat of a car as it twisted and turned up a steep hill, a lengthy period of manhandling, as though he was being delivered like a parcel through many teams. And then he knew by the jerking and jogging of his horizontal frame that he was being carried over rough terrain on a stretcher. He heard whispered voices and smelled the rich and musty scent of the forest floor. And what now came into view he knew he had seen before in another of his dreams.

Ric saw the fringes of the umbrella pines and the angulated sweeping limbs of the oaks and between them, as if drifting through some winding corridor, he saw the bright stars as they looked down at him, twinkling and chattering, watching over his slow progress up the mountain. And just as in his dream, he came to rest in a dark room with a high casement window. Manou was there, somewhere. He did not see her so much as feel her presence.

When the dawn rose, Ric woke too. He found himself confined, lying on a straw mattress on a wooden cot in a cramped, stone room. Although the dawn air was chilled, he was not cold for there were layers of heavy blankets laid over him. His right leg, hip and groin hurt like hell, but he managed to lean up on his elbows.

Beside him, placed on a rough wooden shelf, lay a baguette of bread, a pair of *figatellu* sausages and a roundel of *ottavi* cheese. There were also a couple of bottles of St George's water, an old bone-handled folding-knife, an old enamel plate and a box of matches. An oil lamp hung from a hook inserted in the wall, and a small-handled axe was suspended from a nail in the facing wall. The pungent aroma of goat hung in the air.

Beneath the blankets he was naked but for the bandaging about his thigh. He ran his hand over his leg. Someone had done a professional job; the bandaging was clean and fresh, and there was no evidence of any bleeding through the dressing. Ric looked at the rather makeshift door that led outside and considered getting up. But with his contemplation came enough pain from his leg to banish the idea of any further activity. He lay back down, understanding too that he was suffering under the soporific weight of some anaesthetic. Soon he fell asleep again.

Later, he woke up hungry and ate the food. Ric saw that some clothes had been left for him. He dressed, moving very gently otherwise some unseen devil doused his right leg in burning oil. There was no mirror for him to assess his face, but by running his hands over it he could tell it was swollen and bore all the hallmarks of having been beaten; the skin was tight and split at his lips, most of his knuckles were skinned and his ribs were bruised. Dressing tired him and he fell back on the cot and slept some more.

He was surprised to find when he woke again that it was dark and he realised he had passed a whole day in his stone-walled retreat. He had no alternative but to get up as he needed to answer a call of nature, so he straightened up and lit the oil lamp. Feeling less drowsy, he surveyed his surroundings. Though the light was different from his first visit, he recognised the room as being the inside of the *oriu* he had seen the day he had walked up through the forest at Carbini with Manou. The lamp had been hung on the hook that would have more usually suspended the cooking pot over the hearth. The walls and ceiling were smooth to touch as though they had been plastered, but the rock was natural; it had been disgorged in molten form

373

from the depths and cooled smooth on contact with the air. Ric unhooked the latch on the wooden door and hobbled outside.

As he opened the door he saw, leaning against the wall, a slender staff of wood almost as tall as he was. The shaft was carved in a gnarled but rounded ball, which was smooth, suggesting that more than one generation of hands had polished it that way. The wood was hard and heavy, and ebony in colour, and as he limped through the doorway leaning on the staff, he was reminded of Manou's father whose spirit he had met that night by the tomb; her father whose troubled spirit could not rest until his murderer had been slain. Ric wondered where his spirit had gone to rest and whether there were many others like him prowling the maquis in search of retribution and the release the settling of old scores might bring.

The next day, Ric felt the anaesthetic begin to leave his body. His fingertips were no longer numb and his teeth belonged to him once more. The pain was still strong; strong enough to prohibit him from walking far from his refuge, so he limped outside and sat on the bare rock and looked across the mountainside at the craggy peak above the village of Carbini. Though autumn was not far off, the forest was rich in the many shades of green; there were pine and oak, myrtle and cistus, gorse and heather, and the air possessed a stark clarity and clean sharpness.

Ric heard the old woman Mariucca whistling before he saw her.

She smiled her gap-toothed smile and produced from the sac slung over her shoulder some *coppa* and *lonzu*, and some more bread and water. She had even carried a bottle of *fleur-de-myrte*, which Ric considered unnecessary until he realised she had bought it in order to help him stave off the pain of her inspection. She nodded, whistled and mumbled to herself as she stripped the dressing off his leg. She dusted the wound with a white powder that smelt of herbs and bandaged him up with a new dressing. After she had helped herself to a generous slug of the liquor, she patted Ric on the head as though he were an obedient dog, collected her sac and set off back down the mountainside.

He observed her path down through the woods so that he might be more vigilant in future. Ric did not expect a visit from anyone other than Mariucca or perhaps Camille, or even with a little luck Manou, though he harboured mixed emotions about seeing her again. He missed the light-blue of her eyes, the deep almond of her skin and the silken touch of her fingers.

For a few days Ric remained and watched the mountains, the broad wings of the eagles as they soared on the thermals, and the great green swathe of forest below, the peace of which was broken only now and then by the occasional discharge of a shotgun. The echoes bounced around the hillsides, in and out of the gullies, and rolled like boulders down into the valley below. At night he watched the forked lightning cleave the night sky and listened to the thunder deep in the distance. Some nights stayed cool and dry, and on others the humidity rose so high that a torrent of rain burst upon his rock roof, as though released from the damn over the peak at Ospédale.

Mariucca came and re-dressed his wound every day. Ric knew she did not drive which meant someone had brought her up from the coast; Manou, possibly, probably.

Ric lost count of the days. It may have been a week, it may have been ten days, but one cool and clear morning as he watched the path up from below, he noticed a figure strolling in his direction. The white haired man carried a gun and a sac over his shoulder; a long, double-barrelled shotgun, but not the short-handled, sawn-off type he had seen Camille give Bosquet-the gun the old boy had loaded with dud cartridges.

"*Comu và*, my friend?" he asked, leaning his gun up against the wall of the *oriu*.

Ric stood to welcome him. "As you can see, Camille, my nurse is doing a remarkable job. She's not much of a one for conversation though."

They grasped each other's arms in a familiar and emotional greeting. The old boy studied the younger man's eyes. "*Bellubè!* It is good. You are recovering well." Camille unloaded his sac. There was a small feast inside; *pain di morti, charcuterie,* cheese, fruit and a couple of unlabelled bottles of red wine stoppered with rough corks. He handed Ric one of the bottles and spread the rest of the food out on a cloth. They talked about the land before them just as Ric had with Manou. Camille named the peaks around them and noted the best areas to hunt. They discussed the weather. Camille told him what to expect over the coming days, which Ric took to mean he would be lying low for a little longer. They talked about the war of more than half a century before. Camille pointed away to the north and told him the story of how, as a very young lad in the Resistance, they had destroyed the bridge between Carbini and Levie, and kept so many troops occupied for so long that the Axis commanders were convinced they were fighting an entire, professional army in the hills.

But Camille was more than reluctant to talk about Manou. He interrupted whenever he anticipated Ric was about to ask; he possessed that uncanny prescience in conversation similar to Manou.

So after a time Ric gave up the idea of asking after her. He just listened and was happy to be educated by one who had seen much, much more than he.

Before he left Camille told him to be ready to leave in the evening of four days. There was no other information, no consultation with the fugitive, merely an instruction to be ready.

Then he sniffed the air like an old bloodhound, got to his feet, clapped Ric on both arms, bid him *a dopu*, gathered his sac and shotgun and left. The sun was settling into the valley, and Camille's shadow grew long as he walked away down the path.

The next day Mariucca came and went; whistling as she busied herself removing the protection of the scab that had formed over his wound, cleansing it and replacing the dressing and sniggering to herself whenever he winced in pain.

On the second day she behaved much as she had on any other previous day, but Ric had the feeling he might not see the benevolent old crone again. He did not understand where the feeling came from; he merely perceived it.

So just before she left and when she was least expecting it, he kissed her on each cheek. His action startled her, but did not offend her. She looked up into his face, raised her pudgy left hand up to his forehead and traced the circle of the birthmark above his right eye.

"*L'occiu*," she whispered, as though she was seeing something wonderful for the first time. "*L'occiu*."

"Yes," replied Ric, still not properly understanding her fascination: "The evil eye."

Mariucca did not come on the third day.

That bothered him a little; the break in routine. He waited patiently and watched the approach up through the forest. If he was honest with himself, he had known she would not be coming again and that was why he had kissed her. After all, he had sufficient food to see him through to the next evening when Camille had said he should be ready, and his leg now felt dry and less painful when he walked.

As he sat eating the small round *pain di morti*, the sunset delivered Ric an array of reds such as he had never seen; the bright copper of flames, the bold crimson of regimental colours, and finally the warm, purpling claret of dusk. The last rays seemed long in dying and the glow of the sun beyond the horizon held the stars at bay until late into the evening.

Ric's thoughts turned to Manou and Franco, and he wondered whether they had seen the last of Petrossian. He wondered too whether he had been dazzled by the Armenian's glare in the same way Manou had when she first met him in Paris. Perhaps, like the moths of the forest drawn towards the oil lamp hanging in the *oriu*, they had both been blinded by the flame of Kamo's exuberance.

He was gazing down the valley at the dark carpet of the forest roof when there was a noise to his left and he started.

"Ric?" Manou spoke softly from the shadows.

He turned towards her and waited for her to walk into the light.

She sat down beside him.

They listened to the mountain whispers and the sounds of each other's presence.

After a while she laid her head against his shoulder and he could feel the faint breeze of her breath on his arm. Faint though each breath was, soon enough they had fanned the embers of the fire within him and he could no longer resist turning to kiss her.

Manou didn't resist him.

Even though Ric wanted to consume her the way the wildfire had consumed Renabianca, there was nothing frantic about their lovemaking. There was no desperation about their being together, and yet neither did they linger in their touch as though afterwards they would want to recall every caress, every movement and every pleasure.

Later, they lay on the bare rock and for a while lost their thoughts in the stars.

Manou would not look at him when she talked. She admitted she had lured him into her conflict with Kamo, and for her deceit and dishonesty she apologised. She wished it could have been otherwise, but she felt it was important for him to understand that Kamo was gone now and so things were and could be very different.

Manou admitted that she knew Ric's wife had been taken from him, but that she did not know the words to express her very great sorrow. And she told him that though she did not expect him to believe her, she wanted him to stay and perhaps if he went away only for a while and came back in the spring, by then the dust would have settled.

Manou told him how Franco had screamed at her when she told him it was unlikely Ric would stay. How the boy yelled he would never have a father because she would never allow it.

Ric accepted her confession without reaction. He had completed much of the jigsaw during his solitude of the preceding days, but when she mentioned Franco, Ric tightened.

He closed his hand gently over her mouth. "I know," was all he said.

And it was all he needed to say. Staying would have been difficult and complicated; even though both of them understood it was exactly what the other wanted. But in the same way that Manou had lived in the shadow of knowing that Petrossian would one day return for Franco, there was no way Ric would ask her to live in the knowledge that at sometime in the future others might come for him. Even if she was prepared to put up with the risk, he wouldn't put the boy through it. That much he had already decided.

And besides, though he could not tell her, he knew he would not rest easy in the knowledge that a stranger might one day call at his door; the pale stranger named Doubt, beneath whose feet trust was spoiled.

They got up, dressed, and moved into the *oriu*.

Manou gave Ric the small leather-bound notebook of proverbs and translations that she had lent him on their second date. He assumed it was her way of telling him she had not trusted him before, but that she trusted him now. "Franco said you spoke from the book when it was important. I want you to have it."

He wanted to refuse it, but instead he found himself saying simply, "Thank you."

Then she took from her sac a white soup plate and candle, and beckoned Ric to sit beside her.

Manou placed the plate upon the shelf and lit the candle; it was scented with incense. She took a pair of small scissors from her skirt pocket, cut a lock of hair from Ric's head and placed it beneath the plate. Next she poured some water into the plate and crossed herself three times with her right hand. Taking the oil lamp, she dipped the little finger of her left hand into the oil reservoir at the base, crossed herself again and dripped three small droplets of oil onto the water. Then she put the oil lamp back on the hook and took the small-handled axe down from where it was hung on the wall and placed it on the shelf beside the plate.

It struck Ric as a rather quaint and charming process. The shadows thrown by the oil lamp made it difficult for him to see the plate clearly, so Manou moved the candle closer so they could both make out the three small pools of oil floating on the water.

Manou then began to pray. She half-closed her eyes and recited some phrases, which by their intonation and constant reference to the saints Ric understood to be an appeal to the spirits of the dead. She maintained her hypnotic incantation for a few minutes; Ric was not sure for how many minutes because a curious and lengthy lethargy descended on him.

The next thing he knew, Manou was standing beside him, holding the axe a few inches above his head. Even though he felt increasingly drowsy, the strange charade unnerved him as he wondered whether she had the strength to hold the axe in such a precarious position for so long.

She continued to recite her prayer, her voice increasing in volume until she was shouting out, asking the saints questions to which, when they went unanswered, she provided her own response.

It was at this point that Ric decided it would be better to try and stay alert rather than drift off in case he found himself the subject of some ritual sacrifice, the axe buried deep in his head. He opened his eyes, having not realised they were shut and concentrated on the yellow flame of the candle.

Her chanting echoed in the small stone room and reached a deafening crescendo.

Then Manou silenced abruptly.

She opened her eyes wide. They burned with the cold blue of flame, as though her thoughts had suddenly been ignited by some hellish spark. She put down the axe, picked up the plate and dipped her finger in the oil, dispersing the droplets into innumerable fragments.

Manou stood up, pushed open the door and threw the plate outside. It shattered against the rock with a loud crash, the splinters of porcelain ricocheting and sliding off down the mountainside.

Manou talked to herself for a while. Satisfied or unhappy with whatever it was that she had learnt from the oily water, Ric could not tell. The air lay thick with the incense of the candle.

Manou went outside.

The whole episode took not more than a few minutes and left him with the distinct impression that he had upset her. He felt as though he may have said or done the wrong thing, although he could not recall speaking or moving during the entire, curiously haunting ritual. He waited until he felt he had the strength to face her before going outside.

Ric wanted to ask her what she had seen, wanted to know if there was any great conclusion to her ritual, wanted her to tell him if it, whatever it was that she was trying to cast out of him, was gone. But, somehow he could not bring himself to. He was concerned that she would want to know if he perceived some alteration in his state, and he did not.

But instead of talking they sat and watched the stars and listened to each other's breathing.

Ric slept so deeply through the rest of the night that he did not wake when Manou left. There were no intrusions into his sleep, no unwelcome dreams and no faces of the dead or flashed images of rank carnage. Neither was there any sickening falling and no great collision with the earth that usually woke him drenched in the sweat of his exertions. There was just sleep: deep, pure and simple, and rewarding.

In the morning there was not much else to do other than try to memorise the view as it was laid out before him. He knew he would need to carry it with him wherever he would be going, and whilst that set him to thinking where it was that might be, he did not allow his many and intricate uncertainties to spoil his last hours on the mountain. He wondered how many other souls had taken refuge in the *oriu* over the years; how many *bandits d'honneur* had holed up in the tiny mountain refuge after their bloody assassinations?

Camille came for him not long after dark.

Having been told by Bosquet that Camille was a council member of the FLNC, Ric half expected him to arrive flanked by a troop of combat suited and balaclava wearing flunkies, but he did not. There was just Camille, this time with a larger sac in place of the shotgun.

They greeted each other.

The old man studied Ric's face as though he was appraising his charge's physical state. He stood back and smiled. Then he shook his head as if he should have known better than to doubt the power of Mariucca's nursing. His sac contained a selection of clothes that fit Ric better than the tired cast offs he had been wearing, and they were recently purchased judging by the shop tags. He wondered whether Manou had chosen them for him as they appeared to fit him well enough; they were mostly dark colours, modern materials; fleece-lined and functional rather than fancy.

The two men strolled down through the dark forest, Camille carrying the oil lamp to light the path for Ric so that he did not fall and damage his much repaired leg. The walk was not without pain for him though and he relied on the slender staff for support. When, eventually, he arrived at the foot of the slope, Ric realised he was exhausted.

An old blue Renault van was parked beneath a holm oak. Ric hauled himself into the passenger seat. In the back of the van were piled half a dozen wooden crates; the heady scent of mountain herbs filled the cabin. On the floor beneath Ric's feet were some old newspapers, which, when Camille fell silent to concentrate on the winding road, Ric read by the dim light of a pocket torch he found under the dashboard.

When he saw the headline article he realised Camille had left the paper where Ric would see it. *The Corsican Daily* was dated a few days before.

He translated the side item, reading it aloud as if alone: *The body of an unidentified male has been found near the beach at Renabianca, the scene of a terrible bushfire two days before. Neither the identity of the man, nor the reasons for his presence at the campsite, have yet been established. Local sources suggest the man was interrupted in the process of looting from the campsite, which was uninhabited at the time. Cause of death has been established as shotgun wounds to the abdomen. Police are still searching for the victim's right hand, which had been removed.*

So that was what Camille was doing emptying his shotgun into Bobo's corpse; he was disguising the bullet holes from Seraphina's Beretta.

"The use of a shotgun," the old man explained, "has perhaps a more acceptable place in what is termed an excusable or justifiable homicide. Every house has a shotgun; they are used for hunting, for protecting one's property, or one's life. If a pistol is used – because one does not use a pistol for hunting boar or shooting duck-it demonstrates a different intention from the beginning." He paused to let his information sink in, and to give Ric time to respond. When he did not, Camille said: "I see that you understand, Ric. It is good. Most people think this reasoning is *passé*; I am pleased you do not think so."

"You removed his hand? Is that some kind of ritual?"

Camille sighed. "The ring did not belong to him." He paused. "Now do you have any more questions that will not wait until our destination?"

"The crewman, Alex?"

"Oh, yes; the Russian," Camille replied. "He saved your life. If it was not for him you would be still floating in the Tyrrhenian. Well, but for him and Franco. Brave boy, eh? Like his grandfather. You told him to go back to the beach, but he did opposite; he followed you with the boat. Like his grandfather; one mind." He paused, the proud uncle enjoying his recollection of the boy's actions. "But the man Alex will be okay. As I told you, we are in touch with many old Russians from long time. Is there something else you want to know?"

So Ric repeated the tale of Manou's strange ritual; her divination and her throwing the plate out onto the rock.

The dull lights from the dashboard betrayed Camille's smile and he was quiet throughout Ric's recounting of the tale. When he had finished the old man sucked on his teeth and then chuckled.

"Manou is *Signadori*. I have said this," he began. "And you have, or perhaps we can now say you had, the evil eye." He pointed to his own forehead, not daring to lift his concentration from the winding road. "This mark on your face; it is nothing more than a birthmark, yes?"

Ric nodded in the darkness and then added: "For sure."

"It is possible, Ric, that Manou took this as a sign, like the word sign is used for the name *Signadori* because they make the sign of the cross, a sign that you have the evil eye. Some people think that the *Signadori* can control the *Mazzeri*, the dream hunters, like some people think the *Mazzeri* can predict death, or that they can recognise the spirits of the dead." He paused to negotiate a series of sharp hairpins.

When the road straightened he continued: "The legend states that those under the spell of the evil eye suffer from *depréssif*: headache, bad sleeping, no appetite, *scuràghjine* like sickness. They are often people who suffer from a fragile mental state; they cry much, they find difficult their emotions; you would say they are at the mercy on their emotions. It is said they suffer the attentions of a restless spirit, or perhaps *la lutte des envies*-the struggle of envies. Who knows?" He shrugged his shoulders, taking both of his hands off the steering wheel as he did so. "Perhaps Manou was under the impression that these symptoms were present in you." This time Camille risked a wry and amused glance at his passenger. "Would you know if you suffer this way, Ric?" He chuckled again; a laugh that shifted several layers of the dark tobacco coating his lungs. When he had finished coughing, he continued: "This ritual, as you call it, it is one the *Signadori* use to cast off the evil eye; it is for the purpose of casting out the spirit or cancelling out the envy. The smashing of the plate is the moment at which the bad spirit is cast out and the eye is made no longer evil."

In the dim light of the cabin Ric had no way of knowing whether his birthmark had disappeared. He felt inclined to touch the red mark above his right eye in case it had gone and left some scar in its place. When he did, he felt no change and felt stupid for even entertaining such an idea.

However, Camille took his right hand off the steering wheel and turned the rear view mirror Ric's way. "*Attinzioni*," he said.

Ric picked up the pocket torch, shined it at his forehead and studied his face in the mirror.

Neither spoke through the next few bends.

"Have you seen the *cignali*, the animal in your dreams?" Camille asked.

Even though he knew the other man could not see him, Ric nodded. "The boar, the *sanglier*? Yes I have seen it, and killed it in my dreams."

Camille sighed and coughed. "It is said that the animal comes to the *Mazzeri* as an omen of death. It is the fortune teller of death." He paused for a moment and then went on: "It is better that you see it and fight it; this means it is not your death that will come but the death of another."

He had seen the boar. It came to tell him of the death of his wife and he had dismissed it as nothing more than a bad dream; a natural result of the many strains and stresses he and many others suffered while on operations. But then he had seen the boar again and from it materialised the face of Bobo, the man who killed Manou's father, the man who Seraphina shot. That second time Ric put the dream down to sorry coincidence, nothing more. The third time he hunted the boar in his sleep he had been met with the face of René Bosquet, the obsequious policeman who ended up dying by his own hand. The sanglier had not foretold Ric of death by his hand; it had spoken to him only of the death that would come to others. It had informed him, it had not instructed him to carry out its will.

"And Manou?" Ric asked.

And like an adultery concerning two old friends that had been put to one side for too long, both men understood that *enfin* they would have to talk of her.

"*Signadori*," Ric repeated the word, trying to get a feel for it.

"It is so," replied Camille, but he offered nothing else.

"And I am a *Mazzeru*. Or was it the drugs that hijacked my dreams?" Ric was not inclined to let the old man off so lightly.

Camille winced and leant his head from side to side as though 'this question' he was considering at great length. "These things are difficult to know. They have been handed down from mother to daughter for many centuries; from village to village, from tavern to tavern, from darkness to light. It is said they make these *puzione*, these potions, from the cactus and the agave. It is a form of mescal, like the Tequila the Mexicans drink; people say it encourages the user to see things they do not want to see. This cactus is not, as you would say *indigéne*, not like the Zizula. It has been brought to our island by those who have visited us from other lands.

"But I do not think her intention was for you to come to any harm. I do not think her purpose was to abuse you. If Manou gave you drugs, I am sure she would have done so to help you see something that was not so easy to see."

"Perhaps," was all Ric could muster in reply.

They drove towards the half-moon. Ospédale gazed down like a contented chaperone over Porti Vechju and the north-eastern isles of Sardinia. Lights twinkled and shimmered in the distance and the air, the denser they descended, warmed Ric's bones; the chilled mountain atmospheres of his nights in the *oriu* weighed down by the heavy blankets seemed already lost long ago.

Camille took the left turn at Palavese and slipped down the back road through Gialla and Ribba, and almost as soon as he joined the main coastal road heading north he turned right for San Ciprianu. Before arriving at the bay though, he turned for Cirindino and then, having passed the pale tomb at the bottom of the drive up to the house where Ric had spent the last few weeks, Camille dropped down into the bay at *la Tozza*. The old van rattled as it rolled down the dusty and bumpy track in the moonlight.

Once at the bottom of the hill Camille parked the van and they sat in silence, content without conversation in each other's company. But most silences are a prelude to activity, so the old man had told him. Camille opened his creaking door, got out and disappeared into the shadows thrown by the maquis.

Ric bathed in the heady aroma of the herbs crated in the rear of the van. The unmistakable scents of arbutus, juniper, myrtle, rosemary, boxwood and thyme lay thick in the air. They reminded him of nights spent listening to the crickets whirr and Manou's soft breathing. The perfume of lavender brought back to him the feel of the soft, silken skin at the nape of her neck.

He got out and looked for Camille on the beach.

Out in the bay the rock stood proud. The moon lit a shimmering path straight out to the granite tower. Again this evening the stars and the moon illuminated the landscape and heightened the contrast between the two worlds; one in light, the other in dark. The world was to be measured in height and width only; that other dimension depth was abandoned to the shadows.

He found the old man standing, waiting at the back of the beach. Ric removed his espadrilles so that he might remember the feel of the fine sand between his toes, and stood beside the old boy surveying the still, straight horizon and the sail boat lying in the shadow of the rock. There was, he noticed by the rhythmic rise and fall of the boat, a gentle swell.

Camille handed him the plastic bag Ric had hidden in the branches of the holm oak at the back of the beach. The feel of it made him smile. It was just as Manou had told him; the maquis saw everything. In the bag he recognised his wallet and money, but there were also two passports, the sight of which caused him to hesitate, an envelope, which he did not recall putting there, and the signet ring with the *Catochitis* stone that Camille had removed from Bobo's cold, dead hand.

As he went to open the bag, the old man closed his own hand over Ric's. "Franco told me you should have this."

"I can't keep this, Camille. It should stay here."

"It is better that you take it. Manou was ashamed that she doubted you."

"You give the ring to Franco, please Camille?" Ric asked.

But again the old man closed his hand over the bag. "Franco will have my ring when it is time. This ring," he paused, "Manou wanted you to have this. Keep it close, eh!"

Ric felt himself sway for a moment, as though a zephyr had unexpectedly filled his sail.

They stood in silence for a time. Ric was not sure for how long exactly. He felt bound by the island, as though it exerted some curious gravitational pull over him and was reluctant to release him.

Eventually Camille spoke: "The motor bicycle we have disposed of," he said in a way that suggested his information warranted no comment. "Your car we have taken to Nice. It has been left in the Rue Neuve; it is a district with many popular restaurants, but it is also close to the recruitment centre for the *Légion Étrangère* in the Rue Sincaire. If anyone should look for you, the trail will end there, for now.

"The passports in the bag are two that were left behind by the campers after the fire; the pictures are not good, but if you should by chance drop them in the sea it will help to improve your looks, eh? Perhaps it would be best if you used one of them for a time; perhaps until things have settled?" He chuckled at the fact that he had seen the pictures, but that Ric had yet to enjoy that dubious pleasure. "The names we could do nothing about; I am sorry. Maybe you can choose the face, but not the name."

"Where are we going?" Ric asked.

Camille exhaled as though there was much beyond his control that he would like to have held greater sway over. "The adventures of my sailing days have become a little too exciting for me in the last few years. Perhaps it is time for me to find a different avenue for my vacations."

"Camille, I can't take your sailboat."

The older man hesitated. His curly white hair glowed in the moonlight, like the bubbling, silver froth at the water's edge. "Yes," he replied, "you will. It is for the best; it should be so. She should be with a man who is strong enough to see her through the storms."

Ric shook his head and chuckled in approval, "You crafty old soul, Camille! You've had this planned for a while. That's why you brought the *Mara* over from the marina in Porti Vechju."

He rubbed his scalp and his teeth shone out in the dark, "*A volpi perdi u pelu ma micca u viziu.* Like the fox," he said, "I lose some of my hair, but I hope not my cunning. This saying, it is in the book she has given you.

"But I find some storms are these days too strong even for me, and learning to sail the *Mara* will keep the devil from making use of your idle hands; especially now that the evil eye has left you." Camille winked theatrically.

They pulled a small dinghy out of the cover of the scrub at the back of the beach and, rather than start the small outboard motor, Camille rowed Ric over to the *Mara*.

The breeze from the north was strengthening and cooling, and the sheet lines tapped against the mast.

"You can sail my boat?" he asked, as he brought the little dinghy alongside the wooden hulled sloop.

"Bit late for that, Camille," Ric replied. "Though you might need to come on board for a moment and show me some of the ropes, so to speak."

They tied up and boarded, and Camille gave Ric a potted instruction into the running of the boat: the rigging, the electrics, such as they were, the navigational equipment – or rather the lack of it – the charts, the helm and, perhaps most important of all, the head with its miniscule shower.

When he'd finished, Camille seemed to be in a hurry to disembark. But as he stepped down into the dinghy he stopped, turned and looked up at Ric, leaning with his hands on the rail.

"Go surely and go far, Ric." He sniffed the air. "First go south; it would be best. *Addiu*, my friend."

Through the clear darkness of the shadow thrown by the slender moon, Ric could make out the gentle lines of sorrow creasing the old boy's face. Ric hoped the lines were written as much for him as for the beautiful sailboat that was about to become his new home.

"*Mara*," Ric said trying to pronounce it the way he had heard Camille say it. "Manou's mother?"

Both names seemed for a few seconds to suspend in the air between them. "It was so," Camille replied, but he kept his eyes fixed on the young man who leant down towards him from the deck. "We were..., we were very close at one time."

"I saw her name in the tomb near the house," Ric told him. "It's the Pietri family tomb?"

Camille waited for a moment longer and then said with a profound and enduring sadness, "*Mara*..., Yes, *Mara*. Like her daughter, she was very beautiful." He hesitated as no doubt a vision of her face came to him. Then he said: "All names have meanings, you know. *Mara*," he repeated as though he might never say her name again. "It means *amertume de la mer* – bitterness of the sea."

Out to the west Eos was spreading her rose-tipped fingers along the broad horizon and, as he tacked round the southern point, Ric shivered in the cool dawn air. He knew the maquis was watching.